RETURN OF THE AFRICAN DIASPORA

Exodus Village

OTHER BOOKS BY LINDA PACE SAMUEL

Book I

Return of the African Diaspora
A Mother for Celeste

RETURN OF THE AFRICAN DIASPORA

Exodus Village

_____

LINDA PACE SAMUEL

'N Gratitude Publishing
Aquarian Age Books

Published in the United States by 'N Gratitude Publishing Company
Atlanta Georgia

www.NGratitude.net

ISBN 978-0-9833150-0-1

Printed in the United States of America

First Edition - Paperback

over Design by Sean Collins - www.TenTen71.com

~~~

Cover Photography by Jina Wilson for Joni's Heart Photography - www.JoniHeartImage

*To my father – one of the smartest people I've ever known.
Thanks for passing on your thirst for knowledge
and fascination with politics to me.*

For My Grandsons -

Quincy McArthur Stewart and Kamren Amir Reynolds,

and for my new friend, Miss Kayla Madison

Acknowledgements

Many of the people who supported me in writing my first book in the **Return of the African Diaspora** series: *A Mother for Celeste*, have remained in my corner throughout my work in releasing this second installment, *Exodus Village*. Many listened to Spirit in making their miraculously-timed calls, or sent me emails of encouragement on the days that I needed them most. Others gently pointed out the areas where improvements were sorely needed, and I am grateful to *you* in more ways than you will ever know.

I would like to say thank you in particular to both my parents for their support. Thank you to my big sister Mena; who has always encouraged me to be the person God made me to be, since the time that I was born. I appreciate the many "hook-ups" you've given me over the years, and as I find my way in marketing my books and growing my publishing company. Many thanks to my aunt Nellie, and to Khari, James, Linette, Lorraine, Theada, Jen, Super Jr., Jay, Woubit, Kibb, Marcus, Marlon, Leslie, Marjorie, Mike, Ann, Rev. Sandy, Bet, Ruby, Brenda M., Ramona, Vyann, Corliss, and Deborah. A big thanks to my cousin, Jan, for helping me get ready to "meet the press;" and to my friends, Cassandra and Brenda L., for your help in getting this second volume to the presses.

I am also deeply appreciative of my high school classmates for having faith in me, and for helping to make my first book launch such a success. A special thanks to Bettye Morgan, for helping me get the series added to the collection of the Macon County/Tuskegee Public Library. And thanks, to Tuskegee Mayor Omar Neal, for your continued caring attention and devotion to our fine city, and for making my first radio interview the positive experience that it was.

Finally, I would like to express my deepest gratitude to my Aunt Mamie, my cousin Emma, and to my friend and classmate, Ernestine. I can't thank you enough for all you've done to make sure everyone you knew had my first book in their collection.

I truly appreciate all your enthusiastic and nurturing support.

Special Thanks To:

John Inman, Anthony Murray and Mena Pace
Kellogg Hotel and Conference Center
Tuskegee University
~~~

Iowa State University Library - Special Collections
George Washington Carver Exhibit
~~~

Petre Bridges and Bettye Morgan
Macon County - Tuskegee Public Library

Main Entry[‡]: di·as·po·ra

a) the breaking up and scattering of a people:

<u>MIGRATION</u> <the black *diaspora* to northern cities>

b) people settled far from their ancestral homelands <African

diaspora>

c) the place where these people live

Main Entry: ex·o·dus

Etymology: Latin, from Greek *Exodos,*

a) literally, road out, from *ex-* + *hodos* road

b) a mass departure

Chapter 1

Kristin And Winston

*K*ristin peered into the distance at the slowly approaching figure, propping herself up from a prone position on their borrowed cotton blanket for a better look. Whoever the person was, they were still at least a quarter mile away—too far to make out a face or even know for certain whether it was a man or woman. But she sensed it was Winston somehow, and after a few minutes more she could make out the distinctive walk that left no doubt in her mind. Her new husband was finally on his way back to her.

They had reluctantly left their love nest in the hotel earlier that morning; only pulling themselves away to spend more time on the beach before they had to leave the island. The cool darkness of the early morning had barely begun to lighten as they started out from the hotel. They reached the sugary white sand just as the sun began its ascent over the crystal Jamaican waters.

Even with the Florida coast being only a three-hour drive southwest of Tuskegee, their trip had been Kristin's first experience with the ocean. And it had been love at first sight—a love she discovered she shared with Winston and the handful of people from their hotel that they came across that morning. They all smiled and nodded to each other as they passed; acknowledging their common eagerness to be out on the beach so early, their kindred passion for witnessing the sea front come alive.

The couple stood quietly at the water's edge for several minutes, taking in the marvels of nature as a new day began to unfold. Then they strolled hand in hand on the nearly deserted beach, heading east long after they could see nothing of the Montego Bay Golf Resort and Hotel. They walked as far as the landscape would allow them to go, stopping only now and

1

then for a quick kiss to affirm their delight in being together. They sought out the privacy that newlyweds often crave until they came across a small ravine that unexpectedly blocked their path. It had been created during a violent storm that had eroded the wide expanse of sugary white sand that once evenly blanketed the coastline. Despite its minor flaws, the pristine beach was still a marvel to Kristin; the energy it emitted made their early morning venture seem even more surreal.

She had packed several pieces of fruit from a basket that was delivered just after they checked into their hotel. She and Winston carefully laid out the large blanket they thought to bring with them across the sand. Large bottles of water secured it against the mild breeze that the gentle currents coming in from the sea brought with them. They had relished their love for each and their time together under the tepid Jamaican sunshine, staring into the other's eyes and exchanging frequent smiles. They ate their breakfast unhurriedly, as rhythmic waves crashed loudly in the distance. Afterwards, they lay back on the blanket together in silence; listening to the sounds of sea gulls flying overhead contentedly, with eyes closed.

Later, as the morning sun began to rise higher across the dazzling sky, the light ocean breeze that had first caressed their skin began to heat with increasing intensity. It wasn't long before they had second thoughts about not taking one of the beach umbrellas they had spotted in a bin near the hotel pool—both convinced by the cool morning winds that one wouldn't be necessary. Since they were determined to spend as much time on the beach as possible, Winston volunteered to make the long trek back to fetch an umbrella and Kristin watched him until he had disappeared completely from sight. She lay back on the blanket alone, missing him almost immediately.

It wasn't long before she began to feel baked by the heat of the sun. She walked closer to the water's edge to find relief, sticking one foot into the sparkling blue-green water tentatively and then the other. Gradually, she dug her toes down into the soft wet sand and even further until it closed in around her ankles. Firmly anchored, she stared out at the sea, her attention captured by a ship passing in the distance. She felt as one with the ocean in that moment and watched intently as the ship made its slow progression across the horizon. Dolphins broke the spell periodically, as they jumped from the water in a flash of movement; only to quickly dive back underneath it again.

Suddenly claustrophobic, Kristin freed her feet from their imprisonment abruptly. She turned to walk down the beach in the direction of the hotel, closer still to the water's edge. The morning tide brought ever stronger currents rushing toward the shoreline, forming crooked patterns across the wet sand. After walking a quarter-mile or so Kristin turned to head back. Eventually, she left the cool shelter of the sea breeze once again to stretch out on their blanket and wait for Winston's return.

He had been close to her thoughts the entire time he was away. She could still barely believe that the love of her life had asked to marry her so soon after they 'officially' started dating—or that she had said "yes" for that matter. They had only known each other for a short while but her heart felt as though she had known him forever. Kristin knew it was right from the beginning; somehow, she could tell instantly that Winston was "the one." She had recognized him from a distance. She had her first glimpse of him walking toward her from across the campus, with the same swagger that she now watched move toward her from down the beach. He appeared from out of nowhere that day as she sat idly on "the Fountain," watching the latest group of new students arrive for the fall semester.

Her sister, Rena, and two of her high school classmates had started the ritual of "freshman watching" a few years earlier. Rena was four years older than Kristin and already living on the sprawling campus. Her dorm sat smack in the middle of the most active part of student life at the predominately Black college. They had started people-watching with Rena that day on the steps of White Hall, her sister's dormitory, certain at first that it was the best possible vantage point to take in all the sights. But later, Rena led them to sit on the top landing of the fountain - a large rectangular structure that sat right in the middle of the most popular area of "the yard."

The original intent for the massive water fountain had long been abandoned and the water long gone; instead, it had morphed into one of the most popular places to be on campus, a well-established gathering place for meeting up with friends between classes. The fountain provided the perfect view of everything going on around them. Rena started a contest to see who could pick out the largest number of freshmen from among the crowds of students. Even though Kristin and her friends were still in high school themselves, they took delight in joining to spot the newcomers. They starred into the faces of students looking for clues, as they walked along the sidewalks that crisscrossed all around the fountain's borders in front of them, until it was finally time for Rena to leave for the cafeteria for dinner, at Tompkin's Hall.

Growing up in the small town had meant passing through the campus on a regular basis, since the main road linking the community led through it. Kristin had visited the campus frequently with her parents as a child; they would often attend nationally acclaimed plays and concerts at the Chapel or at Logan Hall, the main venue for student entertainment. She had daydreamed about becoming a Tuskegee student all through grade school. It began with her very first interaction with the "practice" teachers who came regularly from the college to help her teachers in their elementary classes.

She had known since she was six years old that Lewis Adams Elementary had been named for the former slave who had been responsible for bringing Booker T. Washington to Tuskegee. Her school's principal had been Adams' granddaughter and she made certain they learned *all* there was to know about the college's history. She made sure they understood that history began with her grandfather coming up with the seed money to get it started; expanding on the vocational training that he and his wife had already begun providing to newly freed slaves in the area surrounding Tuskegee. Adams wanted others to benefit as his family had from its thriving businesses. He had *hired* Washington to work at the newly established Tuskegee State Normal School as its first principal, one of three commissioners designated to supervise the school and its new state budget. She and her classmates learned the more widely-known history too, about Washington's success in transforming that first school into the famed Tuskegee Institute. But more so than other residents of the college town, they knew that Lewis Adams became a successful businessman after having been freed from slavery, and that he had been a community leader who spoke several languages. He had been known for his negotiating skills that had also resulted in a political deal being struck with white Alabama state senators to secure the two thousand dollar annual funding for the college. He had delivered the vote of newly freed slaves in the area, and the senators kept their word by convinced a then all-white Alabama State Legislature to provide the school money.

Kristin had felt a part of the college for nearly all her life. After graduating from high school, she had waited anxiously all summer long for school to begin again and her chance to watch the new freshmen class arrive on the well-manicured campus. This time they would be members of her own graduating class.

The first time she saw Winston, she thought for sure that she already knew him. It wasn't until after he had walked close enough for her to see his face more clearly that she realized that wasn't the case. The realization made the strong sense of familiarity she felt that much more surprising.

That first day they had only exchanged glances, both already engaged in conversations with other people. After that it seemed that she would see him wherever she went around the sprawling campus. At any given point in time, she could look up and there Winston would be—usually making his rounds from one eager young female student to another. She had tried as best she could to ignore him; all evidence pointed to him being just another scamp, as her grandmother would say. She had no intention of becoming one more plaything for him. For a while, she would turn away from him quickly whenever their paths did cross before there was time to make eye contact. She did it just to prove her point; to let him know she refused to be another sheep he could add to the flock he was apparently collecting around campus.

Still, there had been something about him that haunted her thoughts and kept her from dismissing him altogether. Once she realized he was an engineering major, she decided to reserve further judgment until she had gathered more facts. Apparently, he wasn't nearly as empty-headed as she had first assumed. She was surprised when she caught herself hoping they would have a class together the next semester. She could get to know him better that way, she told herself to justify her thoughts—as a friend, of course.

And sure enough there he was; the first person she saw when she walked into Dr. Keenan's spring semester History class. Winston's face lit up as bright as a Christmas tree too, when he saw her. And she smiled back in spite of herself, moving forward inside the third floor classroom of Huntington Hall toward a vacant seat. By the time the class ended she had managed to regain her composure; she deliberately left the room ahead of him, without so much as a glance in his direction. Kristin felt proud of herself, some unnamed victory in a game she found herself playing. But she couldn't deny how flustered she felt when Winston caught up to her.

She had walked quickly down the wooden steps that led to the first floor of Tuskegee's main academic building. She felt her heart pound faster, thrilled that he had hurried to keep pace with her.

"Want some company?"

She had practically held her breath for the first few minutes that he fell in line beside her. They passed the reading lab and exited a side door, Kristin struggling to appear nonchalant as they walked together hurriedly toward the opposite end of campus. By the time they reached the steps leading down to the George W. Carver Museum, they had begun making slow but steady small-talk. Both of them slowed unconsciously as they neared Dorothy Hall, the converted guesthouse and lunch counter that was one building down from the museum. The former girls' trade building was just inside Lincoln Gates and close to the main entrance of the well-kept campus grounds. It would be the point where their paths would lead them in different directions toward their next classes. Winston would keep straight in the direction of the engineering building, where he would have classes for the remainder of the day, while Kristin veered off to the right for her music appreciation class in the Chapel. It was strange how even the painful vibrations screeching from her classmates' cheap plastic flutes sounded like sweet music to her ears that day.

She had still been excited about their encounter as she described it to her friend Niyla later that afternoon. Niyla, however, was quick to point out that Winston was known to be seeing a young woman who lived in her dormitory. Kristin tried her level best to hide her disappointment at having her bubble burst so quickly, and sadly resigned herself to having only a platonic relationship with him. But much to her surprise, their after-class walks continued; it soon became a ritual that the two of them followed every Monday, Wednesday, and Friday morning. In those brief times of being together, Kristin had discovered that she liked Winston quite a bit. They had lots of things in common too, especially considering that they had been brought up in such different environments.

She had been born and raised in small-town Tuskegee, a sharp contrast to Winston's native hometown of Washington, D.C. But they found that they liked the same kinds of music and they mostly agreed on politics—a subject that was near to the hearts of most students at the time, to some degree. By the end of that semester they had become close friends, though the young woman who lived in Niyla's dorm had remained off limits in their conversations. They both felt an undeniable chemistry building between them though neither of them acknowledged it.

Kristin didn't think to conceal her joy on the day that Winston purpose-fully told her that he and the young woman were no longer seeing each other. Neither did she pretend to be unaffected when he announced, in nearly the same breath, that he had been selected for a NASA internship. She was elated for him, of course, but she knew right away that it meant he would spend the summer in Houston, instead of there in Tuskegee with her. Her hopes of developing an even closer relationship with him during summer school, when there were fewer students on the campus and an even more intimate atmosphere, were very short lived. She didn't even have time to start daydreaming about it, as she often did.

Winston reacted to her distress with a broad smile across his handsome face. Initially, she felt her temper spike at the realization that he was laughing at her so blatantly, but she could only smile herself when she realized it meant her carefully orchestrated ruse hadn't been as convincing as she once thought. It was obvious that Winston knew all along that her true feelings for him went well beyond friendship, and it apparently tickled him that she would miss him so much over the summer.

※※※

"Hey Sweetie. Did you miss me?" Winston dropped to his knees next to his bride on their cotton blanket. The question came as though he had read her mind, which was often the case.

"Always, my love, always—whenever we're apart for more than a few minutes." She smiled, rising slightly to meet his wet kiss and then she came fully onto her knees to hug him warmly. Kristin felt the same loving energy between them when their bodies met as she had felt since they came together as a couple.

They had spotted each other at nearly the same moment that next fall after the internship in Houston that had separated them over the summer. She had been hurt at first when she didn't hear from Winston all summer, as she had expected, but realized how much the job with NASA meant to him. She knew how important the opportunity was to his career; if they were to be together, she would have to get used to his long hours at work. They were standing in separate lines in Logan Hall when their eyes first drifted toward each other and locked into place. The school's well-utilized gym also doubled as its student movie theater, and was the main venue for a variety of other events—from off-Broadway plays and renown symphony performances, to campus talent shows and step shows. They were both nearing the end of a very long and tedious process to complete their registrations; standing in the last of several lines that snaked slowly across the well-worn basketball court.

It had literally taken hours to maneuver through the first tortuous round—each competing with other students for one of a limited number of keypunched cards for each class they wanted to take. The cards were distributed from various points around campus, and *anything* could happen during the process. That day, much suspense had been created by members of a certain popular fraternity that had been notorious for executing conspiracies and using trick-nology. They posed as student assistants and periodically made phony announcements about the availability of the most sought after class cards. At some point during the day, the academic vice president had decided to open new sections for several classes, based on a larger-than-expected enrollment. Kristin and Winston had both waited in line for hours after word of the new classes began to surface. They remained vigilant until the class cards were in hand, knowing that a few unsuspecting students had been deliberately thrown off guard in their quest to get theirs. They had been duped into giving up their coveted positions in line — especially the ones for Dr. Keenan's classes.

It had been a very stressful process to get to the point where they were when they saw each other. Like most other Tuskegee students, they felt they had proven how much they wanted an education there, by virtue of their perseverance through the registration process. If one of the cards for classes that had been approved by their faculty advisor wasn't available, it could mean shuffling everything around to make a new schedule fit. In some extreme cases, it could even mean having to start the whole process again from the beginning.

But somehow, Winston and Kristin had managed to fit everything together for their schedules. When they first made eye contact they were both in lines on the downhill stretch, nearing the quarter-mile mark to the finish line. Slowly, they kept making their way toward the Finance Office windows and Winston was first to reach it. He paid his tuition and room and board fees with the blank check his mother had given him, then leaned against a side wall to wait for Kristin. As soon she had, they stood together in the last line to take pictures for their student Ids, finally completing the tedious process and becoming official students.

Her parents had insisted that she live at home during her first year, but Kristin had managed to convince them to let her stay on campus her sophomore year. The night before registration was to begin, she moved most of her clothes and several boxes of pictures and books from home into the small room that she and Niyla were to share. Everyone called their residence hall "O. D." but the dorm's official name was Olivia Davidson Hall, built in honor of the second of Booker T. Washington's three wives. But as it turned out, she and Niyla ended up being roommates in name only since she and Winston became inseparable early in the semester.

Kristin vividly remembered each minute of their first date under the

"Wine Tree" still. The towering thick evergreen stood close to a busy sidewalk running along Campus Avenue, and had two large branches growing close to the ground horizontally, near the bottom of its massive trunk. The seats they formed were nearly perfectly straight at 45 degree angles, with smaller branches that had been stripped clean over the years. The smoothed out surfaces of the branch seats could accommodate several students. The sidewalk crossing in front of the tree led to buildings that were a main part of student life. There was lots of foot traffic but the fullness of branches visible from the outside provided all the privacy that they needed.

There were groups of students known to frequent the Wine Tree for reasons that would have surely been frowned on by the administration. And many a pledgee had quickly escaped by ducking under its shelter after spotting a big brother or sister near Campus Avenue. The fullness of the tree provided a solid shield; the narrow opening leading into its inner sanctuary was furthermost from the sidewalk, so its occupants were usually hidden entirely from sight.

Kristin had been quite surprised by the intimacy created within the tree as Winston led her inside; it felt magical because it was so unexpected. He had packed a small basket of chicken that he had picked up from The Chicken Coup beforehand. The restaurant was the only one within walking distance of the campus and one of the only places to eat off campus in Tuskegee, period. She had to force herself not to grimace at the sight of grease stains on the napkins he had used to wrap the chicken. She was so smitten by him that before she realized it she had actually eaten a small piece. She even drank a few sips of the Boones Farm Strawberry Hill wine that he poured into two paper cups, and she was reminded of the toast promptly as she awakened the next morning.

They spent hours together under the Wine Tree that afternoon, laughing and talking and finding out more about each other than their time between classes the previous semester had allowed them. Winston brought a portable cassette player with him too, and began introducing her to musicians she had never heard. She listened to the Last Poets for the first time, to Pharoah Sanders, Flora Purim, and several other favorites of his that were never played at WBIL, the local radio station in Tuskegee. When it was finally time to leave their haven under the tree, Winston abruptly moved toward her. When he was close enough, he touched her lightly in the middle of her stomach with his index finger. They stood facing each other quietly for several minutes after he had done it, as though something much more significant had taken place. Then he leaned down and kissed

9

her softly on her lips. It was their very first kiss and it left her certain that she wasn't alone in the way that she felt about him.

They were together constantly from that day on and Winston's friend, Tony, began teasing her whenever they saw each other at their off-campus apartment. He would always tell her that she had Winston's nose "wide open," but she had still been surprised when he proposed one night while they were studying for finals.

※※※

"Look what I brought you." Winston reached deep inside the pockets of his cargo shorts with a wide grin on his face. He brought out a handful of almonds, still in their beige cork-like shells and held them out, patiently waiting for Kristin's reaction.

"I just happened to look up as I was leaving the hotel and noticed the tree near the pool. It was loaded with 'em and I got one of the security guys to help me shake these down." She responded with a coy smile although she had no idea what he was holding out to her.

Winston had spent summers in Jamaica with his grandfather as a child. As their plane circled the airport to land, he had told her the island felt as much like home to him as Washington did.

Quickly, Winston turned his attention to the task at hand—protecting them from the sun's now intense rays. First, he dug a small deep hole in the sand and plunged the large umbrella he brought back as far as it would go. He secured it with a large mound of damp sand and packed more sand all around it. Once the umbrella was opened there was an area of shade large enough to cover their blanket and provide instant relief.

He seemed quite proud of his accomplishment, and that he had thought to bring back the almonds. He pulled out a few from his pocket and showed her how to get inside the thin casings covering the nuts. He began handing her the sweet meats out of the shells. They were very tasty and Kristin ate several between sips of fruit juice that her husband brought back for their mid-morning snack. After she had her fill, Winston deposited the rest of the nuts from his pockets onto the blanket.

"Sweetheart, you'll never guess what happened while you were gone." Kristin had stretched out lazily beneath the umbrella. "I had the strangest conversation with a security guard who walked past here."

"What?" Winston was instantly on the alert at the mention of the strange man. He had been uneasy about leaving her alone in such an isolated spot in the first place, especially clad in a swim suit.

"No, no Honey. It was nothing like that..." She could read his thoughts almost as easily as he could hers. There had been nothing threatening about the polite young man who had stopped to talk to her, and she hastened to let him know.

"He said he had to walk the whole length of beach in front on the hotel's property line several times during his shift. It's part of his security check."

"Well, what did he want?" Winston wasn't about to be deterred from his interrogation.

"I was the one who started the conversation, baby, because of these strange thoughts that were popping into my head out of nowhere."

The expression on his face told Kristin he had no idea what she was talking about.

"Just before he walked up," she went on, before Winston could ask. "I was sitting here thinking about you—about how nice our trip has been.

"I've never been so happy in my life." She smiled at him.

"Me either," he agreed, wistfully. "I almost wish we didn't have to go back to Tuskegee."

She smiled because the exact thought had crossed her mind.

"It was just so weird," she went on after a bit. "I have no idea where these thoughts were coming from; it was like being in some kind of trance. I had been staring into the ocean in the direction of the sunrise. My mind was just drifting—you know?" She looked for signs that he might under-stand what she was saying and found none.

"All of a sudden, it dawned on me that Africa was on the other side of all this water," she shared her epiphany enthusiastically, "right over there—just thousands of miles away. I found myself having a strong urge to go there to see it for myself. It was more of a longing to go, really."

"Maybe we can get there for our fifth anniversary," Winston offered with a smile. "I should be making some real money by then." He was eager to please Kristin but still unsure of what she was getting at. They had talked about going to Africa many times in Tuskegee, especially during their political debates with friends. After James Brown's hit back in the 60s, black college students had begun to openly claim kinship with Africa—something that had never happened before. And after they heard what Elijah Mohammed was teaching to the Muslims he converted, there was even more radical change in the air. A new trend soon developed on many of the historically black college and university campuses. Female students wrapped their hair in colorful cloth the same way that many West

African women still do; and both male and female students alike began wearing dashikis to class.

"I would love for us to go there together," she agreed. They punctuated this new resolve with a kiss, smiling into the other's eyes and imagining what their married life would be like by that time.

"It was all so strange..." Kristin resumed the conversation as soon as they had released their embrace. "It was just weird how the thoughts kept popping into my head the way they did...And I had such a strong urge to go to Africa; I can *still* feel it.

"Then I looked over in that direction," she said, pointing north, "and I started thinking about the triangular slave trade of all things—how the ships brought African captives to the Caribbean first to sell as slaves. From here they headed north to trade the slaves they had left for tobacco, in the American colonies. They would fill up the space that the captives took up while they were still crossing the ocean with sugar and rum, and they sold that in the colonies too. They would leave there with tobacco they bought from colonists and sell it in Europe, creating a triangular shape trade route across the Atlantic Ocean for hundreds of years.

"I kept thinking about the slave auctions too, as if for the very first time. I thought about how some people who had been together on the ships were separated in the Caribbean. Then they were separated yet again once the ships reached the auction blocks in America—from their family, friends and even those they only came to know in the slave castles or on the ships.

"...Anyhow, before I knew it, I was thinking about Marcus Garvey." Kristin's tone emphasized her further confusion. " I mean I was *really* thinking about him.

"It's hard for me to explain it now, honey, but they weren't thoughts that were coming from me."

"What do you mean by that?" Winston was even more perplexed than ever.

"Well, it's like I was saying before, I started out thinking about us—that's really all I *wanted* to think about. We're on our honeymoon for goodness sake. I just wanted to cherish every moment that we have together here, before we have to head back to Tuskegee for school.

"But then there I was, with these really deep thoughts about slavery and Marcus Garvey that I couldn't get out of my head..."

"Maybe it's because of what Grandpa was telling us," Winston countered. They both smiled at the mention of his grandfather, who Kristin had met for the first time on their trip to Jamaica. The couple had spent their second night as man and wife in Kingston—a welcomed wedding gift from Grandpa Bailey. Their marriage ceremony at the Macon County courthouse in Tuskegee had been hideous. When the judge first entered the courtroom where they waited, it was all that either of them could do not to laugh out loud. The man had instantly reminded them both of one of the regular characters on "Hew Haw," a country comedy show that had been very popular on television. It had been hard for them to hold in their laughter the whole time they were saying their vows, and they smiled every time they thought about it.

They had decided to get married right away after Kristin accepted his proposal. Winston's grandfather had been the only one of their relatives who knew anything of their plans. They had called his mother and her parents from the airport in Atlanta, just a few minutes before it was time to board their flight. To say that their announcement had been unwelcome news was an understatement. The general consensus was that they were too young to even think about marriage, and everyone kept saying that they hadn't known each other long enough for such a big step.

But Grandpa Bailey seemed genuinely happy for them. He told the couple he heard love in their voices when they called to tell him they were on their way. He had insisted on sending Winston money to pay for their trip; it was a chance to meet his new granddaughter, he said, since traveling had become such a chore. He had arranged a small reception in Mandeville, his hometown in Manchester Parish. Mandeville sat in the mountains in the center of the island, nearly two thousand feet above the sea.

Kristin was excited just to be on the island where her husband had spent so much time growing up. It was a fascinating place and on the way to Grandpa Bailey's house, they drove past young boys holding gigantic lobsters up for sale. Their cost was far less than the price of chicken from the Chicken Coup, and Kristin's mouth watered each time they passed one of them. She finally insisted that their taxi stop at a stand on the way up the mountain to buy some mangoes. She was anxious to taste something of the enticing foods that the vendors waved in their direction as they passed, and the fruit didn't disappoint.

The unspoiled beauty of Mandeville had taken her by surprise, and she fell in love with it right away. Grandpa Bailey had hung colorful decorations up to welcome them, and fifty or so well-wishers were on hand to greet them. Some brought sweet treats along to complement the barbecued goat, pigeon peas and rice, plantains, and other side dishes that Winston's grandfather had prepared. They danced for hours to the music of a small reggae band in his back yard; the party was set against a spectacular backdrop of mountains with lush vegetation growing in the valley below.

Everyone laughed when his grandfather made a point of telling Winston the goat he had cared for as a boy was still among the living. And there wasn't a dry eye in the crowd as he proposed a toast to officially welcome Kristin into their family. He told the newcomers to the community that he was standing in for his only son, who he had lost to an automobile accident when Winston was only nine years old. Several people who had known his dad came up to them before the party ended, and told stories about what his father had been like when he was Winston's age.

Grandpa Bailey had insisted that they spend at least a week in Jamaica when they were making their plans. He surprised them with arrangements he had made to have them stay at the bed and breakfast in Kingston after all their guests went home. It was owned, he told them, by some friends and he had hired a taxi to pick them up the next afternoon to drive them the sixty miles to the southeastern coast. Kristin had been thrilled to hear him describe the secluded cabin they had stayed in for the next two days. It was steps away from the ocean that she had waited all her life to see.

As their conversation dwindled, Grandpa Bailey mentioned that he met the owners when they had all worked together for Marcus Garvey. His statement revived their conversation for at least another hour.

"What?!" Kristin and Winston chimed in unison, not sure that they had heard what they thought they had. In all the time that they had discussed Garvey in Dr. Keenan's classes, it never dawned on them that Winston's grandfather might have actually known him.

"Yes, that's right." He responded proudly, surprised by their interest.

"I worked for Mr. Garvey for around three years as his apprentice— that was back when he was publishing *Black Man* magazine and *The New Jamaican* newspaper. It was right after he was released from those trumped up charges brought against him in New York. He moved to London not long after that though, and that's where he died eventually."

Winston and Kristin were practically speechless by the familiarity in his voice as he spoke about the man they had studied in school.

"I got the job after convincing my dad to let me try something different for a change," Grandpa Bailey was saying, "to take a break from farming for awhile." He was looking directly at Winston with a smile, and they both recalled his days of rebellion about taking care of his goat and helping on the farm. Apparently, Grandpa Bailey's father had used a much gentler approach on him, but by then Winston knew that his grandfather had been deliberately hard on him, to toughen him up because his father wasn't there to do it, he said.

"Wow!" Wait 'til I tell Dr. Keenan about this!

"He's our History teacher at Tuskegee," Winston explained, "very eccentric but I think you'd really like him, Grandpa. He has us thinking about all kinds of stuff."

"Sounds like my kind of teacher, alright. So, they're teaching you about Garvey at Tuskegee?" He seemed satisfied in knowing the answer to his question.

"He was going to start a school here like the one in Tuskegee, you know."

Kristin and Winston looked at each other to see if either knew anything about what Grandpa Bailey was saying.

"I never knew that!" Winston was in awe. "What was it like to work for him, Grandpa? I can't believe you actually *knew* Garvey."

"Well, that I did, indeed." They could hear pride in his voice.

"There were many of us who looked up to him around here—especially the farmers. We're the planters of African descent here on our island," he explained to his bewildered new granddaughter. "Our class is considered beneath the "coloreds" like your mother, I'm afraid." He had turned back towards Winston as he finished his sentence.

"Her people are mixed African and European blood," he said, "unlike my ancestors who're African and Indian on both sides. Thousands of Indians came here voluntarily as indentured servants after slavery was abolished. Most ended up as landowners—compensated with land to make up for unpaid wages and promised transportation back home after their period of servitude was over.

"And I'm talking about to India," he said, winking with a smile. "I'm not talking about the people who were native to the land and just called "Indians" because somebody wouldn't admit to being lost." His reference was made to early European explorers who stumbled their way upon the "new land" trying to get to the Far East for spices."

"India?" Kristin was surprised and still smiling at the comment.

"That's right, "A large group of Indians and Chinese came to Jamaica to work the sugar plantations after slavery was finally declared illegal here. The Chinese weren't as suited for the climate, but many of them stayed here anyway.

"It was the Indians who first brought the ganja here, as he called marijuana, and curry. Eventually, they intermarried with the worker class—the Africans, and some of them married the coloreds if the planter had large enough farms.

"Garvey started the Universal Negro Improvement Association right here in Jamaica, you know, back in 1914 when I was barely a teenager. I remember my dad and my uncles sitting around the table talking about him. He had travelled around Central America and Europe for four years before he started UNIA and everyone looked up to him," he told his fascinated grandson and his wife. "He talked to as many people with African blood as he could, and you could tell he had given a lot of thought about how to help everyone recover after slavery. He put all sorts of information together about it; an inventory of what we all had available, as a people. That's why he was so keen on getting together with Booker Washington, but it just didn't work out."

"But why wouldn't it?" Kristin wanted to know. "What happened?"

"It had to be in Divine Order, is all I can say; Washington up and died just before Garvey's trip to Tuskegee. He was gonna meet with him and Dr. Carver about the school he wanted to build here."

"Wow! That would've really been something! Can you imagine what would've happened if they *had* met?"

"I guess that's something we'll never know for sure, Son." Grandpa Bailey was quiet with his memories for several seconds.

"He had already been deported from the U. S. by the time I met him," he said after a pause. "...After Hoover set him up, that is."

"What?" Kristin searched her memory for something she vaguely remembered Dr. Keenan saying in class once. He started telling them something about J. Edgar Hoover, the first director of the F.B.I., but he had stopped in mid-sentence and let them draw their own conclusions. She wondered whether it had anything to do with what Grandpa Bailey was saying.

"That's right." He confirmed her suspicions in a resolute tone, as though reading her mind. He was thrilled that his grandchildren were interested in hearing his stories about the old days and was eager to share his experiences and the history he had lived through.

"Hoover had just gotten out of law school; he was still wet behind the ears when he lucked into that job at the Justice Department. "But that didn't mean he didn't know how to take advantage of an opportunity— I'll give him that. He built his whole career by fabricating a criminal case against Garvey, and it did the trick too because it killed all his plans.

"And all of it was motivated by the blind quest for money, as usual," he said, dryly. "Garvey was interfering with the powers-that-be who were looking for reduced costs in the production of automobiles for sale. They had to squelch all that pan-African talk he was spouting to have any chance of being successful. What Garvey was talking was revolutionary; it still is, with far-reaching consequences."

Grandpa Bailey settled back into his arm chair, still pleasantly surprised that his grandson and Kristin were so captured by what he was telling them. They hung onto every word.

"Sometimes, when we were between deadlines in the print shop, he would tell us things about his experiences in America. I had a chance to ask him all sorts of questions and I discovered some very interesting things."

"Like what?"

"Well, for example, he ran across Booker Washington's *Up From Slavery* when he came back after his travels in 1914. He was fascinated by that book and what Washington was doing at Tuskegee. He was always disappointed that he missed that opportunity to meet him, but Washington inspired his creation of UNIA. Garvey had a tough time trying to get it going in Jamaica but he was only twenty-eight. When Washington died a few months before he was ready to travel to Tuskegee, Garvey ended up going to New York instead. And the climate was ripe for UNIA there, as I'm sure you probably know. It hadn't been that long since the race wars," he ended, referring to the racial violence in New York in the early 1900s.

"It sure would've been interesting if he had met up with Washington." Winston's mind was still busy sifting through the possibilities.

"You're right about that." His grandfather agreed. "That Washington had a lot more business savvy than a lot of people gave him credit for, that's for sure. He played a big role in financing *most* historically black schools in America, not just Tuskegee. According to what Garvey told us, the money people would always ask Washington for his opinion before writing checks to any Black school. That's why Garvey had such high hopes for Jamaica.

"He modeled UNIA after some of the founding principles of Washington's National Business League, organized to promote Black commerce and financial development. It was a good move too because UNIA ended up with over thirty branches and two million members in just a few years after Garvey opened the New York office.

"But he would speculate about it too sometimes," he said thoughtfully, "what else he might have done here if he had been able to work directly with Washington, or at least spend some time talking to him face-to-face.

"By the time 1920 rolled around, he had close to a thousand local divisions of UNIA in the U.S., the Caribbean, Central America, Canada, and several African countries too. He was becoming quite successful, which is what caught Hoover's attention in the first place—that and his plans to organize African Americans to go back to Africa. Garvey was very vocal in urging African descendents to help free the continent of colonialism; he collected large sums of money through UNIA to fund the movement.

"But a lot of effort went into discrediting him," Grandpa Bailey concluded. "Did you know that the first Black FBI agent had Garvey to thank for his career? He was hired solely for that purpose—to infiltrate UNIA and spy on Garvey. He helped Hoover build the case for mail fraud against Garvey, in connection with the UNIA fund raising. He was tried in 1923 and spent a few years in federal prison in Atlanta before he was deported to Jamaica.

"Garvey would tell us one story after the next about his plans to return the Diaspora back to Africa," Grandpa Bailey reminisced after another pause. "He told us it was his plan to start a UNIA colony in Liberia that had been his downfall. It posed a big threat to certain business interests because plans coincided with the time that the American auto industry was just getting off the ground. There were lucrative business deals being negotiated for rubber production in Liberia and the cheap labor there was a big part of that equation.

"Garvey used to say that it was the first nail in his coffin, so to speak, the minute he started interfering with all of that profit potential.

※※※

After giving it some thought, Kristin reluctantly agreed that their conversations with Winston's grandfather may have played a role in her strange beach experience.

"...That's probably part of it," she conceded finally, after several minutes of silence. "...But I haven't even told you the strangest part."

"I admit that what Grandpa Bailey told us blew me away and we talked about Garvey in Dr. Keenan's class a lot too, but I wasn't consciously thinking about any of that. I promise you, I was content just to lay here and think about you." She leaned over and gave Winston's cheek a loud smack and then raised her head higher so that he could cradle her in his arms.

They had checked into the Montego Bay hotel to spend their last two days in Jamaica—another surprise wedding gift from Grandpa Bailey. The next day they were to board their flight back to the United States. Kristin knew she would never forget their trip, just as she knew she would always love her husband.

She tried a different approach in explaining. "The thoughts I was having were so intense that when I looked up and saw the security guy coming this way, I felt that I *had* to talk to him since you weren't back yet. And this is the *strangest* part of it for me...

"I started talking to the guy about the triangular slave trade and after a minute or two I realized he had no idea what I was talking about. At first, I thought it was a language barrier; his accent was pretty thick and I thought that since I was having a hard time understanding him, he might not understand me either. Eventually, I realized that wasn't it at all; he didn't *know* there had been slavery in America. At one point, he even said he had heard *rumors* about it—he actually used the word "rumor." Can you believe that?"

"Well, as a matter of fact I can, sweetheart." Winston hesitated, knowing he would leave her more confused than ever by his response.

"What do you mean? How could he possibly *not* know about American slavery?"

"I know it may sound strange to you," he told her, "but you have to understand the dynamics of slavery here. There were many Africans brought here to work the sugar and pineapple plantations; it didn't take very long before they outnumbered the Europeans—and by very large margins. The Europeans were terrified, of course, after they realized it; they were in great fear of reprisals almost from the beginning. They did some awful things to keep their captives under control over the years, and after their fears became realities things only got worse. There were many slave revolts in Jamaica; many of the African captives escaped into the mountains and never came back down. You can see for yourself how thick the vegetation grows around here. The Europeans had no way of accounting for the escapees and you can just imagine what a frightening experience it must have been for them."

"Yeah, I'll bet." Kristin agreed, without an ounce of sympathy in her voice.

"The thing is," Winston went on, ignoring her sarcasm, "when they saw that they stood little chance of catching the escapees, they began keeping their captives as isolated as possible so others couldn't escape. They were kept in ridiculously unhealthy living conditions and when word got around about the violent slave rebellions in Haiti, things began to go downhill fast. The Haitians outnumbered the French by even greater margins than the British were outnumbered here, but they were forced into such poor conditions that their death rate was high. The solution chosen by the French was to keep bringing in more slaves to replace those who had died. The uprisings began in earnest during the late 1700s and large numbers of Europeans were killed. It was like a pressure cooker boiling over and it kept getting worse until the Haitians finally won their independence in 1804.

"What with all the bloodshed and violence, the sugar industry suffered greatly. In the end, the French decided it just wasn't worth the trouble of keeping the Haitians enslaved, but they forced them to pay outrageously severe reparations for the property that had been lost during their rebellions."

"Yeah. I remember Dr. Keenan telling us that the Haitians were forced to pay for winning their freedom, and were *still* paying for it."

"You wouldn't believe how large an assessment they were charged. It was so excessive and severe that the freed slaves were never able to recover," Winston agreed. "That's the main reason for the extreme poverty in Haiti to this day. And of course the British in Jamaica knew all about those rebellions, and about the ones taking place in the United States. They used extreme tactics to keep their forced labor under control and it just kept getting worse until the rebellions grew more persistent and ended slavery in Jamaica too."

"But I still don't get it, baby," Kristin spent a few minutes in thought before speaking, her tone once again highlighting her confusion.

"That happened a long time before slavery ended in the United States, but most people I can think of know there was once slavery in the Caribbean too. I just don't get what you're saying."

Winston decided to try a different approach to helping her understand the island's unique culture.

"Things have always been more complex here, I'm afraid. Take the missionaries who came from Europe to teach the former slaves here, for example. They didn't do it for free the way that education was offered to America's freed slaves. That made the biggest difference, I think, but the other major factor was that the coloreds were always treated better than those who were purely African. It's kind of the same way things were in New Orleans with some offspring of slave owners there. The coloreds in Jamaica had money and they owned property long before slavery ended here. They were just as used to the finer things in life as the Europeans.

"My mothers' family, on the other side of the island, was always able to afford an education—from the time that the missionaries first came. The coloreds only make up a small percentage of African descendants here in Jamaica and the majority of them treated the black workers worse than the Europeans ever did."

Kristin was shocked and amazed by what her husband was telling her, yet it all finally made sense. It also explained why he didn't suggest visiting his mother's family while they were on the island.

"It sounds to me like your friend who stopped here might've been born into a family that has never been able to afford school. There're still plenty of them, you know—literally generations of people who've never had the money to pay for an education.

"This is all mind boggling!" Kristin was stunned as she realized she had probably talked to many Jamaicans since they arrived who had no idea that American slavery ever existed.

Winston was eager to change the subject after Kristin was left with her thoughts for a few minutes. "Listen, baby. The guy who helped me get the almonds down offered to take us into town later tonight, if you wanna go."

"Of course I want to go!"

And just like that her mood seemed to lift, although she never forgot her conversation with the security guard. She did make an effort to put it out of her mind though, because her husband was trying so hard to show her a good time.

Winston expected the prospect of a trip into town to distract her. He knew how much she loved dabbling into other cultures, and listening to their friends at Tuskegee who were from the city talk about their experiences.

"Great, let's go then. The only thing is we're going to have to wait until he gets off work. We have to meet him at the security booth at the edge of the hotel grounds too. The people working here aren't allowed to fraternize with the guests, I'm afraid. They're just supposed to wear colorful uniforms and smile all the time." He was being sarcastic now. "The hotel owners don't want us to know what their lives are really like because it might spoil the whole happy tourist thing they have going."

"That's unbelievable." Kristin thought about it for a moment. "But I guess that explains why that guy seemed so hesitant to talk to me.

"And thanks for arranging for us to go into town. Seeing more of the *real* Jamaica will make our trip complete."

She decided to get a grip on herself and shake off whatever it was that had taken hold of her. She would concentrate on enjoying the rest of their honeymoon trip. But their trip into "Mo Bay" turned into more of an outing than she expected.

※※※

"Pssst."

Kristin looked in the direction that the sound had come from, surprised that she could even hear it over the noise in the club. So far, she had been reeling from their adventure into downtown Montego Bay. She and Winston had walked to the security booth near the hotel's property line as planned, and they waited for the thin young guard who had helped Winston collect almonds from the tree. After he signed out, they walked further up the gravel street with him toward the main road to wait for a jitney cab.

They stood in the pitch darkness of night for what seemed like an eternity before a distant light finally approached them from down the dark road. Kristin would've been terrified had Winston not been there with her. The pine trees in Tuskegee cloaked everything in a velvety blackness too after the sun went down, except for those few places where streetlights were installed. But there was a different kind of darkness in the Jamaican night. She clutched Winston's hand tightly, imagining all sorts of wild animals to be lurking in the nearby woods. The light finally grew stronger until a small car roared to a stop right in front of where they stood. They all piled inside the already crowded vehicle and William, their security guard-turned tour guide, gave the driver money for the ride. After they were settled the car took off again in the same direction, still traveling at a break-neck speed.

The colorful voices of passengers in the car were alive with laughter—at least until Kristin made a comment to Winston loud enough for them to hear. After that, all their conversations came to a halt, and it took a few minutes before she realized it was because of her American accent. In a short time, the warm vibrations they had felt when they first got into the cab were replaced by a wary distrust. Kristin's feelings were hurt. She had several Jamaican friends back home, as well as friends from a number of African countries. It was hard to accept their suspicions of her, and she discreetly mentioned it to Winston as soon as they were out of the car. He merely brushed it off as an offshoot of Jamaica's complicated class system, so she tried to forget it.

First their guide took them to an area downtown where the streets were filled with people. Most seemed to be making their way home from work, dashing into shops quickly and returning to wait among the crowds around bus stops. Their voices held the same enthusiasm as the passengers in their taxi, as old friends greeted one another.

William led them to a westernized club next that was a few streets over from where the cab had dropped them. There was a band there that played many of the same songs they listened to in Tuskegee. They danced to a few tunes to appease William, who was clearly proud of himself for having taken them there. After a bit, Winston took him aside. As tactfully as he could, he told him that as good as the band was, they really wanted to do some of the things that *he* would normally do in town. Smiling, William led them to a tiny bakery a few blocks over where Winston happily bought several beef patties and coco-bread that he had been longing for. The spicy meat pastries had been heavy on his mind from the time they left their hotel, and he quickly polished one off. He had been able to find plenty of good patties on Georgia Avenue in Washington, but had no such luck in or around Tuskegee. He ate his fill and afterwards, he insisted on stopping at a small stand to buy chicken sandwiches that were cooked right on the street in a tall drum of hot grease.

"My grandfather used to buy these for me when I came down for the summer," he managed to say between bites. "He used to go into town every other week for supplies and he always took me with him."

Kristin enjoyed the beef patties as much as Winston, but she shied away from the street meat. She had a history of stomach issues and didn't want to take a chance on eating the chicken so far from their hotel.

She had learned her lesson in the jitney cab and said very little as they walked along the streets. They went virtually unnoticed as they mingled with the December crowd. It was a warm night so she kept asking William to buy ginger beers from the money Winston had given him. She had downed several of the strong sodas to try and quench her thirst and before long, she was urging him to find a place where she could relieve herself. William immediately led them down a narrow alley and into a darkened reggae club filled with music. It also reeked of ganja, but she was in no position to protest by then.

The act of doing her business in the dingy bathroom turned out to be more of a challenge than she expected, but she managed to balance herself carefully over the well-used toilet. She kept one hand pressed firmly against the unlatchable stall door at the same time, and somehow, completed her mission. She encountered the old woman as she left the cramped room. She heard her hissing sounds as she looked for a space to wait for Winston, who had disappeared into the men's room.

"Do you mean me?" She looked over her shoulder before asking the question to see if someone might be standing behind her. The crumpled woman looked to be in her late 70s and she had piercing eyes that fixed on her. As soon as she responded the woman came forward quickly.

"Yes, Miss." Her voice had an ominous tone, and she held up a well-worn deck of tarot cards as she continued to stare into Kristin's dark eyes. "There is much that I can tell you about your future."

It was only then that Kristin realized the woman was asking her whether she wanted to have her fortune told. Normally, she would have jumped at the chance, especially after her friend Niyla introduced her to astrology. The composite chart she created to represented her relationship potential with Winston had been fascinating, and Kristin vowed to use it in the coming years to keep their relationship on track.

She was surprised by her level of anxiety at the prospect of hearing what the woman would read from the cards. She seemed to see straight through her, for one thing; she had known right away that they weren't Jamaican when they had managed to keep it from nearly everyone else in town. It was all Kristin could do not to run out of the noisy club and wait for Winston in the alley.

"No, thank you," she mumbled weakly. "My husband and I have to leave soon to get back to our hotel."

"Ah yes, I see." The woman responded, as though she knew much more about them than Kristin was comfortable having her know.

"No worries—I understand, my dear." The knowing look on the woman's face did little to ease Kristin's concerns. And after she finished speaking, she continued to stare deeply into her eyes.

"Just remember, my dear—one day you'll have to choose between him and your destiny."

"Are you ready Sweetie? This is a first—you finishing up in the ladies room before me." It was something that had been a point of contention whenever they went out together.

Winston had walked up behind her unaware and startled her at first. She turned toward him quickly as she recovered, relieved after recognizing his voice.

"What's wrong, Baby?" The look on her face made him don his protective posture again right away. "What happened?"

"I'm okay." She gave him a quick assurance after seeing how upset he was becoming. "It's nothing; I was just talking to this woman..."

She turned back to where the old woman had been standing but she was already gone. Kristin didn't know what to think of that and found the whole encounter to be unsettling. But she definitely wasn't about to repeat what the woman had said to her, not to her husband.

"Never mind, baby. There was just a woman here who wanted to tell my fortune, that's all." She turned again so her face wouldn't give her away.

"Oh, okay." There was relief in his voice after learning she hadn't been in any danger with him no there to guard her safety. "I'm sure there are plenty enough fortune tellers around here, that's for sure, but it's time for us to go find William I think. We should probably get back to the hotel so we can pack to fly out tomorrow."

They found William standing outside in the alley, waiting patiently for them to come out of the club. He quickly hailed a taxi that took all three of them back to the hotel—this time to the lobby entrance since they were riding in an official cab. Winston had already given him what he had asked to be their guide for the evening, but he gave him a generous tip before they said their good-byes.

When they were finally back in the hotel, Kristin tried her best to rebound from the disturbing encounter with the old woman. But she was never able to fully relax after the woman's ominous warning. She lay awake for hours after she and Winston made love one last time before they had to leave the island and end their honeymoon. She kept wondering what the woman in the club had been so intent on telling her, and asking herself whether she should have taken the time to listen.

Chapter 2

If I Could Turn Back The Hands Of Time
Twenty Five Years Later

*T*he large iridescent fly walked back and forth across the wall facing Kristin's desk. She had been watching it for several minutes, intrigued by how much it reminded her of an expectant father pacing outside a delivery room. She couldn't remember an insect being in her office at any time before. She had been in Ghana the whole time their administration building was being built, and she had witnessed its solid construction for herself day-by-day. Like all the other buildings in Exodus Village, the administration building that also housed her apartment, was designed to be free of pests. Each structure built in their transformation haven featured a screened entranceway filled with colorful pots of citronella, marigold, lavender, basil, and thyme. The plants were all natural repellents to mosquitoes, flies and similar insects and formed a shield leading to each building's inner door. To be where the fly was when she spotted it meant having to make its way past those natural barriers, as well as travel down two hallways and through three doors that were normally kept closed. How it came to be on her wall at all was a mystery that she had become intent on solving.

It was the perfect diversion from the stacks of papers piled on her desk and her self-imposed deadline for going through them. Her assistant, Amina, and her staff had already sifted through hundreds of applications from people who wanted to be their first residents. Once again, the young woman had proven herself to be a lifesaver. Kristin couldn't imagine how they would have ever accomplished all that they had without her.

She had been a godsend from the moment they met, almost eight years earlier. The strikingly beautiful young woman had been a history teacher during the same time that Kristin had been in Ghana on loan from Hunter

University. She had been a visiting professor at the University of Kumasi—formerly named the Kwame Nkrumah University of Science and Technology, and Amina had been assigned as her liaison. Kristin quickly came to rely on her for help in navigating the then-unfamiliar West African culture. A trusted friendship had grown between the two women that had lasted far beyond her two-year teaching assignment.

Amina and her four-member staff had spent weeks narrowing the list of applicants who would be eligible to become transitional residents of Exodus Village. The Diasporan Exodus Foundation had received thousands of applications for their pilot program, even with the announcement being sent to a limited number of organizations. It had been a painstaking process to sift through them all but her group had finished ahead of schedule as usual. Now, it was up to her to make the final selections of who they would invite to participate in their six-month pilot, along with the applicants who would be their alternates and placed on a waiting-list. For the past two days she had struggled with her contribution to the process since the unexpected phone call she had from Winston; a call that could change everything.

A tentative knock interrupted her thoughts and a few seconds later Amina walked cautiously into the room. Normally, she would have respected the closed door's suggestion and taken it as a signal that Kristin didn't want to be disturbed. But the younger woman was too worried about her to stand on ceremony. They could all see that the wind had been knocked out of Kristin's sail after the call from her ex-husband. She had never been very good at concealing her feelings and this time she didn't even try.

"Kristin...?" Amina's voice was as tentative as her knock. She knew they were working against a deadline but she wasn't sure if she should leave her friend alone.

"Do you need anything? Are you okay?"

She had already learned from the server who brought Kristin's meals that she had eaten very little of her lunch. The two had breakfast together that morning, as they did whenever Kristin was in the village. She had been careful about moving food around in her plate, but Amina noted how little of the food made it to her mouth.

The concern in her voice brought immediate tears to Kristin's eyes. Her mind had been overstimulated for weeks, even before she answered the phone to find Winston on the other end. She had already been finding it difficult to focus; thankfully, they were ahead of schedule because she had found it impossible to concentrate after his call. Her emotions had been all over the place for a month—starting with her excitement in receiving final confirmation that their pilot program was on track. She had also been pleasantly surprised when Winston conceded to allowing Celeste to come with their son to spend time with her in Ghana, shortly thereafter. And the same night that she picked Celeste and Trazi up from the airport, her son had absolutely thrilled her with news that he was being discharged from the Navy. It had convinced her that 1998 would be a magical year; her son would leave the military a year before his commitment was scheduled to end, just as she had prayed.

His announcement had been the perfect start for the two weeks they had spent traveling across the country together. There had been enough of Exodus Village built to give them a true sense of the Foundation's mission. By the time they boarded their flight for Zurich, they were both as excited about the Foundation's chances for success as she was. Then, before they could land at Dulles airport in Virginia, she was on the phone talking to Winston.

She had been so flustered by the sudden sound of his voice that she nearly missed the pain that was underneath it at first. She braced herself to find out why he was calling. She had been terrified that he would say something had happened to the kids, but still, she found little relief in learning the real reason for his call. He was calling about Angela, he said, in a tone that she had never heard before.

"Thanks, Amina...I'll be okay," Kristin answered her finally. "It's going to take a little time—that's all. It's just hard for me to get Celeste's mother off my mind."

"I didn't realize the two of you were so close." Amina took her comment as a cue and walked more fully into the room. She automatically adjusted the blinds to let in more light, still alert for signs that her friend wanted to be left alone. But she had a feeling that talking might force Kristin to confront her grief and she decided to give it a try.

"She was a freshman at Tuskegee when we met," She said after a pause, "when Winston and I were just going into our junior years. We were planning our first anniversary celebration, and Trazi was just a few months old. For some reason, Angela caught my attention the first time I saw her on campus."

Kristin looked up from a preoccupation with her fingers. "Some of the guys would refer to them as the latest "crop" of freshmen. They came like clock-work every fall—new groups of beautiful Black women on campus everyplace they looked." She was smiling.

"It was months later before we actually met." There was a hint of sadness in her voice. "That's when I found out she was one of Winston's home girls."

She had put a slight emphasis on the term that had evolved in meaning so much over the years. In the current culture, there had been a gang-related tinge attached to its meaning but at the time they were students, it meant something much more innocent. It simply described classmates who had close hometown ties and could be counted on to look out for each other.

"One of the first things I noticed about Angela was how pretty she was," Kristin continued. "In all the time I knew her, she was always stylish— even in her worse moments." She dropped her head and resumed her fascination with her fingers for a few seconds before looking up at Amina with a bittersweet smile.

"Celeste is stylish too; she has the same sweet personality that I picked up from her mother when we met all those years ago." Her smile brightened as she mentioned her adopted daughter's name, and there was a mischievous look as she relayed how Winston had nightmares when Celeste became an adolescent overnight.

"She's pretty *and* shapely, just like her mother; it nearly drove him insane there for a while." Kristin laughed weakly for a few seconds.

As she talked to Amina it dawned on her that she had never felt threatened by Angela's relationship with Winston—not even after things turned out the way they had. She hadn't minded at all when her husband started looking out for Angela at Tuskegee; she liked her too, and the kind of informal connection they had was common around campus. It didn't even bother her when she noticed Angela following Winston around sometimes. Their two-year age difference had seemed quite significant back then. They both treated Angela more like a little sister than anything else, and she could remember thinking of it as little more than a harmless crush. Now that she looked back, it seemed odd that she didn't feel a threat when Winston mentioned running into her at an alumni Christmas party, after their marriage ended. She wasn't even overly concerned when he told her that he and Angela started dating. None of it registered with her because Kristin didn't believe Winston had ever stopped loving *her*—not for a minute.

It was only later that she realized how much in denial she had been. She believed that his love for her would make all the difference; she never once considered that what they had might be in any real jeopardy. But before any of them had time to adjust to Winston's and Angela's quick marriage, they found out Celeste was on the way. Everything had changed when she was born and their fates were sealed.

"We had a very unusual friendship," she told Amina. "It's remarkable how it withstood the test of time, especially considering the way things were..." Her voice trailed off.

"We never had one disagreement between us," she started again. "Trazi was barely four when she and Winston got married. I turned my focus to making sure my son wouldn't be negatively affected by our divorce. It led us to a closer friendship; much closer than the one we had at Tuskegee."

And it was true. Their relationship had taken dramatic turns throughout the years, but it had survived even after Angela and Winston were divorced. That's why she was finding it so hard to accept. Her friend's transition from the Earth had come so suddenly, just when she was starting to get her life together. The years of treating her depression with drugs and alcohol were finally behind her, but they had apparently already taken their toll. Angela's kidneys had failed and she was already gone by the time her neighbors found her in her house.

"I know in my heart that her death was the ultimate healing from the torment she went through for all those years. I can find comfort knowing that her Spirit is eternal, that her soul is finally at peace."

She smiled a few seconds and then her face became wistful again. "It's just going to take some time, that's all, to get used to her being gone."

She got up from behind her desk to take a closer look at a photo she had taken of Angela and Celeste when she was eight years old. Her friend had taken very little interest in the child until recently but Kristin had always held out hope that their relationship would take root one day. She made a point of taking pictures of them together as often as she could, as Celeste was growing up. She was glad that she had because now she could put them in an album and send them to her. Kristin picked up another photo of mother and daughter and stared at it for a moment. Sad again suddenly, she put it back on the credenza.

"I was worried about how the news of her mother's death might affect her." Kristin had been standing with her back to Amina and she turned to face her before walking back to sit down heavily behind her desk. "She seems to be taking it well though—all things considered."

There was hope in her voice, but Amina knew her smile was forced. Kristin had told her that Angela and her daughter had finally begun to consciously develop a relationship, fifteen years after she was born. They had made plans to start getting together at least once a week so they could start over and get to know each other. They were supposed to start right before the kids came to visit her, but there had been some kind of a mix-up about a vaccination Celeste needed before boarding her flight.

Kristin got up and went to stand near the window. "It's all so sad."

"She seems pretty self-assured." Amina paused before making the comment, hoping the observation would bring her friend some relief. They all knew how conflicted she was about not going back to the States for Angela's burial. "She seems to have a good head on her shoulders for a girl her age," she added.

"She does." Kristin agreed readily. "Before I could even bring up the subject of Angela's service she was already convincing me that I didn't need to fly back to be there for it. But if I thought for one minute she really needed me there, I would have gladly made the sacrifice."

She turned toward Amina after the unnecessary explanation. "I could've found a way to work on these on the plane." Kristin waved her hand toward the applications piled on her desk.

"But after the kids saw what we're all about here, they understand now how much work we have ahead of us."

"I don't think anyone would expect you to travel so far," Amina reassured her. "It's good that you were able to spend so much time with Celeste and your son while they were here." She hoped the reminder would help change Kristin's focus to happier times. She could see that she was just as upset as she had been on the first day they met. Amina had seen it right away as she walked toward Kristin to introduce herself. She could tell that she was being tortured by something and she had watched over her carefully during her first few months in Kumasi. She didn't find out until later what that was all about.

And right on cue, Kristin began talking about her ex-husband as she frequently did.

"The thing that surprises me most is the way Winston is reacting to Angela's death." She looked up at Amina as though expecting some explanation.

"Celeste put him back on the phone and I had to tell him I wasn't coming to her service. He all but lost it when he knew I wouldn't change my mind."

Kristin had grown close enough to Amina to confide in her even more than she did with her old friend Niyla at times, probably because there was little chance that she and Winston would ever meet. It was like having an opportunity to share your deepest secrets with a stranger on a train, some-

31

one you would never likely see again. It had taken years before Kristin finally told her about the baby that she and Winston lost; it was late one night as they worked on plans for her travel agency's grand opening. And she seemed instantly relieved once she told her; no longer all alone on those times that she was pulled under by grief by the loss of their baby.

She and Winston had only let down their guards once after he and Angela got married. She never told him anything about the little girl they created that night. Their baby girl would've been close in age to Celeste if it hadn't been for the miscarriage.

She had only carried their second child for a few precious months. It took Nana Adwoa to help her begin a healing process from the emotional scars she carried for years. Her friend and elder offered comfort to her smiling, telling her the soul that had occupied her infant's body had merely played a trick on her. It *pretended* to come to live with her, knowing it would only stay a short while. Nana advised her not to spend more time in mourning because the baby could come back at any time she wanted. The knowing look on her face had convinced Kristin that what she said was true, especially after Nana assured her that the baby would find its way back to her one day.

As unlikely as it seemed, that had helped her accept her loss in a much different way. She was still sad on days that she had vivid memories of her happiness in feeling the child grow inside her. She also felt tremendous guilt because she never told Winston about the baby.

At first, she didn't know how. She could already see that he had never forgiven himself for having a moment of weakness with her that night. His grandfather had taught him that being a man meant being in control at all times. What happened between them had definitely not been planned, and once it was set in motion, there had been little that either of them could do to stop it. She knew Winston was still wracked with guilt. Angela had never been the same after she had Celeste, when he had been so happy about their new baby.

Kristin had carried her own guilt about the night they were together, but only because they were never truthful with Angela about it. Now it was too late.

"What did he say to you?" Amina wasn't sure whether she was prying.

"It wasn't so much what he said," Kristin answered her slowly, "as how he reacted after he realized I really wasn't coming back. I could hear in his voice how upset he was; terrified by the prospect of going through it all without me. He didn't even try to hide it." She rested both elbows on her desk with her hands gently cradling her face.

"I was tempted to remind him that he got married a *third* time and he still has one wife left to comfort him." A devilish smile told Amina she was kidding.

"Unfortunately, I couldn't do it. I never could stand it when he was feeling down about something; not even when I was mad at him."

She looked at the small clock on her desk and saw that it was nearly five o'clock. Angela's service would be starting soon and everyone in Washington was probably getting dressed for the chapel.

"He still feels guilt but I'm the one who went through loosing the baby. I've lived with scars that he knows nothing about.

"I still feel sick at the prospect of telling him about her." She looked at Amina with a look that asked to be rescued from her dilemma. "But sometimes I think I won't be able to put it behind me until I do tell him."

She knew the regret Winston had to live; how he responded to Angela after he lost patience with her. It had been obvious to everyone that she had checked out of their marriage early on, and for a while, no one knew for certain whether she ever intended to check back in. After he gave up on her being a real mother for Celeste, Winston had become indifferent to her struggle with alcoholism and depression. Kristin had seen his resentment grow over the years, knowing how trapped he felt. A part of him probably still resented her, even as he wrestled alone with his guilt.

But none of it could be helped by anything that she did. She had already rearranged meetings that had been scheduled during the children's visit. She couldn't afford to reschedule them again—especially since Celeste seemed to be okay. She had too much work to do even if she *had* been inclined to go back to help Winston get through the day.

But flying all that way back to the States wasn't going to help Angela. She didn't need help from any of them anymore.

Chapter 3

Living For The City

*L*awana sprinted the last twenty yards to the bus stop and still barely made it before the No. 42 bus pulled out. She held her breath until she was on the steps because if she had missed it, she had little chance of getting home in time. Even with that she had to pray that the D. C. traffic would be light all the way. It still meant running the last two blocks after she got off but with a little luck she just might make it.

The last caseworker had been much nicer but she had to up and quit her job—right after Lawana figured out she could trust her. It was just her luck that the woman found somebody who wanted to marry her; now she didn't even *need* a job anymore. It wasn't that she wasn't happy for Ms. Steele, she was just the one person at Social Services who didn't treat her like something on the bottom of their shoe. It had been a big blow to find out the woman was leaving.

Half the time, she couldn't tell whether some of the others even heard her answer the fifty million questions they always asked—every time she had to be recertified for benefits. But not Ms. Steele though; she was different. Lawana didn't realize it until right before she left but she could see that she really cared what happened to her and her kids. She didn't just check off all the boxes on the long forms like the others, like she was in a hurry to get finished. A lot of them acted like they could care less, no matter what you might be saying.

Ms. Steele had some good ideas too; she told her how to get the boys to cooperate with their counselors and get along better with their teachers. None of those problems came up until after their daddy died. She knew it was because they didn't want anybody else telling them what to do.

Ms. Steele had talked her into going back to get her GED too; she even helped her fill out the application. But that woman who replaced her was more like the heifer driving the bus at that time of day. The man she rode with since she started working full time always looked at his side mirror, to see if anybody else was coming instead of just pulling off the way that woman did. If the other bus driver saw you were close enough not to be holding everybody else up for too long, he always waited if you hurried up. The witch driving the bus she was on now acted like she barely saw you half the time. She always closed the door real fast like you were lucky that she had waited as long as she did. Sometimes, the heifer wouldn't even turn her head in your direction when she gave you a transfer.

Lawana figured out a way to save some money right after she and the kids moved into the apartment. She could ride the Columbia Road bus down to Safeway and get a transfer and if she could get in and out fast enough, she could use the transfer to get back home. All she had to do was walk three blocks over and catch a bus going up 16th Street instead. It meant walking four blocks home with her groceries, but she saved the extra fare. And without Jabari, she had to try to save money any way that she could.

She routinely passed up several seats closer to the front and kept moving toward the back as the driver pulled out into traffic. Never once did the woman consider the people who might be standing or trying to find a seat; the bus accelerated just as jerky as it usually did. Since Lawana always made a habit of checking out the person sitting next to any empty seat she saw first, she was forced to trot the last few steps down the aisle before she swung into an empty pair she finally spotted. Everyone she'd seen along the way either looked crazy or like they might start yapping until one of them got off the bus. And the last thing she needed was to have someone filling her head up with all *their* problems, or rattling off a bunch of empty words just to hear themselves talk. She already had enough to think about of her own, without cluttering her head up with stuff like that.

The first thing she had to do was figure out what to do with George, before he messed everything up for all of them. Her youngest son had made her miss a half day of work with his foolishness at school. She was going to be short four hours again in her next check, when she couldn't afford to be short on anything. And all she would have to show for it would be time spent talking about her son with somebody who didn't know either of them, asking *her* why he wouldn't do what he was supposed to do at school.

Mr. Henry didn't look none too happy either when she gave him the bad news about having to take the afternoon off. She was praying that she would still have a job when she got back. The restaurant was what most people would call a dive—a real "greasy spoon" she heard one lady call it. But the food was cheap and it didn't taste that bad once you got used to it. At least working there meant she had a steady paycheck every week, and sometimes Mr. Henry boxed up food that was left over: chicken, or fish, and one time he even gave her some oxtails to take home for her kids. She took the pork chops he gave her too but she always put them in a separate containers. She gave them and the livers she got from the restaurant to Lacrecia's baby sitter, but since Mr. Henry was nice enough to give her the food she didn't want to hurt his feelings. He didn't know that she and the children didn't eat pork or liver.

He was a good man alright, almost like a father. But she had taken off at one of the busiest times of the day on the busiest day—Friday. She tried to tell her case worker that when she scheduled the appointment but she acted like she didn't hear her. So, Lawana had no choice but to leave Mr. Henry with one cashier to handle all the people in the drive-thru, plus the ones who came inside. It was easy enough for one person to handle the inside crowd, because all you had to do was take their orders and their money as soon as they walked inside the door. After that, they didn't have much choice but to take a seat, or stand around and wait for their food when the restaurant was real busy. Mr. Henry knew most of them didn't have much time off though. He had everybody work real fast during the breakfast and lunch rush, but there was always a chance someone waiting in the drive-thru might get tired of waiting. It was easy for them to pull out and go some place else to eat, even if they had already ordered. The drive-thru was where they made their money if they could keep the line moving. But she had to leave in the middle of the lunch rush to make it home by two o'clock— she really saw no choice.

She looked down at the Rolex her new boyfriend gave her the last time he went to New York. She knew he must have bought it on Canal Street, but it was hard even for her to tell it was a knock-off right away. She was secretly glad the watch *wasn't* real, as long as it kept good time; she had already learned *that* lesson with Little Man's daddy. Still, she had to give it to him. Willie had treated her like a queen from the first day they met.

She fell in love with him right away but she had been very young at the time. Willie had bought her a *real* Rolex and many other things she thought she would never have. She had heard the name before but he finally had to tell her how much he had paid for the watch. He probably figured he'd better tell her so she wouldn't just set it down someplace and loose it, or let somebody steal it from her. She was only fifteen when he gave it to her, but Willie waited patiently for her sixteenth birthday before he accepted the thanks she tried to give him. She might've been young but Lawana knew exactly what he wanted from her, even if he was willing to wait for it. Thanks to her mother's boyfriend, she already knew what most men wanted.

But Willie took her away from all of that. He was six years older but he looked much younger and their ages didn't make a bit of difference to them. She met him at the mall one day when she went to get out of the house. She surprised herself when she agreed to let him buy her lunch. Having a boyfriend was the last thing on her mind because all she knew was how her mother's boyfriends treated her.

She and Willie had talked for hours that day and they met in the same place every day for weeks. Finally, she mustered up the nerve to tell him about her mother's boyfriend—the way he was always at their apartment and would "accidentally" walk into the bathroom when she was in it. There wasn't a latch on the door, she explained, so he could do it whenever he wanted; trying to catch her without clothes on. And her mother got mad when Lawana told her what he was doing. Telling her didn't make any difference at all and he kept coming to their house like nothing had happened.

Willie brought her home to his condo that same day, but she had her own bedroom at first since she was so young. He was the first drug dealer she had ever met, although she had seen plenty enough of them around. Willie told her he had started out selling weed when he was thirteen; by the time she met him he had moved up to selling "rock," as he called crack cocaine. He was nothing like she would've expected a drug dealer to be. He never smoked any of the stuff he sold himself, although he brought home pot every now and then. He never sold drugs on the street either; Willie had other people who did it for him.

They lived a good life in his condo in Southwest Washington; it had a fantastic view of the Potomac river from the balcony and they would eat breakfast there when the weather was nice. He always brought home presents for her too—really nice clothes and the jewelry to wear with them. He took her to some of the best places to eat in town—all over the city. They would drive up to the Inner Harbor in Baltimore in his shiny black Mercedes often, and they always went to the best shows that came to town. Everything had been going perfect for them, until the day this young dude who worked for him messed it all up.

Willie had always told them that if they got arrested, they should keep their mouths shut and wait for somebody to get'm out of jail. He never brought much of his street life to their place but sometimes he would tell her things when he came home. He told them all to keep quiet and wait. That's all they had to do but this one guy panicked. She found out at Willie's trial that the cops had come to the shop with their guns out. This guy pulled a gun out too and started shooting, instead of putting his hands in the air like everybody else. He got the gun from a stash of weapons they always kept in the shop. He just pulled the gun from a drawer and shot one of the cops—right in the chest. The poor guy bled to death before the ambulance ever got there.

Willie's luck couldn't have been any worse. If he hadn't been in the shop at that exact moment, his lawyers would've been able to keep him out of jail as they always had—even if the police traced the business back to him. Now he had to be in prison for the rest of his life. Everybody who was there was going to stay in prison, and it was all because that one idiot went and killed a cop.

Willie told them all the time that the guns were only for the young bloods who got up the nerve to try to rob them, or the crackheads who showed up desperate for drugs with no money. Nobody was gonna care if one of *them* was accidentally shot and killed, he used to say. The guns were meant to protect the shop, that's all; not to have a gunfight with the police for Heaven's sake. But then she found out at the trial that the shooter was only fourteen years old. He was the same age that Little Man was now, and only five years older than George. Now, she realized he was just a kid who should never have been mixed up in Willie's drug business.

She had been planning to tell him about Little Man that night when he came home for dinner. She had suspected she was pregnant for a few weeks but she finally took a pregnancy test that day that she bought from the drugstore. She waited up all night to tell Willie he was going to be a father but he never came home. His lawyer called the next morning to tell her she would have to move out of the condo so he could sell it to pay for Willie's defense. He had been in jail only one other time since she'd known him. He had been there for a few days but that was because it was so close to an election and some prosecutor wanted to make a point. Nothing had changed for Lawana during the brief time he was away. Nothing changed for his business either, and everything still worked smoothly without him.

Willie was seldom in the shop himself and that's why Lawana couldn't believe it—that he had been there when the cop was shot. Normally, he would meet the men he dealt with for lunch, or they might sit in the park or some other public place to work out what they needed to work out. This time everything had been different because the police shut down Willie's whole business.

They took all the drugs and money that was in the shop. All of it was gone, except for the fifty thousand dollars Willie always kept at their condo. He used to tell her it would be enough to get them out of Washington if they needed to go in a hurry, or to use until he could get to a bank. She knew that Willie would never tell his attorney about the money because that fifty thousand dollars was all that would be left for her. The rest of his money and the good life they had been living so freely were all gone.

She had moved back to her mother's apartment just long enough to give birth to Little Man, and 'til she could get approved for public housing. The day after he moved her to his condo, Willie had gone to her mother's house to give her some money and talk to her boyfriend about her. He had never told her exactly what he said, but it was apparently enough to keep the boyfriend from looking in her direction again, even when everyone knew Willie was in prison for life.

The place that she and Little Man moved into wasn't all that bad. It was close to the rental office so it was safer than some of the other buildings. She found a job that paid enough to pay rent when her son was three months old, plus she qualified for food stamps and for WIC to buy the baby's milk, juice and cereal. She and Little Man were doing pretty good on their own all-in-all.

Then she met George and Lacrecia's daddy. Lawana knew right away that she had lucked up again because Jabari fell in love with her *and* Little Man. It wasn't long before she was in love with him too; it was much easier than she thought because Jabari didn't try to force her to pretend like she had stopped loving Willie. He was in prison that's all, and they all knew he wasn't getting out. It was just like he was dead and she knew she had to move on. She didn't want to upset Willie with news about the baby while his trial was still going on and once the trial was over, she decided not to ever tell him about their son. What would be the use? She knew he was worried about how she would be taken care of. He would only worry more knowing about the baby, without being able to do anything about it.

She visited him regularly for a while and started sending letters instead when her belly got bigger. She made up all kinds of excuses for not coming to see him at first, and finally stopped mentioning anything about coming at all. It broke her heart to see him locked up like an animal and she hated to hear the sounds of those metal doors in the prison. She kept writing him though, less frequently as the time went by. But she still made a point of sending a card every year on his birthday so he would know that she had never forgotten about him.

His son had still been a toddler when she and Jabari met. Little Man had always thought of him as his father, mainly because that's the way Jabari treated him—even after George and Lacrecia were born. He was such a good man and he worked hard every day to take care of his family. He didn't have a lot of money all the time like Willie had, but then again, they didn't have to live life on the edge all the time. And whatever money Jabari *did* make, he always brought home to her—every penny of it. His friends would tease him all the time about it, but he didn't care. He was proud of the way that he took care of his family.

That was what got him killed in the end because he refused to give up his wallet to that man who tried to rob him, even with a gun waving in his face. Every week after Jabari got paid they would all take the bus to Safeway together, as soon as he got home. On the way back, they would stop off at the Chinese place on the corner to get take-out, with all of their groceries too. Jabari used to let the boys order anything they wanted off the menu. As soon as the policeman told her, Lawana knew right away what had happened. She knew that he fought that man so he wouldn't have to come home without the money he always brought home on Fridays. He didn't want to disappoint his family, and he had died because of it for the Chinese restaurant. They never caught that man who killed him either and that was what made it harder for the boys.

Lacrecia was only two, so she never understood anything that was happening. She barely missed her daddy after a few weeks but her boys hadn't been the same since. They were on their way to meet their father at the bus stop when it happened, just like they did every Friday afternoon. They had been just close enough to see the man shoot Jabari, but he was long gone by the time they got to where their daddy was. They watched him die right there in the street, and they couldn't even say what the man who shot him looked like. That was what hurt them the most. They felt like they were responsible for letting the man get away with it.

And it wasn't long after that when Little Man found out Jabari wasn't even his real father. That first social worker just blurted it out, right in front of him. She was there for their first home visit after Lawana applied for welfare and didn't even seem to notice how shocked he was. She just kept right on going, asking her whether she thought Willie had any chance of getting out of prison. It all happened so fast that she didn't have time to react, to do something to keep her son from hearing what the woman said. The thought of going to jail was the only thing that kept her from slugging her. Then, her children wouldn't have nobody because Willie was in prison and Jabari was dead. He had been a great provider but the money from his life insurance barely covered his funeral. She had to borrow money from her mother until the insurance company paid up, and by the time she got the check she realized it would only leave her with three thousand dollars after repaying her mother for the funeral. Her husband had worked too hard for her to have his children see him buried in a pine box, so she did right by him.

She still remembered how quickly Little Man's brow had shot up when he heard what the social worker said. She had a quick flash of Willie; his brow shot up the same way his father's did when he was surprised. The look on her son's face was forever etched in Lawana's mind— it was a look of betrayal. First watching Jabari die, and now this; he was twelve when Jabari was shot and George had just turned seven. Now her son wasn't sure whether he could trust his mother, and she knew he would never be the same.

Lawana looked at her watch again and saw that she was cutting it real close, thanks to the bus driver. It was the woman's last route before her shift ended as she knew all too well. She used to catch the same bus every-day when she was working part-time at Mr. Henry's restaurant, during the breakfast shift. The bus driver had tortured her with her slow driving every day, when all she wanted was to get home in time to catch her "soap" on the TV. It was much easier for her to loose herself in what the residents of Genoa City were doing, than to face up to her own life.

She hurried to the back door just as the bus pulled up to her stop. Lawana wanted to be the first one out so she wouldn't run the risk of being behind the two older women who were sitting across from her. It would probably take them forever to get down the steps to the ground, and her grandparents had taught her to always respect her elders. Her mother moved her and her older brothers to Washington when Lawana was in the third grade, but she still remembered living in South Carolina and going to Sunday School with her grandmother every Sunday.

After she had safely passed the bus door off to a teenage boy standing close behind her, she was off and running down the sidewalk. She ran down one block and then walked fast down the next, until she was finally at the front door of her run-down apartment building. She was hoping to have time to get out of her smelly uniform before the social worker got there. She ran up four flights of stairs instead of waiting for the elevator because it was slow as molasses. She knew she wouldn't have to hear Ms. Wilkens' mouth about her not being home when she first got there, and she breathed a big sigh of relief. The last time that the woman had to wait all of five minutes she had been on her way out of the building as Lawana ran up. She had been scared that she wouldn't be able to coax her back inside that day so she had used Lacrecia, who she carried on one hip with a bag of groceries balanced on the other, to charm her back in the apartment.

She wondered whether George was at home yet and thought again about how much she wanted to strangle him for putting her through his nonsense. And she just might do it too after the social worker left. She had tried just about everything else; she even went to sign up for a big brother for him and Little Man. But by the looks of things, *both* her boys would probably be grown before they moved up enough on the waiting list to actually get a big brother. The next thing she knew, one of her own brothers showed up and then her small apartment got even smaller.

Reluctantly, she had switched bedrooms and let him move into her room with the boys. She had to admit that the extra money did come in handy for a while, but him being there created all kinds of headaches at the same time. In the end, she realized the money just wasn't worth it. She finally put him out but the damage had already been done. George brought some of the dirty magazines he left at their apartment to school and that was what got him into trouble this last time. His teacher had apparently flipped out when she saw them, but George had only been nine at the time and Lawana couldn't see why his teacher was making such a big deal out of it. She knew he shouldn't have had the magazines at all, much less at school, but it wasn't like he had killed somebody or set something on fire. She could tell that his teacher was sick and tired of him too, because they were only three months into the school year. The magazines were just the latest in a series of bad behavior and it always ended up with everybody else being punished for what George did.

She could just hear Ms. Wilkens now going on and on about it, questioning her about where she had been when George was getting ready for school. She would probably ask her why she didn't know he had the magazines in his bookbag—like she had time to watch a nine-year-old's every move with everything else she had going on. She would have to grit her teeth to keep herself from asking whether the social worker knew what was in *her* children's bookbags at all times.

All Lawana knew was that her boys had been doing just the opposite of what they would've been doing in school before Jabari died. They were both mad about it for different reasons, and they were taking everything out on her. Ms. Steele had tried to help her with it before she quit her job. She really tried hard. She made her see that it would be easy for them to get her in trouble with Social Services. Ms. Steele made sure she understood what a nightmare her life would be if that happened—if the District decided to take her children. She knew it was possible that she might never see them again. That scared Lawana to death because her oldest son was out of control, and his younger brother wasn't far behind him. She didn't even know where Little Man was half the time.

And when he *was* home, she didn't know whether to be happy or sad. George had always looked up to his older brother, even more so since their daddy died. Willie had been selling drugs for more than a year when he was the age their son was now. Maybe there was no chance for him, just like her boyfriend Frankie always said. He and Little Man seemed to hate each other on sight, and she was beginning to think that maybe she should stop seeing him. Maybe she and the kids should start going to the Masjid on Fridays, like she and Jabari had talked about doing. The mosque wasn't far from their apartment and she knew she'd find a good father for her children there.

Jabari already told her that the women and children sat in the back of a large open space during prayers, and while they were listening to the Imam, the mosque's leader. He told her that they put the men in front so they wouldn't be distracted by all the beautiful sisters. Everyone sat on the floor except the older women, those women who were on their cycles, and the new mothers. The subtle scent of a fertile woman was apparently a distraction too, Jabari told her. They sat along the side of one wall and were set apart from everyone else, along with the women who just gave birth.

If she went to the Imam and told him what was happening with her boys, Lawana knew that he would help her. He would introduce her to a good man from the community and that man would help her raise her children.

※※※

"And just exactly how long do you expect your brother to be living here?" The social worker had been busy scribbling notes and marking blocks on the long form she pulled out of her satchel. She spent the first fifteen minutes or so asking questions that made absolutely no sense. She knew that Lawana wasn't blind; she could see that she still didn't have any other physical handicaps and that she lived in the same place as before.

Did Ms. Wilkens really think she would be dumb enough to slip up like that? If she *had* been lying when she told her that Miles had moved out, did she think she would fall for her tricks and say something stupid? All of her brothers were much older than she was, and Lawana used to fantasize that they would protect her from her mother's boyfriends if they had lived nearby. Miles had moved to New York not long after their mother moved them all to Washington. Since he was already eighteen, her mother didn't try to stop him. A few years later, her other brothers both moved to Nevada and had both been working at one of the casinos out there for years. Lawana hadn't heard from any of them in a long time before Miles showed up at her apartment door.

She had no idea how he had even found her; she hadn't talked to their mother since right after Jabari died. By the time her brother showed up Little Man and George had both started doing bad in school. She knew they felt responsible cause they couldn't tell the police what the man who killed their father looked like. The counselor that Ms. Steele helped her find would have been great, but her boys stopped going to see her. Lawana didn't know anything about it until months had gone by. They had been pretending to take the bus down to her office twice a week. How could she keep track of them while she was working at the restaurant.

She kept nervously glancing toward the front door the whole time she was talking to Ms. Wilkens. She knew the woman didn't realize her boys weren't in the apartment; she probably thought they were back in their room playing video games. Lawana had been on pins and needles while she went through all her questions, wondering how long it would take before she found out. Lacrecia had also been doing a great job of distracting her. Her baby girl was as cute as a button and the four-year-old was the only family member that Ms. Wilkens seemed to have a soft spot for. This time, Lawana didn't try to hold her little diva back as she usually did, and insisted she show the social worker that she knew how to recite the alphabet. The baby sang it all the way through, giggling at the end. She was a real star in the making, and smart just like Jabari. All of her kids were smart; she just couldn't get her boys to go to school and do right.

She was still half-way holding her breath in suspense when the front door finally opened and George walked in alone.

Chapter 4

Malaya

"Why so glum, honey?"

Uncle Paul's question startled Malaya, who had been in the sitting room for nearly an hour, staring out the window into her grandmother's rose garden. He had entered the room too fast, momentarily forgetting how jumpy his niece had been since the day of her stepfather's violent death. They had tried everything they could think of to shake her out of it; everyone hoped she would find some comfort in living in her grandmother's old house again. And she had recently given signs that it had helped, that she might be ready to move beyond the state she had been in since the day she and her younger brother arrived. Up until then, she had remained virtually unchanged since the events of that awful day.

"Hi Uncle Paul." Malaya did her best to appear less affected by his quick entrance than she was. He had gone through so much trouble to be nice to her—everyone had, even the twins. Her older cousins had always seemed distant to her before. They were unwilling to put their psychic conversations on hold long enough to include her when her mother, stepfather and brother came for their monthly family dinners. But they had volunteered to let Malaya have her old room back when she came to live with them, although it had been their room since their grandmother's death. They even helped her paint it back to the color it had once been but she was still uneasy with their sudden niceness. They never had time for her before.

These days, Uncle Paul seemed only a shadow of the grumpy old man she had once imagined him to be. She turned slightly so that she faced him as he sat down in a chair across from her. It had been her grandmother's favorite chair and Malaya would sometimes imagine that she was still alive and sitting in it. They had admired her roses together often from the room when she was a little girl.

She could see from her uncle's face that he still felt bad about the fiasco that her visit with her mother turned out to be, but no one could have imagined it would go so bad. She tried to convince him that she had put it all behind her, but in reality she knew that was far from the truth. Every night she would lie awake in her old bedroom trying to think of a way to let it all go. She had to if she stood any chance of getting on with her life—at least that's what her doctor kept saying. So far, nothing had come to mind that could possibly explain it—why her mother blamed *her* for Sam's death. If he was still alive he would probably be doing the same horrible things he used to do to her, or worse. Was that really what her mother wanted?

"Where's SJ?" Paul pretended not to notice the distressed look passing across his niece's face. Her brother's name had been a constant reminder of her tormentor; at some point they had all made an unspoken agreement to call him only by his first and middle initials, instead. Malaya had cringed whenever anyone said his old name because it was still painful to hear. It was a reminder that made it that much harder to keep the monster image of Sam out of her mind. Thankfully, her brother had never been anything like his father and she prayed to God every day that he never would. SJ had always been a sweetheart; they had formed an instant bond the day their mother brought him home from the hospital. She loved her little brother, even if his father had used him as an excuse to be in their room.

One of the twins had been the first to start calling him "SJ," and since he was almost in middle school now he didn't mind the change at all. He thought that name made him sound much older so SJ became his new name officially over night.

"He and Nathan left a few minutes ago," Malaya responded finally. "I think they went to play basketball."

Her cousin Nathan had been the one who had walked in and caught her stepfather trying to have his way with her that day, nearly seven months ago. She still shuttered to think what might have happened if Nathan hadn't come when he had. Sam had been so determined. He flew into a jealous rage because she had been spending so much time with her *cousin*. It was a climax to the years of abuse that she had lived with since her mother married Sam.

Less than a month after they were married he had started coming into her room late at night. After SJ was born, he came more frequently on the pretext of checking on his infant son, whose crib sat next to her bed. She had lived in torment since she was six, always in fear of what Sam might do next, or worse still what might happen if she told anyone about it. After she turned thirteen and her mother told Sam she had started her period, he stopped bothering her except for leering when no one else was watching, making her feel like she didn't have on any clothes.

She had struggled against him with all her might that day, after he grabbed her and pushed her down on the couch. Sam had left home earlier that morning with her mother and SJ for one of her brother's soccer games, something Sam rarely did. He came back unexpectedly without them and found her waiting for Nathan to pick her up to take her to the museum. Her cousin had just finished restoring an old car after months of work. He wanted to show it off, he told her, otherwise, she would have taken the bus to meet him at the Smithsonian, as she usually did.

The smell of alcohol on Sam's hot breath had immediately quickened her panic, even as it turned her stomach and threatened to make her physically ill. She had fought hard to keep him off her but Sam was heavy. She hadn't been able to get him to budge an inch, and had nearly worn herself down when Nathan walked through the front door. God had answered her desperate prayers and sent her cousin in time to save her.

When they had all left that morning, Malaya had been relieved that Sam would be out of the house—if only for a few hours. Then, Nathan had called out of the blue to invite her to see the new exhibit at the Hirshorn.

She would never forget the look on her mother's face when she walked in and saw her husband lying unconscious on the floor. In the split second before the tragedy unfolded, the accusatory look in her eyes distracted Malaya. She had been confused by it and it kept her from focusing on the scene still going on around her.

If only her mother had believed Nathan's explanation—maybe one of them would have noticed Sam's lethal motion. They might have seen him come to and crawl toward the kitchen for a weapon he could use against the younger man's strength. If they hadn't been so caught up trying to convince her mother that Nathan wasn't at fault, maybe all of them would have paid more attention. They might have seen the murderous look in Sam's eyes; how driven he was to make Nathan pay for interrupting his plans. But it had been *Sam* who paid the ultimate price; he and her mother had both paid.

"Why won't she believe me?" Malaya seemed almost desperate for an answer, and she looked sad and dejected when her uncle couldn't give her one.

It was the first time he had a verbal indication that his niece was ready to talk. It was the sign they had all been waiting for since Paul arranged for her to see a therapist. The doctor had warned them all to wait until Malaya was ready to talk about what happened. He made arrangements for her sessions right away—as soon as an attorney cleared Nathan of legal responsibility for the fatal blow to Sam's chest. The two men had struggled for control over the knife that Sam wielded, and Nathan did the only thing he *could've* done to stop him. It came down to kill or be killed before it was all said and done, and Paul was grateful every day that his son had survived Sam's attack.

Malaya's doctor told them that Malaya would let them know when she was ready to talk to anyone outside of their weekly sessions. Paul had insisted on making appointments for Nathan too initially, until he and the therapist were both convinced that his son wouldn't be haunted by traumatic scars. Secretly, Paul held himself accountable for everything that happened, knowing there was no way he could have predicted things would end the way that they had. He was the one who had asked Nathan to start spending more time with his younger cousin in the first place; he just never did anything about what he found out.

"I'm so sorry baby," he said finally, with a sadness in his voice.

He waited until she had turned in his direction before he stretched his arms out to her slowly. She was hesitant at first, glancing toward the door; afraid to believe that she could trust even him in that moment. But Uncle Paul had been so kind to her. He had opened his home and his heart to her and her brother, and he treated them as though they were his own. It hadn't been long before SJ was getting into regular mischief along with his cousins, who were close in age, and getting punished with them too. Everyone had still been treating Malaya with kid gloves though, not sure what else to do. Now she had finally signaled that she was ready to start opening up.

She moved forward toward the edge of the sofa so her uncle could put his arms around her, and finally relaxed after a few stiff seconds of silence. Then she clutched at the back of his shirt as relief began to flood her body. After a few seconds, Paul pulled her to her feet so they could stand together and he could hold her tighter in his arms. They began to feel like her grandmother's arms to Malaya, and she remembered the last time she had hugged her on nearly the same spot. She had almost told her about Sam that day, and there had been so many days afterwards that she wished she had.

After he had moved his family in, her uncle made changes to her grandmother's house right away. Many of the rooms, like the kitchen, looked nothing like they had when Malaya was younger and lived in the house. The sitting room had been her favorite room and it had been her grandmother's favorite room too. She could still feel her Spirit when she went there, and when she was outside into her rose garden too. She felt her grandmother all around her there and it felt just like being wrapped between her uncle's strong shoulders. She was finally able to release the tears that she hadn't been able to cry—for all the years that she had spent in misery.

After a while Paul realized he was crying too. He felt so guilty that he hadn't done anything to help his poor defenseless niece; such regret for failing to protect her from his brother-in-law for all those years. His sister Anna, who was two years younger, had tried to make him see it a year before everything blew up. She came to his house for that express purpose; to talk to him about it. She said their brother's wife and even his *own* wife were all worried about Malaya. There was something going on at Vivian's house, she told him, that just wasn't right. They had all noticed the extra attention Sam was giving the child at their family dinners.

"I'm telling you, it's just not natural!" his sister had argued. "He watches her like a hawk, all the time; like we're some kind of threat instead of Malaya's blood relatives. He's paying *way* too much attention to her and I'm telling you that it's just not right!"

But Paul had let his ego get in the way of his better judgement. His sister had come to him because their father made clear that Paul was to be the family patriarch when their mother died. They all took his wishes seriously, Paul especially. But he chose to overlook that he was the oldest son and logical person for the job. Instead, he had put all *his* energy into convincing everyone that he was a "born leader" and not one to be questioned.

None of them had any idea what it took for him to work his way up at O'Hare airport, at that time the busiest airport in the world. He hadn't told his sisters and brother how hard it was for him to get the kind of respect and recognition he deserved all those years in Aircraft Operations. He didn't want to come off sounding weak, so he never shared those experiences with them.

He had finally retired just before his mother died and the timing had been right to pull up his family's Chicago roots and move back home to

D.C. Once he got the house like he had always wanted, his main focus had bee in rubbing his siblings' noses in the trust their father had put in him. He made light of any one else's hard knocks if they came to him about it, and eventually transformed himself into the bully that he had never been while they were growing up. In a way, he took everything out on them that he had suffered while he put in his thirty-five years at O'hare. It was too late before he realized what he was doing, and how much he was letting his father down in the process.

Paul would have given anything to go back in time and if he could, he wouldn't be so quick to dismiss what his sister told him about Sam. He would have realized it was serious, or otherwise she wouldn't have taken time to make a trip to his house to talk to him about her fears. But his ego kept him from seeing any of it at the time. All he remembered thinking was how Anna had some nerve to come to him like that, implying that he wasn't doing his job. And as it turned out, he really hadn't been.

He had always known the other women in the family didn't approve of Vivian's marriage to Sam. They all thought he was too controlling of their younger sister; and in all honesty, Paul didn't like him very much at first himself. He had only decided to give him a break because everybody else seemed to dislike him so much. And he also gave Sam the benefit of the doubt because he was from the old school himself. He believed a man was supposed to have control over his household—and *especially* over his woman. Paul had always been in control of his own household; his wife knew which areas she could be in charge of, and which ones she needed to talk to him about before any changes were to be made. And besides all that, he didn't think it would do any harm for him to pull his baby sister in a bit.

But he had still asked around the old neighborhood about Sam, just to be on the safe side. Once Vivian announced she was planning to marry him, Paul took the time to find someone who knew Sam and his folks. He went to their old neighborhood when he brought his family home for Christmas that year, and he found out through the grapevine that Sam had been raised by his maternal grandmother. His mother, the word was out, had moved from Washington right after Sam was born. And the neighborhood gossip had it that the white man his grandmother worked for, had really been Sam's father. He was a fairly well-to-do businessman whose family had run a general merchandise store in the neighborhood for decades. His grandmother was their housekeeper and everybody that Paul talked to said that Sam looked just like the man's three daughters. But of course, no one could say for sure. Apparently, Sam's grandmother had let him have his way when he was growing up. Most people thought she was making up for him not having parents to raise him; and she was gone from home all the time, looking after his father's family.

Paul couldn't very well blame the man for how he started out in life. He even thought he understood him better after finding out more about his background. *Their* mother had spent a good part of her time with the white family she had worked for too, until their father finally got a steady job with the railroad and made her quit. By then, Vivian was just about out of high school and Paul was already in the military, doing his second tour in the Air Force.

He still remembered how shocked he had been one day when he had gone to the house where she worked with his father, to pick her up. The children in the family were treating her like she was *their* mother and she was talking to them like they were her children. They all hugged her good-bye, just like he and his brother and sisters did when she left their home to go to work. It was a picture that had stayed in his mind all his life.

Vivian had taken their mother's absence from home much harder than anybody else did, probably because she was the baby of the family. The older kids gave her lots of attention automatically, but apparently that wasn't enough for his baby sister. Everyone else could see how hard their parents were working by then, but Vivian was only embarrassed by them having to scrape to get by. Paul remembered thinking that she and Sam might just be good for each other because they had so many things in common. He figured Sam had probably done some of the things he did to compensate for what he missed out on as a child, like the way he always dressed to the nines.

Paul pulled his niece away from him to look at her face evenly.

"I really don't know why your mother is acting the way she is, Malaya." He answered her with the simple truth. Her therapist had made them all aware that there was a huge amount of work ahead of his niece. The most promising chance of a recovery was for her to develop a close bond with the uncle who had taken her in, so she could have a positive father-figure to replace the experience she had with Sam. They had only started to get to know each other after he moved his family back from Chicago. He knew Malaya would have to trust him if there were to be any chance of developing that kind of relationship with her, and telling her the truth was the only way to make it happen.

"I wish I did know, honey. I only know how sorry I am about all of it."

It had taken quite an effort for him to visit his sister in the rehab center; the hospital visit had been bad enough. He had been stunned when his son called to describe what happened so vividly. The blow that had been meant for him had plunged into Vivian's back instead. She had made an unexpected move toward Sam just as he was attacking Nathan, and her spinal cord had been severely damaged as a result. It was doubtful she would ever walk again although she had undergone three surgeries in as many months. There had been little improvement in her condition and Paul barely recognized her when he walked into her room.

The sassy smile that his little sister had been known for was gone, twisted into a permanent scowl. There was little resemblance to the stylish woman she had always prided herself on being. The visit had started out as well enough, but he soon picked up on her reluctance to hear anything he had to say about her children—even SJ. She never once asked after her son or her daughter; she didn't even seem curious about how they were doing after having their lives turned upside down.

After a few awkward minutes, Paul had steered the conversation toward Sam's death; how she ended up being paralyzed and the situation that they all found themselves in. He started by telling her how proud he was of his son because he had risked his own life trying to protect her daughter. But he soon realized he wasn't getting through to Vivian at all. As hard as he tried, Paul couldn't convince his sister that his son and her daughter had told her the truth about her husband.

"...Even if Malaya *was* lying about some of the things she said Sam did to her, and I'm not saying I believe for one moment that she *is* lying; *Nathan* had no reason at all to lie. He told the truth about what he walked in on. I believe him, Vivian, because from what he saw there can be no doubt about Sam's intentions. My son literally walked in your house and caught your husband trying to rape your daughter—in broad daylight!"

He had raised his voice in spite of his resolve not to do it. On the way over, he had promised himself that he would remain calm as he talked to his sister, no matter what. But he had soon lost his patience when he saw that she still refused to hear the truth about Sam.

Eventually, Paul had begun to notice some of the things that Anna had told him about Sam himself. He made a point of paying more attention when everybody came for dinner. Usually, Paul and the other men at the table would be so caught up in their conversations that they would take little notice of anything else. But after observing his brother-in-law more closely, Paul had been troubled by what he saw. He had asked his son to spend more time with his cousin since they both loved art, and he was only slightly older. His suspicions had grown even stronger after Nathan began reporting back. He was convinced there was something going on that wasn't quite right in his aunt's house too.

Paul had been beating himself up for months because he failed to put it all together sooner, and even when he had, he still didn't do anything to help poor Malaya.

"She missed out on a lot growing up." He offered the explanation finally, then quickly followed with, "Don't get me wrong. I'm not making excuses for her. I'm just trying to make sense of it too, really, so I can maybe help you understand your mother a little better."

He searched Malaya's face. "*I'm* trying to understand her better because I left home before she was out of high school."

"When we were younger," he went on after a few seconds, "our folks worked all the time just to keep a roof over our heads. There were five of us kids you know, and we barely *saw* our mother once she started working for those people. Us older kids learned to adjust but for some reason your mother never did. Maybe it was because she was the youngest of the bunch, but she took everything harder. The rest of us had our memories too, of when things were different and Momma used to stay home to take care of us while our daddy was away working. We didn't have much money back then either, but that never made a difference to the rest of us. That was before momma started working for that white family."

Malaya was looking at her uncle expectantly, hoping he would say something that would help her understand everything.

"It's like I said before," he said finally, after realizing he had been distracted by a trip back in time. "I'm not trying to make excuses for your mother at all. You've got to believe me on that. I'm on your side—the whole family is."

A fleeting look of sadness traveled across Malaya's face and reminded Paul of his focus. Tears started to form in his niece's eyes again and he had to force himself not to intervene. He stopped himself from telling Malaya not to cry because her doctor said it was part of the recovery process. They had all been so worried because no one had seen her shed a single tear since the day Nathan brought her across the bridge to their family home.

Paul had rushed to pick up his young nephew from his friend's house as soon as Nathan called him. SJ had gone there after his soccer game, and Paul had been panic-stricken thinking the poor boy would go home and walk right into the aftermath of the violent scene in their living room. His blood had chilled as Nathan told him how Malaya kept screaming even after everything was over, until paramedics gave her an injection to calm her down. She had gone to sleep in the car and was soon back to sleep after he got her home and her aunt and cousins had helped her into bed.

She had stayed in her room for over a week for the most part, and even when she did venture out she was very quiet. Paul knew it was a good sign that she was releasing some of the emotions that were pent up inside. It marked the beginning of her resurrection from the horrible life she had been living. He was heartbroken by how much she had suffered under everyone's noses, and by how little he could do to help her now.

"Your mother always seemed to need much more than our parents could give to any of us," he said to her. "I don't know—maybe she needed to make up for not having momma around."

At the mention of his mother, Malaya's tears began streaming down her face. She missed her grandmother so much. She had spent days thinking about how different her life might have been, if only she had been strong enough to tell her. But her stepfather had convinced her that no one would believe her even if she did tell. Or worse, they would blame *her* for it and she knew she would have died if that happened. She had been far too afraid to risk it; to find out whether what Sam said was true.

"Momma would bring us clothes home sometimes," her uncle was saying. The expression on his face was set in the past again. "They had belonged to the children in the family she worked for— hand-me-downs that they outgrew. Sometimes they were new or looked new; stuff they decided they didn't want anymore. And they were pretty well-off so there were some really nice things, mostly. Momma would throw away anything that didn't look like it was brand new but she always waited until she was home to do it."

"Did my mom wear the old clothes too?" Malaya asked the question shyly after her tears finally stopped flowing. Somehow she couldn't picture her mother in anything that was a called a hand-me-down, no matter what.

"She did at first." Her uncle surprised her by his answer. "But not after she got old enough to know where the clothes came from, and that they weren't new. After that, she wouldn't have anything to do with 'em."

"What did Grandma do?" Malaya never knew her grandfather, because he had died before she was born. She had only heard stories about him from her aunts and uncles, and some of her older cousins. Her grandmother had been the sweetest, loving person that she ever knew, but Malaya still did what she said to do.

"Your mother was the youngest of the bunch, like I said." There was regret in his voice. "I'm beginning to think that might have been a part of the problem," he added wistfully. "Maybe we went too far for her. All of us let her have her way too much, and she just got used to having it.

"I couldn't begin to tell you how our folks managed to do it, but I can guess why, now that I'm a parent myself. Somehow, they always came up with new clothes for your mother to wear, from the time she started junior high on up. And she still complained about most of them..."

Paul's voice trailed off as he thought back to his sister as a young girl Malaya's age. He could see now that things had gone wrong with her much earlier than he had first thought. "...I guess we just let her get away with murder," he finished sadly. "Pretty soon, she didn't think about anybody *but* herself—not even when she got old enough to understand how much it took for our parents to buy her things they couldn't afford."

"But she *did* love you, Malaya." He used his index finger to lift up her face. "And I'm sure she still does." He corrected himself quickly after realizing he had used the past tense. "That's the hard part to understand. Your mother changed quite a bit after you were born, and she did it all on her own. She was very protective of you after your father...."

He left the sentence hanging. Vivian had married Malaya's father soon after they finished high school together and their daughter had been born seven months later. They were broken up by the time that Malaya turned two years old. Paul had spent months trying to find Jonathan. But Vivian had been out of touch with him for years and they had never known his family.

"It had to be Sam's money." Paul changed the subject abruptly. "He bought your mother all the stuff she ever wanted."

'*Was that it then?*' Malaya wondered. Was her mother upset because she couldn't buy nice things anymore with Sam's money? Was that why she never noticed what he was doing to her?

That night as she lay awake she thought about what her uncle said. She thought back to the night that her mother had come home so happy that she was going to marry Sam. It all began to make sense.

She didn't have all the answers yet, but talking to Uncle Paul had helped just like her therapist had said. And for the first time in a long time, she didn't feel quite so alone.

Chapter 5

The Gold Coast

*W*hen it became clear that she wouldn't be getting work done that day, Kristin stretched out on the overstuffed loveseat in her office to gather herself. It was a beautiful piece of furniture, carved in ebony and covered in a rust colored silk fabric that was embroidered with the Adinkra symbol she had chosen for Exodus Village. The English translation for 'sesa wo suban' was "transform your life and character." It expressed her exact intent for their residents of Exodus Village. Just like the last time, the translation had stood out from a list of symbols as she searched. She was proud that their relocation village would live up to its meaning, just as their foundation had lived up to the Adinkra symbol chosen to represent it. 'Boa me na me mmoa wo,' which means "help me and let me help you," exactly represented the Diasporan Exodus Foundation's mission in Ghana, and she had taken express measures to make sure that it would remain so.

She found herself looking at her clock frequently after Amina left, picturing Angela's service as it was likely taking place. Talking to her had forced Kristin to relive portions of her past that had been closed off for years. It had helped her put things in perspective—in her mind and in her heart. Feelings were reawakened that surprised her yet again; the strong bond she had always felt with Winston. She was conscious of his pain whether she wanted to be or not—even with an ocean between them.

For once, she didn't force all thoughts of her ex-husband from her mind before they had time to settle. She allowed herself to remember their past together, and think about the life that they once had. She let herself wallow in her memories; questioning how things could have changed so much between them. How had they let things get so bad?

Then, before she could conjure the guardian of her mind's gate to report for duty, another thought slipped quietly by: *'Maybe Angela's death would make it possible for us to fix it now; maybe we could be together again after all.'* She chided herself immediately for the thought, the guilt overwhelming her. She forced herself to refocus and compelled her attention to the official opening of Exodus Village; anything that would help her escape the thought that had betrayed her by its blunt passion.

Within a year's time, fifty families would be brought aboard their ship docked in a harbor near Baltimore Maryland. They would sail to Elmina, a coastal town on the Gulf of Guinea, after stopping for orientation sessions in the Caribbean. Kristin would allow her inner Spirit to guide her in selecting the families who would participate in their pilot. If she came across an application with a scribbled signature that caught her eye, for any reason, she planned to separate it from the stack to read more about the family's circumstances. After the initial list was down to one hundred and fifty applicants, selected for various reasons. She would go through a similar process to cut that list in half. Each family she selected from that list of seventy-five would be scrutinized carefully. She would allow herself to be sensitive to feelings she might pick up as she studied their applications, until she felt a certainty about each of them. Only then would they be sent letters of conditional acceptance. She would select an additional ten families using the same technique; those who would be wait-listed and taken through the same screening process, in case of prohibitive issues were later discovered with the selected families or there were cancellations.

As she began the process, she was aware of a faint tension in her body; she blamed her lingering reactions to events of the past weeks. No matter how small, Kristin knew that it would block the flow of Infinite Knowledge that was always available from the Universe. She would only receive its intuitive guidance if a clear vessel was available to receive it. She tried meditation and found that she was unable to still herself or her thoughts.

She was aware of the impact that a missed deadline for finalizing the list might have on their project plan. It could mean pushing back dates for several other tasks that couldn't begin until details regarding the selected families were known. But she felt it was even more crucial to select the right mix of people—those who would be best suited to accept the dramatic changes of their new environment and to their lifelong habits. They would have to be able to peacefully coexist with a diverse group of strangers and share a limited space for five years. The Exodus Foundation needed their first residents to be as cooperative as possible; to embrace the program's structure without the need for exertion on the part of their staff. They didn't want to spend unnecessary energy in enforcing rules with the first group of residents, when that energy could be better used somewhere else.

The pilot residents would help them discover flaws in the implementation of the programs they would offer. They would help point out adjustments that the Foundation would need to make before they brought their village to full capacity. The first residents would be a decisive element for that very reason; they would be pioneers—leaving all they had ever known behind and putting their complete trust in the Exodus Foundation. Eventually, the press would come to them for interviews; they would be asked to confirm the Foundation's successes to the rest of the world. Kristin believed they deserved to have the best that could be provided for them in Exodus Village, and her intention was to make sure that they had it.

The final decision on the families she would select was too important for her to undertake the task in her current state. She felt off-kilter so she gave up on the task again, refusing to bow to mounting pressures of deadlines looming before her. She decided she would take some rare time off—though technically the day had ended since it was long past six.

She kicked out of her sandals to get more comfortable and lay back on her loveseat, letting her legs dangle over the sides. She tried to think of something that might bring a smile to her face and her thoughts went immediately to the children's recent visit. It was hard to believe how happy they had all been just one week earlier, just like things had been when they were younger.

It hadn't been long before they all knew Angela would never be the mother her infant daughter needed—she just didn't have it to give back then. Kristin had run into Angela's sisters once, by chance, when they had all visited her at the rehab center at the same time. They told Kristin that Angela had always been what they called "high-strung" growing up. They confided that they weren't at all surprised by the way things had turned out. Angela's pregnancy had thrown her off balance even further and she needed a much longer time to recover than what was considered normal. Before anyone realized what was happening, she had gone from an addiction to the drugs she was given for her postpartum depression to out of control alcoholism.

Kristin and Winston had agreed when they first separated that it would be best for Trazi if he lived with his father once he started grade school. They wanted him to learn all the "manly" things from Winston, so he would stay with her on weekends and travel between both houses during the holidays. By the time he was ready for first grade, Celeste was nearly two months old. They decided they would stick to their original plans, though things had changed quite a bit in Winston's life.

Before she learned to walk, he had started packing up his daughter's things on Thursday evenings along with Trazi's, making sure they had everything they would need for a weekend at her house. Angela had still been in a state so Celeste became a part of their son's weekly ritual, almost from birth. She had grown up spending as much time with Kristin as Trazi had. And for her, having Celeste come with her son every weekend had been like a gift to Kristin and seemed the most natural thing in the world. She had felt a tremendous bond with Celeste from the second she laid eyes on her, the day her parents took her home to recover from her birth trauma.

Their connection that day had seemed almost mystical. Without a doubt, Kristin knew the Spirit of the daughter she had just lost played a role. She had been delivered prematurely just before Celeste had been born and had lived only a short time. Later, Kristin realized the daughter that Winston still knew nothing about had left the Earth at nearly the exact same time as Celeste had entered it. Her attachment to her ex-husband's daughter had been so pronounced that Kristin had deliberately kept her distance for the first few weeks of her life. She had been afraid that her feelings might interfere with Angela bonding with her infant daughter. It was only later that it became clear that Celeste needed her in her life as much as Kristin needed her.

The first weekend that Winston brought her over, Kristin had handed him her car keys as soon as she spotted the baby's overstuffed diaper bag in the back seat of his car. Without so much as a word spoken between them, she had unstrapped the giggling baby from her car seat to pull her out and handed her diaper bag to Trazi, who followed her and Celeste into the house. Winston had been left in the driveway so he could switch out his daughter's car seat and secure it to the back seat of Kristin's Saab. It gave birth to a new ritual that differed only slightly from their routine as new parents to Trazi when they were students at Tuskegee.

As Kristin continued to reminisce about the children's visit to Ghana, she found herself laughing out loud as she thought back to how badly she had unknowingly scared them, as they traveled around the country. She had been caught up in reciting local gossip about the behind-the-scenes negotiations for repair work on a bridge that crossed the Volta River, just outside Atimpoku. The kicker was that they were still driving across the eight hundred and five-foot suspension bridge at the time. Thank goodness Amad had looked in the rear-view mirror in time and noticed the kids' ashen faces. After he signaled her and she looked in the back seat, she realized the panic she had caused. Quickly, she had assured them that the bridge was structurally sound. She had only been referring to some cosmetic changes that were needed, she told them. It had been a controversial topic because of the large amount of cedis, Ghana's currency, that the project would cost to complete. But the damage had already been done by then. They were almost out of the Eastern region on their way to Kumasi, by the time Trazi and Celeste relaxed again.

She had found herself staring at her son frequently because he looked nearly identical to the way Winston had looked at the same age. And she could barely believe the overnight transition Celeste had made, from cute little girl into a beautiful young lady. She remembered thinking how much she looked like Angela, although she also wondered whether anyone else noticed that the teenager's eyes were still exactly like her own. They were nearly the same rich shade of dark blue that Winston had once teased her about when they first met. He had jokingly said he feared they would hypnotize him, if he stared into them long enough. She knew he did it without thinking, but he had even called his infant daughter "Baby Blue" for a while, just as he had once called her.

Both of the children had been awestruck with Ghana, just as Kristin had been on her first trip. She had given them a full overview of her organization's mission as they traveled around the countryside. Thanks to generous donations from their American and Ghanaian supporters, she happily told them, their goals were finally beginning to materialize.

Most notable among those had been the gift of land donated by Asanteman, the Twi speaking Akan nation. The ethnic group made up the largest percentage of Ghana's population. Exodus Village was being built on a beautiful stretch of land that bordered the rain forest in the Ashanti administrative region. It had been presented to the Exodus Foundation by the Asante king himself, also known as the "Asantehene." The gesture had been grand and very timely; the kind of assurance that would put many African Americans at ease. They could allow themselves to believe that they were welcome in the West African country.

The Foundation had been given all the land that it would ever need, even enough for all the commercial enterprises they planned in the region. Exodus Village had been under construction for months before the children arrived, with key structures like their administration building and its attached apartments already finished and in full use. The hard work that so many people had put into Kristin's vision had finally come to fruition. They would soon begin bringing home the African Diaspora that had been living in America and on islands in the Caribbean, for centuries. Her hope was that they would expand to Mexico and South American countries too over time, where many of the African captives had also been taken.

The Foundation was to assume full responsibility for residents of its five-year relocation village. She knew the majority of Black Americans would return home to Africa without any recognition of their homeland. Most would come knowing little, if anything, about the glorious kingdoms that once existed in Africa or about the many progressive things going on in African countries today. At first they would think that none of what they would be taught in their orientation classes would have anything to do with them, personally. The majority wouldn't grasp a connection between themselves and a country that had lost millions of its citizens to human trafficking during the slave trade. It would be months, perhaps, before it would fully sink in that the people who had been captured and taken away from Ghana might well have been their ancestors.

As they drove along in her Land Rover toward Kumasi, Kristin had explained the groundwork that was being laid to consciously bridge the cultural gaps between the two now-alienated cultures.

"It'll be our way of preventing more obstacles from forming as our residents get acclimated here. We may seem completely different to each other at first glance," she said, "but once you get to know the people here, you can see where many Black American traits originated. Our differences are usually based on superficial things; those things we use to judge how other people stack up against "the norm." Once we're conscious of it, we can choose to see things differently; we can see that our similarities outweigh our differences."

"How do you mean?" Celeste was puzzled.

"Okay, let me give you a good example." Kristin answered after a brief pause. "Take the average West African family new to the country that you might run across in Washington, for example. A mortgage is probably a foreign concept to them, since it's not normally part of owning a home in their country. They may choose to live in a less expensive area of town, so they can pay as little as possible for rent while they save enough money to buy a house at the price they want to pay.

"Most of us would tend to assume that they can't afford to pay the higher rent that many of us choose to pay; but that assumption is based on *our* "normal" habits. The cumulative track record in the African American community is to pay rent on a permanent basis. Many people have never even explored the possibility of buying property of their own—it's that far out of the realm of possibilities for them. And that's something that many West African families in America may not be able to understand, based on what's "normal" for them.

"Or, we might form an opinion about the financial worth of a West African we see in the States based on the type of clothing they might wear. The truth is that you might just as easily find a West African millionaire shopping for children's clothes in KMart. We might find that strange, even when we all know how quickly children can either tear up their clothes, wear them out, or outgrow them." She was smiling.

"Given those circumstances, it should be easy for us to understand why they're puzzled that we choose to spend so much of *our* money on clothes for children. Or, why, for that matter, so many of us spend every cent of our disposable income on fashions that will change every year, or on bar drinks when it's a struggle to put food on that same person's table. They see us buying the latest gadgets on credit when we clearly can't afford them—just because our friends have them, starting a cycle that perpetuates itself. It shouldn't be surprising at all that many people from other cultures view this practice as fool hardy."

Kristin described more of what her foundation was doing to chip away at stereotypes that could feed the fire and further ignite the cultural divide.

"We expect to find cultural biases both ways," she said. "There are still those African Americans who never saw beyond the fictional persona of Tarzan and that show's subtle endorsement of colonialism, a system that consumed much of the continent."

Kristin had found out later that her son remained unconvinced. He challenged her about it in nearly the same as his father would have done.

"I just don't know, Mom." His doubt was directed at the summary she had just given him of the Foundation's diversity plan.

"There's just so much mistrust all around. You see it all the time in Washington," he reminded her, thinking back on how hard it was sometimes for him, as a Black man in D.C., to get a cab to stop for him that was driven by an African cab driver. He knew that many of them were probably afraid that they would be robbed if they stopped, but that was only because they knew of others who *had* been robbed already by some misguided African American youth.

"It's gone on for so long," he pressed. "Do you think it's even possible to change it?"

"Oh yes, baby, I do. Everyone on our board does." She suppressed a smile of pride about his sharp mind. He was asking all the questions that she and her board members had wrestled with during hours of discussions, for months on end.

"We believe that with all our hearts because *everything* changes with time. Just look at the relationship between black and white America, how that's changed over time," she pointed out. "Now, when you go into a place like Walmart and see a white person who, in passing, you might easily picture at a klan rally; you might ending up seeing the same person minutes later and get a completely different picture. You could very well see them on a different aisle helping their spouse to lovingly herd up their rambunctious, coffee-colored grandchildren to get them to move along through the store."

Trazi finally agreed that she had a point, but Kristin kept going when he admitted that he was still not fully convinced.

"We're also taking into consideration that most young adults like you have no way of knowing how much things have changed in the last fifty years," she told him. So, we're using documented facts about our history to teach our participants; we'll start with the first Africans who were brought to the U.S. in chains as indentured servants, who were then later freed to live freely in America after their years of servitude. We know it doesn't register with many in your generation how much of a dream the things that Dr. King had talked about in his famous speech really were, at the time. That in itself is a testament to how much things have changed, especially for those of us who lived through it and still remember it vividly.

"Nowadays, our kids may quietly wonder what was so bad about sitting in the back of the bus."

"You're right," her son quickly conceded. "I remember how we always thought of the back of the bus as the fun place to be, where everybody wanted to sit when we went on school field trips.

"Exactly my point," his mother chimed in.

"We have to keep our history alive, for the same reasons that Jewish people took responsibility for keeping the history of their persecution in Europe alive. Everyone else wants to forget about the atrocities that people have committed against each other, and still commit in too many countries. But if we forget that it's possible for things like that to happen, they can't be stopped in their tracks the next time around. It's up to us to shed the light of truth on our history because chances are, no one else will do it. There is very little about the Civil Rights Movement in the average public school text book nowadays. They'll never be taught what actually happened during those years of struggle in most schools—nothing about the actual Movement itself.

"But we'll be teaching our residents about all of it here, and we'll start when they are on their way over. They will be very clear about it by the time they graduate from our programs, and I think it will be a tremendous help for them to see themselves as survivors starting out to make changes on their own, rather than as victims. I don't know anyone who wants to associate with being a victim."

Both Trazi and Celeste agreed.

"By the time we're done, they'll know the strength that runs through each of their veins. We'll have at least the majority of them feeling much more confident about tapping into their inner strength, so they can create legal businesses going forward and find new ways to express their creativity. It has to start with removing the chips that many have carried on their shoulders all their lives, so their reconciliation with Ghana and West Africa will stand a real chance. Once they start coming en masse on a regular basis, it's just a matter of time before the same thing happens that happened in the States, after forced integration was carried out. Blacks and whites were forced together in schools, where they lived, worked, and where most played. We've already seen it happen here too with the Black Americans who have moved to West Africa on their own, many who've been here for decades. It would keep happening naturally over time, just as it happened for many of the city kids who came to Tuskegee to go to school, by the time they graduated.

"We have to help the process along, that's all, because we only have five years to do it. Our residents' successes will hinge on a willingness to drop the past and come correct in the future. We're going to tackle that head-on so I can confidently predict there will be remarkable changes for everyone who comes to live with us—including our volunteers and mentors.

"The same child who might have grown up to become a violent criminal in America will learn to respect their elders again here. They'll no longer be a threat to them and that in itself will be priceless."

"But how?" Trazi still needed more. "How will you make that happen?"

"Well, for starters, anyone who has a long-term affiliation with our Foundation will have to go through our sensitivity classes. That way, everyone will start out on the same page. We're putting together curriculums based on whether the person was born in Ghana, in the U.S., or in the Caribbean. The first half of our classes will be geared toward people born in one of these three specific places; but after that, all three cultures will come together for the final part of our classes. Those classes will start twice a year, as soon as the latest group of residents arrive at Exodus Village.

"We're going to use them to flush out misconceptions and stereotypes on both sides of the ocean. There will be plenty of opportunities for open and honest dialog, in a moderator-controlled setting. We anticipate buried feelings to be stirred up so at the end of each class we'll have group meditations to transform those released emotions into the light of understanding. It's all part of the transformation process that we'll guide our residents through, with a graduation ceremony at the end of their fifth year."

They had made their way just north of Kumasi, their next stop after Kristin's meetings near Lake Volta. Celeste had been so intent on finding more presents for her mother that they stopped twice more before finally heading for their hotel. There were young vendors who crowded around them as soon as the Land Rover pulled to a stop in Bonwire, their first destination.

The popular tourist spot known as "Kente Village" sits about twenty kilometers—twelve and a half miles, off the main road leading into Kumasi, northeast of the city. Few tourists ever expected the exquisite collection of silk fabric they found packed inside the tiny stores that were clustered at the end of a long dusty road. The kente is created exclusively by the men of the village, who weave four-inch strips together and sew them into rectangular parcels. There were stacks and stacks of kente in the shops that were rarely seen in America, all folded neatly on shelves or inside glass counters of the shops' displays.

After they left Bonwire, they made the short drive to Ntonsu in the Kwabre district, still north of Kumasi. They stood with a handful of tourists in the back yard of a large house, watching a small group of men mix dyes together in black kettles that swung over open flames. Once the colors were deemed properly mixed, the men block-stamped Adinkra symbols onto cotton cloth of different colors. Each stamp itself had been carved from a calabash, a long-shaped melon that was normally used as containers and other such purposes, rather than for food. After the melon is cut in the appropriate shape, it is left to harden and dry in the sun so it could be used over and over for stamping.

"Adinkra symbols have been a part of the Asante culture since the 19th century." Kristin's voice was hushed so she wouldn't disturb the energy coming from the scene they watched intently. "They have been used to express spiritual beliefs, and as points in history, philosophies, and even religious proverbs. They originated with the Gyaman clan of the Brong Region in the 16th century—back when the Akan states were spread across Côte d'Ivoire, known to Americans as the Ivory Coast. The Gye Nyame, probably the most recognizable of Adinkra symbols, represents the Omnipotence and Immortality of God.

"According to the history passed down by the griots for centuries, the Brong king, who was called "Adinkra" had plans to copy the Asante's golden stool, which has a rich legend of its own. In short, the golden stool was declared to be the soul of the Asante nation, by the chief spiritual leader of the Asantehene at the time.

"King Adinkra's plans were considered to be a major offense against the Asante; it prompted a fierce battle that ended in him being beheaded. He had been well-known for the robes he wore that were painted with symbols, and they were taken by the Asante as a spoil of war. At the same time, their meanings were also passed on and many other symbols were later added by the Asante nation over time. In the beginning, the garments were worn exclusively by royalty and spiritual leaders, or during special ceremonies."

"Wait, back up...Did you just say that the Asantehene beheaded King Adinkra?" Celeste asked.

"I'm afraid I did. That was a popular form of justice all over the world at the time. The same king who unified the Asante states was responsible for having King Adinkra beheaded, and he took his robes as pay-back for him planning to copy the sacred golden stool."

"Wow—I guess they were really serious about it then." Celeste observed.

Everyone appreciated the quiet reprieve in the backyard of the house, especially after the hectic pace of their shopping experience in Bonwire Village. By the time they arrived in the Kwabre district, Celeste complained that her head had still been spinning. Most of the time they spent watching the men make dyes, the silence was only occasionally interrupted by the sounds made by the rooster and chickens running around the yard. The formulas the men used had been set to memory and passed down to the next generation for centuries.

After they had watched the whole cloth-making process from start to finish, they moved to a different area of the yard to look at the items that were displayed for sale. She had helped Celeste select a beautiful beige bedspread for Angela that had Adinkra symbols stamped around the hem. After making the purchase, they drove on toward the Garden City of Africa, reaching Kumasi just before sunset.

It had still been early the next morning when they arrived at Kumasi Market, and relatively uncrowded. The market sprawled across a large tract of land in the middle of the city, with parts extending into several alleyways. It would have literally taken all day for them to explore the whole thing so they limited their tour to a small section. They made several trips to drop off purchases with Amad, who read the morning paper at a nearby restaurant patiently and waited with the truck. They weaved in and out among the rows of stalls filled with goods brought from countries all over West Africa. There was jewelry made of gold, silver, and other precious stones wherever they looked, with bolts of silk fabric, woodcarvings, beautiful works of art of all kind, and nearly everything else imaginable.

From the time they arrived in Ghana, Kristin had been telling them that they *had* to see the tomato markets in Kumasi. As soon as they turned down the narrow alley leading to it, the kids knew immediate why she had been so determined that they see it. They had both stopped short, rooted to the spot, bedazzled by the sheer volume of perfectly ripened red tomatoes that filled stalls on either side of the alley. There were more tomatoes than either of them ever imagined seeing in one place—rows and rows of the juicy luscious red fruit, as far as they could see. The image stayed with them for hours after they had left the market, and Celeste finally asked her that night who would buy so many tomatoes before the sun had a chance to ruin them. Kristin had told them early on that many of the people they saw on the street didn't have refrigeration so the vision of so many tomatoes in one place remained a mystery to her.

The following day saw them headed south, in the direction of Exodus Village. As soon as they were outside the Kumasi city limits, their discussion turned to the subject of colonialism. Kristin tried to explain the organized efforts that had been made to keep Africa separated from the Diaspora, once slave trading finally ended. There had been deliberate thought given by the British especially, in making certain the Diaspora was kept at odds with Mother Africa, leaving little hope in reuniting the two.

"Many people don't stop to realize how seamlessly the British occupation of Ghana was. They began along the coastal areas and planted the roots of colonialism soon after the slave trade was forced to an end. We shouldn't forget that the fittest among the people had been the primary targets to be hunted down and captured at first, either. They were the ones who were thought to stand the best chance of survival in the slave castles and the ships."

"I still don't understand how the British were able to do it?" Celeste was confused.

"It happened overtime, honey, and in a variety of ways. Part of their success was in keeping the Diaspora apart from the continent. Take the situation with Chief Alfred Sam, for instance."

"Who's that?" The young girl asked.

"Exactly my point." Kristin pounced as soon as Celeste asked the question. "I had never heard of him either, until Amina told me all about him.

"But who was he?" It was Trazi's turn to ask.

"Chief Sam was an international businessman from the West Akyem District of Ghana, once known as "The Gold Coast."

"Hey—that's where Daddy said he and Aunt Grace lived when they were little." Celeste seemed confused. "Is that the same place?"

"Oddly, yes." Kristin answered. "That's where the neighborhood in D.C. where your father was born got its name; it's right above Rock Creek Park. That was what the Europeans first called what is now Ghana, back when they traded for gold; before the human slave trade was in full bloom.

"Chief Sam's business was rubber exports; he was quite ambitious, and had business connections in Europe and America. One of his main goals had been to help open up trade opportunities for West Africans in the world market. He started his American trading company in 1913, and he used it as the vehicle to promote his other major goals—that of making it possible for African Americans to emigrate to West Africa. He failed, obviously, but he tried his best to make it happen."

"Really?" Kristin could see that Trazi had been caught unaware.

"I've never heard of him before." Celeste joined her brother.

"Well, don't feel bad because even with two history degrees I'd never heard of him either," Kristin admitted. "His *Ethiopian Steamship* line was the forerunner to Marcus Garvey's *Black Star* line. And given the timing, I think it's likely that Garvey must have drawn on Chief Sam's back-to-Africa movement for his inspiration."

"Really?" Trazi asked.

"Yes. Chief Sam was popular with African Americans in Oklahoma," she told him. " Many of them had moved that far trying to avoid racial violence and inequalities in other parts of the country. But some ran into the same kinds of situations there; hundreds were frustrated enough to pay

Chief Sam twenty-five dollars for the cost of passage back to Africa. He had at least five hundred people ready to leave on his broken-down steamship from a port in Galveston. At the last minute, he scaled back the number of passengers to less than a hundred before they courageously set sail."

"So what happened?" Trazi was curious. "Don't leave us hanging."

"Well, it's hard to say," Kristin answered bluntly, "especially considering who was keeping records of everything at the time. I think the resulting failure was a combination of misfortunes: inadequate planning, and British interference once the ship left Galveston. From all indications, the British and American governments joined forces on a misinformation campaign about Chief Sam. There were insinuations that he had committed fraud against the people who were ready to follow him. You can still find statements of record to that affect with wording like, he was "supposed" to own land in Africa, to cast doubt on whether such land ever existed.

I personally believe his motives were sincere but he was up against a lot with the campaigns that were purposely launched to discredit him. There were road blocks set up every step of the way. Now that I think of it, that was probably where Hoover got the idea to go after Marcus Garvey the way he did, a few years later. He just expanded on what the British did."

Kristin shared a bit of what their great-grandfather had told her and their father when they were in Jamaica on their honeymoon.

"A great deal of effort had apparently been put into stopping Garvey's movement too, and the tactics used against both men were very effective. The best evidence of that is that most Black Americans have no idea that a West African businessman came to America in the early 1900s, to arrange to get us back to Africa. It ended badly for Chief Sam, but I can't think of many who would've left the port of Galveston at all with all the obstacles stacked against him. But he persevered through most of it, including interference by the British that caused his ship, the *Liberian,* to be diverted to Sierra Leone before it could reach Ghana. Even more trouble had been brewing for him after he finally docked his ship on the Gulf of Guinea, because back then it was a British Colonial territory.

"Chief Sam's story may have had a tragic ending, but that was then and this is now. There's no one who can stop us now because the truth is no longer hidden. After we get a handle on reconciling our cultural differences, we'll be able to work everything else out. We'll get beyond it the same way that Americans finally got beyond the stereotypes and myths about Blacks that had been universally accepted over time. It took blacks and whites living and working together, going to school together, and eventually intermarrying before both groups realized a person's race had little to do with one's character. The way we are accepted now is often taken for granted, but it didn't come about until after the majority had finally settled down after forced integration. By that time, it was clear to anyone capable of thinking for themselves that there are Blacks and Whites of *all* kinds— and that goes for people of other races and nationalities too.

"So what's going to happen when everybody gets here?" Celeste wondered a few minutes later. "How is that going to work?"

"Well," Kristin started slowly, "the majority of our residents will come from a group of African Americans that we feel are lost; they've had no real purpose in America for many years. I was motivated to create this project as a way of coming to their aid. I started focusing on them after my first trip to Ghana—really thinking about them," she added. "I've convinced our board members that many of their ancestors fell between the cracks emotionally, both during and after slavery. They were too traumatized by their experiences, by the violence that took place after Reconstruction ended, and couldn't move forward. They never made a full recovery; they didn't get a firm enough footing to create productive lives for themselves and their families when they were finally free to do it. They didn't know how, so they couldn't teach it to their children, who couldn't teach their children, and so on; until we end up with the Black American "underbelly" that we have today. Just think about it— people drifting aimlessly for decades, choosing mates from similar backgrounds so their offspring are left in the same boat. Maybe the spouse has a different brand of trauma to contend with, but it's usually something that has saddled them since birth.

This group still had a legitimate place in America until a few decades ago, even if it was being a dependable source of cheap manual labor. Now, the few who still try can't find jobs that require no particular skill. There have been many groups of immigrants, including some from Africa, who have moved to America in large numbers since then, and have taken those menial jobs that haven't been taken over by machines. Those immigrants have been going to America en masse since the second "Great War" ended, or what we call World War II. They arrive all psyched up to succeed, and with a hunger to take advantage of any opportunities they find. Unlike the African Americans they replaced, it's easy for them to create pictures of success in their minds. They use the unskilled jobs they find as a stepping stone on the path toward fulfilling their American Dream.

"In contrast, many among the underbelly are only one step above slavery. Many still look to someone else to provide their substandard housing and monthly allotment of food. Their hopelessness is generational, but it's buried so deep that many of us fail to make the connection to its source."

"That paints a pretty bleak picture." Trazi was quick to say.

"We could choose to see it as bleak, yes," Kristin responded. "But that's been done for years and it didn't help anything; in fact, it's had the opposite effect. It reminds me of the consequences of global warming, whose effects can easily be seen now. From what I understand, most of the negative consequences of our past actions in not doing what is environmentally sound, could be reversed over time. All we have to do is start changing the way we do things, like the way we dispose of trash, for instance.

"What we've decided to do is to start off with the assumption that the underbelly is going to need quite a bit once they get here— including basic education, skills training, and for some, social guidance. On the other hand, some people will only need to be retrained in a trade or helped in tweaking their skills so they're a better fit here."

"But how will you tell one from the other?" Trazi's brow was wrinkled like his father's. He longed to satisfy his curiosity.

"Well, we think we have that part figured out too, son," she answered. "When they arrive in Jamaica, all the adults and older teens will be given an aptitude test covering what they've told us they want to do here. Everyone within a certain age range will have to start school or some kind of occupational training once they get here, if needed.

"Is that it?" Trazi questioned her again. "Do you think that's enough?"

"For some of them it will be, but many others will have more deep seated issues, I'm afraid. That's one of the reasons our re-education programs will be so thorough, and why our participants will have to take classes for all five years. We're going to tackle everything head-on so it shouldn't take long before our residents understand how they ended up in the situations they were in. More importantly, they'll see that any other African American could have easily suffered the same fate, if circumstances were different. A huge factor during slavery was in the luck of the draw; that, and the ability to hold on and have hope, which some people are just better at than others. Once everyone understands how they got to where they were, I predict that most will find success here. The misery felt by many before they left the States will gradually fade, after they've boarded our ship. We're going to help them form a vision for their God-given potential.

"But I still don't understand how you'll do it?" Trazi persisted. Kristin forced herself not to smile; he sounded much like Winston.

"I understand, and I'm not saying it's going to be easy, baby; but our

71

residents will be nurtured here. For many, it will be for the first time in their lives. That in itself will take time to get used to, because they have to learn to trust us as well. But our expectations are high, and we'll have strict accountability for the simple plan we'll implement to transform their lives. We'll gently, yet firmly, guide them into a new style of living that's different from any that most will have had before.

"Our organization will operate very similar to a small city government back in the States, except that everybody living in Exodus Village will have to make a contribution to their community, in one way or another. We're not creating some new form of welfare state here; that's something we'll make clear from the beginning. I don't expect it to be an issue once we get started though, because we'll have families to showcase their success stories. They'll become role models for others—examples of what is possible. Their friends back home will be able to visualize their own transformations from hearing about our residents' experiences.

"We'll offer all kinds of on-the-job-training once we get started. Exodus Village will be self-sufficient; our residents will learn to be well-equipped to care for themselves and their families after they leave us."

"But what happens when they leave?" Trazi was still not satisfied.

This time Kristin couldn't resist a smile. "During the second phase of our mission we'll start our commercial operations," she answered, still smiling. "We'll start in the Ashanti region initially and gradually expand to other areas. We expect each plant to create hundreds of jobs—not just for our graduates but for native Ghanaians too as part of our agreement."

"What kind of commercial operations will you have?" Trazi asked.

"Well, first and foremost, everything we do will be eco-friendly—we're going green all the way. Ghana is a beautiful country and we fully intend to protect the environment to make sure that it stays that way. We even have some restoration projects in mind for later down the line. Our first commercial projects will be food-based, though. We have nutritionists already in place, working on products that we think will appeal to native Ghanaians as much as our residents will like them. The main ingredients for many of them will be soy, and several products will be made using the seeds or leaves from the magical Moringa plant.

"What's Moringa? I don't think I've heard of that."

"It was new to me too, a quietly kept secret that can alleviate many issues that are faced by people of limited resources. The Moringa plant grows really tall and it thrives on the climate here. It's extremely versatile and has a full range of nutrients and other amazing properties. We can actually use the seeds to sanitize water for drinking!"

"Wow." Trazi commented.

"We've started growing it on our farms already so we'll be able to tap into the many benefits right away. Amina will explain it all after we get to Exodus Village. She can tell you about the Moringa plant when she shows you around. Everything we produce in our plants will be nutritious and affordable—from our soy milk and cheeses to our meat substitutes, cookies, and other snack foods we have in mind for later. Everything will be simple and high in protein, calcium, iron, minerals and other stuff that the human body thrives on. We're only using fruit or fruit juices as our sweeteners, and only fresh ingredients so our products are natural and healthy. We've decided to start with cookies since they'll be the least expensive to produce and buy. Our nutritionists have come up with great recipes and they won't have to be refrigerated because they won't be made with dairy products or eggs. That means packaging and storing will be easier too."

"That's a great idea," Trazi agreed.

"As soon as the cookie business is running smoothly, we'll start work on our solar plants," his mother added. "We've already started unofficially; we're building our own solar panels now for all our buildings. With the intensity of the sun here, there's no reason that electricity shouldn't be available to everyone who wants it. We're making that it a major goals—to make solar energy affordable for as many people as we can."

"I never thought of it that way, Mom. You're absolutely right, solar energy should be a no-brainer."

"Well, we're committed to making it happen, and sooner, rather than later. It was quite the task to set our priorities, because there's so much we want to do. I believe that we're going in the right direction though. We've been thorough in our planning and we're taking things one step at a time.

"Our next big task will be to recruit enough Black Americans with the skill sets we need to run our village to get us started. They'll be the ones who help make everything else happen—even if they only stay for a couple of years, or even a few months. Amina has a separate group working on that now and we'll use our travel agency to make that as attractive an offer as possible. We must have commitments up front for certain critical tasks, with several lines of backup for most of them as well. We won't be able to go beyond a certain point until we have the people we need to run Exodus Village. Amina's group will be pitching the idea of sabbaticals, so my baby boomer classmates will have another option available to them for coming to work with us. And I'm betting our offers will be attractive enough for some of them to move here permanently."

"That's a great idea, Mom. I'm surprised somebody didn't think of this sooner. But how can you be sure you'll get the people you need?"

"We're banking on it, sweetheart. Back in the '60s, Black students dreamed about coming to Africa one day. By this time, they've already raised their children; most have proven themselves in their careers, and have done everything else they've wanted to do. We're going to reignite their passion for Africa and help them remember their forgotten dreams. We'll make it easy to fulfill too, because we'll be taking care of their travel and living expenses after they get here. All we need from them is their knowledge and skills, and they'll get an experience of a lifetime in return.

"This group of Black American's are the ones whose predecessors still had something left of themselves after their slave experience. They may have been brought here as indentured servants instead of slaves, with blood lines that lived free in America hundreds of years before slavery ended for everyone else. Either way, after a point all Black people were considered as being one-in-the same by most others in America, negating the distinction of how they got here or how long they were enslaved. We all have a stake in paving the way for the underbelly's transformation; we'll make it easy for our mentors to come."

"But how do you start the process?" Trazi persisted, taking in what she said. "How do you convince people to leave all they've known to come?"

"I already have my sights on some of my old classmates from Tuskegee," Kristin confided, "and I'll be reaching out to them personally soon. I know they'll be a great fit too, once they realize they won't have to give up all the conveniences they're used to having. I'm hoping to get them here for our first few years of operation, in particular. Eventually, we're calling on all historically black colleges and universities across America, through recruitment fairs that we're organizing now. To start out, we're targeting Tuskegee, North Carolina A & T, and Nkrumah's Alma mater, Lincoln University. We'll eventually reach out to junior colleges and technical schools too, in America and the Caribbean.

"But some of them are going to really need our re-education program first, though." Kristin thought back to Saturdays, when she was growing up, and how she had rushed through her chores so she could sit and watch *Tarzan* on TV. Now, she realized how the colonialist-inspired show had been a means of justifying what the British were doing in Africa; the same way that racist stereotypes had been first used in America. Tarzan was a young boy who was lost in the bush somewhere in Africa, after his rich parents were killed in a plane crash that he somehow survived. Through some miracle, he was adopted and raised by apes in the jungle who were still smarter than the native tribes they taught Tarzan to dominate."

Amina surprised her one night over dinner by describing what her parents' generation had been taught about African Americans—basically that they were ignorant, lazy buffoons. Their misinformation was courtesy of British colonialists who took over in 1821 and occupied Ghana until 1957, when Kwame Nkrumah led the fight for independence. The British controlled the government, the schools, and nearly everything else in the country for over a hundred years. Its cultural influence was substantial.

"I had no idea that so many of the people here put Black Americans in the same "Good Times" pigeonhole, just like our assumptions about them based on something we saw on Tarzan. Many still seem to fall back on it whenever they interact with Africans they happen to run across."

Amina had told her how the British drove wedges between traditional rulers in Africa and those with no power—the majority. The colonialists' presence led to a corruption of the customary relationship between tribal chiefs and the people they governed, one that had existed for centuries before the Europeans came. In many cases, the chiefs' role as protector and provider became tainted over the years and as you might expect; many eventually succumbed to their own self interests, instead of the best interest of their people. They allowed themselves to become puppets in exchange for wealth and social lifestyles that only benefited themselves and their families. Many allowed their greed to replace the responsibility that traditionally went with their positions of power.

"It's a complex process; I'll give you that," Kristin admitted. "But I'm betting we'll be successful. We've been planning for this for a long time, so we know what it'll take to run the village day-to-day at maximum capacity. There's a specific number and type of skill sets that we'll have to have to operate; people who will serve the community as medical professionals, nutritionists, food service workers, engineers, construction workers, farmers, and people experience in working in plants of all kind. We'll need teachers, social workers and administrators too, all trained and ready to go by the time our pilot residents get here. If we don't have our volunteers in place by a certain time, we'll hire consultants in the interim.

"They'll help us repay our obligations to the people of Ghana for giving us this opportunity. The evidence of our success will include a positive contribution to the country; we'll have to present evidence of it to Parliament on the sixth year after our regular programs officially roll out. We'll be asked to show a significant impact made on the region as a result of Exodus Foundation activities. By our projections, on the Ashanti region it will be as high as twenty percent; most from the employment opportunities we'll be providing—both inside and outside Exodus Village.

After we get our bearings, we're going to build at least two schools in the surrounding areas too," she mentioned, "and bus some of our children out to them every day. That's going to speed up the process of culture blending in the long run as we continue to help one another other. The very best will be extracted to form a new hybrid society over time, from both cultures. And what better place to do it than in the Ashanti region?"

They had talked about the role that the Akan played in the African slave trade earlier, motivated by a quest for dominance over an unstable region that was free for the taking. It would have been impossible to imagine what American slavery would be like at that time; or that it would be worlds apart from the traditional system of captivity that was practiced in West Africa and in other countries around the world at the time.

"I'm sure there'll be other dependencies that pop up," Kristin admitted, "things that we won't have much control over. The very nature of West African politics requires us to remain flexible," she added, smiling.

"Things are moving along quite well though; they're falling into place and we only have to gear up for one last push before we start our pilot."

After a long pause she added confidently, "we're planning for success. My dream is that what we do in Exodus Village will catch on across all of Africa. I'm hoping that some day it will have the same domino effect that Nkrumah's revolution had. The spirit of freedom he ignited in Ghana spread quickly throughout Africa until the entire continent was set free."

Trazi had a look of pride on his face. "I had no idea you were working on something this big," he confessed candidly, finally satisfied with what she had told him. "I want to come back to work with you myself, some day."

"Me, too." Celeste chimed in, although she wasn't quite sixteen and had no idea what role she might possibly play.

"I'd like that," Kristin admitted. "In fact, I'm counting on it."

"I can't wait to tell Daddy about everything," Celeste added, infected by her brother's excitement. "I know he'll be proud of you too."

"I'm going to do a much better job of keeping you guys up-to-date from now on." She made the promise hurriedly, wondering whether she had blushed and shown too much after Celeste made the unexpected comment.

"Once our pilot residents are here and settled, I'll be free to travel more frequently, she promised. Hopefully, I'll be able to update you in person."

Chapter 6

Man-Child In The Promised Land

'Where in the *hell* is Little Man?'

Lawana paced the living room floor in front of her window overlooking Euclid Street. Sweat had started popping out over her plump face so she finally sat down on the couch for a minute to rest. Eating left overs from Mr. Henry's restaurant had really started to take its toll. She had recently started taking medicine every day to regulate her blood pressure, and she could almost feel it spiking every time one of her boys got in trouble.

Her grandmother always told her that a watched pot would never boil. Maybe that was true. Maybe if she stopped looking out the window then her son might come home before Ms. Wilkens got back from down the street. But a sinking feeling in her stomach told her that her good luck had finally run out. She had been just as shocked by Ms. Wilkens pretending to have to make a phone call down the street to give her some time as she had been by George coming home alone. Something was very wrong and she knew it. The look her social worker gave her as she left her apartment told her that she knew Little Man wasn't at home and that she would have a limited time to find him and get him in place.

Lawana's luck had held out for her all day; she even got home early enough to change out of her greasy smelly clothes before she picked her baby girl up from the babysitter's down the hall. She had only been at the restaurant a few hours but she could still smell the stinking odor of burning pork grease that had saturated her hair. She had always come home smelling like that when she had worked the breakfast shift. The daily special was a sandwich made with two stiff pieces of bacon stacked on top of two scrambled eggs. They made them with either white bread, or that thin gummy wheat bread that Mr. Henry would buy wholesale.

They wrapped the sandwiches tight in waxed paper and the brown paper bag they packed them in was always greasy by the time they handed them across the counter. The sandwiches sold like hotcakes until it was time for their breakfast menu to take a back seat to lunch. The whole place would still smell like frying pork until after eleven o'clock, when Mr. Henry finally turned on the exhaust fan and pulled some of the smell out. Now, since she was there all day, the pork smell from breakfast would gradually mingle in with the smell of hot grease they used to cook their lunch specials: always some kind of fried fish sandwich and french fries. Then later, the smell of baked ham and those nasty chitlins would blend in with all the other smells from the kitchen, as Lawana helped get the salad bar ready for the dinner crowd. The smells would always saturate her thick hair and she usually wreaked of the combined stench by the time she got home, now that she had moved up and was working at the restaurant full time.

She knew that Jabari would have never let her work at Mr. Henry's restaurant, even if they had been as desperate for money as she was now. Mr. Henry was a nice enough man but Jabari wouldn't have been able to take her coming home smelling like pork every day—or "swine" as he always called it. He had started going to the mosque around the corner regularly right before he got killed. He had been trying to figure out a way to change his work schedule around so he could get Friday afternoons off. He wanted them to start going to Jumu'ah every week together, with his friend. He had already started studying the Qur'an with him. He had been talking to her about going for evening prayers one Friday, after the muezzin sang out the stirring call to prayer, the adhān.

They could hear the man's melodic voice singing out the ritual call in Arabic from their house. Jabari told her it was to let all the Muslims in the community know that it was time for prayers. He had brought some books home for her to read too and said he wanted her to study Islam with him. He had been getting more and more excited about it everyday, although it still seemed somewhat foreign to Lawana. She never did get a chance to read any of the books her husband brought home, but she loved Jabari and she trusted him. She would have gone with him to Jumu'ah and anywhere else he wanted her to go.

She couldn't believe how unfair life had been to her; she had just turned thirty a month earlier and already felt as though her life was over. She was only holding it together for her kids. She had no idea what was going to happen with the boys but Lacrecia was only four years old and she had a long way to go with her. She had to figure out some way to get them out of that neighborhood before her daughter got older, and started taking up with boys who acted just like her brothers.

Her luck had held out for most of the day. George had been at home when she home from work, still looking sheepish because she didn't even try to hide how mad she was with him. Any other day, Helena would have called her as soon as she got to work to tell her that George had slipped out of the apartment. But that day had been different, and he at least had the decency to cooperate after causing so much trouble.

It was Little Man who was nowhere to be found and that had set off red flags for her right away. She had expected her oldest son to be home by the time she got home—that maybe he would've picked up Lacrecia from Helena's apartment so she wouldn't have to do it. She had sent George over near Malcolm X Park to look for him as soon as she realized he wasn't there, since Ms. Wilkens still hadn't made it to their house yet by that time. She told her youngest son to check the block-long street that ran just off of Euclid too, a few blocks away from their apartment building. Her brother had told her that he saw Little Man there once, and she had prayed that George would be able to find him. But she knew in her heart that there was something wrong, otherwise Little Man would've been home. She had told him that the social worker was coming the last time she saw him. Little Man knew all of them were expected to be there, and she knew he would never put his family in jeopardy like that—not if he could help it.

These days, he was only going to school whenever he felt like it; usually when he wanted to spend time with his friends. But she had never had one call about him skipping school yet; their policy was to try to reach her at least once before calling Social Services. The school considered that there was always an off-chance that he might have had a legitimate reason for being absent, so she assumed that the school hadn't called Social Services about his truancy yet. Unfortunately, that hadn't been the first time their social worker had to set up this kind of home visit though; every time they did it had something to do with George. He kept getting into more and more trouble in school and she didn't know why his teachers couldn't see how much he enjoyed being suspended. *She* was the one who was being punished because every time, his antics caused her world to be turned upside down. She had to pay Helena extra to make sure he stayed inside their apartment until she got home from work. Otherwise, she would have to take off work herself to stand guard over him.

It was all fun and games for him though, because just like his father, George wasn't afraid of anything. He was only nine so he still didn't really get it, otherwise, she was sure he would never have started them down the road they were on. She had tried to shield her two youngest as much as she could; she didn't want to scare them about what might happen next.

But Little Man knew exactly how serious things were with Social Services. He knew they had to jump through any hoop that was held up for them to jump through. She also knew her oldest son felt like he was the man of the house since their father wasn't there to protect them anymore. Sometimes, she found herself letting him play that role too. She told him how the welfare people were threatening to take all of them from her and put them into foster care; although she didn't think for one minute that Little Man would ever go with them. He would run away for good before that happened; but she knew he loved his brother and sister and it wasn't like him to take that kind of chance with them.

Her sinking feeling only got worse when Ms. Wilkens gave her a break. She knew for sure then that it was going to be real bad if Little Man didn't come back in time. But her luck was still trying to hold out and the woman said she had to make a phone call, right after George opened the door and came in alone. She didn't say anything to him, not even to say hello like she normally did. She only looked at him a quick second and told Lawana she was going to the sandwich shop on the corner for a few minutes, to make her call. Then she said she would need to talk to her and *all* her children when she got back. She had given her more time in the hopes that all three children would there when she came back to officially start her home visit.

Lawana looked at the clock again, knowing that Ms. Wilkens was bound to be back at any minute. George had wanted to go back out to look for his brother after finally sensing the seriousness of what was going on. She thought about letting him go too, because then the State would only have her baby girl. Maybe at least she would see her boys from time to time if they both ran away to the streets.

It seemed like Little Man was determined now to follow in Willie's footsteps, ever since Jabari died and he found out his real father was in prison for life. Soon after, her son found his father's people in Anacostia—before she had time to figure out what to do next. He took a bus there all by himself one day and one of his uncles brought him back home the next day. They didn't even call her right away to let her know he was alright; they just let her worry about him all night. By the time he got back, they had turned Willie into some kind of super hero and Little Man had stayed mad with her for a real long time for not telling anything about his father.

She wished he had just stayed mad because after that he tried to *be* like Willie. She couldn't lie to him, so she had to tell him that she loved Willie too and that he was a *good* man. She didn't want to tell him that because her son knew now that his father had been a drug dealer, and one of the best. He made lots of money too and he was generous with it. He had taken care of all his family when he could, so she knew his uncles had filled his head with all kinds of stuff that a thirteen-year-old boy didn't need to hear.

Little Man had even tried to force her to take him to see Willie once, but she drew the line at that. Then he begged her to take him to the prison for a visit; she didn't know how to tell him that she had never told his father anything about him. His family didn't keep in touch with Willie after he went away, so his daddy *still* didn't know he had a son as far as she knew.

But that didn't keep Little Man from trying to be just like him.

Lawana jumped when the phone rang and she knew it would be bad news before she picked it up. The policeman on the other end said he was calling to tell her that her son, William, had been arrested for drug possession. She held her breath until the officer told her that they had caught Little Man selling nickle bags of weed. She was relieved because she knew right away that it wasn't a felony and since he'd never been arrested before, he would probably get off with one of those first-time offender programs. One of the girls at the restaurant had just gone through the same thing with her son. Lawana had been afraid the policeman would tell her someone was dead or something, but thank God nobody was. Her son was arrested but he was still alive. She knew where he was and that he didn't have enough pot on him for any serious trouble; she knew he wouldn't get any hard jail time like his father.

She didn't pretend to be surprised that Little Man was selling drugs of some kind. Whenever he did turn up at their apartment lately he was always dressed like somebody doing pretty good in life. She knew she hadn't bought the clothes he wore and besides that he always brought presents for George and Lacrecia. He had brought presents for her too at first, just like Willie used to do. He switched to flowers after she kept making him take whatever he brought her back, but she just didn't have the heart to make him take the presents he brought for George and Lacrecia back. She knew she should've done it and that it wasn't setting much of an example for them. But they didn't have much of anything extra for them anymore, not with their daddy dead.

Little Man was so much like his father now that she thought it would scare her to death. She had finally told Ms. Steele about her grandmother down in South Carolina, because of Little Man. She tried to find her while Ms. Steele was their case worker so she could've helped her take her children and move down South. But then she found out her grandmother had already moved, and she had no way of knowing whether she had moved out of the neighborhood or out of the state. Her mother had moved too, since she last spoke to her. Lawana had thought about going back to live with her for a few months, just until she could save up enough money to move South on her own. But when she called, she found out her number had been disconnected and an old friend came into the restaurant not long after that. She told her that her mother and her boyfriend had moved out of the house a long time ago.

Lawana wished to God Ms. Steele was still her caseworker, but in her gut she knew even that wouldn't matter now. With George being suspended from school again, the best she had hoped for was to have Ms. Wilkens tell her she would keep a closer eye on them and schedule more home visits. That would have been bad enough, but with her oldest son arrested she knew *that* was no longer an option. She didn't have the money to get Little Man out of jail either and she knew better than to call his father's people. They only paid attention to Willie when he was buying them things; they stopped all contact with him after his money ran out and they knew he was never getting out of prison.

But she couldn't be worried about Little Man right now; she was too scared the State was gon' take her other children.

And sure enough her biggest fears came true.

Chapter 7

Lake Bosumtwe

*A*mad drove south on Lake Road on leaving Kumasi and continued south on the Ejisu-Bekwai Road that connected the two towns. By that time, the conversation in the car had whittled down; everyone had been quiet for several minutes until Kristin turned toward the back seat.

"I hope you guys won't mind, but I've asked Amad to make one last stop before we get to Exodus Village." Celeste groaned.

"I know, but we're going to be driving too close to Lake Bosumtwe not to stop, honey. It's such a special place that you kids really shouldn't miss seeing it. But don't worry, we'll only stop long enough for a quick look."

"Sounds good to me, Mom. I was hoping we'd get a chance to see it."

"Good. I'd like to take a look at our architect's latest drawings while we're there. I want to compare it against the scenery but it still won't take us too far off schedule."

She knew the children were anxious to see Exodus Village but it was no surprise that her son would say what he had. He loved being around water almost as much as Celeste did. They had been talking about Lake Bosumtwe over dinner the night before and she had told them that it had been created after a huge meteor fell to Earth over a million years ago. It formed an almost perfect circular depression on impact with the Earth and it had filled up with water during rainy seasons over the passing years.

After another minute Amad made a sharp turn heading east, on a road that took them through the town of Kuntanase. He drove past the government hospital that provided care to many of the people in the region, and a short time later they arrived in the town of Abono, driving as close to the lake's boundaries as possible before turning to head north.

"Solomon used his father's influence to help us negotiate with the chiefs of towns closest to our property," Kristin said of her friend and business partner. "That made the process of getting permits for our travel agency's spa much easier than it likely would have been otherwise."

She had only learned that Solomon's father was a powerful chief in the Ashanti region after they began negotiations to buy Heavenly Travel. She had met him at the University of Kumasi when she taught there briefly before moving to Ghana; their bond had formed as fellow professors.

Kristin reached under her seat and pulled out a long black cylinder that she had been given before they left Atimpoku, in the Volta Region.

"I asked our architect to scale back his original designs for the spa after I fully understood this area's spiritual significance," she said.

"What do you mean by that?" Celeste was curious. She perked up when she caught her first glimpse of the massive lake.

"There was a famous battle fought near here centuries ago, a fierce one between Asanteman ancestors and a rival kingdom. Many warriors lost their lives fighting to protect the nation and they were buried in a mass grave in Ekoho Forest, which borders the lake."

She told them the story that had been passed down for generations past about a hunter who had once chased a deer through the forest bordering the narrow road they were on. The deer escaped into a small body of water that had accumulated in the hole created by the crater and apparently saved itself after taking cover behind a large bolder in the middle of what is now Lake Bosumtwe. The deer managed to disappear completely from the hunter's sight and the boulder became known as the "Abrodwum Stone." She added that it was likely all that was left of the meteor that fell.

"It's wouldn't be surprising to me if it still carried some of the energy it brought from space," she speculated. "The stone is considered the lake's spiritual center, and this whole area has been regarded as sacred for centuries. It is still respected in honor of the warriors who sacrificed their lives for the survival of the kingdom. Only wooden boats are allowed to sail on it; no metal or gas powered machines. As a matter of fact, the people around here took such good care that it's one of the few remaining areas of the rainforest that's still in its pristine condition."

"That's interesting," Trazi commented, "and goes to show that giving care to our use of the environment is effective. This place is certainly beautiful. I can see why you'd want to build something here."

The Land Rover had just passed a section of the road that gave them a clear panoramic view of the lake and surrounding landscape.

"It is beautiful," Kristin agreed, "We're planning to build more elaborate quarters closer to Ekoho Forest but those will be exclusively for the Asantehene and his guests. According to legend, the lake was created on a Sunday so it is honored during the Akwasidae Festival. Other more traditional ceremonies have been held near here privately for centuries, probably with the original protocol of libations being poured in honor of the warrior ancestors and other sacred traditions.

"Culturally, it's one of the few places with little western influence from the British occupation. There are sacred places here that are off limits to everyone except for the king and highest level of traditional leaders.

"Wait...Was that what we saw at the palace in Kumasi yesterday? The Sunday festival?" Celeste was finally putting it all together.

"That's right, honey. The word "Akwasidae" translates as "Sunday" in English. The celebration at Manhyia Palace has been held there since 1926 for the general public. That's when the British built the palace for the return of Asantehene Prempeh I, after his years of exile in Elmina.

"This area is rich with tradition and once I found out more about the lake's history and its importance to the Asante nation, I completely agreed with Solomon. We'll only bring a select group of clients here at all, and we're only sending out announcements about our new spa to a select few; clients that we know to be at a certain level of spiritual and cultural awareness."

"Really?" Trazi questioned. "I'm sure this would be a popular destination for people looking for a hide-away retreat."

"We think so too," his mother agreed, "but it's more important to us that it stays as beautiful as it is now; that's part of our agreement. We promised the chiefs here that we would cause minimal disruption to the lifestyles of the twenty-seven local communities built around the lake." She explained their architect's design around the existing landscape. They would clear only those trees that he couldn't see any other way around.

"And even with that, we'll have to get approval from the counsel of chiefs first, before any cutting takes place."

They had reached Heavenly Travel's property line and Kristin pointed to a small sign nearly hidden on one side of the road.

"That's going to be our only visible sign from this road," she told them. "People will have to already know we're here and roughly where to find us. Our spa is going to be nestled between these beautiful ancient trees," she said pointing. "And you're right, Trazi, seclusion will be our main selling point. Solomon, Amina, and I have had many conversations about it before we agreed to provide an option for our guests to make weekly excursions into Kumasi. We'll arrange for one of our minibuses to take them shopping at Kumasi Market and for a visit to Manhyia Palace and that's all."

At her request, Amad kept driving past the entrance and they proceeded to continued the twelve and a half miles around the lake. She wanted to give them a better feel for the area before they stopped for a closer look.

"Oh, yes. I forgot to mention that the depth of the lake still shifts some-times with heavy downpours during the rainy season. Some villages have been forced to relocate to higher ground because of flooding."

"When is the rainy season?"

"We're in one of them now, actually," Kristin answered Celeste. "As you can see, it doesn't necessarily mean that it's going to rain every day, and if it does rain, it doesn't necessarily last all day."

It had only rained once so far since the children had been in the country.

"The regions in the northern area of the country only have one rainy season that lasts from April until September," she added.

Kristin had shown them a map of Ghana on their first night there and they knew the combined size of the Northern, Upper East and Upper West regions was close to the area of the country below the North, which was where the majority of people lived.

"All the other regions have two rainy seasons, including this one. They usually last from April to July, and then get started again from September to November. That also means that this area gets nearly double the average rainfall every year that the North gets, usually around forty three inches."

"Holy Toledo! Okay, now I understand how rain could create such a large body of water." The puzzled look left Trazi's face after everything had fallen in place in his mind,

"Trust me, you'll definitely understand it once it really starts raining around here," she agreed. "The meteor carved out the perfect space to collect water after crashing."

"Do you really think the Abrodwum Stone is all that's left of it?"

"It makes sense to me, son," she answered. "Energy from the stone might even explain some of the mystical powers associated with this area."

They had come full circle and were once again nearing Heavenly Trav-el's property line. This time, Amad turned right onto a narrow unpaved road that eventually led them into a large clearing. They got out of the Land rover and took in an unobstructed view of the lake front, while Kristin pulled out the architect's revised sketches.

"This is exactly what we had in mind." Her tone was filled with excitement as she carefully unrolled the blueprints to let the children take a look. "Solomon is going to love this."

She pointed out that most of the accommodations would be built on an elevated tract of land that they hoped would be high enough to avoid damage during any projected flooding.

"We're only building a handful of cabins here at all," she told them, "and only two of them will be built at the lower elevation." She pointed to a thick area of bush below where they stood. "Both are going to be built on stilts; one will be for Solomon, and I'll use the other cabin as a get-away without my having to leave the country and Amina will use it as well. We'll have a shared dock and a platform with stairs on either end to lead directly into the water."

The kids wanted to follow a nearby footpath that led them to a higher elevation before they left. They took another look at the lake from that vista and after they were back in the car again, Amad retraced the route they had taken back through Abono. They drove westward through Kuntanase, turning the car south toward Bekwai, a small town of less than three thousand people with a disproportionate number of schools. Outside the city limits, Amad picked up the Kumasi-Yomaransa Road that took them in a southeasterly direction through a small range of mountains in the direction of Exodus Village.

"Mom," Trazi started, "what else are you planning for your new residents when they get to Jamaica? Three months is a long time." His mother had mentioned during an earlier conversation the three-month lay-over their residents would have in the Caribbean, before crossing the Atlantic.

"It is, and we plan to get a lot accomplished during that time. Aside from time spent in their classes, everyone will get a chance to start getting to know each other too. We have social interactions planned each week that they're there; the people coming from America will be linking up with people who start their journey in the Caribbean there. We'll do as much as we can to help prepare all of them for their new life here, and as part of that process, we'll expose our American guests to people in Jamaica that I've always referred to as the "real Jamaicans." They are mainly from the "black" or "worker" class," she said, remembering her introduction to the culture when she and Winston were in Jamaica on their honeymoon.

"They make up the majority population although they've historically been on the lowest end of the totem pole according to how they've been treated. They've generally had the least exposure to European culture too, so their lifestyles are very similar to that of West African culture.

"We're going to highlight Marcus Garvey's successes with the Universal Negro Improvement Association (UNIA) there of course, as well as his thwarted plans to further Pan-Africanism—the unification of all people of African descent world. African people were taken all over the world during the slave trade and Garvey's vision for economic and cultural recovery began with uniting African descendents worldwide.

"Did you know that your great-grandfather once worked for Marcus Garvey?"

"No I didn't." Trazi responded in surprise. "Dad never mentioned that his grandfather knew him personally."

"Well, apparently Grandpa Bailey spent quite a bit of time with Garvey between 1927 and 1935, after Garvey was released from federal prison in Atlanta and deported. He worked with him on the newspaper and monthly magazine Garvey started in Jamaica, until he eventually moved to London.

"He suffered an illness a short time later that left him paralyzed. It was apparently after reading a story about his death in the papers that he suffered another attack, and died as a result of that. Or, at least that's what the reports say. There was so much criticism of him after Hoover's campaign that many people don't realize just how successful he was with his ideas about economic development. I wouldn't have known much about it either if it hadn't been for Grandpa Bailey.

That's why our foundation is determined to share as many details as possible about what Garvey was able to accomplish, in spite of obstacles stacked to limit him. Back then in the '20s, when he was in full swing, Blacks hadn't been guaranteed equal protection under the law yet. The first major elements of organized crime were running rampant too, which probably made it easier for Hoover to justify doing his thing. Now, thanks to the Freedom of Information Act, anybody can see proof that the FBI played a major role in discrediting Garvey, just as it did with later Civil Rights leaders like Dr. King.

"But the Freedom of Information Act has one major drawback."

"How so?" Celeste asked

"Well, by the time something is finally released to the public sometimes, the people who were originally interested are either no longer alive or no longer care enough to pursue their concerns."

"I get it," Trazi said. "Someone like me would never know to look."

"Yes, and that's exactly my point."

"Your great-grandfather was working for Garvey when he made his well-renowned prophesies about Haile Selassie's coronation as Emperor of Ethiopia," she announced after a pause. "Or Abyssinia, as it was once known. He told me and your father that it created quite a stir in Jamaica at the time. Garvey quoted scriptures that supported his predictions of the Emperor's coronation in 1930 and announced that it would be of great significance to people of African descent. That led to the start of the Rastafarian movement you know, which in many ways became a self-fulfilling prophesy."

"What do you mean? What did his predictions about the emperor have to do with Rastafarians?"

"Everything really," Kristin answered her son. "The movement's name came from the name that Haile Selassie had been known by before his coronation as Emperor. He was given the name Tafari Makonnen at birth, and he was later bestowed the title of "Ras" in 1916, which means "leader" in the Amharic language spoken in that East African country. Ras Tafari headed successful military campaigns that led to the coronation of Zauditu as Empress of Ethiopia, and to his own ascension to the throne of Shoa in 1928. That position was a junior line of Ethiopia's Solomonic Dynasty, and he became known as King Negus Negusta during his coronation. Empress Zauditu died two years later however, and he was proclaimed heir-apparent to the throne. He ascended the imperial throne of Ethiopia in 1930 and was when he was crowned Haile Selassie."

"In Amharic, the name literally means "Power of the Trinity," she added. "And, like all other Ethiopian emperors before him, Haile Selassie was said to be a direct descendent of King Solomon and the Queen of Sheeba. That, makes him part of the same bloodline as both Mary and Joseph, of course.

"He was also bestowed the traditional title held by all Ethiopian kings—"King of Kings, Lord of Lords, Conquering Lion of the Tribe of Judah." It fulfilled the prophecy that Garvey made about his coronation long before the world had ever heard of the man who was crowned Haile Selassie."

"That's an interesting story..."

"It is, and what's even more interesting is that Haile Selassie later embraced the Rastafarians who sought refuge in Ethiopia, although he remained an Orthodox Christian himself throughout his life. Ethiopia is a very unique country in that it's the only country in Africa to successfully repel Europeans who tried to colonize it. They drove the Italians back in

1896, after almost two years of fighting.

"But on the down side, slavery was still practiced in Ethiopia a long time after it ended in America and most other places.

"What?"

"Yes, I'm afraid so. People were still being taken as slaves until Selassie, while pursuing membership in the League of Nations for Ethiopia, finally bowed to pressure and officially ended the practice. At the time, the League's somewhat elastic definition of "civilized" meant those countries that had abolished slavery and slave trading. When Mussolini was ready to invade Ethiopia again in 1935, the definition had evolved once again and the Italian leader then gained permission to send a large force of troops there to make certain Italy wouldn't be defeated a second time."

"Another interesting thing is that His Imperial Majesty was exiled to the United Kingdom for six years during the Italian invasion. He and Garvey ended up living in Europe at the same time."

"Wow. So did they get together to plan their next moves?" Celeste was intrigued by the timing.

"Not exactly." Kristin had no choice but to disappoint the young teen. "By that time, Garvey's opinion of Selassie had changed dramatically; he was extremely disappointed on learning that slavery had still been going on in that country. Selassie himself owned slaves and their treatment was apparently harsh—although it didn't compare to American slavery.

"From what I've learned, Garvey was also outraged when Selassie fled the country after Italy's second invasion, leaving his countrymen without a head of state to fight off the Italians. He wrote a rather seething editorial about it in a London paper, which probably contributed to the Emperor's paranoia once he finally returned to Ethiopia in 1941. And things pretty much went downhill fast once he went back, I'm afraid, although after he was restored to power, he ended up giving the Rastafarians five hundred acres of his personal property to live on. A group of them still lives there to this day," she continued, "even though their belief in Selassie as the second coming of Christ clashes sharply with orthodox religious views in the country. It also puts them at odds with those who lost faith in Selassie during the time of his exile.

"It was all very complicated and controversial, but I think that learning about that part of Africa's history will be good for our new residents too. It'll be part of the process of opening their minds to new thoughts; reconditioning their old outdated ones. We're hoping to get some of the Rastafarians who have visited Ethiopia or lived there to stop by at some point in Jamaica, so they can answer any questions about the settlement there.

"Something else we have planned is to start classes that will expose our new residents to traditional values still held in Ghana, like family responsibility, respect, and spirituality. We're going to start wellness classes in Jamaica too, and introduce residents to the art of using herbs and spices for medicinal purposes and to maintain good health. Other than fish, there won't be any meat or meat products to be found in Exodus Village. We're being proactive by conforming to the results and recommendations of many studies that show the negative impact of consuming large quantities of animal products, on the human body. At one time in history, most people only ate meat during holidays or when there were special feasts."

"Really?" Celeste was surprised.

"That's right, as strange as it may seem now, I can remember that we only ate turkey on Thanksgiving and Christmas, as a child. And chicken was a once a week treat. I think that over the years, people started associating their ability to eat meat regularly with wealth, although they seemed to miss the association that the same rich diet had with gout and other diseases that wealthier people tend to develop."

"But don't you think the 'no meat at all' thing is a little strict?" Trazi challenged. She had always encouraged him to question everything until it made sense in his mind.

"It probably is," she admitted, "but we can't afford to be lax. We need to keep everyone as healthy as possible for the five years they'll be living with us, and we know that good eating habits will take them far beyond that. We have to look at it from a practical perspective because we have limited resources. We can't afford extensive medical care that bad diets eventually lead to.

"That's why we've added the mandatory requirements for physical exercise to go along with our ban on meat. It may seem extreme at first, but I can guarantee that their new diets will help rid our residents of many of the health issues they arrive here with."

"But what are you going to do about their emotional health?"

"That's a good question, son," she complimented him. "That was a big topic of discussion because we expect our residents to bring a variety of emotional issues with them. After the first six weeks in Jamaica, our staff will meet with each family as a group, to assess whether some type of intervention might be useful. We're hoping this will help us predict areas of concern before it crops up; issues that some groups of residents might be prone to develop, or have already developed before they join us.

"Unfortunately, we're not equipped to handle extreme cases, though, so our staff will most likely recommend an end to an individual's participation in some cases. Like, for example, if they've already been flagged as rehab provisional when they're accepted and our staff feels they pose a strong risk or, we later learn they will have a need for other extensive counseling; we'll have no choice but to gently remove them from our programs. We're hoping that this will only affect a small percentage of the people we accept, but we won't waste our limited resources trying to deal with imbalances that we're not equipped to handle. That energy would require us to move too far away from what we aim to accomplish.

"Mom, you just mentioned something about rehab—are you talking about substance abuse?" Kristin wondered whether her son had picked up on her mention of their policies that address people with addictions.

"How are you going to handle drug abuse? With that many people, I guess some would be bound to have that kind of problem."

"That's very true, and something else we've had to think hard about," his mother admitted. "We agreed that there will likely be a large group with substance abuse problems, especially given the percentage of Americans who feel the need to get high everyday off *something*. We usually hear more about people who use illegal drugs, but the drug of choice for many might be alcohol or prescription drugs—whether they be legal or not. We think we've found a way to handle that too, though."

"Wow, you guys really did think of everything."

"Well, I'm not so sure about that, but I guess we'll know for sure by the end of our pilot," she was smiling again, pleased by her son's approval.

"What we've decided to do is send out provisional letters of acceptance to the affected people, about nine months before the ship is scheduled to leave Annapolis. Before anyone goes anywhere, they'll all have to go through a basic health screening. It will be for everyone's protection although I'm hopeful that the day will come when we won't have to turn anyone away. But we're not at that point yet, so we'll be looking for serious health issues that our medical staff deems high risk, like cases of active tuberculosis, hepatitis, and other infectious diseases. We've put together teams of volunteer African American doctors, nurses, and lab technicians who will run tests for people who don't have health care; we're arranging to set up shop in designated cities and they'll be on standby to test anyone we accept who is without insurance.

"That's when we'll also do our drug and alcohol screenings to identify people with addictions; to prescription, non-prescription, legal, and illegal drugs. We're flagging people with blood alcohol levels over a certain threshold too, which would indicate alcoholism.

"I guess that will eliminate a lot of people." Trazi observed.

"Well, not necessarily," his mother corrected him. "We're not wasting time or money trying to identify the recreational pot smokers; we'll have other ways of keeping that under control once they're here. What we'll do for people who test positive for other drugs is notify them of their test results first. We'll request a response within a certain length of time and we'll use that to help us decide whether to take a chance on them or not."

"How so?"

"I think we came up with something that will make the process simple," she said. "If we get the usual denials back from someone who clearly shows evidence of an addiction, we'll have no choice but to send them our regrets along with suggestions for rehab facilities in their area. That's all we'll be able to do really—encourage them to get clean and let them know that they can apply again after they have.

"But on the other hand, if they respond in a way that shows they accept responsibility for their addiction and that they're ready to rid themselves of it, we may still accept them conditionally."

"But what exactly does that mean?" Celeste wondered.

"As soon as our ship docks in Jamaica, the people we've identified as being in need of rehab services will be discreetly separated from the others. They will be directed to a make-shift residential rehab facility, where they will stay for the first two months they're on the island. We're not equipped to handle any addiction issues during our pilot though, and I don't know that we'll ever be prepared for dealing with addicted minors. It all just gets too complicated for our setup and resources.

"The condition of acceptance for our adults will hinge on their cooperation with rehab counseling, and on their willingness to submit to random testing throughout the entire five years they're living with us. If things go well with their two-month rehab in Jamaica, they'll in effect be outpatients for the remainder of their time with us. We're deliberately making our programs intense too, to weed out those that we don't feel have a better-than-average chance of making it without a relapse.

"And, they'll still have to take the other classes that everyone else will be taking at the same time," she added. "The drug-related sessions will be extra, which in itself may become a deterrent for some. But if all goes well, we'll integrate those people who are successful in rehab with the rest of the group for their last month in Jamaica. They'll have to pass another unannounced screening before they can board the ship, and on top of that, they'll be assigned to AA or NA sponsors and expected to cooperate fully."

"Wow, that's going to be tough."

"It is. We're giving them all the support they need to stay clean because there will be zero tolerance for relapses. We're going to make that clear before they leave Annapolis too. Anyone who fails our random testing will be subject to immediate removal without appeal, and they'll be taken back to the United States as soon as their travel can be arranged.

"Man!" Trazi commented. "That's hard!"

"I know it may sound drastic, son, but at least we're giving them a chance. Hopefully, we're talking about circumstances that aren't likely to happen, but we have to be cautious about who we accept in our program and who we bring to Ghana. We're planning for success, like I said before. At this stage of the game, we can't allow ourselves be bogged down with issues that we're not comfortable with or prepared to handle.

"Some recreational drug use has become acceptable in American culture over the years, although it's still illegal in most places. The last few American presidents have openly admitted to smoking pot, for example, but in countries like Ghana there has never been that kind of tolerance or acceptance. We have no intention of jeopardizing everything by allowing drugs to become a factor in Exodus Village.

"All of our operations have to be tight because of the number of people we'll be dealing with. We've been trying to think of everything ahead of time so that we can document our procedures and handle any eventuality.

"We already know Exodus Village won't be a good fit for everyone, so it's in everyone's best interest that we reach that conclusion sooner rather than later. It's much better for all concerned to do it in Jamaica, instead of after the person has traveled all the way to Africa.

A few minutes later, Kristin announced that they were close to a side road that would lead to the gold mines in the town of Obuasi. She said it was close to the turnoff for Exodus Village too, but it still seemed like an eternity to Celeste and Trazi, who had grown anxious from their anticipation. They rode in silence for another few miles before Amad finally began to slow down. Shortly thereafter, he turned onto a gravel road off the main highway. It stretched out before them after they drove around a small curve, as Kristin simultaneously announced that they had just reached the southwestern property line for Exodus Village.

Chapter 8

The Thrill Is Gone

*C*harlotte appeared to be calm as she sat passively next to her husband on the couch. In reality, she was struggling to ward off a blood-curdling scream—one that would be aimed directly for Winston's ear. For the past twenty minutes or so, she had found it increasingly harder to control the urge. With each passing second, her frustrations grew along with the impulse to do it.

She turned to watch his profile as he continued to watch the television set, barely conscious of her being in the room. The one thing that kept her from screaming was the realization that it *still* might not get his attention. That would have been far too pathetic and as she considered the consequences, she realized she had no idea what she might be capable of doing next. She couldn't say for sure what she might do to herself; or better still, to Winston. He was so aggravating that she honestly didn't know!

She forced herself to control her breathing instead, fully aware of its rhythm until it had slowed to a steady pace. Gradually, she felt her impulse to do him bodily harm subside a bit until the rejection that it had grown from once again took its place. She had foolishly tried to convince him to take her to a party that evening—one that Pam, her line sister, always gave and was considered the event of the year. Everyone who was anybody in their circle always made an appearance; every one of her sorors who lived in the area—everybody. Last year she made the mistake of going alone after Winston bowed out at the last minute. She could still see the look of pity in the eyes of her friends as she lied about some business emergency that he had stayed behind to get under control. She had prayed that he wouldn't come up with one of his lame excuses again this year. She had hoped, as she waited for him to get home, that maybe, since it was on a Friday this year and the beginning of the weekend, he just might take her.

But, surprise, surprise, he had begged off again; just as he always did these days. Even when she told him she had practically promised the girls they would be there. This time, his excuse had been that he was too worn out from being stuck in traffic for over an hour. For the life of her, she couldn't imagine what else he had expected to happen. He scheduled one of the few meetings he still had outside his home office for downtown, and on a Friday afternoon. Nearly everyone in Washington who could always took off early on Fridays, as often as they could. They all wanted to be someplace else because the traffic was *always* worse as the weekend got started.

She had been disappointed, to say the least, when he told he wouldn't go, but she made a decision to play the role of understanding wife this time, instead of giving him a dose of her usual pouting. She had recently been made aware that somewhere along the line that ploy had lost its effectiveness, so she had empathized with him about the traffic for a few minute s instead. She went through all the motions and even gave him a back and neck massage to help him relax from his drive. She feigned concern for his tense muscles, trying to forget that he probably had no intention of taking her to the party in the first place. And they hadn't been out together in months!

Still hopeful, she had made a special trip to Whole Foods on her way home that afternoon, knowing how prone he was for turning crazy about the least thing when he was hungry. She picked up an assortment of chicken and fish dishes, plus a nice green salad with all the things she knew he liked. She went all out to make sure he would have a good meal before they left, so he wouldn't get tired at the party and want to come home early. Little did she know they wouldn't be going anywhere at all.

This time, she had good reason to hope. Winston actually got along with Pam's husband; whenever they had been at the couple's house before, the two men usually drifted off to watch a game on their gigantic television screen. But her husband had dashed her hopes this time, right after he got home. Then, it had taken nearly an hour for him to wind down and after he finished eating, he quickly lost all interest in her altogether.

As a compromise, they were supposed to be watching television together; once again, she had taken that to mean there would be *something* in it for her. Instead, he had been engrossed in a stupid documentary he had harassed her into agreeing to watch. He didn't even notice that she had been staring at him for almost a half hour. It seemed there had always been something that stood between them from the very beginning. It was either his children, his job, his crazy ex-wife who kept going in and out of rehab, and now, this television show. Charlotte never realized their marriage was in so much trouble until after his daughter left on her trip to Africa. The complete lack of attention he had shown her when his favorite distraction was no longer around, finally made that clear. Now she only hoped that it wouldn't be too late to fix it.

"What time is this show going off, honey?" She yawned casually and at the same time draped her arm across his shoulder; a move that was borrowed from the average teenage boy's repertoire of tricks. She even leaned in closer to give him a whiff of the perfume she had picked up in Fairfax—an often-used teenage girl's trick. The woman at the cosmetics counter told her that the chemical secretion of pheromones in the perfume would send out a magnetic appeal to the opposite sex. She had practically assured her that she would get the kind of reaction that she wanted from her husband, so Charlotte had bought the largest bottle that they had. She had hoped Winston would suddenly find her alluring again without realizing why. She heeded the salesclerk's warning that too much of the perfume might overwhelm the senses and have the opposite effect. Charlotte misted herself sparingly after taking a quick shower, and she only sprayed a tiny bit into the air of their bedroom when Winston called to say he was a few blocks away.

Now she had to wonder whether she had sprayed too little of the expensive scent. After almost two hour, it had *still* failed to do its job.

"Huh? Oh...I think it should be off in another thirty minutes, or so..." Her husband's distracted answer was another bad sign. Another few seconds passed before he finally turned to look at her, as though it had just registered that she was sitting next to him.

"Did you want to watch something else?" She could see the recognition slowly sweep across his face. Apparently, he had finally remembered they were supposed to be spending the evening *together*. But even at that she could see that he was being pulled back toward the television set. The commercial had just ended and the host was introducing the next segment —something about a water conservation project in Botswana or some godforsaken place in Africa. As if that had *anything* to do with them or she should care.

Charlotte decided to be passive/aggressive for a few minutes, taking far more time than was needed before responding. She decided she would keep his attention focused on her for as long as she could manage, knowing that he was dying to get back to the television set. She pretended not to notice and pasted what she hoped would pass for a sweet smile on her face.

She had been quite surprised when her husband agreed to let his precious daughter go to Ghana with her brother. Everyone knew how protective Winston had always been of Celeste, so at first she had taken it as a sign that he had noticed their marriage was in need of attention too. She had almost convinced herself that her husband saw them growing apart as she did, and that he was just as anxious to fix things between them. She figured the two weeks that both his children would be out of the country would be enough time for them to rekindle their romance. She had been excited about having him all to herself for a change, so much so that she had been extra nice to his daughter, and even helped her pack for the trip.

But his kids were already due back in less than a week. She had yet to attract his attention without hatching some sort of scheme to get it. Instead of cutting back on the long hours he was working as she had hoped, Winston started working even longer hours after Celeste left the country. It had probably never crossed his mind that they should spend time together refocusing on their marriage. Apparently, he never thought about it, or her, at all.

She had a sudden flashback to how surprised she'd been when he up and quit his job. He never even discussed it with her, and the year before he had been given a big promotion. That should've been her cue that something was amiss. She had worked almost as hard as he had, entertaining his bosses and coworkers who headed the projects he wanted to work on.

His promotion meant he would finally be working at NASA's more prestigious offices on "E" Street. Another one of her sorors, whose husband worked on Capitol Hill, had set it all up once he found out Winston was a fellow Tuskegee alum. The new position came with lots of growth potential too, not to mention that it paid much more money. There was an added bonus, because he no longer had to drive all the way out to Greenbelt everyday. And even more important than that, it put them right inside the Washington social circle she had been dying to get into.

The new job was in NASA's legislative affairs office, and with quick thinking she had asked his new secretary to copy her on all the invitations that came into the office when they were introduced. They got invitations to all sorts of events around town, including VIP passes to all the best parties during the Congressional Black Caucus Legislative Weekend every September.

Everything had been going great, as far as she was concerned, until Winston decided to start his own business. He never consulted her about anything; all of it had been put into motion before she knew anything about it.

After the initial shock wore off, Charlotte still tried to make the best of it. She had hoped his working from home would mean more time for them to spend together, but she couldn't have been more wrong if she tried. His business seemed to take up every minute of his day; at least every minute that wasn't spent trying to keep track of his daughter's every move. His working out of the loft did not translate into any more time for the two of them; they didn't even eat breakfast together most of the time. By the time she woke up, Winston was usually in his office with a big bowl of cereal and already working on his second cup of coffee.

Something had definitely gone wrong with their marriage and she had no idea what that was.

"No, no, Honey, that's fine," she lied. "I was just curious—that's all."

Charlotte had always been a practical woman; she decided early on that there would be no advantage in struggling to get Winston's attention. She could already see that it would be a loosing battle this time too. But one thing was for sure, she would definitely have to figure something out. She didn't like the way things were going at all.

"You know what?" She had waited patiently this time for a commercial break before speaking, hoping that it would somehow play in her favor.

"I think I'm going to head upstairs and leave you to your program."

She waited for a split second, still hoping in vain that her comment might at least prompt an apology for ignoring her. She saw right away that none was forthcoming and her ego took yet another hit. The look that she saw flash across her husband's face was clearly more akin to relief at knowing she was leaving the room.

"I feel like soaking in a long hot bath all of a sudden." She continued her lie with an exaggerated yawn, trying to disguise her disappointment.

She pecked her husband's cheek and stood up dramatically to leave, adding an extra sashay to her walk as she exited the room. This time, when she looked back over her shoulder her ego was nearly laid to rest. Not only had she not gotten the reaction she had hoped for but the documentary had come back on just as she started to leave. Sadly, Winston hadn't even turned in her direction.

They had only been married for six years but for the life of her, Charlotte couldn't remember when their relationship had started to fizzle. Their compatibility in the bedroom had been the one thing she had always been able to count on—at least until recently. Now, she was beginning to feel that her husband had grown disinterested in that too; and with a man like Winston, she knew that could only mean *major* problems down the line.

Once in their bedroom she opted for a shower instead of a bath. Why should she even bother? Her husband clearly preferred watching people slowly die of thirst in Africa, to spending quality time with her.

She sat on one side of their bed with her robe partially opened, her still-wet short curly hair wrapped in a towel. It was the kind that one of her girl-friends at Boggs Academy had always referred to as "good hair," and she had to admit to feeling special at the Presbyterian boarding school. She had screamed bloody murder when her parents first broke the news that she was being shipped off to the private high school for African Americans in Keysville, Georgia. But after a few months, she was used to it and even grew to like it there by the time she graduated.

Most of the girls washed their hair every Saturday afternoon,and she and several of her friends always shampooed each other's hair. They had maneuvered around in the cramped shower room of the oldest dorm on campus; it had been built shortly after the school was founded in 1906. Her hair was a different grade than nearly all the other girl's on her dorm floor— a much "better" grade. While everyone else was tortured by hot straightening combs, Charlotte had set her hair on curlers and let it air dry.

Saleh, himself, had taken over from her high school girlfriends as her stylist, as soon as she had graduated and moved back to Washington. The House of Saleh on Georgia Avenue was her first stop now every Saturday morning, as she busied herself with preparing for the coming week. Saleh kept her hair cut in the latest short style; all she had to do was blow dry it after she was out of the shower. Although she wouldn't easily admit it, she was well aware that nowadays *anybody* with the money could pick up a cheap kit at the beauty supply store to get their hair to do the same thing.

Charlotte stood in front of the vanity mirror and examined herself critically for several seconds. She turned from side to side, looking at her lightly tanned skin for signs of aging, and leaning in for a closer look at her face. She would be forty years old in a few months and thought that she looked fairly decent and could still hold her own. The one thing she and Winston had never argued about was the amount of money she spent on maintaining her appearance. Everyone in Washington knew that appearances went hand in hand with success of any kind; anywhere in the Metro area. D.C. was the kind of place where you might easily find yourself doing a double-take at someone you had not realized at first was homeless, especially in certain parts of the city. Even down on their luck, some still tried to give off an air of success; they were easy to picture in a prominent position in their not-so-distant pasts. Some still wore business suits everyday, and carried well-worn leather briefcases that hinted at successful careers in years gone by.

Being a part of Washington's inner circle had kept Charlotte satisfied for as long as it had lasted. Unfortunately, that had not been for very long. Everything ended when Winston started his own business and although they weren't exactly homeless, he wasn't making nearly as much money from his business right away. And he didn't want to do anything outside of that so she decided to look up some old friends from law school and friends from her sorority as a diversion. She made the effort to start socializing again just to keep herself busy, except that it didn't last very long either. Most of her friends were doing pretty well and many were well-connected. It wasn't long, however, before she saw no point in doing it; there was far too much that she had to do before she could go out.

She had to make sure Winston had a decent meal and plenty of snacks, so he wouldn't get hungry again and be clowning by the time she got back. She had to get her car washed for valet parking, because Winston would only do it on Sunday afternoons. But the biggest issue was having to drive around late at night in Washington. She finally made the decision that it just wasn't worth it for her to go out.

She couldn't believe now how much she had thought they were made for each other on that first night that they met. One of her firm's clients had invited some of the attorneys in her office to accompany them to the fisheries lobby reception on Capitol Hill. That reception and the one given by the ice cream lobbyists were legendary; there was always an abundance of their products available at both events every year. Each of them served the best of the best to their guests. At the fisheries lobby reception, there was every kind of seafood you could imagine, cooked every way your could think of. But Charlotte had all but forgotten about the feast that lay before her in the Merchant, Marine and Fisheries Committee room. As soon as she walked in and saw Winston, her mind was focused on him and nothing else from that moment on.

He had been standing in a small group of people, balancing a plate of food in one hand as he talked. She checked him out discreetly as she picked up a small plate of herb encrusted flounder that had been stuffed with crab meat. She took a tiny bite of the yummy dish and then gradually positioned herself so she was part of Winston's group. There were several lobbyists and another NASA engineer and after a few moments of listening, she made casual comments, all in response to something Winston said.

Eventually she had found a way to branch into a conversation with him away from the rest of the group. She found him to be as charming as he was obviously handsome. Charlotte had always been a pretty girl herself. She had no difficulties in getting a date so she hadn't been surprised when Winston asked for her number before he left, and called to ask her out.

Never once did he mention a ten-year-old daughter though, or that he had a son who was nearly fourteen. Charlotte didn't know about any of that until after they had been dating for almost five months. By that time, she had already decided he was a good catch so she recovered as best as she could, determined not to let it distract her from reeling Winston in. She would just have be a stepmother, she thought, because it would clearly be a requirement for being Winston's wife. But she still had no idea his children actually lived with him year-round; not until the evening that he finally invited her to his house to meet them. She recognized their instant dislike of her right away, as they all struggled to get through dinner.

It had been easy enough for her to send the son packing not long after they got married. It only took a bit of exaggeration on her part to pit father against son; Trazi had been the perfect age to do it. She had cornered him one day and told him she suspected that he had a crush on her, although he was quick to tell her the suspicions she had couldn't have been more wrong. But that didn't stop her from making the same suggestion to her husband of one year that very same day. As soon as she had Winston thinking his teenage son was hitting on her behind his back, everything else was set into motion and just a matter of time. All Charlotte had to do was to step back and watch it happen; until all that testosterone came to blows.

Unfortunately, she had no such luck in getting rid of his daughter. Thanks to that dysfunctional mother of hers, there was really no use in trying. Charlotte had tried to fake it with Celeste in the beginning, when she sensed that she was making an effort to be nice too, unlike her brother. But over time Charlotte could tell that she wasn't falling for her act either; and now that she was a teenager, it was all that she could do to keep the spoiled brat from interfering in her marriage.

Charlotte walked back into the bathroom to put a thin layer of greenish goop from a small bottle over her face. She would have normally waited until after Winston had left the house before giving herself a facial, but at the rate things were going it hardly seemed to make a difference anymore.

She was glad she had her mother-in-law as an ally; her only one in the close-knit family. She wouldn't have been able to handle it if Winston's mother gave her problems too. But Mother Bailey seemed to appreciate her; especially after she found out she had a law degree. Charlotte had her eating out of her hands after she mentioned she had passed the bar in all metro jurisdictions. And she found out later that it had been his mother who had urged Winston along in their courtship, once he started stalling toward the end. Apparently, it was Mother Bailey who convinced him he should propose to her too, and that he was lucky to have found her.

The two had become like mother and daughter. Her mother-in-law had amazingly good taste so Charlotte enjoyed their occasional shopping trips, once thought of as an obligation. She even managed to convince her mother-in-law that Winston's children were only balking because of their resistance to the firm discipline she handed down that all children needed. Even *she* had difficulty believing she would be able to pull *that* one off.

As she looked back on it now, Charlotte could see that their marriage had always been more work than she had ever imagined she would have to put into one. But she had invested far too much energy on Winston and his spoiled children to give up now. She had obviously made a mistake by not paying close enough attention to their marriage; things had changed drastically between them and she had no idea when that had even happened. But she wouldn't just stand by and let things unravel without a fight.

She had been afraid at first that it would be Angela who would never be completely out of the picture—what with all her neediness and all. But when he finally had enough of her, Winston cut off all communications except for those that he couldn't avoid. And he did it on his own too; that was the best part, that he didn't need any prompting from her. It felt so good after he finally stopped pampering Angela so much and Charlotte was convinced that it had helped the woman get a grip on herself. *She* had been the one who convinced Winston to let Celeste spend time with her, she just omitted the part about being glad to have her out of the house.

She and Winston had been married almost five years before Charlotte gave any thought to Kristin at all. Only recently had she considered that her husband's first wife might be a factor in their marriage. After all, she had been living in Africa most of time they'd been together; their son moved to her house not long after she and Winston were married. Charlotte remembered the chilly vibe from Kristin when they were introduced.

She had chalked it up to jet lag at the time, but now she wasn't so sure.

She certainly hadn't missed the spark in her husband's voice when he was on the phone with her, coordinating arrangements for Celeste's trip. His first wife had made herself scarce during those first years she was back in the country, after she and Winston married. Kristin had moved to Africa for good not long after that. The more she thought about it though, the more she realized Winston had never been the same after the night that Trazi left home. She knew there had still been some tension, but she always assumed it had to do with his relationship with his son, rather than with her. Then she remembered that he had been at Kristin's house all night, supposedly waiting for Trazi to get there. She had been so focused on staying above suspicion after all the insinuations she'd made about his son, she never once thought what the two of them might have been up to.

Was it possible that her husband still had a thing for his first wife?

The clock on the dresser told her she had been upstairs for over an hour. She could still hear the television going and she pictured Winston sitting in the same spot where she'd left him. He probably hadn't thought about her at all and she dwelled on that as she took off her facial mask and put on her night cream. She plugged in her blow dryer and brushed her hair until it was dry enough to lay down against her head with the help of clear jell.

For the thousandth time, she wondered how she had let things deteriorate so much and what she could do to put herself back in the driver's seat. A few minutes later, she heard Winston switch off the television set, followed by sounds of locks rattling as he checked the front door. For a split second, she thought about hopping into bed and pretending to be sleep, but she was still too wound up for that.

She thought about her friend's party and all the fun that everybody else was probably having. Resentment begin to creep back in but being the practical woman that she was, Charlotte fought hard to suppress it. It wouldn't do her any good at all and she refused to let her emotions distract her from her purpose. It was only Friday and she wouldn't give up on their weekend together just yet; they could still salvage part of it, but that would never happen if they were fighting. She would stay focused and make the most of the few days she had left, before Celeste would be back home from Ghana.

She was still standing in the middle of the room when Winston finally swung open the partially closed door. Almost immediately, she dropped the robe she had been wearing to the floor, and donned a smile to match the one on her husband's face as he hurried toward her.

Chapter 9

Exodus Village

"**H**onestly guys. We're almost there, I promise."

It would have been hard for Kristin to miss their groans after Amad's last turn, or the way Celeste's face had fallen. They were on yet another country road with thick foliage growing on either side of it. Kristin knew that to Celeste especially, it probably looked much like the last road; they all seemed to lead nowhere on the first visit to Exodus Village.

She raised her voice to be heard over the sound of gravel crushing under the Land Rover's wheels. They had to drive slowly for the first few miles on their property line; the gravel had been laid thick to keep the road intact during the rainy season.

"We have twelve buildings so far that are finished and already in use—that's not counting our administration building with adjoining apartments, or the houses in our first community. We've begun work on several other buildings too and they're all in different stages of construction. Things have finally begun to take shape for us, I'm proud to say." There was no response from the back seat.

"I know I've said this before but everything has truly been in Divine Order to bring us where we are today. And from the moment I started consciously *looking* for signs that would point us in the right direction, they've gotten much easier to spot..."

Kristin hoped her start of a new conversation would distract Celeste and keep her occupied for a few minutes more. She was so happy to have the children with her and excited to have them see Exodus Village first-hand. Maybe it would help make up for some of the time she'd missed with them, when they had both needed her so much. She had wanted so badly to be in both places at the same time, but even with all the magical things that were happening that still hadn't been possible. She didn't want Celeste to be agitated when she had her first look at what their foundation had accomplished—the end result of all she had worked for during the years she was away.

"...This one particular morning," she continued, "I found myself thinking about some of my former students—right out of the blue."

She turned to the back seat to watch the young girl's face for signs of interest. Poor thing, she seemed so distressed; her patience was finally worn after the roundabout route they had taken to get there. She knew that the kids wanted most to see their village and the fruit of her hard work more than anything else on their trip. Instead, they had left Accra the morning after they flew into the country, and drove east to the Volta Region for a day, then Northwest through the Eastern Region to reach Kumasi; and finally south again to Exodus Village.

"Which ones?" Celeste had wearily taken the bait.

"Well, over the course of the day I thought about four young women altogether, all students that I once taught at Hunter—first one, then another. I had just meditated, as I still do every morning, when a passing thought about the first student popped into my head. The thought was quick and had soon drifted in and out. I probably wouldn't have thought more about it except that I became conscious of having similar thoughts about the three other students, all in the same day. Casual thoughts about each of them passed through my mind—briefly at first. I would dismiss them idly as they occurred until they became more persistent and frequent. By that time, I was feeling a strong urge to contact the young ladies so I could talk to them about our foundation.

"I mentioned before that we're planning to reach out to HBCUs in the States. Before the day that this all happened, I had been mulling over sine ideas about the timing of the recruitment fairs that we're planning to have each year. At some point, we hope to involve all historically black colleges and universities in our mission. But, for some strange reason I felt pressed to reach out to this group of students; and sooner, rather than later. I couldn't imagine why at the time, but after the thought formed in my mind it stayed there. By the end of the day, I felt obliged to make contact with them and right away.

"But how could you even do that from here?" Celeste wondered. "Did you know where they were?"

"No, not at first. And I couldn't imagine how I would find out, either.

They had graduated a few years before I left the States; I couldn't even remember their names at first, only their faces. I decided I would dismiss the whole thing and resume focus on what I had been working on before all this started. But just as I was gaining momentum on that project, I remembered that the young ladies had all been business majors. They had taken several of my History classes together as a group, for the same reason Dr. Keenan's classes were always so popular." She smiled, thinking back to her favorite professor at Tuskegee and his unorthodox grading policies. "Apparently, it freed up blocks of time for the business case studies they were always being assigned as a group.

"Now, mind you, I'd forgotten about all of this. Then, I remembered I had literally run into the same group of students at the end of the spring quarter before I left. They had been back at Hunter for a symposium that the alumni association sponsored. We recognized each other at just about the same time in the middle of our apologies for the collision. They asked me to have dinner with them to make up for it, they said; assuring me they planned to "expense" the whole thing.

"On a whim, I accepted their invitation; strange, because I was knee-deep in packing for my move here. I still had a mountain of things left to do before I could travel and had to finally stopped calling old friends around the District to let them know I was leaving. If I hadn't, I might still be there going out for one last get-together with friends."

She smiled thinking back to that time, about the friends she had made in the twenty years she had lived in Washington. For many years they were friends she had shared with Winston. She'd been out of touch with many of them for a long time so saying farewell had been hard to do.

"Looking back, I guess I must have considered that "chance" encounter as a good excuse to take a break from the whirlwind of activities I was involved in," she said, a minute or two later. "I kept telling them how proud I was that they had done so well. All of them were working for a top-five accounting firm. Each young lady was on track for moving to the particular rung of the corporate ladder that she had her sights on. We had such a good time at dinner that we decided to go for drinks afterwards. We must have talked for at least another hour and it gave me a chance to get to know them on a different level than when they were students."

Kristin could see that her distraction was working; Celeste was absorbed in her story, bless her heart. She could only imagine how long the three miles they had to travel before seeing any parts of Exodus Village must seem to her. Amad had no choice but to drive slowly and they were practically swallowed up by the ancient forest, with its loud chorus of birds, crickets, and frogs calling out from the trees and thick ground cover. There were lush ferns growing in huge clusters and spots of brilliant color emitting from flowering plants that grew close to the stately trees. The trees' density blocked nearly all of the sun's rays in some places but soon afterwards, they saw flickers of light as they drove forward until the sun was once again shining brightly above their heads.

Kristin paced her story, deliberately allowing several minutes to pass before continuing.

"I finally remembered that they all had given me their business cards that night," she said after a lull, "when it was time for us to part ways. I had completely forgotten until I drove down the mountain again another morning after meditating. It suddenly came to me that I had stuck the cards in a folder that night after I got home. I can remember all of it now like it was yesterday, although it's already been over three years since I left. It never crossed my mind before then that I'd have their business cards here with me all that time, and I can't imagine why I kept them at all. I was about to leave the country soon after they gave them to me, and I guess that was the reason I hadn't given them any more thought..."

"Wait—you mean you brought them here to Ghana?"

"I did. Can you believe that?" Kristin smiled because it was hard for her to believe it herself.

Whittling her earthly belongings down to fit shipping limits for the move to Ghana had been a challenge. After she had given away many of her most prized possessions to friends she left behind, including her Saab to Celeste; she donated much of the rest to Goodwill. She had limited space available for shipping all her possessions and although she was excited about buying new things when she arrived for her new life in Africa, the piece-by-piece consideration of each item had given her pause. As she separated the final few items into piles of 'Must Keep' or 'Donate,' she had been forced to give measured thought to those things she ultimately couldn't bear to be without. She never expected that her students' business cards would be among them.

"I had the cards all the time," she continued, "and you can just imagine how surprised I was to find them. When I did, I was looking for something else altogether—a paper written by another student for a class I taught before leaving Hunter."

She failed to mention that she had given that student a final grade without ever reading his paper. She had strangely started thinking about Kioni too, soon after the business students popped into her head.

"I found the business cards in the same folder where I found the paper. Don't ask me how they ended up there," she followed quickly, "maybe I just couldn't bring myself to throw them away. But finding them caught my attention, that's for sure. There's no such thing as coincidence, you know; those magical things we sometimes notice are synchronicities, sent by the Universe to guide us in the right direction. There are always signs to lead us toward our highest good."

"That would be the only explanation about your finding them that I can think of, alright." Her son agreed.

"But once I found them, I didn't hesitate. I reached out to all of them that same day. I sent emails describing the Foundation's mission—what we aim to accomplish here. I didn't know for sure the young ladies would still be with the same firms—three years can be a long time in the business world. But I can't truthfully say I was surprised to find they were still there, either; and they were all receptive to our mission. I can't tell you what a blessing they have been to us; they have given us the boost in our long-term stability that we needed."

"How so?" Trazi was curious. "What exactly did they do?"

"Well, after getting feedback from everyone, I set up a conference call to give them a chance to ask any questions they had—so everybody could hear the answers at the same time. After that, they got together on their own to set things in motion. Before I knew it, they had quietly begun steering some of their wealthier clients toward the Exodus Foundation for charitable contributions. They also helped me set the Foundation up in the U.S. and the response was immediate and has been generous. Apparently, we've become a popular new tax shelter, causing us to have to expand our public relations staff months ahead of schedule. I have to admit, though, having to make that adjustment to manage donor relations was the best predicament we could've had." She was smiling again.

"The generous gift of land from the Asantes gave us a solid foundation. Now, thanks to my former students, we have sizeable donations coming to us on a regular basis through the foundation. We're taking in enough right now to cover salaries and living expenses of the people we have on staff. It's put us in an *excellent* position because we own everything you'll see in Exodus Village—free and clear."

"No debt? Really? That's wonderful!"

"Yes, it is. But don't forget, mortgage loans are virtually unheard of here in Ghana. We have no choice but to pay as we go, but thankfully, we've completed construction of the first of five communities our residents will live in at full capacity. We've not had to take out a single loan for anything and we have substantial cash reserves too. We're handling our good fortune and resources wisely, as though every cedi we spend might be our last. And we have measures in place to make sure that it stays that way for as long as the Foundation operates.

"Our village will be sustainable and as self-reliant as humanly possible. We're building our own plant to make bricks, for example, so we can use them to construct buildings for other projects going forward. We're using the same formula that Dr. Carver used when he taught Tuskegee students how to make bricks to build the original classrooms.

"By the way, the clay they used came from a big hill that was near my parents' house at one time; the name everyone called our community was "Brick Yard Hill."

"...And speaking of Dr. Carver," she said a second later, "our youngest board member is a Tuskegee native and reminds me of Dr. Carver in many ways. Dr. Levy will be taking a five-year sabbatical so he can head up our agricultural enterprises, to make sure we have it right. He's a brilliant scientist and I couldn't be happier. I've recently learned that he even meditates in the early morning hours just like me and Dr. Carver."

"He did?"

"Yes. As a matter of fact, he credited meditation as being behind all his scientific discoveries; he says he heard the whispers from God.

"Dr. Levy already has ideas for outreach programs he wants to create here, especially in the communities closest to Exodus Village. He wants to help people in rural areas with farming issues, just as Dr. Carver once reached out to the people of rural Alabama. Dr. Carver was inspired to share his unique knowledge about the soil and how to heal plants and keep them healthy. He taught his techniques freely to everyone—black or white; rich or poor. His discoveries about soil restoration virtually saved the economy of the South during a time when it was agriculturally based.

"Wow—I didn't know that either." Trazi admitted. He had visited the George Washington Carver museum in Tuskegee several times.

"Well, it's true," she assured him. "He received national and international recognition for his scientific innovations; it helped put Tuskegee on the map. Booker Washington was a brilliant businessman for sure; he turned the two thousand dollar investment that Adams bargained with the Alabama State Legislature for, into an endowment of nearly $2 million by the time of his death. It was an amazing feat, especially for that time; but its endowment wasn't what gave Tuskegee its notoriety.

"The college would've been well-funded, yet quite ordinary, had it not been for Dr. Carver. He was the first and only Black person to have a national monument dedicated to him—the George Washington Carver National Monument in Diamond, Missouri.

It was established in 1943, years before our Civil Rights movement even started."

"Wow." Celeste was impressed.

"Most people don't realize Dr. Carver's career had already taken off long before he decided to come to Tuskegee. That's right, he was a well-respected researcher at Iowa State College of Agriculture and Mechanic Arts, as Iowa State University was known at the time. He did experience isolated racial prejudice when he first arrived as a student, but his personal and professional reputation soon put an end to that. He was credited as an accomplished artist as well as a scientist. He made his own paints from clays and plants, like his famous Egyptian blue dye, a pigment used by the Egyptians for thousands of years before its usage and the ability to formulate it was lost. Carver's paintings were often exhibited in national fairs and he won many prizes for his work.

"He kept in close contact with his Iowa colleagues too, all his life. To this day, there's a special exhibit dedicated to him in Iowa State's main library. He only left because he wanted to use his talents to help his people; but his nature was to be generous in sharing knowledge with anyone he came in contact with. He was a humble man who only wanted to use his gifts from God to serve others. He downgraded his style of dress after moving to Tuskegee; he was mistaken for a derelict once, when he traveled to Washington to testify before Congress in support of a tariff on imported peanuts. His testimony convinced Congress, and southern peanut farmers had him to thank for saving their livelihood.

"He was of great influence on the young son of Henry C. Wallace, one of his professors at Iowa who later became Secretary of Agriculture in 1921. When his son, Henry A. Wallace was a young boy, he became fascinated by Dr. Carver's soil studies and his research techniques. The young Wallace loved to hang around Carver's lab and watch him do his experiments; he also grew up to become U.S. Secretary of Agriculture, as well as Secretary of Commerce, and later, Vice President of the United States.

"So you'd better believe that Dr. Carver was responsible for bringing in his share of money to Tuskegee too, to add to its coffers. His achievements could only bolster Washington's ability to persuade benefactors to fund programs and new buildings for the school. It was Carver's reputation that motivated Morris Jessup, a New York banker and philanthropist, to sponsor a mobile lab set up inside a wagon that was equipped with every-thing Dr. Carver needed to do his outreach work. It was called the "Jessup Wagon" for the man who also co-founded the YMCA. Dr. Carver used the wagon to teach botany, soil restoration, and to minister to the sick all across rural Alabama."

"I still can't believe he left home when he was only nine-years-old and all by himself—just so he could learn stuff." Celeste added the thought after a moment. She had been as captured by the story of Dr. Carver's early life as Kristin had been, as a child.

"Me either," she agreed. "He was one of a kind, for sure. He poured his heart and soul into Tuskegee and gave up a very promising career in Iowa to go there. But his relationship with Washington was not good; Carver complained to friends about being bogged down with administrative tasks that he wasn't very good at. It held him back from making progress with his true talents. It wasn't until after Washington's death in 1915 that Carv-er's more well-known accomplishments at Tuskegee were made.

"It's one of the main reasons I feel so sick every time I hear the mention of the so-called "*Tuskegee Experiment.*" The irritation was rising in her voice. "I know in my heart that if Dr. Carver had lived longer, the U. S. Public Health Service wouldn't have been able to do what they did. Carver had been dead for a few years before penicillin was discovered as a cure for syphilis. The men who initially signed up for the study were wrong-fully denied access to proper treatment for decades, although none of that was revealed to the general public until the early '70's.

Since Celeste had never heard of the *Tuskegee Experiment*, Kristin filled her in. She explained that a group of uneducated black men in the rural areas near Tuskegee had been duped into becoming human guinea pigs.

"That name has always bothered me because it sounds like something our school came up with it," she said, exasperated. "We have such notori-ety for research that the name makes one think of the study as something the all-Black doctors at John Andrews Hospital came up with, to find a cure for a poor black man's disease. In reality, nothing could be further from the truth.

"In fact, it was a *U.S. Public Health Service experiment,* conducted at Tuskegee; a big difference. At the time, syphilis had been known in the medical community as the "great imitator" because it was so hard to diag-nose and treat. It was a disease that knew no color or class bounds either, which was the reason the government funded the study in the first place. They had no stake in whether poor Black men in Alabama had the disease; finding a cure for syphilis had become important to the health and well-being of the country."

"Really?" Trazi was curious again.

"Of course—think about it. There were a number of noteworthy people throughout history who were reported to have contracted syphilis; people like Franz Schubert, the composer, Charles VIII of France, Hitler, Mussolini, and even Tolstoy. Many others were said to have died when it was left untreated and that list includes Christopher Columbus, George Washington, and Napoleon.

"From what I've read, the PHS study started out with noble enough intentions. And I'm sure that when Dr. Moton was approached about it, he saw it as another opportunity for Tuskegee to shine. He became president after Booker Washington's death and it must have seemed like such a coup to play a role in research that might lead to the cure for such a dreaded disease.

"But, on the other hand, Blacks weren't exactly in a position to refuse a request by the Public Health Service either, not in the 1930s. And unfortunately, the rights of the all-Black subjects were severely violated; available medical treatment was withheld from them and they were left unprotected without any safeguards to fend against the diseases's destruction. There were no regulations at the time to prevent the kind of sinister use the study evolved into, once the initial administration of the Public Health Service changed hands. After that, the study merely traced the progression of the disease into death, mental illness, and a host of other foul ends.

"And, apparently, they used the sweet smile of a black female nurse to help lure men into participating—unknowingly, I'm sure. But there were others who were probably eager for those overnight trips to Tuskegee that they were promised. Staying at the hospital on the school's campus would have been enough enticement for some to volunteer; that, and getting those "special" health exams they were to be given as participants. The reputation that Dr. Carver had built by providing medical outreach in the surrounding communities, probably lent much to the study's credibility.

"I'll bet you any amount of money that Dr. Carver wouldn't have allowed them to do it; they wouldn't have been able to inflict that kind of medical abuse on unsuspecting people. And he had the connections to stop it too, at the highest level of government. He would've seen what was happening after penicillin was discovered as a cure, and put an end to what was happening in Tuskegee. Those men wouldn't have been allowed to suffer needlessly, I'm sure of it."

Kristin was quiet for a few seconds. "I still can't believe I was born in the same hospital and at a time when the experiments were still being conducted behind closed doors," she said finally. "I can just imagine what Dr. Kenney would have thought about it, had he known," she said of the Black doctor who started the first community clinic in the all Black hospital. John A. Andrew Hospital was named in 1913 for John Albion Andrew; Massachusetts' 25th Governor, who headed the state during the Civil War. He was a guiding force behind the creation of some of the first U.S. Army units composed of Black men—including the famed 54th Massachusetts Infantry. The hospital was made possible through a donation from Andrew's granddaughter, and it served much of that area of Alabama.

"But, it gained its stellar reputation through the wisdom and leadership of its first medical director, Dr. John Andrew Kenney. Dr. Kenney came to Tuskegee fresh out of an internship at Howard University's Freedman Hospital in 1902, just two years after the college's existing hospital services for students were extended to the community. Blacks from all over the state came to John A. for medical treatment, through the hospital or the John A. Andrew Clinic founded by Dr. Kenney. It operated in the tradition of Dr. Carver's Jessup Wagon and provided an opportunity for medical interns at the all-Black Meharry Medical College in Tennessee to complete their internships and residences at the same time.

"You were born at John A. too, I'm afraid." Kristin looked remorseful as she acknowledged her son's surprise. "But don't feel bad, I didn't know anything about what was going on either—not for a long time."

After another brief pause, her mood began to lift. "I have such a good feeling about Dr. Levy coming here, though." She changed the subject and the scowl on her face was replaced by a weak smile. "Dr. Carver thought about coming to Africa too, you know, when he was ready to move on from his career at Iowa State. Did you know that? He chose the "pride of the swift-growing South," as Tuskegee is called, and the documentation about his research and scientific experiments was put in the Carver Museum, after he died, using money he had willed to the school for that purpose. He wanted the people of Alabama, especially poor Black people, to have access to it so they could learn from it. That's why the students went ballistic when the school administration moved so much of its contents out, when we were in school.

"He saw a Black man being hanged once too," Kristin added after a brief pause. "It was when he was still young; all alone and starting out on his quest for knowledge. Seeing what happened stayed with him all of his life.

Kristin had told the kids stories about the so-called "night riders" who had taken George's mother when they were small children. They were men who would look for opportunities to ride in on horses and steal slaves away from the shacks they lived in during the night and sell them to farmers in other areas. She told them there were many bands of these thieves who were active toward the end of slavery. They sprung up especially after Congress finally banned the importation of African slaves and the slave ships stopped coming in with their seemingly endless supply of captives. Several state legislatures had banned the practice of slavery completely by the time the infant George and his mother were kidnapped.

"Rough riding along the borders of slave-states like Missouri and non-slave states like Illinois became a regular practice because the slave quarters were usually isolated and unarmed. From all accounts, the Carvers, who lived in Diamond Grove, Missouri, treated George and his older brother quite well, under the circumstances. George had been born toward the end of slavery and he was very sickly as an infant. The Carvers hired someone to look for him and bring him back, knowing that his very valuable mother was probably long gone, as she was. They nursed George back to health in kindness and he was excluded from doing any strenuous work. He had plenty of time to learn from the only book they had at their farm, and that's when he developed his passion for nature and plants. But the image of seeing that Black man being hanged was forever etched in his mind. It made him determined to do something to help his people.

"He had his sights on going to live in the Liberian Colony too," Kristin added, "although I'm pretty sure he didn't know that settlement took root and was built on land that the rightful owners were forced to give up at gunpoint. Dr. Carver was trying to come here to help; he wanted to do something to restore communities in Africa and to help farmers solve some of their agricultural issues.

"And now that we have Dr. Levy on board," she ended happily. "We'll be able to have the kind of community outreach that Dr. Carver might have started, after all."

The gravel road they had been traveling on suddenly opened to a much wider street. "Is this it?" Celeste's voice was instantly excited again. "Is this Exodus Village?" She turned to look at one side of the road and then the other, taking everything in at once as she and Trazi had done when they first arrived in the country.

"Yes, we're here—finally," Kristin confirmed. They were just driving past a large gated fence that marked the official entrance. Three large flags waved proudly from the top of a nearby building, caught up in a breeze that also stirred the ancient tree tops. At the top was a large red, yellow and green striped Ghanaian flag, with its black star centering the yellow. She explained that the Adinkra emblem on the middle flag represented the Diaspora Exodus Foundation; symbolizing the cooperation and interdependence that was at the core of their mission. Flying underneath it was the flag that had been adopted for Exodus Village. The Adinkra symbol for transformation combines the morning star, representing a new start, with the wheel surrounding it to signify independent movement.

"Both Adinkra flags capture our aspirations perfectly," she said of the symbols. "Our residents will only have a set five-year period to transform their lives but we will take them as far as we can before they leave us."

Amad drove toward a modern structure in the distance that stood tall among a scattering of smaller buildings on a large parcel of land. It was the administration building, Kristin told them, although it would serve other purposes as well. The grounds were immaculate, as they always were, and neatly manicured. There were massive coconut palms and tropical vegetation staged in clusters around the building. They could soon see that there were several apartments attached to the rear of it as well. As Amad pulled the truck into Kristin's parking space, she pointed toward a medium-sized structure that stood a short distance away from the others.

"That's the Asantehene's quarters, or will be once it's finished," she told them. "We wanted to make it easy for him to join us for special occasions or whenever he chooses to visit, since we're somewhat isolated here. Members of the royal court are working with our staff to make sure it meets his expectations."

Trazi and Celeste were captured for a moment by a grove of stately baobab trees that grew near a picturesque mountain, shaping the distant scenery. The screened verandas attached to all the apartments were perfectly aligned so people sitting in them could enjoy the view at any time. Kristin explained that the architect used the mountain as a positioning point in designing the building. He also gave their living quarters a degree of separation from all the hustle and bustle they anticipated when the village was operating at full capacity.

"We're planning to have a large courtyard over there." She pointed to a spot beyond where the Land Rover was parked as everyone began pulling out packages and luggage. "The entire thing will be enclosed and have tempered glass walls and ceilings that will protect us against the elements. We'll be able to use our Olympic sized swimming pool in any season, and there will be sliding doors connecting everything over here," she said pointing again, "that will lead from the courtyard into a much larger space. It's all going to flow into the atrium that's being built adjacent to the building. We'll use that area primarily for receptions and social events," she finished.

"That sounds fantastic." Celeste's eyes began to sparkle as Kristin described details of the design. "I can't wait to see it when it's all finished."

Kristin showed them around her apartment and a door in her sitting room that said would lead to a short hallway. It connected to her office, she told them, giving her easy access at any time. Her modest three-bedroom suite was colorfully decorated with objects of art she had collected as she traveled around the country.

"Our other suites are on a much grander scale," she pointed out. "They're reserved for our board members and other VIPs that we'll be inviting, at some point, as overnight guests for our evening events."

As they pulled out the last of their packages, Amina emerged from one of the smaller buildings that was set to their left. It housed the residences of their essential staff and families.

"Amina's apartment is much larger than others," Kristin told them, as the young woman came closer. "She has private meetings with the traditional leaders from time to time and the staff of Ministers who we are working closely with. They always prefer a more intimate setting for conversations, but I would make sure Amina was comfortable if there weren't a business reason for her more formal quarters. I've never lost sight of the role that she and Solomon have played in getting us where we are; they've been instrumental in making both our travel agency *and* Exodus Village successful. They're both very sharp people with invaluable connections here."

Amina introduced herself after greeting Trazi and Celeste with warm hugs. "I feel as though I already know you two," she said, smiling. "I've heard so much about you over the years."

And to prove it, she recounted some of their more memorable escapades that Kristin had shared with her. Most were from times when they were much younger and they both grinned sheepishly as Amina talked. They were strangely comforted in knowing she knew so much about them. It was reassuring to know that they had been as much on Kristin's mind all those years ago as she had been on theirs.

She told them she would show them around the village the next morning since it was already late afternoon. She gave them a preview of what
they would see; some of the environmentally friendly features they were
incorporating in all their buildings.

"All of our residential and commercial buildings have passive designs,"
she told them. "They're framed at just the right angles to take advantage of
the natural lighting. We also minimize the amount of heat coming through
openings, and our windows are angled to capture the natural air flow. From
what Kristin has told us, it works the same as the old shotgun houses did
that were built in the southern part of the United States.

"I'll tell you more about that tomorrow." She moved towards the door.
"And I'll be back later to show you around our administration building."

She excused herself and headed back to her apartment, giving Kristin
a chance to show Trazi and Celeste her apartment and get them settled.
Kristin gave them a full tour, taking up where Amina left off in describing
the apartment's eco-friendly features.

"We only use tankless water heaters here," she said, after they were back
in the sitting room. "All you have to do is select the temperature you want
before the water starts coming out. That alone will save millions of gallons
from just running back down the drain unused. When our toilets flush, a
sensor controls the amount of water that gets released; never more than
what's required to do the job," she said laughing.

She led them into a brightly painted room that was just off her kitchen.
There were large recycling containers stacked against the wall.

"Every house here has a similar room with a compost bin built in one
corner," she said, pointing it out. It's not going to be optional either; we'll
collect everyone's trash each week to either be recycled or added to a community compost. We'll use it to fertilize our community gardens, which is
where our residents will "shop" for their produce." They all had a laugh
at the thought of someone using a grocery cart like the ones used in the
States; wheeling it through the rich black soil of Ghana.

A short time later, Amina reappeared at the front doorway and took Kristin aside to brief her on a few issues that required her attention. Afterwards, Kristin went to her office to return phone calls, while Amina led the
kids to the front of the building. She gave them a top to bottom tour and
they saw how much the layout looked like government service buildings
back home.

"As I understand it, the major difference is that we're missing the large waiting rooms," Amina commented. "We won't need those here because we'll issue appointments for business that our residents can't handle over the phone." She explained that their security force would set up a station at the main entrance.

"They will confirm appointments or get authorization before anyone who isn't working here is allowed inside the building, when there's nothing special going on. We'll keep a close eye on the flow of traffic too, when people come for appointments. The ideal situation will be to have them wait no more than ten minutes although our target is for less than five."

When they had reached the ground floor again they were on the side of the building that was closest to the residential area in back. Amina showed them a series of conference rooms close to the existing entrance that were connected by sliding partitions.

"We can quickly convert the rooms into small and mid-sized ballrooms," she said, "and once all the partitions are removed we have our own grand ballroom—and it's a huge space. That's where we'll have our dedication ceremony," she said, "but we'll use it for other occasions too. We made sure this was all a comfortable distance from Kristin's office and apartment, by the way. This whole side will eventually lead into a glass-enclosed atrium," she added, pointing toward the entrance. "Construction is scheduled to start on it in just a few weeks."

They had come full circle and found themselves back at the end of the long corridor where they had started their tour. Amina pointed the way toward Kristin's office but before she left, she arranged to meet the kids early the next morning to give them a tour of the village. They wandered along the hallway aimlessly, reading each sign on the doors before they reached the front door of Kristin's office. She was on the phone and motioned for them to come in while she completed her call, signing off on one last report that needed her attention after she had.

Trazi and Celeste busied themselves by examining the plaques, artwork, and photos hanging in the large office. They were instantly pulled toward a large framed photograph of Rosa Parks on the wall facing Kristin's desk. Then they spotted the table of family's photos, where they were prominently featured in several candid shots. There were several others of Winston and Angela, as well.

After Kristin finished reviewing the report, she led them through the rear door and down the connecting hallway that led to her apartment. She excused herself again to go through more mail that had arrived in her absence. It was only after she had left that it dawned on Trazi and Celeste that they hadn't eaten anything since breakfast, other than the fruit Kristin packed for their drive. They stood in her doorway and teased her about it, giggling.

Trazi accused her of forgetting that her only son was in Africa as soon as she got back to Exodus Village. She laughed herself after he assured her that he didn't really feel neglected. The kids were still wound up from their long drive south so they grabbed whatever they could find to munch on in the kitchen. They watched television as they ate and talked about things they had seen and done in Ghana, until they were finally ready to call it a night.

Kristin was still asleep when they woke up the next morning. They ate more fruit and nuts for breakfast and Trazi scribbled a quick note for his mother before they went to the veranda to wait for Amina. Within minutes of finishing their fare, they saw her walking out of her apartment and went out to meet her. She led them to the opposite side of the building and to a small uncovered lot. There were several solar-powered carts parked in it, all with the Adinkra transformation symbol painted on their hoods.

Amina unplugged the back-up battery attached to one cart and tucked it, along with cables, inside a cargo area. She pointed out modifications that had been made to the cart, including changes to the steering mechanism that would allow them to drive faster than was safe to do in a regular golf cart. It was powered directly by solar panels attached to its rooftop, and continuously replenished by the powerful rays of the sun. The generated energy fed into a battery beneath the cart's hood; the backup battery provided ten additional hours in the evenings or whenever direct sunlight was unavailable.

After signaling them to get in, Amina got into the driver's seat and started the engine. A second seat had been added as another modification and Celeste sat in the back as Trazi got in the front with Amina. She started down the drive toward the front of the administrative building, answering questions about their use of solar technology as they rode along.

"Our solar business will be one of our first commercial enterprises," Amina volunteered, repeating what Kristin had already told them, "right after we introduce our line of cookies.

"We've developed a relationship with a Chinese supplier already— a very reputable businessman, who can furnish us with all the materials we'll need. He'll send us photo voltaic cells, micro-inverters, charge controllers, and even the deep cycle batteries we'll be using. He can get us a good price on wires, soldering irons, and the other smaller materials we'll need too.

"I know it's hard for you to conceive of so many people here being without electricity." Amina started. "Americans are quite used to it, we know, so the prospect of living here without it would be most unappealing."

Both kids smiled sheepishly because neither could imagine life without electricity, except for those rare occasions like when their father took them camping once, overnight.

"After we started pricing the individual components for the solar systems we needed, we concluded right away that it was more cost effective to assemble our own panels. The plans we started out with quadrupled from there. Now, we intend to provide low cost solar electricity to families all over Ghana. And that gives us a new avenue for creating jobs too, especially in rural areas. We're beginning with Exodus Village and we'll gradually expand to other areas of the Ashanti Region, linking the systems together with our smart grid technology to manage our usage efficiently.

"Our first installation outside the village will be at Manhyia Palace, of course," she went on. "From there, we'll link to Ejisu and other prominent cities of the region. By that time, we should be ready to start production of the other solar products we have planned, like a portable system with three electrical outlets built-in. We'll make that our first product, so we can make electricity available to as many families as possible; those who aren't able to afford anything other than the portable units. Three outlets may not seem like much compared to what you have at home, but trust me, having just one of our units will make a big difference to families who had nothing before.

"And all our systems will be upgradable too. Once our customers are ready, they'll be able to add more units or upgrade the portable ones if they're kept in good condition. Down the road, we're going to manufacture small solar ovens, refrigerators, and similar household appliances. We'll sell them all as close to production costs, as possible. We'll be able to do it because of all the money we'll be saving by constructing our own panels. We've hired consultants to review our plans and they've already given us the green light for the capacity that we need.

"I'll show you our solar plant later, but right now I want to take you to see the first of our residential communities. It's where our pilot families will live next year when they come and where each new group of residents will spend their first year at Exodus Village."

"Hold on back there!" Trazi advised Celeste, as Amina swerved to avoid a dip in the road. He still protected his little sister as he had done since he was six years old. Amina said they had all agreed with Kristin's assessment that it made no sense to pave the roads until all the heavy equipment had stopped traveling back and forth.

"There are some tricky places that have been worn thin by the weight of gigantic trucks," she added as she maneuvered the cart around the damaged places in the road. "Everybody has been working long hours to get things finished," she noted. "This road is set to be resurfaced in another six months."

They picked up more speed when she made a right turn onto a much wider street, after driving down the gravel road in front of the administration building for about a mile. The road, she said, would connect all five communities.

"You'll be able to go much faster in these carts once the roads are paved."

"You're right, Trazi. They're engineered safely for speeds up to thirty-five miles an hour," she said, "but our speed limits will be twenty miles. The FOI is going to issue citations for carts that go any faster than that.

They knew FOI was short for Fruits of Islam—the somewhat controversial arm of the Nation of Islam. Kristin had told them earlier about running into an old friend from Tuskegee who had been involved with the organization for decades. She hadn't known until then that they had contracted with several city governments across the United States to provide building security details, and they had an excellent reputation. Her friend had come to Ghana at Kristin's request and the FOI was handling all aspects of security inside Exodus Village. Their foundation had opted to take responsibility for their residents when the choice was given to them by Parliament. Kristin felt very secure in her choice with Brother John there and in charge.

"I'm sure it would be fun to go faster, but we had to set lower limits to prevent potential accidents." Amina anticipated Celeste's protest.

Smiling, she described the agonizing level of coordination that had been required to get construction of their first community off the ground. She said they had carefully documented their experiences along the way.

"That way, we'll be able to improve processes for our next phase," she added, "making use of all lessons learned. That's a strategy we've adopted for all our projects; each time we undertake something new, we'll use the first implementation out of the box to develop best practices for the next one.

They had driven a short ways further and Amina turned right onto another gravel road. There was a prominent sign in front of them that was printed in block letters near the turn. It read: *"Welcome to Marcus Garvey Community."* And painted underneath, in slightly smaller letters was the tag line that Garvey adopted for the Universal Negro Improvement Association—*"One Aim, One God, One Destiny."*

"The name is certainly fitting," Trazi observed.

"Yes, we thought so. Kristin put a great deal of thought into the name of each of our five communities, as well as the roads that run through the village. Most of them will honor a person who played a significant role in securing the freedom of African slaves held in America or who helped their descendants in some way. We agreed that it would be a great way to emphasize your history to our residents and to everyone working here.

"The next community will be named in honor of the man who had been the house slave and coachman to Jefferson Davis, the president of the Confederacy during your Civil War. From what Kristin tells us, William Jackson's position made him privy to highly sensitive military information. General Davis apparently planned strategies with his aides right in front of Jackson, talking candidly about battle plans against the Union army as though he wasn't there. Jackson risked his life several times crossing into Union territory to pass on information to military commanders there, repeating the high-level battle plans he overheard. It would have been easy for him to remain in the safer territory of the North after his first escape, but he kept going back for more information. He provided intelligence to the Union army that was said to be crucial in the victory over the Confederates. He made a tremendous contribution; it went a long way toward winning the Civil War and freeing the captives that were still enslaved.

"The street we were just on will be dedicated in honor of Harriet Tubman. Many of us here knew about her because of the Underground Railroad, of course. She physically led hundreds, if not thousands of slaves to freedom; all in spite of severe medical problems that could cause her to loose consciousness without warning. But there were other details of her life that we only learned recently, from Kristin," she continued. "I had no idea that she had been the most infamous of all captives who spied for the Union Army during the war, for example. We thought it only fitting that the street connecting all our communities be named *Harriet Tubman Boulevard.*

Amina pulled the cart into a small parking lot that was off to the right and turned the engine off. It was big enough to accommodate carts for those families who would live in the three triplexes that formed a semicircle around it. At the opposite end, a small plot was being developed into

123

a park. As they approached the first group of houses, Amina pointed to a similar tract farther down the road. She said they were temporarily being used as housing for some of their construction crews.

"It makes it possible for them to start work soon after daybreak," she said, "when temperatures are much cooler."

Celeste was ahead of Amina and Trazi and peaked inside the front window of the first townhouse they approached before they all went in for a closer look. It was a modest one-bedroom home designed for an individual or for a couple with no more than two children under the age of two. It was efficiently designed with lots of built-in storage like Kristin's apartment. There were wall beds, a built-in laundry hamper, and plenty of pull-out shelving; the style minimized the amount of furniture that would be required by its occupants, eliminating the associated cost of repairs and replacements.

Celeste got a kick out of exploring the houses, opening doors and cabinets in each room searching for hidden features. Each triplex was designed as dual multi-family dwellings with a single residence separating them, or there were two single residences with a multi-family unit connecting the two.

"When we met with the architect we asked him to design several models, ranging from single dwellings to four different designs of multi-family units. They'll be mixed in randomly in each community to give each street its own look and feel. This community is closest to the administration building. Kristin hopes she'll be able to keep a close eye on their newest residents here and get to know them when she's not traveling so much.

"The number of Ghanaian families living in the first community will always be at a ratio of 1:5. We want to keep the number sufficient enough to help with resettlement adjustments. There are certain customs from our culture that will be strictly adhered to in Exodus Village," she said. "For example, there won't be any tolerance for disrespect, especially toward our elders. We expect that it will be a learning experience for many but we'll help them make the adjustment in a strict, and loving manner."

She had a smile on her face as she said it. Trazi and Celeste laughed with her, thinking the Foundation had its work cut out for them.

"I have to admit to being surprised at learning the lengths that many of your ancestors went to in order to free themselves," Amina confessed later. "Fortunately, these are the kinds of things that will be taught during our cultural sensitivity and history classes, so everyone will be exposed to your freedom fighting history. And they'll learn our history too," she added, "which sometimes connects with yours. One thing I neglected to mention, as we toured the administration building yesterday was that it will be named in honor of Chief Alfred Charles Sam during our dedication ceremony. And the gravel road leading into Exodus Village will be named for Queen Yaa Asantewaa, the Queen Mother of Ejisu, after it's paved. She led the final Asante rebellion against the British in 1901, called the *War of the Golden Stool.* It was the last physical resistance and the only major battle the Asante lost after a hundred years of fighting the British.

"The British took advantage of the civil wars going on in the Confederacy of Asante States between 1883 and 1887, and that's how they were able to gain control. Queen Yaa Asantewaa led her rebellion almost four years after the Asantehene, King Prempeh I, had been captured and exiled to Elmina. Ghana, Amina explained, is a matrilineal society. Each person's lineage is determined by their mother and women retain it even after marriage. They often hold considerable power too, although it's usually exercised behind the scenes. Queen Yaa Asantewaa was outraged after male members of the council allowed the British to take their King without firing a single shot. She rallied the people to do something about it for years but unfortunately her plans to do battle were anticipated. Thousands of British and Indian troops were brought in to defeat the army she raised. She was captured and exiled to an island in the Indian Ocean where she could be of no further threat to anyone."

"And that was where she eventually died," Amina ended.

Chapter 10

Keep Your Head To The Sky

"*L*awana???"

Eleanor stopped dead in her tracks. "Is that you??" She had been walking quickly away from Woodies' 12th and G Street entrance toward the train station, a central hub connecting three of the five color-coded Metropolitan Area Transit Authority lines. The rail system was the second busiest in the United States and Metro Center had been designed to connect to D.C.'s first department store, Woodward and Lothrop. She had spent most of the morning combing through the sales tables at Woodies, as it was called by locals, and had decided it was time to make her way home. She wanted to be far away from the downtown area before it came alive with the lunch crowd.

Eleanor thought the woman sitting near the escalator that led down to the trains looked familiar but she had pegged her for a "bag" lady when she first noticed her. Then she realized the woman didn't have the customary bags stuffed with all her belongings, and it suddenly dawned on her that she might be one of her former clients.

She stopped for a closer look and saw that the woman's body was partially blocking the top landing of the escalators. It *was* Lawana sprawled out on the well-worn cement flooring, and judging from the way she was propped against the wall, she'd been sitting there for a long time. Had she been drinking?

"Why are you sitting here like this? Are you all right?"

The blank expression that greeted her questions was all the answer Eleanor needed. Lawana *had* been drinking—and apparently quite a bit! And it wasn't even lunchtime yet.

She had certainly seen enough people in the five years she had worked at Social Services to know intoxication when she saw it. Quite a few of her clients had shown up high on alcohol or something. It had been hard for her to tell what was what for a while, and some of the ones who *weren't* high were so incoherent that she thought they were. She had to struggle to figure out what they were saying, although she tried her very best—with every last one of them. After all, she had majored in social work in college for a purpose; she wanted to do something to help her people. Lord knows it wasn't because she expected to make a lot of money from it.

But the real surprise had come when she found out just how little time she would have to do *anything*. The volume of cases transferred to her caseload every month had overwhelmed her from the start. It wasn't so much the gruelling pace or the mountains of paperwork they had to fill out to comply with federal guidelines; she knew she had no choice about that. Her grandmother had made certain that she and her siblings knew not to waste their time on things they couldn't change. Nana had come to live with them after their grandfather died and the first thing they knew, she had completely taken over "their 'ligion," as she called it. Before they could blink an eye, they were all going to Sunday School every Sunday and to bible study on Wednesday nights. And every night before they went to bed, they had to each say their prayers out loud. After they had all finished, their grandmother would make them recite the Serenity Prayer in unison:

> *"God grant me the serenity to accept the things I cannot change;*
> *the courage to change what I can; and the wisdom to know the*
> *difference."*

"If you can get that you're gonna be way ahead of the game," she would tell them every night, after they had finished.

Eleanor knew that Congress was in charge of making the laws; all she could do was follow them. She wondered when the people who always complained about the welfare system would realize that. People cheat to get on food stamps because they can, and many end up with more stamps than their families really need every month. Quite naturally, some are going to sell those excess stamps to get the money they also need. But the opportunity to do it is made possible by the *same* regulations, and carrying them out is what took up nearly all Eleanor's time.

As hard as she tried, she seldom had enough time to talk to her clients after their mandatory interviews. She was kept far too busy verifying stuff that had no bearing on anything, as near as she could see. She wasted valuable time everyday—and paper, copying the same identification cards and social security cards over and over again.

But she had no choice if she wanted to stay in good graces with her supervisor. Eventually, she figured out how to tell whether her clients were incoherent because they were high on drugs or alcohol. She could tell as soon as they started talking and it became an invaluable asset over time. By the time Greg had talked her into quitting, she had been able to tell whether the drug was legal or illegal. It saved her from wasting time with people she couldn't realistically expect to help; if she didn't get the right response after she brought up the subject of rehab, she merely moved on.

She had no idea what the realities of being a social worker would be when she enrolled at North Carolina A & T, especially working in a place like the nation's capital. Otherwise, she would likely have gone in a different direction altogether. Maybe she would've gone to law school like Greg, except, she would probably have tried to start a community law center by now, instead of going for the money like her husband had. She knew from her clients' stories just how much legal help was often needed for lower income families. Lives were constantly being destroyed when some fatherless child was picked up for selling a small bag of marijuana. The real crime was in being from the wrong family; otherwise, the whole thing might well have disappeared with a particular-sized donation to the police benevolent fund—all without leaving so much as a legal trace.

She had begun using her personal contacts around town as much as she could. Eleanor had tried to make a positive impact on all her clients, everyone whose path crossed her own. Still, she knew that in reality she was no more than a pencil pusher, or mouse clicker, as would be more accurate now. She had finally admitted that to Greg, that he had been right about it all along. She had been fighting a loosing battle and that's why she let him convince her to quit.

But the whole time she had been there, she listened carefully to what her clients said to her, far beyond the answers she needed to complete their interviews. She had been alert for hints of anything else she could do to help them—especially when it was clear that they were trying to help themselves. Sometimes, it was little more than giving them a direct number to an agency they needed to call, or the name of someone they could talk to for assistance. That was sometimes a big help to people who were easily discouraged; those who were quick to give up when confronted by bureaucratic runaround.

Eleanor had all sorts of clients at Social Services and Lawana had shown promise of being able to pull herself up to make it some day. She had never known her to be in any way irresponsible; she was too worried about her children for that. Lawana had talked about her boys constantly when she was her client, and she seemed to appreciate any advice she was given. What she saw now was definitely out of character for her former client, especially since it was the middle of the day. She thought that her life must have taken quite a turn; for a split second she heard Greg's voice in her ear and considered whether she should keep walking. After all, she had already quit her job a year earlier.

But there was something odd about the way the woman was just sitting there, and a much louder voice told Eleanor to stop.

"Are you okay?" She asked again and took a step closer. She put her hand on Lawana's shoulder to help her focus.

The woman looked up at her, still with a blank expression for the longest time. Then, slowly recognition filtered through her dull eyes.

"They took my children." Her voice was slurred.

"What? Have you been drinking, Lawana?"

That question failed to get any response.

"Who took your children? Are you talking about Social Services?" Eleanor thought she knew the answer but she didn't know whether she should hope that was what Lawana meant, or that the children had been kidnapped. Either way, with no money she probably stood an equal chance of getting them back. She could see little hope for the poor woman in either case but Eleanor couldn't help but try to think of something.

Lawana kept staring at her for several seconds, still blank. Then she looked like she might cry.

"You tried to warn me, Ms. Steele," she moaned under her breath. She lowered her head onto arms folded across her lap, and it became nearly impossible for Eleanor to understand her after that.

"Lawana, listen to me." She shook her shoulder slightly, trying to get the woman to focus. "You have to tell me what happened."

"Come on." Eleanor decided to take charge of the situation after there was still no response. She grabbed Lawana's arm firmly and pulled her to her feet with one of her arms still draped across her limp shoulders, until finally Lawana was standing on her own.

"Let's go across the street and get some coffee," she urged. "Then you can tell me what in the world is going on. Okay?"

And just like that, Eleanor was a social worker once again; driven to get through to Lawana so she could find a way to help her.

She hadn't been in that area of the city in months and had decided to go to Woodies on an impulse that morning. They were having a great sale, although thanks to Greg, she didn't have to use a calculator when she shopped anymore much less having to buy things on sale. Besides that, there was honestly nothing she could think of that she really needed. Her husband had a great sense of style and would often bring home dresses for her as well as jewelry, pieces she had never dreamed of owning.

The trip downtown had been more of a distraction than anything else, something for her to do with her time. She felt like she was on an adventure as she hurried toward "M" Street to catch a due-to-arrive bus to the G. W. train station that morning. She decided to get off a few blocks before Metro Center, window shopping and people watching the rest of the way. She would've missed Lawana altogether had she decided to take the same route back home.

She and Greg were married two months after he finished law school; he studied for the bar while she and her girlfriends added finishing touches on the wedding plans. After they were back from their honeymoon, Eleanor busied herself with sorting out presents and sending the proper thank-you cards; then she took on the task of decorating their new house. Greg had lived in a tiny efficiency off "M" Street while he was in school. It had been the perfect location for them and they had been reluctant to leave, despite the size. They were spoiled by being able to walk to all their favorite restaurants, or to Blues Alley when Greg took some rare time off from studying. They weren't used to having to fight the Georgetown traffic anymore or having to circle the block looking for a parking space in one of the most popular areas of the city. So it had been quite a thrill for them to find the townhouse, just as they were ready to give up—and it was only a few blocks from Greg's old place.

The previous owners had moved to Europe and their tasteful furnishings were included in the sale. But there were still lots of changes that Greg and Eleanor wanted to make and coordinating the renovations had kept her busy for months. To live in Georgetown meant having much more time to spend together; since the young couple was still very much in love. Getting them settled into their new home became her number one priority. Greg had been with his firm for just over a year and he spent a great deal of time working, so any time she could help carve out for them was all the better.

On the day that her husband proposed, he told her he would give her the world, and he was well on his way in keeping his promise. An uncle, who had been an investment banker on Wall Street for years, pulled some major strings for Greg when he was still in school. He got him a job clerking for the prestigious firm on "K" Street where he now worked. At the time, the practice hadn't exactly been known for its diversity, but they liked Greg and he had graduated near the top of his class at Georgetown Law. They offered him an associate's position soon after he passed the bar and hired him for their commercial litigation division, no less, where all the big money is.

Soon after she quit her job and gave up her apartment, her husband-to-be had Diner's Club send her a credit card. She had used his American Express card for all their major purchases for their wedding and his Diner's card more sparingly. Now, his only request of her was that she give him a heads-up whenever the balance on her Diner's Club card rose to over five thousand dollars. That way, he could move money around and minimize their interest charges, he said. Once he got his own clients, she would use it to manage the social end of his career. She was convinced that time would soon come because he was well on his way to proving himself to the partners.

They had both been brought up in large families in North Carolina but they had decided to wait a while longer before they started their own family. There was a good chance that Greg might be transferred to the Hong Kong office, especially if he continued to excel. He had always had Hong Kong in his sights; it was one of the first things he told her that night learning Chinese, even back then, and he had tried to impress her with his skills. Although English had been the official language in China since the British occupation in 1842, Mandarin had remained the language of the people— as far back as the days of Imperial China. His motivation for learning the language was to show the proper respect for their culture, he told her, when the time came for him to live there. He had even hired a tutor to help him with his inflections.

That was the kind of guy that her husband was, and a big part of the reason that she loved him so much. He had taken her out for dinner the next night after they met and they had been together ever since. Things couldn't have been better for them as a couple, but Eleanor had still been quietly feeling that there was something missing in her life. Running into Lawana that day had helped her realize exactly what that was.

"Oh Lawd!" Eleanor kept shaking her head and moaning under her breath. She had finally told her about all the events of the previous day: about George being in trouble again, Little Man being put in jail, and ending with Lacrecia and George being taken by Social Services.

"Oh my goodness, Lawana." She struggled to think of something positive to say but that was all she could come up with. It had taken two whole cups of hot coffee before the woman had started making any sense. And when Eleanor *did* finally understand her, she was left with a sinking feeling in the pit of her stomach. This was serious.

"Listen Lawana, this is bad," she admitted, finally. "I won't lie to you and there's no point in trying to sugar coat it. We don't have time for that." She was hesitant because she had no idea what her former client's reaction might be in the state she was in.

"I'm going to make some calls, okay?" She made the promise firmly. "I'm going to see if there is something I can do to help you. Okay? But I've got to tell you, this won't be an easy fix."

The two women sat in silence for several seconds. "What about your oldest boy? Have you seen him since he was arrested?" She had been so focused on the younger two that she had nearly forgotten to ask.

"I can't stand to see him behind bars, Ms. Steele. I just can't do it." Lawana started crying all over again at the thought of the heavy iron doors clanging into place behind her baby. She thought about her visit to see his father when he was arrested that first time. Willie had been calm because he knew he was gonna be out in a few days, but she hadn't been so sure. She had been traumatized seeing him locked up like that, just like an animal.

"Ain't no way I could stand to see my baby locked up behind bars, not when I can't do nothing to get him out." She released a big sigh and sat back in the booth they were in with both hands covering her eyes.

"I just don't know what I'm gon' do. Every last one of my babies is gone." She started crying all over again.

"Listen to me Lawana." Eleanor's voice was firm, as she reached out to grab her by the forearm. They were past the point of niceties, and she needed her former client to focus. "I don't know whether I'll be able to do anything, but I promise I'm going to try, okay?"

Lawana had stopped crying, but her face was filled with such sadness. "Thank you, Ms. Steele," she said gratefully.

"Call me Eleanor. I don't work at Social Services anymore."

That, surprisingly brought a brief smile to Lawana face. The first since all her babies were taken. She would never forget the look on George and

Lacrecia's faces as they were driven away in the back of Ms. Wilkens' car. They had looked so scared.

"Okay...Eleanor." Lawana felt some of the weight she had been carrying lift and Eleanor felt it land squarely on her own shoulders. She had no idea what she could really do to help Lawana but she would try her best.

"I'll do everything I can to help you, Lawana, but you'll have to promise me one thing. You have to promise me that if *I* don't give up on trying to get your kids back, you won't give up either.

"And you're going to have to pull yourself together, too," she warned, "starting today. You can't just throw yourself a pity-party every day; not if you expect to get your children back. I have to be perfectly honest and tell you that fixing this won't be easy and I don't know if it can be fixed; but I can guarantee that you'll never get them back if people start seeing you like I found you earlier."

Lawana looked sheepish because she was now sober. She had never been one for drinking at all so it had taken very little of the tequila her boyfriend left at her apartment to get her drunk.

"Social Services is *supposed* to do their best to fix whatever caused the problem," she told the now-alert Lawana, "as a first resolution. Whenever children are removed from their homes they're supposed to do what's in the their best interest and get them back to their own homes, if possible. You and I both know that's not always the case," she admitted candidly. "But I still know a few people down there, so I'll make some phone calls to see what I can find out about your kids.

"I have to tell you though, they give caseworkers a lot of leeway in these situations and very little interference is allowed in their decisions—no matter what the source. There are a lot of frustrated people working at Social Services too, unfortunately; many with huge chips on their shoulders. Some of them seem to even enjoy being able to make their clients jump through unnecessary hoops—just because they can. So, no matter what, you have to remember not to let anyone bait you into saying or doing something that you'll regret later, okay?"

"You've go to stay on the good side of whoever the social worker is who gets your case too, because your kids won't be released as long as they keep your case open. I'm sorry to have to say it, but that's just the way it works."

Lawana looked terrified.

"I have some other ideas I'm going to work on too," Eleanor assured her. "I don't want to tell you anything yet, in case they don't pan out.

"You just need to get on the bus and go home, Lawana, and start thinking up ways to make yourself look like the best mother who ever walked the face of the Earth."

Lawana felt much better going home than she had ever expected to feel after waking up that morning and remembering what had happened. Now, she had hope because she knew that Ms. Steele—Eleanor, would help her. She had once fantasized that the woman was her older sister, as she waited for an appointment. She had missed the advice that she would sometimes get from her and she could smile again because she no longer felt so alone.

By the time she joined her husband in bed that night, Eleanor had put several things in motion. Greg's firm did pro bono work but it was mostly for structuring small businesses. He contacted Terrance, one of his classmates from Georgetown though, whose firm had some of the best criminal attorneys in the metro area. Terrance did pro bono work through his firm and he was pretty sure he could get Lawana's oldest son off with probation, since it was his first offense. He would get the process started the next morning but the main problem would be figuring out where he would go after he left jail. Under the circumstances, he told them, no judge would release him to his mother.

She had also managed to get in touch with Barbara Wilkens about the other children, and she confirmed everything that Eleanor had already told Lawana. She did learn that George and Lacrecia had been placed in a temporary home with a very nice couple, Barbara said. God was on their side because the children hadn't been separated yet or put directly into foster care. There was excellent news for her to give Lawana when she called her the next morning—about all three kids.

She had known Barbara for only a short time before she left the agency, but they had talked at length about all the nonsense rules they had to follow at Social Services, at the beginning of their conversation. Eleanor had convinced Barbara to help them, and she had seemed eager to do it because they were breaking some of those rules. Eleanor had been surprised by her candidness and very encouraged by it. She began to think that she might really be able to help Lawana after all. What they needed most now was to buy her more time.

She could help her get a better handle on her parenting skills and guide her into becoming more stable financially, because that was always a factor. From what she knew of her circumstances, Lawana had practically grown up at the same time as her oldest son. She had a hard life, true, but she still needed to step up to the plate again and do what needed to be done now.

As she poured all her energy into helping Lawana and her kids, she felt a new lease on life. After she kissed Greg good night, she told him she had a feeling that fate had sent her downtown that morning, just so she could run into Lawana. As she fell asleep, she wondered how long it would take her to convince Greg to let Lawana's children live with them, so they wouldn't have to go into foster care. She had already passed all the background checks that were required for foster parents, and Greg had to go through all sorts of security clearances for his job.

The very first thought she had when she opened her eyes the next morning was about a conversation she had with her sister's husband, several weeks earlier. It started when he asked here if she was familiar with one of the History teachers he had at Hunter University. They had discovered some time ago that they had both been students there at the same time. He had been very excited about a program this teacher had started in Africa, and he had proceeded to tell them what he had read about it in the paper.

By the time it was late enough for her to call their house that morning, Eleanor had already decided how the program would fit into her plans for Lawana and her kids. The more she thought about it, she knew it would be the perfect solution for them and she only hoped that Lawana would be receptive to it.

Her heart was beating faster by the time she finally dialed the number.

"Hey Val," she sang out, as soon as her sister answered the phone. Her optimism about the family's future was beginning to make her feel giddy.

"It's me," she said, stating the obvious. They both knew that Val always checked her caller ID before she picked up her phone.

"I need to talk to Kioni. Has he left for work yet?"

Chapter 11

Moringa

*A*mina breezed along on the well-worn gravel road and urged Trazi and Celeste to hold on as she hurried toward the next stop on her tour. She had been honored that Kristin had ask her to show them around Exodus Village; everyone knew how much the project meant to her personally. There was much for them to see and Amina had carefully chosen a few projects that would give them a complete picture of the foundation's plans.

Kristin had always seemed to her like a sister—a kindred Spirit that she had recognized immediately when they first met, even with all Kristin's emotional distractions. She had been the first African American woman that Amina had known personally; though she had often run across them in London, while traveling with friends and family. She had also seen them when she studied in London before returning home to teach at the University of Kumasi. To be expected, she had found much difficulty in adjusting to the climate in the United Kingdom, but the culture had not seemed at all unfamiliar. She had grown up influenced by the residual culture that had been left in Ghana after more than a century of British occupation.

She had been conscious of that influence from an early age; both sets of grandparents had been determined that she and her siblings follow the traditional ways. All through their primary and secondary grades, they were aware of sharp differences between what was said and done at home, versus school. The British culture still influenced many areas of Ghanaian life; ranging from the structure of the national government to the prevalence of Christianity throughout much of the country. But the traditional religion had survived too, although forced underground in part during British occupation—and far away from Western eyes.

136

Amina had often noted the contrasts between European classmates that she came to know well at her school, and their American counterparts. Most Americans she had come across in London seemed quite smug in their lack of sophistication; almost proud that they were culturally deprived. Between the African Americans she saw on television and brief encounters with them in the shops near her university, she had little desire to get to know one. But meeting Kristin had changed all that.

She remembered to slow the cart down in time to avoid a familiar dip in the road. A few seconds later, she stopped and pointed out a set of structures that were built along a nearby lake; one of two were within Exodus Village. "Those buildings are part of a mixed-use entertainment facility for the residents who'll be living in our first two communities. That first building will house a library, movie cineplex and several television rooms. The building next to it will be used as an auditorium and for theatre productions, and that small building a short distance from the others will house a health and fitness center.

"Once we're at full capacity, we'll have close to five thousand residents living here at any given time. There will be three of these same pavilions to are to be shared among our five communities."

Amina made an abrupt turn to the left, which brought them to another wide road that she continued down. After a half mile or so, she brought the cart to another stop and pointed south toward a stretch of distant land. There were groves of baobab and ebony trees growing half-way around the perimeter.

"That's where we're planning to plant most of our ground crops," she told them, "and our moringa will be grown over there." She pointed to a different area of land that lay in the opposite direction.

"Aunt Kristin mentioned moringa a few times on the way down. She said you could tell us more about it because neither of us have heard of it before."

"Well, you're not alone, but we're going to change that around here," Amina answered her. "Some people call it a magical plant, because each part can be used for one benefit or another. It does produce beans, but they're not meant to be eaten.

"The moringa has been coveted by different cultures around the world for thousands of years. It has wonderful benefits for maintaining health and is very versatile. A single plant can quickly grow to up to three meters in height.

"Oh, I'm sorry," she added, noticing their puzzled looks. "That's about

137

twenty feet—as tall as a tree." Amina automatically thought in metric measures, as did most of the world. She had briefly forgotten that Americans were the only world citizens who didn't use the metric system, although the U.S. had enough influence to make everyone else within the international community still have to learn the standard system that Americans use too. Their residents would have to begin learning the metric system as soon as their ship set sail.

"Kristin has been insisting to us that the moringa is the same plant described in your children's story: *Jack and the Bean Stalk.*" Amina was smiling now, and so were Trazi and Celeste. They were also very curious about the plant and wanted to learn much more.

"The most potent part that's used for consumption is the leaf," Amina went on. "After the leaves are properly dried, they can be ground up and used as nutritional supplements. We steep them into a delicious hot tea and our chefs sprinkle the more finely ground version into many of the dishes they've created. Moringa leaves are very rich in vitamins A, the B vitamins, C, D, E and K, with minerals like calcium, copper, potassium, iron, phosphorus and zinc, plus many of the essential amino acids," she added.

"It's practically life sustaining because of all the nutrients it contains, but that's not the most amazing thing about the plant. Its seeds can be dried, ground up and then used to purify water." There was excitement in her voice.

"That's what Aunt Kristin said, but its hard to be that it can really purify water.

"Well, amazingly it does," Amina answered, with another warm smile. Her ebony skin had a beautiful glow in the warm morning sunshine. Trazi hadn't missed how pretty she was and she was smart too. He smiled to as he caught her gaze.

"We can grind up the seeds, put them in dirty polluted water and miraculously it becomes crystal clear," she told Celeste, turning back to her, "once the water had been left to stand for a short while."

"Wow. That's the most incredible thing." Trazi was still fascinated by the discovery. "The possibilities for something like that really are endless."

"Well, we definitely agree," Amina assured him. "We see the moringa plant as a true God-send and we've expanded on its intended uses nearly every day. Our moringa plants will become a big part of our commercial operations and so far, the sky is the limit."

She had pulled the solar cart back onto the road and continued driving in the same direction they had been headed.

"We're very proud of this next area that I'll be taking you to see, our hydroponic farms," she said.

"You have those here too?" The previous school year, Celeste's class had completed a project on hydroponic farming. Their science teacher brought in a small device that she and her classmates had used to grow strawberries without any soil. They fed nutrients to the plants directly into their roots, through the water that they grew in.

"Our farms are going to be structured like those that will be used to feed athletes and coaches during the 2000 Olympics in Australia," Amina informed them. "The only difference is it'll be on a smaller scale. Those farms in Sydney are expected to produce tons of high quality and vitamin-enriched fruits and vegetables. They'll be eaten by the nearly one hundred thousand people expected in Sydney's Olympic Village and they will depend on it every day.

"Somehow, we were fortunate enough to get the same gentleman who's managing the project in Sydney to come here, to inspect the system we're setting up and to provide us with his guidance." The tone of her voice was excited again as she described their initial meeting.

"I still don't know how Kristin got him to come here in the first place. He took time out from a very busy schedule for our meeting and a site visit; her presentation was so moving that he was hooked on the spot. Once the Olympics are over, he's going to come here and take full charge of our hydroponics division; for him that will also mean postponing a lucrative opportunity in Denmark in order to do it. His being her to guide our operations will help us make major contributions to our country; eventually, we'll be able to provide locally produced, high quality food in those communities where soil erosion prevents any substantial farming."

Amina turned left again and drove them in the opposite direction they had been going; only this time they were on a side road off the main street. After another mile or so, the road veered sharply to the right and she turned into a parking lot adjacent to a large building, after negotiating another sharp curve.

"This is our experimental station," she announced after they got out of the cart. "It's where we test our soybeans and moringa to determine their optimal growing conditions." Amina had walked Celeste and Trazi inside the solar-powered plant and showed them a small parcel of soybean and moringa plants, sectioned off into various stations.

"We will use rainwater from our catchment system for both our hydro-

139

ponic and traditional farms," she told them, "using irrigation techniques. We're testing our automated lighting systems here too, in a different section of the building; our researchers are documenting the growth records of our plant specimens for further data analysis. That's how we'll be able to identify the most favorable conditions once we start production. We have nutritionists and botanists on staff too, experimenting with different combinations of seeds. They are all working together to analyze the nutritional content of the crops we're going to be producing."

They walked further into the building and she led Trazi and Celeste into a lab at the end of a large hallway. There were a number of smaller test stations set up inside the lab.

"Kristin always says this area reminds her of Dr. Carver's research lab at Tuskegee. I hope to one day have a chance to visit his museum, so I can see the products he learned to preserve and see the place where he conducted his research." Trazi agreed that it looked a lot like parts of the Carver Museum.

Amina directed them into a greenhouse at the rear of the building with rows of thick soybean plants growing in varying stages. The plants all reached toward the solar-powered light fixtures suspended above them.

"Our researchers have been using us as guinea pigs to rate the quality of soybeans produced in that section." She pointed to a far area of the greenhouse where there were several rows of more mature plants.

"How? With bake-offs?" Trazi joked, and used it as an excuse to flirt with Amina again She was only about six years older and he hoped she would think his comment funny.

"No," she answered smiling. "They pick the beans and get them to our cooks with a request that they be served on the same day of their harvest, before any of the nutrients are gone. We are given little forms to fill out; they ask for our opinions on the taste, texture, and so forth of what we've been served. Our construction crews eat here for free too and they add their opinions.

"We haven't found anyone with expert experience in growing moringa yet, but by all indications, it's fairly easy to grow. We've had an unexpected endorsement of our plans from a prominent leader of your Civil Rights Movement too. It seems that Ambassador Young has been trying to wake the world up to the benefits that moringa can bring for many years now, especially to those in countries that may need it most. I'm sure Dr. Levy will be getting the word out about the benefits of moringa here, through his community programs.

"I'm amazed that no one has been on a crusade before—especially with it purifying drinking water. And with all those nutrients too." He commented thoughtfully.

"Well, what you must remember is that the focus has often been on what can be taken out of Africa. The most damaging, of course, was the millions of our people who were taken away from the continent, but our gold, precious stones, forests of ebony and other hard woods, our produce, and our oil—it's all taken out every day with not nearly enough benefit to our people. There have always been those with good hearts who have come here with good intentions, but many more have come only posing as such. They come to gain the confidence of the people they seek to rob first.

"Interestingly, there was an international report about moringa published in Accra not long ago," she reflected. "You wouldn't believe how much it down played the plants' importance and usefulness. Kristin says it's because it's so easy to grow; there won't be a lot of money to be made from it, once people realize they can grow it on their own. And we're planning to teach them how to grow it here. Contrary to the findings in that particular report, the indigenous cultures of India, Haiti, and several African countries have benefited from the moringa plant for thousands of years.

"We have put the commercial production of it very high on our list of priorities. We'll package the dried leaves to sell and we'll eventually sell moringa seeds in the medicine markets at very affordable prices.

"What are medicine markets?" Celeste asked, curious.

"Think of them as apothecaries—or pharmacies, as you call them. It's where the medicine people in the villages go to get their herbs," Amina was pleased by the interest both of them showed in learning her culture.

"...At least the ones who don't grow their plants for themselves. The majority of people still use traditional medicine in some form or fashion. Making moringa more widely available and educating people on using it will have a huge impact on the country. In a few months we'll be ready to start testing our seeds; they develop inside the long pods that grow from the plants. After the seeds are dried, all the oil is removed and the remaining part of the seed becomes a natural coagulant; that's the part we use for water purification and treatment."

"A what?"

"Coagulant" Amina repeated. "It's the stuff that pulls the toxins out of the dirtiest of water we've tried it on it. It makes the water clear and safe to drink. But there is a potential issue that we'll need to overcome," she added. "We may get some local resistance at first to cleaning the water.

Some may have fears of disturbing the Spirits living in the water."

Neither Trazi nor Celeste showed the slightest surprise in Amina's reference to spirits. Kristin had told them quite a bit about the strong spiritual beliefs of the people and the role it plays in their every day lives. It was as much a part of the culture as a belief in angels in western cultures; only in Ghana, their belief is not limited to Sunday mornings. Spirits were openly acknowledged and played an underlying role in almost every social practice. The longer the kids were around so many who all believed the same thing, the more natural it was for them to believe it too.

"Kristin may have mentioned that we'll be using soy as a chief ingredient in our consumable products," Amina changed the subject. "We've started work on campaigns to help introduce our residents to the health benefits of soy, moringa, the other vegetables that we'll grow here. We'll use spices to transform the meat substitutes into delicious meals for our residents, in addition to the health benefits the spices also add. At the same time, we'll educate them on the issues associated with consuming large quantities of meat without periodic cleanses, and consuming dairy products in general. We won't have any of it here in Exodus village, of course.

"We'll teach them that dairy is particularly harmful to people of African descent, because they're usually lactose intolerant," she said. "There are serious health consequences down the line beyond a potential breach of manners in a social setting. Once they know how harmful cow's milk is in the long run, we're hoping they won't be so ready to fall back on their old habits once they graduate from our programs and leave."

Trazi and Celeste knew all too well what Amina meant; Kristin had made a point of keeping them away from dairy from the time they were small. She made certain they understood that the soy milk she bought for their cereal was much different from cow's milk.

"Kristin said something that I'd never thought of before," Amina admitted. "She told us once that the advertising people were to be given credit, along with your national agriculture department, for their dairy product ad campaigns. They had managed to brainwash the world; people everywhere now believe that God created man to be nutritionally dependent on a cow for survival. She told us the activist, Dick Gregory, had been first to make her realize that the milk a cow produces is designed for nutritional support needed for the development of a calf into a cow—not an infant into an adult human.

"I never realized it before she said it, but mammals apparently loose all ability to process the milk coming from their own mothers after the age of two. We humans are the only mammals who continue to want to drink milk well beyond our infancy; and we're also the only ones who seek out the milk of other mammals, except for in dire circumstances. We've blindly accepted all the ads that have told us we need cow's milk, just like it was the gospel.

"Vitamin D, one of its touted benefits, comes naturally from the sun, and many plants have a much higher source of calcium. Even the protein that people get from eating beef is an indirect source," she added. "The cows eat the plants and the protein that's in them; and then we eat the cows. Most people don't ever stop to consider that cows grow strong and lean by eating plants as *their* only source of protein. And when you stop to think about the animals that *do* eat other animals, you soon realize many of them are forced to rest in the shade all day, in order to digest the meat they've just eaten. A lot of energy is required of us to digest meat too.

"We're going to produce a full range of meat substitutes down the line too. The list will be very close to the list of products Dr. Carver created from his experiments using sweet potatoes and peanuts. The only difference is that we'll be using soybeans instead. We're going to start by introducing it to the communities near us through their schools, and our first product will be our delicious cookie line.

By the time they arrived back at Kristin's apartment, she had finished all her business for the day. They sat down together for their evening meal and she tried to prepare them for their trip to the coast the next morning. Celeste fell asleep trying to picture what it would be like to be in a slave castle.

Chapter 12

Reach Out, I'll Be There

Malaya inched closer to the top of the oak staircase, reluctant to go down the steps. She remembered how her mother used to hold onto her carefully when she was little, letting her slide down backwards along the shellacked bannister that her grandfather had built before she was born. She would follow its curvy path adjacent to the wide polished steps until her small feet touched the shiny hardwood floors below. Her mother had always put one hand firmly against her bottom so she wouldn't fall off on the way down, with the other hand braced across the back of her flannel footy-pajamas. She would walk with her down the steps just like that; holding onto her carefully and taking them one at a time. Malaya would wiggle and laugh wildly the whole time, in excitement; imagining herself on a carnival ride.

As she stepped onto the top landing now, she prayed that she had waited long enough; that everything would be done in the kitchen by the time she got downstairs. She still preferred the isolation of her room to being among people but she had stalled as long as she dared. She knew that if she didn't come downstairs on her own soon, her uncle would only send someone looking for her. That would be a step backwards so she didn't want that to happen; she was trying her best to move forward.

Nearly everyone in the family had come up with an excuse to stop by to check on her already. Now, they were all at the house for their family dinner; the first one in a very long time. The last time they all had come together was before her mother's accident, as everyone was calling it now. Her family had shown Malaya how much they loved her—no matter what. But sometimes it was all too much for her to take. Everything was still

144

always focused on her; what she did or didn't say or do. They kept asking her how she was feeling like she had been down with the flu. So she had decided she would convince them all that she was okay, once and for all, so they would stop asking her. And she would do it when they were all at the house for family dinner.

Uncle Paul had always loved having the family over for dinner but with the exception of the younger children, he was the only one who enjoyed it. Her grandfather had started the tradition and it had passed on to him after Malaya's grandmother died. They all thought he took his job as family patriarch too seriously; he thought nothing of putting them on the spot at a moment's notice. Before her mother's accident, Malaya thought she had been the only one who would be on pins and needles sitting around the table, praying she would get through the meal in one piece. No one ever knew who might be his next target so most of them had cut out coming to the house at all *except* for their family dinners.

Her uncle and his family were the only ones who didn't think it strange that no one came by the house much any more. When her grandmother had still been alive, everyone had come by at least two or three times a week—some everyday. It was how they always saw each other. Her uncle had driven them all away from the family home as soon as he moved his family home from Chicago, and he hadn't even realized it.

That was why Malaya had been especially touched when they all started coming by after she and her brother moved in. They had hid their indifference to Sam's death because of SJ too, and they came together as a family to bury him for the same reason. Since the grandmother who had raised Sam was no longer alive, and they had no idea how to reach his birth mother; they had all just rolled up their sleeves and did what they had to do. Malaya even went, because her therapist had recommended it. As she had felt better seeing Sam buried deep in the ground, for herself.

Luckily, his death had been viewed as just another Black-on-Black crime statistic in D.C., she had overheard Uncle Paul saying once. Sam's death had been small news so they didn't have to worry about anyone on their side of the Anacostia Bridge finding out about it. It made Malaya relax a bit more at the prospect of having new classmates again, when it was time for school to start. She still missed her friend, Celeste, of course, but she could never dream of going back to her old school.

She was starting to feel less afraid again, as she felt the loving energy from Uncle Paul and his family. She and her mother had lived in the house with her grandmother from the time she was born, and it had been filled with the same love, laughter and warmth, now distant memories.

For the longest time, Malaya had believed her grandmother to be the only other person she could call on for help, but her family had shown her that wasn't true. They were all very angry with her mother, even still, and they didn't hesitate to say so, if SJ was out of earshot. And Malaya knew what they wanted from her; why they came by to see her so often. They wanted her assurances that she would be okay—she could see it in their eyes whenever they looked at her. And she wished with all her heart she could give them what they wanted, to stop them from looking at her the way they did. That's why she had convinced Uncle Paul that she was ready to start having their family dinners again.

Everyone would be there and she would make them all believe that their wish had come true. On the day that Sam was killed, she couldn't imagine ever being okay again; but lately she had begun to feel like she just might have a chance. She desperately wanted things to go back to normal, but there had never been a normal for her—not since her mother married Sam. She had learned to separate herself from it over the years; from what he did whenever he found her alone in the house. That was how she got through it—by pretending that it didn't happen, that everything was okay. Her only hope had been that she would be older soon; she would be eighteen when she graduated from high school and no one would have been able to stop her from leaving. She had kept her grades good and she planned to go away to college; it didn't matter where she went.

Her therapist had warned her that her family might start to feel guilt about not helping her sooner, and Malaya felt responsible for that too. She had been so gullible to believe the things Sam said. By the time she was old enough to know better, it was far too late. She had never gotten up the nerve to tell anybody what he did, and now she couldn't explain that to herself. Why had she believed her family would turn their backs on her? It was like a bad dream because everyone found out about it anyway. She was still mortified every time she thought about them knowing—embarrassed, and so ashamed.

It was their whispered conversations about her that she hated the most. She had overheard them speculating about what had happened to her; each giving their own answers to the questions she had never been asked herself. They would stare when she walked into the room, severing conversations so fast that it left no doubt that she had been the topic under discussion. That had been the worst: not ever knowing *what* they said about her. It ate her up inside so she decided she would make it all stop. She would take control of the situation, just as her therapist kept telling her she would one day. She would convince them all that she was okay so they could finally focus on something else.

Malaya forced herself down the stairs slowly; by the time she walked into the kitchen, the twins had just finished setting the table. Everyone had already arrived so they all sat down for dinner on time for a change. No one said anything about her mother or Sam at first; it was like having a pink elephant in the room that no one mentioned.

"Paul tells me that you've been doing some painting." Her Aunt Anna had made a point of sitting next to her, so they could talk, she said.

"How do you like working with oils?"

Malaya had never known about this aunt's love of art until Nathan mentioned it one day, when they were visiting the Hirshorn's new exhibit. Anna had offered an explanation the first time she came to visit her; she told her why she had never visited their house before, when her stepfather was still alive.

"I never cared much for Sam." Her aunt seemed to spit out his name. "And your mother was forever defending him for some reason or another." The latter was said more forcefully, but under her breath; she was trying to keep SJ from hearing.

As she looked around the room, Malaya realized how much had changed about their family dinners—aside from her mother and Sam's conspicuous absence. The men no longer held their own separate conversations, for one thing. Everyone joined in and talked to everyone else around the table, but she still found much of the attention centered on her.

"It's okay, I guess." She answered the question hesitantly, feeling suddenly uncomfortable. Maybe starting these dinners again so soon had been a mistake. But Nathan, who was sitting across from her, was quick to come to her rescue again. He joined in the conversation before their aunt could say anything more, describing some of Malaya's paintings that he liked and saying how good he thought they were. He turned it into a safe conversation that nearly everyone around the table could join in on. They all had something to add: about art, one of the Smithsonian Museums they had visited, or about the crowds of tourists who flocked to the mall every year in the spring to go to them. The stiff mood had finally lifted; the ice was broken and they had officially christened the new start for their family dinners.

But as the afternoon wore on, everyone was still careful not to mention her mother's name. Finally, Uncle Paul tapped his water glass to get everyone's attention and put an end to it in a surprising way. After the room was quiet, he told them he had visited Vivian the week before at her rehab center. For a few seconds, they all seemed to hold their breath, except for SJ. But her uncle kept right on talking as though he never noticed. He told them what the doctors said about her chances of walking again, which was very slim. He gave his impressions of the prognosis he had been given, ignoring their shocked expressions. He kept right on reporting to the rest of the family how their younger sister's recovery was progressing.

He never once mentioned Malaya's name, but he deliberately looked into her eyes when he told them that Vivian seemed to be doing quite well. SJ looked relieved, and his sister looked anxious until Uncle Paul said she would be transferred to a different facility in three months time. Then, it was Malaya's turn to look relieved while her brother's face became anxious. They had never told him any details of what had happened to his mother or his father. He only knew that his mother was badly injured in an accident that had also killed his father. SJ had only talked to their mother once since the day everything happened. He had kept asking to visit her until Uncle Paul finally told him there were age restrictions and he wasn't old enough to go.

They had all silently wondered what would happen when Vivian *was* finally released, so Paul's report had been somewhat a relief to many around the table. But he reminded them in no uncertain terms that she was still their sister and a member of the family—no matter what. He would do what their father had made him promise he would do: he would look after them all. He would protect Malaya and SJ, but he would look after his younger sister too. And by the time he was done talking, the tension had all but left the room.

All the adults and older kids loosened up finally and they were as care-free as SJ and his younger cousins. Everyone thought the dinner was a huge success, although Malaya excused herself as soon as she had helped her cousins clear the table. This time she deliberately left everyone behind so they could talk about her. She wanted them to say what was left to be said before they all went home. She thought she had done a pretty good job of hiding her true feelings, even after Uncle Paul had started talking about her mother. Looking back, she was glad he had done it. Everyone had stopped pretending that her mother didn't exist, or that she and Sam wouldn't have normally been sitting around the table with everyone else.

※※※

148

The easel in the corner of Malaya's bedroom had been covered up for weeks. The dark eyes on the otherwise blank canvas underneath had seemed to follow her around the room, no matter where she went. She had covered it so she wouldn't have to look at the piercing eyes every day.

She sat on her bed and exhaled from her performance downstairs, keeping her back still to the easel. She felt the pull of the canvas but she resisted it as long as she could. Finally, she got up to remove the cloth that had concealed her work and the piercing glare immediately invaded her essence. It was an unspeakable violation that had become all too familiar, before she even started the first grade. Sam's eyes had been a constant source of torment to her; they reflected all her pain and fear.

But this time, she didn't flinch as she looked at the eyes on the canvas. Nathan had seen some of the other pieces she created in art therapy, but her therapist had been the only one to see this painting. Malaya had covered it when she brought it home, inspired to paint the eyes as she absently stroked her brushes across the canvas one afternoon, seeking her comfort zone with oil paints. She enjoyed art therapy because she could easily put what she was feeling into a brush stroke, without any need for words.

When she told Dr. Kenner that the painting represented Sam's eyes exactly as she remembered them, her therapist had suggested that she take the painting home with her. She recommended that she use it to help rid herself of the old fears that she sometimes felt, even knowing that Sam was dead and buried. Dr. Kenner suggested that she keep the painting close by until she no longer had strong feelings when she looked at it.

Malaya could see that she was right; that the painting was helping her release many of her old fears. The more she looked at it, the more she felt them fade away.

But after a few more minutes she realized the feelings weren't completely gone after all, and she covered the painting again.

Chapter 13

Nana Adwoa

*T*razi helped Amad pack up the Land Rover early in the next morning. After a light breakfast together, he and Celeste had reluctantly said their good-byes to Amina before they drove away. As with Amad, they had grown very attached to her in less than two days. She, too, seemed very much like family to them and they waved to her until she was out of sight.

Amad turned onto the gravel road in front of the administration building to be named for Queen Yaa Asantewaa, during the dedication ceremonies. Much sooner, it seemed, than when they had arrived, they were back at the Kumasi-Yamoransa Road. Amad drove south toward the town of Fosu; the Assin South Parliamentary District of the Central Region. They stopped in Assin Fosu for a quick mid-day meal then continued south through the town of Dunkwa, and on to Elmina and the Gulf of Guinea.

There were scores of crowded lean-tos jammed together across from the old slave castle, intertwined with colorful small wooden buildings that seemed to be falling apart. It distracted Celeste from her anxiety about what she might find in the castle, as did the crowd of people she could see standing just outside the main doors. The massive trading fort had been converted from its original design that had catered to the needs of the first Portugese traders, who came to Ghana to buy gold, lumber, and other treasures. It had morphed into a slave mill only after the value of the captured humans grew well beyond profits brought in through other enterprises.

On one side of the towering antique structure was a picture of serenity in the gulf, with waves lapping gently to the shore. On the other side, there was a jumbled assortment of fishing vessels and anglers, all crammed on top of each other as they competed for docking space. When the group had

150

moved closer to the heavy wooden doors of the entrance, Celeste realized the crowd she had seen was made up entirely of vendors, as persistent as the group that had greeted them outside the small shops in Kente Village. It was such an odd occurrence to confront them again in the midst of her emotions; she had been trying to prepare herself as best she could for the reality of what they would find inside the slave castle.

As she sought to brace herself to go in, the assertiveness of the young salesmen distracted her from her focus. The mix of emotions was almost too much for her to bear as she waved them away. Kristin watched, silently empathizing with the look on the young girl's face. She recognized it instantly, as she was still struck by the same emotion each time she visited one of the castles.

The young men's apparent insensitivity to the emotional burdens being carried by most people visiting the forts, and that had always been surprising to her as well. The thought of going inside and being accosted by the realities of what had taken place inside them would certainly affect anyone with blood running through their veins, it seemed. Most visitors left with clear visions of the horrific fate that had been determined for those Ghanaians who had been unable to escape. Surely, anyone would expect some degree of sympathy from those who had not been captured.

But to Kristin, the young salesmen were proof-positive of her theory; one she planned to share with their African American residents at Exodus Village for increased understanding. There were many Africans who still had no true sense of American slavery—to this day. They still didn't know anything about the long-term effects on those who had been taken away from the continent forever, and the continued effects on their descendants. It reminded her of a conversation she once had with a security guard; she had come across him on the beach, during her Jamaican honeymoon. The man had told her he had heard "rumors" that slavery had take place in the United States. She could still remember how shocked she had been to hear him say it.

The vendors outside the old forts proved her point; many in Africa still had no concept of what the people inside the castles had suffered; especially after they were made to board the waiting ships. Forced labor had been a normal consequence of war for hundreds of years in West Africa; a customary system of captivity that had been the practice during the time the Europeans entered the picture; in Africa and other parts of the world. It was a system that had been one hundred and eighty degrees different from American slavery and it had taken hundreds of years for it to evolve into the monstrosity that it became. Those complicit with the Europeans in establishing the slave trade could never have foreseen the consequences.

The castle tour that day had been no less emotional for Kristin than it was for Celeste and Trazi. Except for an occasional sniffle, everyone had been quiet after they were back in the Land Rover and Amad headed the Land Rover toward the Coconut Grove Beach Resort. Kristin had arranged for them stay there to give the children time to heal from their experience. They had all picked through a light meal after settling their things into their rooms. They spent a quiet afternoon on the patio, lounging by the sea in silence. It was the perfect way for them to decompress, to begin recovering from the emotional trauma of the slave castle tour that had nearly drained them.

Knowing that they were both sensitive, Kristin had been hesitant to include the castle on the itinerary she had planned for them. In the end, she realized it was far too important that they see it for themselves. The slave castles were a symbol of who they were, just as they were for every other African slave descendant. She watched over the children carefully all evening as they stared over the cliffs into the rushing waters below. Only occasionally did anyone speak, and then with few words. The waves crashed angrily against the large boulders that formed the patio's foundation beneath them. The sounds of the crashing waves spoke all that was needed to be said; it gave perfect expression to their own sense of outrage at what their ancestors had gone through, even before they left Africa. Kristin knew it was an experience that neither Trazi or Celeste was likely to forget, nor would they ever regret having been there.

The waves gradually calmed at sunset and they were all soothed by the passive sounds of its ebb and flow. Finally, they were relaxed enough for sleep and retired for the evening; up and ready for an early start the next morning. They had recovered enough to appreciate the resort's expansive and tasty breakfast buffet, and they noticed for the first time the colorful art displayed and the beautifully manicured grounds.

Kristin had deliberately planned their trip to the coast for the latter part of their visit to Ghana, scheduling it in the same order that Heavenly Travel scheduled most of their tours. They realized their clients might be too haunted by their experiences in the slave castles otherwise, and not be able to appreciate all that the country offered.

She also knew that what she had planned for them next would distract them further from the dark emotions of the slave castle. It would be a no-brainer, she thought to herself as Amad started on their way. He drove twenty or so miles through a serene stretch of highway to Kakum National Park. The preserve had been dedicated to safeguarding the remaining rainforests in the country; at one time, the rainforest had stretched from Guinea down through several countries into Ghana, and then extended itself to the gulf. She had tried to describe the sensation of walking across the canopy of ancient trees on their drive over, but she knew that nothing she said could adequately prepare them. They were immediately startled as soon as they entered the park by the sight of the trees' massive roots that were raised fifteen feet out of the ground. Both children had loved going to theme parks when they were younger, so Kristin had no doubt they would get a thrill out of what she had in store. They would walk suspended, more than three hundred and twenty eight feet in the air, with only worn cargo netting to hold onto and prevent them from falling from narrow foot-bridges. The bridges themselves were made from wooden planks that were nailed together and supported by steel cables; spaced at four-feet intervals and strung together from tree to tree.

There were seven individual bridges all together, all linked by wooden platforms that had been built into the tops of the trees. Each footbridge stretched for over three hundred meters on its own, or just under one thousand feet. With one person walking across a bridges alone, it made for an exciting experience and the narrow passage felt relatively stable. But after they had walked for twenty-five feet or so, a park official would usually prompt a second person to begin their walk across the same bridge. That person always made the bridge sway a little, and that's when the treetop walk became a bit scarier for the first person moving across the bridge. Kristin remembered that it had been at that point that she first gave *any* thought to whether scheduled maintenance was performed on the foot-bridges. And as she had neared her first platform, she noticed that a few of the planks had separated from their anchors and there were screws missing from the connection to some boards.

When the park official directed yet a third person to join on the walk, the entire adventure became suddenly hairy to the first person walking across. The narrow planks would begin to twist and turn in unison with the net-ting, in response to each new person's weight and walking speed. Kristin remembered that she had calculated her chances for survival at that point, terrified she would fall from the tree tops down to the ground. She also regretted not knowing how long a meter actually was, as she prayed that she would make it across. It had been the first time she had been remotely interested in the metric system since her third grade class at Lewis Adams Elementary School had studied it, only briefly.

But, once she finally forced herself to calm down, she began to appreciate the experience of being so high up in the trees. She looked around her boldly and took in the beauty of the scenery from a bird's eye view. Some of the characters from one of Richard Wright's book entered her mind. She thought of Bigger Thomas and his young friends, routinely jumping from one rooftop to the next; high in the sky as they made the tall city buildings they lived in their playgrounds.

The kids wanted to stop for a minute on the first tree platform, of course, to collect themselves. It was the perfect place for the tourists who visited the park to gather their courage, if they found themselves overwhelmed by the experience. The three walked around the platform and looked down at the foliage from several different vistas. They searched the forest floor in hopes of spotting an endangered animal, but saw only birds and a rustle of brush, as some larger animal darted from one hiding place to another. They were forced to move on when more tourists arrived to congregate on the platform. Kristin had no idea how much weight it would hold safely, so she urged the kids to keep moving until they had crossed the six remaining footbridges and their tour was over.

After crossing the last bridge, they were navigated into the gift shop where they met up with Amad. Each of their legs were still shaky from their experience high above the trees. They sat down for light snacks and a cool drink to recover themselves, with Trazi and Celeste talking about their experience at nearly the same time. A few minutes later they had caught their breaths and calmed down from the canopy walk, ready to move on again. They milled around in the gift shop looking for souvenirs after their snacks, and on their way out, Trazi asked one of the park rangers whether there were visitors who walked across the first bridge and refused to go further, paralyzed by their fears and unable to move again.

None of them were surprised when he answered that it happened frequently. It was his earnest response to Celeste's question, about how the situation was handled, that made them all laugh out loud for several minutes. In a most sincere voice, the young man answered that they would keep urging the person until they finally moved forward again. Having just experienced the canopy walk themselves, they all knew it was the only thing they could possibly do. There was far less danger in moving forward than in trying to go back to where the walk started. And even if there were ladders nearby for them to climb down from the tall trees, the thought of doing so was much more scary than walking across the bridges. The trees grew so close together in the forest that even if a helicopter appeared from out of nowhere, it wouldn't be able to manage a rescue. The only choice left was to keep going forward, because the middle of the rainforest was no place for a tourist to be after nightfall.

They stopped to read about the other tour that Kakum Park sponsored, and both kids wished they had been able to take it. Unfortunately, it was scheduled for the same time as the canopy walk and they would have to wait several hours before the next one started. Kristin told them she regretted it too, because the guide was very knowledgeable and could talk for hours about the many species of plant life growing in the rainforest. He would point out various plants of interest as they walked along a carved-out path through the foliage, discussing the various properties they contained for use in human and veterinary medicines.

"There are plants and herbs to heal wounds, fight infections and fevers, lower blood pressure, cure digestive ills, and many other things. Prescribing them requires a great deal of knowledge, though," she cautioned, remembering her own brush with death after ingesting too much cayenne pepper.

"There are serious side effects and contra indications from their improper use; prescribing herbs requires the same care that's needed for western pharmaceuticals. In fact, many of the same herbs are the primary ingredients for most popularly prescribed medicines. Only here, they are in their natural state without the harmful additives and side effects that come with many of the pills that chemists make from them.

"It's the tar and nicotine added to tobacco that makes cigarettes so deadly *and* addictive," she added. "And I find it very interesting that the federal government *still* barely attempts to regulate their sale. I guess the legacy of the tobacco magnates who can be blamed for chattel slavery, still lives on—even today."

Kristin told them about a partnership that had been formed between a prominent black American medical school in Atlanta and local practitioners in Ghana. The two groups had been working together for a number of years, she said, looking for the best combination of the two modalities in healing.

"A holistic approach to medical care is considered to be best suited to an individual patient's needs, and one of the key physicians involved in that project will head our health division at Exodus Village. He's going to help us make sure our residents get off to a good start in their new lives here in Ghana."

They headed for the parking lot and the Land Rover; the kids were now eager to see what Kristin had in store for them next.

"Well, I guess it's best that we save *something* for the next visit," she said wistfully, thinking of the second tour they would miss. She was trying hard not to focus on the fact that they were leaving the country the following day.

"There's a woman who lives nearby that I want you to meet, though," she offered, as they settled into the truck. Amad waited patiently for everyone to buckle their seat belts before backing out of the parking space.

"She's well respected throughout the region, and considered one of the foremost authorities on medicinal plants from the rainforest. I think she will more than make up for the tour you missed, although she's never had any *formal* education. I met her for the first time when I came to Ghana to teach at the University of Kumasi. Her name is Nana Adwoa Afriyie and we have become great friends over the years. She's an elder who is in constant contact with the ancestral Spirits. I think you will find her fascinating."

Kristin mentioned that Nana Adwoa had lectured in several regions of the country, primarily to medical students. "She is a major contributor in the partnership with the American medical school that I mentioned earlier. I must say that she is a very wise and intuitive woman," she added.

Soon, Amad was approaching Nana Adwoa's house and a few seconds later he had pulled into her front yard. Skillfully, he parked the Land Rover near a large tree.

"It did take some time to get used to her," Kristin admitted, as they approached Nana's front steps, "but now I'm rarely thrown off guard by anything she says or does. There was an instant bond between us, and she has helped me through some difficult times." Her thoughts seemed to drift for a second.

"I'm told that's partially because we share the same soul name," she continued, "Adwoa." It means we share a similar destiny; we were both born on Monday, or Dwo, in Twi, the Akan language. Dwo is the first day of the week in the Akan forty-day calendar; it's a day of quiet, peace, and calm."

"Their calendar has forty days?" Celeste asked immediately, curious.

"Yes, and that seemed odd to me at first too, until Amina explained the calendar and I learned more about the culture. It only makes sense to me now, much more so than the western calendar." Amina had explained in detail how religious ceremonies and rituals are held based on nine cycles of forty days, a number frequently referred to in the bible in relation to the great flood that Noah prepared for, Jesus fasting, and others events.

"I have no idea how old Nana Adwoa is either," Kristin mentioned, as they approached her front door. "She appears to be in her mid-eighties, but age is difficult to guess here in Ghana. Everyone looks much younger to me than their years; for all I know, she could already be one hundred.

"She recently lost most of her eyesight but that doesn't seem to have much affect on her," Kristin said in a hushed tone, after a young woman who opened the door left to fetch Nana. "She recognizes me right away every time I come for a visit," she added, "no matter how long it's been since the last time. Somehow, she always knows who I am before I speak."

Celeste too felt something familiar about the old woman immediately. Curious, she watched her approach them after she had emerged from a back room at the end of a long hallway.

They were all quite surprised when Nana walked directly to Celeste and gave her a warm loving embrace. She appeared happy and excited to see the teen and held her at arms length for a few seconds, as though taking a closer look. Still holding onto the younger woman, she turned finally to face Kristin, who stood still on the other side of the room watching the two women in fascination.

"Ah, so our dear Moses has come back again," Nana acknowledged Kristin for the first time since she had entered. "And I see that you have finally brought my granddaughter with you." She still held onto a very puzzled Celeste.

Nana turned back toward her again without warning, and ran her dark slender fingers slowly across the young girl's face. Kristin had already warned them that the woman would most likely touch their faces; she told them it helped her to form a mental picture of them in her mind. She then would associate the sound of their voices and footsteps with that picture, as well as their natural scent that she could easily detect.

She had also told them that she had been unable to persuade the woman to call her anything other than "Moses." She had been doing it since the first day that she and Amad happened by her house so many years ago, as he drove Kristin around to see the countryside. She had never gotten used it but she had given up on trying to convince Nana to stop calling her that. Later, Trazi told his mother that it was the perfect name for her. Until that moment, she had never made a connection as an explanation of why Nana chose to call her that.

But there was nothing she could think of that would account for the woman's reaction to Celeste. Finally, perhaps sensing the young girl's growing unease, Nana released her abruptly and then moved across the room to give Kristin a warm hug too.

"And who is this fine young gentleman?" She directed her attention toward Trazi at last, after slowly releasing his mother. He had been very surprised by the strange way the woman greeted his sister, and was glued to the same spot he had been in since stepping inside her house. He didn't feel she was a threat to Celeste in any way, but he was still trying to figure out what to make of her.

"Nana, I'd like for you to meet my son, Trazi. And this is his sister, Celeste." Kristin had recovered enough to make the formal introductions finally, after glancing at Celeste quickly first. Kristin could see that she was still confused by the way that Nana Adwoa approached her; she was confused about it herself. She hadn't seen the woman for several months and had no opportunity to even tell her that the kids planned to come for a visit.

Although her introduction may have caused some confusion in the States, it was perfectly understandable in Ghana and many other countries around the world. Polygamy still quietly played a major role in the culture, although it was not usually spoken about openly. It was a part of their culture that the people held onto during colonialism, along with their spirituality and unique way of worshiping God. Kristin didn't expect that Nana would have trouble with her introductions, but it had been she who was surprised when Nana Adwoa referred to Celeste as her granddaughter. Ordinarily, she might have attributed the comment to the woman's increasing age, but she was convinced that Nana was still as sharp as a tack. Eventually, she dismissed it though, guessing that Celeste had perhaps reminded her of one of her own grandchildren.

Nana Adwoa's greeting to Trazi was warm too. She hugged him first and then traced his features with her fingers, a wide smile on her face. Soon afterwards, the initial awkwardness of meeting her had passed. Celeste and Trazi both began to relax and feel more comfortable after she started talking about her work with herbs. Nana shared many things with them about her own childhood experiences; things that she had never mentioned to Kristin before. She told them stories about the restrictions she had grown up with under colonial rule; the difficulties that her family went through during that time. They were all strangely similar to the African American experience before the Civil Rights movement, and the children felt a stronger bond form.

Nana's housekeeper brought in some tea a short time later, followed by a wonderful mid-afternoon meal she had busied herself preparing shortly after they arrived. There was foo foo made with yams, and a delicious soup to dip the balls of doughy pounded vegetables in, steamed fish, and several other dishes that Trazi and Celeste had come to love since they had been in the country. As they ate, Nana continued telling them all about her life as a young adult in Ghana, and how her interest in healing plants began. By the time they were ready to leave, they felt as though they had known her for a very long time.

She hugged each of them in turn as they walked out the front door toward the Land Rover, holding onto Celeste noticeably longer than the others. She also whispered in her ear that she hoped she would see her again soon, before finally letting her go.

Of all the things that she had experienced on her trip, meeting Nana Adwoa was the one thing that stuck out most in Celeste's mind as she drifted off to sleep, on their flight back to Zurich. There had been something about the woman that affected her deeply, and she too found herself hoping that she would have a chance to visit her again soon.

Kristin was still curious about Nana's behavior long after she watched the kid's plane take off from the Accra airport. She was glad that they seemed to have enjoyed their visit. She was also grateful for those few days of happiness they had together before Angela's death changed all their lives.

Chapter 14

From Rags To Riches

*A*ll three of Lawana's kids waited on the curb after they got out of the Yellow Cab, until after Eleanor had paid the driver. Their heads kept turning expectantly toward the escalators that led up from the Foggy Bottom-GWU train platform, just below where they stood. William glanced back for a final check on Eleanor and then grabbed his little sister's hand to follow George, who led the way.

The two boys had made a solemn promise to Greg that they would look after Eleanor and the baby. They had both been diligent in their task too because the took it very seriously. Never once had they wavered from the responsibility they had been given. It made them feel good knowing that Greg trusted them to protect the "women-folk" while he was so far away in Hong Kong.

Eleanor looked proud as she hurriedly covered ground to catch up with the children. They had all been through so much over the past two years; the worst, of course, being the six-month separation from George and Lacrecia. Things could have certainly ended up being much worse for them, that's for sure. But through some miracle, Eleanor had persuaded her former coworkers to intercede on Lawana's behalf. She had only approached a few social workers she had known personally, and only those she knew to have kind hearts. Even still, she had been surprised by the positive response she got, knowing that the most well-intended among them was usually buried under the rules and regulations they had to comply with to keep their jobs. Their main focus had to be on moving their cases along in the system, all within the prescribed SOPs, or standards of promptness.

Many of those she had worked with had all but forgotten their original intent in choosing their professions. She imagined that the majority of them had probably been determined to make a difference when they initially decided to become social workers, as had she. Now, most were so distracted by their own instinct for survival that they seemed almost envious of the clients they served. They watched them angrily in line at the grocery store, buying expensive brands of food that they could barely afford themselves.

But the caseworkers assigned to Lawana's children must have been touched by the Hand of God. No one could convince Eleanor otherwise, because her Spirit had led her to ask for their help, despite the odds. They had all responded, in kind. They had opened their hearts and allowed themselves to actually *care* what happened to George and Lacrecia; not just see them as a statistic—another open case. There were some things she knew they were specifically prohibited from doing by law, once their child protective services cases were opened. But the caseworkers had gone out on a limb for Lawana; much further than Eleanor ever hoped. They had helped her and Greg dig Lawana's family out of the big hole they were in, after William was arrested and George and Lacrecia taken out of the home.

One caseworker even spoke directly to the family that was given temporary custody of the children. And while technically it didn't violate any specific rule, they all knew that action would've been frowned on by agency policy makers. Their expectation was that caseworkers stick to the written procedures that had been created for them; nothing more and nothing less.

The foster parents who had taken care of them had a policy of their own, before George and Lacrecia came to live with them. They were both retired government employees with children who were grown and long gone; they had become foster parents after their last child left home, but they had never kept a child for more than three months. The couple was well-set financially from pensions and had already bought everything for themselves that they wanted to own. They used *all* the money the agency gave them on the children left in their charge. They bought them special things to take the place of favorite toys that had to be left behind, as they were snatched abruptly from their homes.

In their hearts they wanted to do more; but it was much too hard for them to watch the effects of the system on the children as their experiences grew long-term. For many, it was months before they regained any stability; for some it took years, until they had reached adulthood and took themselves out of the system. The foster couple couldn't bear to watch their emotional struggle as they bounced from one home to the next. And the ones who had never been made to follow rules at home were in the greatest jeopardy. They would often respond to the situation they found themselves in by acting out; they made little effort to adjust, but continued doing what they had always done to get their way.

Unbeknownst to them, especially in the beginning, many foster parents were only in it for the money. They would abandon a child at the first hint of trouble; usually oblivious to the correlation between their negative behavior and having been removed from their homes and forced to live with strangers. Many children soon realized their worth had been reduced to the amount of compensation their foster parents were given by the state. The moment their bad behavior went beyond the value of the food and shelter allowances, and the bus passes that the foster family most often used for themselves, as well; it meant they would be subject to being uprooted and having to start the cycle all over again.

George and Lacrecia's foster parents had been shocked at how unfeeling some of the other foster parents had seemed, when they met them at an occasional meeting. There were many who showed no empathy at all for the children in their care. They gave no thought to how traumatized the children must be, after being snatched from the only environment that they had ever known, no matter what the state agency might think of it.

Eleanor had known right away that Lawana's kids would be taken; it was a no-brainer from what she was told that day when she ran into her downtown—what with the family's history, and now William's arrest. And she had known by the time she woke up the following morning that getting through to the court-appointed guardians would be their best chance; before the children could be engulfed by the foster care system. That had been Eleanor's biggest fear as she had put the still-slightly-intoxicated Lawana on a bus for home that day.

Her friends at Social Services had contacted the foster family immediately; they let them know there was a good chance that all three kids could be reunited in a good home. It didn't take long to convince the parents to make an exception in George and Lacrecia's case. They agreed to let the children stay as long as it took, and Eleanor breathed a big sigh of relief when she heard the news. Before George and Lacrecia came to live at the foster parents' spacious and empty home, they had only been able to guess the circumstances of the children who had been left in their care. In the eight years that they had been foster parents, all they had to go on had been the way the children's hair was kept, or the condition of their clothes on the day they arrived.

For some, the abuse and neglect had been obvious, but they saw that others had been raised in loving homes. Some of them had obviously been pampered before being forced into foster care; their lives disrupted, perhaps due to their parents' illegal activities. Or, maybe no relative had stepped forward to take the child home to raise them after a tragedy, but either way, they were all tossed into the foster care system without much ceremony or preparation. To compensate, the couple had poured as much loving care into the lives of those children they touched as they could fit. They tried to compensate by giving each of them something else they could hold onto as their journey continued. They hoped that their token would keep them from giving up when they became tempted later on, and help them avoid being swallowed up by a life of crime.

Greg's friends had called in favors with some of their law firms' biggest clients; those who had influence or knew people who could make things happen through their social circles. Their efforts didn't go unnoticed either: their foster care application was processed in record time and they got the children's case bumped up on the Family Court calendar. The whole process had still taken months to complete; it had been a long time before Lawana's two youngest children could join their older brother at their home.

William's legal problems had been the easiest to get resolved, as Greg had promised. The arresting officer only found fifteen dollars worth of pot in his possession, which meant no felony charges were filed. That meant William was eligible for a nonviolent first-offender program; he was given court-appointed counseling instead of jail time. They all knew how easily things might have been different for him too, if it hadn't been for Greg and his friends. They made sure he was never put in with the general population at the jail; otherwise, he might easily have been involved in an incident that could have ended his life or changed it forever. He could have been sexually or physically assaulted, or forced to assault someone else. Even worse, he might have killed someone. *Anything* could have happened in the blink of an eye that could've turned his minor charges into something else altogether.

But God had been with them; William had one of the best criminal lawyers money could buy. Greg's good friend, Terrance, who took his case, convinced the judge to release Lawana's oldest son into their custody right away, until his case could be scheduled in Juvenile Court. Soon afterwards,

Terrance discovered a technicality on William's police report; it resulted in all charges being dismissed. His record had been wiped clean and it wouldn't come back to haunt him when he was older and knew better. His request to be declared an emancipated minor was granted too, so he was free to live at their house without any court approval.

She had found herself unexpectedly nervous about the reality of having him move in without his younger siblings. Yet, it had become an experience that proved to be the best thing that could have happened for them all. It turned into a trial run to see what kind of parents she and Greg would make, and they had passed with flying colors. But as she had waited alone at their townhouse that first evening for Greg and William to get home, her nerves had gotten the best of her. The heated conversations with her sister about it had suddenly flashed in her head; she had plunged into panic mode for a few minutes, on pins and needles as the time ticked by, imagining all sorts of things that could go wrong. By the time they finally arrived, she had already had second, third and even fourth thoughts about having William stay with them at all.

She kept praying that she hadn't created a world of trouble for herself and Greg, until she recalled a different conversation with her sister's husband. What Kioni had to say finally won out; remembering his arguments had reassured her that they were doing the right thing. Some Black Americans weren't equipped with determination and fortitude passed on my their ancestors to pull themselves up. They needed help from the Black Americans who were and could give them a leg up.

'But what if Dina was right, and William was really some kind of bad seed or something?'

It was then that she realized the last time she had seen him he had only been thirteen years old. It had been that picture of William, as a traumatized boy, that she still carried in her head. She had taken over the family's case only a few months after Lawana's husband was killed. The woman had reluctantly applied for public assistance, only until she could figure out how to support her three children on her own. It had been clear to Eleanor then how badly William and George needed professional help. They were still dealing with having witnessed their father's murder, and Eleanor could only imagine how hard that was for them to do on their own. She thought how she might have coped with something like that herself without help, and had soon convinced a good friend, who was a therapist, to work with them through their recovery.

Then she remembered that Lawana had told her at some point that the boys stopped going to their sessions, and had not gone for several weeks before she even realized it. What if William had turned into someone that she and Greg weren't prepared to deal with at all? What if he brought his young hoodlum friends to their home, and the electronic gadgets that Greg was always buying started coming up missing? Eleanor hadn't given a single thought to any of that until William was on his way to their house to live. If he and his young friends turned out to be budding thieves, she would've put their entire neighborhood in jeopardy.

But the conversations she had with Dina's husband were still the loudest, and she knew that they had to give it a try. Whenever Kioni and Dina came over for dinner or to watch a game, her brother-in-law had always talked about what a little help could do. Something that might not require much from one person could make all the difference in the world to somebody else, he was always saying. And she knew that he was right, that people like Lawana and her children deserved a second chance. She had made some bad choices herself when she was younger—but then again, Eleanor didn't know anyone who hadn't done the same.

She and Greg were from small nearby towns on the outskirts of Greensboro North Carolina, but hadn't met until after they both moved to Washington; her, to get a Master's degree at Hunter, and Greg, for Georgetown Law. On their first date they discovered they had gone to rival high schools and that they'd been Aggies at the exact same time. North Carolina A&T had such a large student population that neither remembered seeing the other before the night they met in D.C. They had both been raised in large families that had little in the way of finances, but they had grown up feeling loved above all else, and very much supported. Eleanor felt a responsibility to at least try to help the people who crossed her path who hadn't had the same safe and loving experience.

And she was soon to realize that her fears about William were unfounded. She and Greg had made plans to sit down with him as soon as he arrived at their house, so they could talk to him about the seriousness of the situation. They had rehearsed exactly what they would say but to her surprise William was already well aware of the role he had played in the whole fiasco. His family loved each other too and he knew his mother had taken care of them as best she could. He had seemed so remorseful that he could barely hold back his tears. Having Lacrecia and George taken away had gotten his full attention; that along with having to spend his fifteenth birthday all alone in a jail cell.

Eleanor had been blown away when he introduced himself as "William" instead of Little Man. She found out from her husband later that he had decided to have a talk with him as soon as they were outside the police station—man-to-man. After they were in the car, Greg started by telling him how glad they both were to have him come and stay with them, and that they were glad to have his siblings come too. Then, he told him how much importance a name has; that it carries the person's purpose on the Earth and vibrates its meaning every time it is spoken in association with that individual. He told him all about the fights he had witnessed as a child, as the non-aggressor's Spirit recognized the harm of being called "out of their name." Greg said he told him that his only condition for living with them would be for him to be willing to say good-bye to "Little Man" for all times. It was only then that Eleanor realized she had never heard anyone call him by his real name before, not until he had gotten into trouble. She had known it to be his name from his official case records, but Lawana had always called him "Little Man" and she had followed suit.

For the first few days William had been very shy around them and very quiet too. It was a challenge to get the two men to talk directly to each other at first and any conversation they had was always carried on through her. The turning point came nearly a month later, after Greg casually mentioned the tickets he had to see the Hoyas play. After that, Eleanor knew that he had a friend in William for life, because Georgetown basketball turned out to be his favorite team.

William had been so excited after the game that he hadn't been able to fall asleep for hours. He kept saying over and over that he had never dreamed of seeing his favorite team play in person—not in a million years. And to top it off, their seats had been inside one of the sky boxes that Greg's firm leased from the Verizon Center every year. They had all kinds of food and deserts there, he told her. He could barely believe it when Greg told him that he and the other attorneys had free reign over most of the season tickets that came with the box. Although Greg did give him fair warning that the partners would occasionally bump them for certain NBA games and concerts. William had still been ecstatic as he drifted off to sleep, still smiling after her promise to keep an eye open for upcoming events.

"Hi Momma!" All three kids shouted the greeting in unison as soon as Lawana's head bobbed up from the escalator. They had positioned themselves to spring out in front of her, just as soon as the other passengers coming from the train platform had cleared their path. Six-year-old

Lacrecia was the first to get to her, with a hug that was so powerful that it made Lawana step back for balance.

"Hey Cre." She wrapped one arm around her daughter's shoulders as she leaned down to kiss her on the cheek.

"Hi guys," She shifted her rolling weekender with her other hand and they all kept walking to get out of the way of other passengers. In seconds, William had taken the bag from his mother and they were all standing next to Eleanor slightly off the busy sidewalk.

"I hope you kids have been behaving yourselves." Both boys leaned down to kiss their mother's cheek on either side at the same time.

"Yes, ma'am." It was their ritual, and had been every week for the past two years. Eleanor had offered to pay for a car service to pick Lawana up on Saturdays, so she wouldn't have to bother with the METRO. But her former client would hear none of it; neither would she hear anything about her buying any more new clothes for the boys, not after she and Greg had bought them everything they would need to go to school in Georgetown.

The public schools where the boys had started that fall were a far cry from Shaw Middle School, where George would have been if they were still in their old apartment; or Cardozo High School, where William should have been that day that he got into trouble. Cardozo had been struggling to make improvements but they still had one of the lowest percentages of graduates who continued their educations beyond high school. And students at Shaw Middle School had always scored consistently lower in math and reading skills than most other schools in the city.

" Hi Ellie. How's everything going?" Lawana finally disengaged herself from Crecia, as her friends at Georgetown Day School had been calling her, just long enough to give Eleanor a proper hug too.

"Thank you so much, Ellie. I can't tell you how much I appreciate this."

That was part of their ritual too; Lawana thanking her for taking care of her children. She told her that every week when they met her at the Foggy Bottom train station; that she had no idea what she would have done without her—and she meant every word of it too. She had been so drunk that day that God sent Eleanor downtown to find her, sitting against the concrete wall outside of Woodies Department Store.

She had never cared much for the taste of alcohol, though she had plenty of opportunities to develop a taste when she was younger. All her mother's boyfriends liked to drink beer, so there had always been a six-pack of something getting cold in their refrigerator. The day she ran into Eleanor had been the first time she had ever been drunk in her life, and she was still embarrassed every time she thought about it. But she had been at the lowest point in her life that day too; even lower than on that day when they put Willie in jail for life, or the day when her Jabari was killed on the street right in front of her boys.

After the child protective services people left with her children that day, Lawana had cried alone for almost two hours after she drank was left in the tequila bottle that Frankie had the last time he was there. She had stopped crying long enough to walk down to the Safeway for a big bottle of cheap wine after that was gone, and she drank half of it before she finally cried herself to sleep. When she woke up again, Frankie, her boyfriend at the time, had been standing over her bed. He had used the spare key that he picked up from her dresser one day after he stayed over at her apartment. He had just put the key on his key ring without any invitation from her, and he kept it there despite her begging him to give it back. Lawana had been terrified that it might cause problems for them with Social Services; that it might get them thrown out of the low-rent program she was in because of her low earnings.

She had still been drunk when Frankie woke her up, and she started crying again when she remembered everything that had happened. Her guess was that he must have been curious about what was going on at first. He had listened patiently to her garbled moaning; but only long enough to find out what all of it might mean for his plans for her that night. Before that night, he had always seemed so nice. He had taken her to the movies sometimes, or out to dinner when she had someone to watch the kids. He even brought her a few presents like Willie used to do, but he had always kept his distance from her kids—even from Lacrecia. She had liked that about him at first, because she had only met him at the restaurant and still didn't know that much about him.

But once she finally got it all out—about Little Man going to jail and Social Services taking her other children, Frankie was out of her apartment in record time. She remembered how confused she had been when he started toward the door, but he quickly lied and said he had to run down the block for a few minutes. He would be right back, he told her, but he had never come back. She had waited for him all night and the next thing she knew it was morning. She knew then that he had never intended to come back. He was leaving her to figure it all out for herself.

Lawana had cried herself to sleep again, when she realized Frankie planned to do nothing to help her. The next time she woke up, she drank the rest of the wine in the bottle and before she knew it, she was sitting on a bus and headed downtown. She had struggled to focus the blurred images of passing landscapes from the bus window. Something made her get off downtown at Metro Center, so she could figure out where to go next. That's what she had been doing when Eleanor spotted her sitting on the cement floor that day.

"You know you're welcome, Lawana," the ritual continued. "Besides, your boys are doing a great job of taking care of me."

"How are things going with you?"She glanced over at them as she said it and they were beaming with pride.

"Things are great, Ellie," Lawana answered, as she always did. "What could I possible have to complain about?"

She still couldn't believe that all her prayers had been answered. She had been so worried about what would become of her children that day, but here they were thriving in their new life in Georgetown.

With Greg working in Hong Kong now and Eleanor carrying their first child, she was glad to be able to do something to return the favor. And even that turned into good news for her and her kids, because they had asked her to move into the townhouse with them. Greg convinced her how much easier it would make things for everyone, and she could save all her earnings for the start of their new life.

After the kids had settled into a routine, he pulled even more strings to help her make that happen. Greg talked to the owner of a popular restaurant on Lawana's behalf, one of his and Ellie's favorite spots for a night out in Georgetown. She had been hired to help out with the weekend crowd, sight unseen, and her savings had been growing in leaps and bounds. The place was always packed with customers, especially on weekends. And since appearances counted just as much in Washington as they did in Hollywood, there were frequent contests held there among customers over who would pay the check. Hefty tips were commonly left in protest by those who had lost the privilege of paying for the meal; large bills thrown in a heap on the table by their departing guests. Lawana had been putting her share of tips in the bank on Monday mornings; all of it to show the judge at her next custody hearing.

Alicia, another of Greg's friend, who would represent her. She had given Lawana a list of things to do in preparation for her court appearance. Things that would make her look like the world's best mother, she said, and the part-time job at the restaurant was a step in the right direction. She had done such a good job there that she had been asked to become a full-time employee after a few months, and that meant even more money that she could save for her family. Lawana never mentioned it to Ellie or Greg, but the restaurant where she worked had once been one of her favorites too. Willie had taken her there all the time, before he was sent to jail.

She still had one more week to give Mr. Henry at his restaurant; giving him time to hire a replacement before she would leave. He had been like a father to her after the children were taken, letting her work as many hours as she could. Now, he teased her that she would probably pretend that she didn't know him anymore after she moved to Georgetown, if she happened to run across him on the street.

"So, what do you guys have planned for the day?" Eleanor asked.

"Nothing right now," was Lawana's quick answer. "We were so busy last night that I was thinking about taking it easy for a few hours, before it's time for me to leave for work again.

"Did you have something in mind to do?"

Normally, they would all have taken the bus back to the townhouse, so Lawana could put her things down. Sometimes, she and the kids would go out again after that for an outing in the city on their own.

"I vote for taking the Circular to Rosslyn to get some cheese steaks." William chimed in, referring to the smaller red, black, and yellow-striped bus that ran through Georgetown. He had been taking the Circular to Dupont Circle every day for the past month and a half, on his way to school. From there, he would catch the red-line train up Connecticut Avenue to Van Ness, and then get on another bus for the short trip to Wilson High School.

The massive school accommodated fifteen hundred students; it was by far the best that the D.C. school system had to offer, with a comprehensive college prep curriculum that rivaled any other public school across the country. Wilson offered twenty-seven advanced college courses that William could choose from, and he was even taking Mandarin Chinese, at Greg's suggestion. He seemed to have quite a knack for learning the complicated language too, one that, along with English, was one of the most difficult to learn as a second language. He would rush to answer the phone when Greg called at his scheduled time every evening. He loved practicing what he had learned at school with Greg and wowing him with the latest phrases.

"That sound's good to me, as long as you're not talking about taking the train," Eleanor agreed.

The Circular ran between Rosslyn, in Virginia and Dupont Circle, in the District of Columbia, traveling through Georgetown on "M" Street. Eleanor usually took it herself across Key Bridge, whenever she had business in Rosslyn. The very first time she took the train to Rosslyn it made an unscheduled five minute stop under the Potomac River. That one time had been enough for the country girl that she still was, and she hadn't been back on that section of the Metro rail since. She had taken the children with her the last time she went to Rossyln, to drop off tax receipts with their accountant. They had stopped for cheese steaks at a popular, albeit, greasy restaurant on Wilson Boulevard.

"I'm with you on that Ellie." Lawana told her. She had heard all about Eleanor's adventure under the river and didn't want to experience it for herself. "Do you think we'll have time to get back before I have to leave for work?"

"Probably not." Eleanor realized, after doing a quick calculation.

They had walked back across "M" Street just in time to catch a near-empty Circular back in the direction of the townhouse. Traffic was hideous as usual in Georgetown, especially for such a crisp fall day like the one they were having.

The kids loved taking the bus, especially Crecia, who had adapted quickly to her new life of luxury. Unlike everybody else, including Eleanor and Greg, she had spent little time on public transportation before moving to Georgetown. Her baby sitter at their old apartment had lived right down the hall, so being on the bus was still an adventure for her. She immediately set about to try to convince the two women that they had plenty of time to get back from Rosslyn, though she had only learned to tell time in the last few days. She had really taken to Georgetown Day School, which Lawana had assumed was a public school too after seeing Wilson and Hardy Middle School.

Hyde-Addison Elementary, where she would normally have gone to school, was as top notch a public school as the two the boys were enrolled in. But it had been Greg's idea to send her to Georgetown Day School, because only the best of the best would do. Crecia had him wrapped around her little finger within a few days of moving in, following him around with her big brown eyes. Greg had once talked about having a house full of boys but that had all changed once he met Crecia. When she told him they were expecting a baby of their own he had said immediately that it didn't matter to him whether they had a girl or boy. A year earlier, Eleanor might not have believed him, but she had watched him get hooked on Crecia in short order. She brought out a side in him that Eleanor had never seen before, and it had changed her mind about waiting to have their own baby.

Greg had been so good with all the children; so welcoming when they were strangers in their home. She couldn't wait to surprise him with her change of heart on his first trip home from Hong Kong. They struck a deal to start trying right away, but neither guessed that she was already pregnant by the time he boarded his return flight to China. The money he made in Hong Kong was quite substantial but he had to spend very long hours earning it; Eleanor would've been left alone there for much of the time. With Lawana moving in, Greg felt much better about being in Hong Kong without Eleanor there with him, especially since Dina and Kioni had left Washington shortly after they learned she was with child. And with William being nearly seventeen now, he was old enough to take full charge of his younger siblings until Lawana was ready to move in full-time.

She would head out for Mr. Henry's restaurant on Monday mornings, after spending the weekend with Eleanor and the kids. In one more week she would be working full time at the restaurant in Georgetown and she would be there to look after Eleanor until the end of the year. The baby was expected to arrive sometime shortly thereafter, but Greg had arranged to work in the States throughout the winter months. Once the baby was old enough, his plans were to pack up his family and move them to Hong Kong.

And if all went as planned, Lawana and her children would be living in Ghana by then.

"Since we don't have enough time for Rosslyn, let's stop by the Junior League shop to see what we can find for the boys." Ellie had leaned in closer to tell Lawana that they needed to talk in a low voice first.

Lawana knew that it probably meant news about their plans to leave for Africa. Since Kioni was in charge of Exodus Village now, there was never much of a cliff hanger about whether or not they would be accepted. Her biggest obstacle had remained her younger children's legal status; she wouldn't be able to take them out of the country until full legal custody of them had been restored.

"That sounds good," she answered, playing along. "Maybe I can find something nice for myself too, this time."

Lawana had teased George and William every week about how spoiled they were getting in Georgetown, but secretly, she was proud of the way that they were holding their own. Their weekly therapy sessions had played a big role, because they had finally been able to talk about their feelings of helplessness after witnessing their father's death. It was like having a ton of bricks lifted from their heads.

Ellie had decided to make things easier for everyone by home schooling the kids during that first year. For one thing, it was the middle of the year when William got into trouble, and he and George had already established a history of sporadic attendance. Their grades were poor and they had both been generally uncooperative with their teachers. There was little hope that they would end up at the same grade-levels in the Georgetown public school district, that they would've been in at their old neighborhood schools. Not having any children herself yet, she had never realized how much of a contrast there was between public schools from one side of D.C. to the other. She and Greg had foreseen major problems if the boys had been forced to repeat a grade too, and the time she spent home schooling them had paid off in spades.

She had poured all her energy that had been pent up since quitting her job into the boys; they had learned more in one year than they had since their father's death. She spent days working on their curriculums and each lesson had something that all three children could learn. Crecia was just turning five at the time, and she had to think of something that would hold George's ten-year-old attention span, while challenging William at the same time. But she had figured it all out, and started taking them on field trips to get them interested in learning even more. When they went to the zoo, Eleanor had them complete the animal fact sheets that she had requested in advance from the Smithsonian, while they were still there. Once they were home, she would connect whatever they learned on the trip to other subjects that they also studied that week. Their spelling words would be names of the animals they'd seen, and she would challenge Lacrecia to learn to spell the names too. She used information that the zoo keeper gave them about caring for the animals in the math word problems that she gave George and William. They would have to figure out how many gallons of water were used in the lion cages every month, based on the amount they were given each day. William's lesson might expand into basics of zoology, while George might be asked to figure out how many monkeys could fit into a specific space, based on the ideal square footage that the zoo keepers said were required to house ten monkeys.

She took them all over Washington, including to the Library of Congress, where she had them research things in their lessons to expand their studies even further. They visited all the Smithsonian Museums, one by one, and went to a few several times. The National Museum of African

Art and the Air and Space Museums were their favorites; they also loved going to the Bureau of Engraving to watch new money being printed and the old money being burned.

Eleanor was motivated by her kind fifth grade teacher each time she made arrangements for their trips. Each person in her class had been asked to bring in ten dollars once for a field trip they were to go on, and her mother had signed the permission slip for the trip. But her father had laughed in her face when Eleanor asked him for the money that she needed, not meaning to be cruel but he had eight other children to feed. Her parents had been good at stretching money and would have been able to make that ten dollars go a long way. Not knowing what else to do, she had given her teacher the signed note but with no money to pay for the trip. Her teacher didn't notice at first, and when she asked about the money as everyone else was about to board the bus, Eleanor's shameful face had been enough to tell the story. Her teacher had quickly reached inside her own purse and took out ten dollars to pay for her. She quickly put it in the envelope with everyone else's money and then without another word, she turned Eleanor around by the shoulders and pointed her toward the line where the other students were boarding the bus. She had never forgotten that teacher or what she had done for her that day.

All three kids were tested before they were returned to public school, since they had been home schooled, and all three of them excelled on the tests. The boys didn't even realize they were in public school for the first month; their new schools were such a contrast to what they were accustomed to having. They had gone from rags to riches over night and they were holding their own with their classmates. Eleanor felt it was a blessing to have played a role in making that happen.

And now, they had but one hurdle left to be jumped.

Lawana had never protested much when it came to buying for Lacrecia, but she had refused to let Ellie buy any more clothes for the boys, except from the Junior League shop. And the boys had no objection at all about where their clothes came from, not as long as they were still blending in with their new friends. There was a Junior League store not far from their townhouse that was filled with clothing donated by people living in their neighborhood. The clothes were sold to raise money for charity projects that the League often sponsored around the city. Practically everything in the store looked like it was brand new, some even had retail tags still left on. Most of the things had exclusive designer labels but were priced

174

at pennies on the dollar. The store near their house had some *very* nice things and Eleanor would have bought some for herself if she thought Greg wouldn't have had a fit. She was fascinated by the bargains they could find there, and tried to get Lawana in the store as often as she could. She had helped her find some cute things for herself too, things that she would never have been able to afford.

Both women knew they needed to stop looking for more clothes for anyone period. What they needed to do now was start thinking about what Lawana's family would leave behind. Eleanor would be moving to Hong Kong after the baby came, and Lawana would need to reduce everything that she and the children owned in order to have it fit the limited number of bags they would be allowed to bring with them to Ghana.

"What's going on?" Lawana asked as soon as they were out of earshot. The kids were all busy looking for clothing in their size. "Did you hear anything back from Kioni yet?" They had been waiting for his input before they decided on their next move.

"He called a few minutes before we left to meet your train." Ellie glanced over her shoulder to make sure the kids couldn't hear. The two youngest had no idea that their lives were about to change radically again.

"Well,...Don't keep me in suspense, what did he have to say?" The two women had become very close over the past two years, and Lawana now knew that Ellie and Greg cared as much about her kids as she did.

"Kioni agrees with the advice we got from your attorney," Eleanor told her, finally. "You and the kids are absolutely guaranteed a spot on the next ship leaving Annapolis, so no problem there. It sets sail on the first of January, so to make it work we'll have to have everything in place by the first week in December at the very latest."

Her brother-in-law had been operating a lucrative engineering firm in Maryland for over five years that morning she had called him about Lawana's family. He and Dina had plans to shop around for land in the Ft. Washington area soon, so they could start building their dream house. Their lives had been successful but fairly routine before she asked Kioni to track down his former History teacher at Hunter. He had finally reached her in Ghana, to find out more about the village she had built for Black Americans, like Lawana. In the process, his and her sister's own lives had changed dramatically too, and almost over night.

Kioni had been thrown off by Kristin's reaction when he announced himself after she answered the phone. As he dialed her number, he wasn't at all certain she would even remember who he was. But she was not only happy to hear from him, she seemed to have expected his call. She mentioned something about having conjured him up with her thoughts, but she talked so fast that he missed a good portion of what was said. There was the mention of some other students' business cards, and an essay that he once wrote for one of her classes. Apparently, she had recently read it, and had been inspired to make some critical changes, she said, in the structure of Exodus Village based in part on what he wrote. Kioni had been even more surprised when she offered him a job with her in Ghana, before he had a chance to mention Lawana's family at all. But after he and Dina learned more about the mission of the Exodus Foundation, they agreed to abandoned their plans for a new home in the States and jumped at the opportunity to go to Ghana.

William had sworn to them that he had only sold drugs before he was arrested and had never used any himself. Still, they had all quietly held their breath as they waited for the results of his medical exam. True to his word, he had passed with flying colors, which left only the younger children's custody status to stand in their way. Technically, as the younger children's foster parents, Eleanor and Greg had some control over their comings and goings, but apparently not enough to legally grant permission for them to leave the country with their birth mother.

"It won't work," Ellie gave her the bad news, "not even if the Foundation broke its own rules and allowed them to board the ship without passports."

The news wasn't all that unexpected; Greg had told them pretty much the same thing. But they had held out hope that an exception could be made. Lawana had no idea where that left them now.

"Kioni said that you and the kids would never be allowed to enter the country without valid passports. Since George and Crecia are minors, their applications require the signatures of their legal guardians; and technically, at least for now, that's the District of Columbia and they've already said no.

"So what happens now?" Lawana asked. She had been quiet for a moment as she sorted it all out in her mind, struggling not to become pessimistic. They had resolved other problems that had popped up over the last two years and she had every reason to believe that this one would be worked out too. Her attorney had given her good reason to hope that the District would restore her full parental rights soon, but the Family Court had yet to make its final ruling. Their case had been scheduled for the Monday following Thanksgiving and that would cut things a little too close for comfort with the scheduled departure for Ghana.

Ellie took a few moments to consider her next words carefully first. "I really think the only other thing we can do right now is pursue the option of Greg and me becoming the children's permanent legal guardians," she said finally. "We might be able to get an earlier spot on the court calendar with Greg's friends pushing it through. With that done, we could expedite the passport application process; I have a friend at the Ghanaian Embassy here, who can get all your visas processed quickly too."

The three of them had sat down together to discuss the alternatives the last time Greg was home, in case there was a delay in Lawana's custody case. The next ship for Exodus Village would leave on New Year's Day, and if they missed that one they would have to wait until July. The ship's departures were timed in conjunction with the celebration of the Emancipation Proclamation, and Independence Day in the U.S. They all prayed they would be able to leave in January, since Greg would be back home by then. But they also knew that as with all babies, Eleanor's baby would have its own way in when it would be born; its arrival would be timed to receive the precise energies that were needed for its mission on the Earth. It was something that only the baby knew for sure, so their family had made plans to move to China in the early summer. A gap in timing would mean making new plans for Lawana and her family for the months after Greg and Eleanor left Washington, and when they could leave on the ship. It was an added complication that they had all hoped to avoid.

"We'll just have to keep our fingers crossed and press forward," Eleanor concluded, optimistically. "We'll get all the paperwork in order, just in case we have to file for legal guardianship. If everything is in place before we file, we have a good chance of pushing it through in time. The kids have lived with us for nearly two years already, and without any objection from you, Greg thinks that will be a very smooth process.

"But either way—we need to start thinking about getting you guys ready for your move to Ghana!"

Chapter 15

Ishmael

(2002)

"*I now release everything and everyone who is no longer a part of the Divine Plan for my life. Everything and everyone who is no longer a part of the Divine Plan for my life now releases me[1].*"

Celeste repeated the affirmation several times, reciting it faithfully as she had done for the last few days. She had carefully copied the verse from Catherine Ponder's book into her diary for a second time. She read it until the spiritual declaration had been committed to memory once again. She could already feel the magic that came after its words were firmly planted into her consciousness; it had begun its work of healing and she could feel a bit of her normal optimism return. She was slowly gaining confidence that she had made the right decision. After all, what choice did she really have?

She had originally discovered the affirmation in a book she found among her mother's things. It had taken several months before she could force herself to go through them but it had been an unexpected and rewarding experience. She had managed to piece together a sketch of the person her mother had once been. Before that day, for instance, Celeste would never have guessed that her mother had been a majorette when she was in high school—never in a million years. She had found a picture of her in her uniform, in a box of family photos she had never seen before. There were photos that had been taken of her parents before she was born. It seemed

---

[1] *"Open Your Mind to Prosperity"* Catherine Ponder, Devorss & Company; Revised edition (June 1984)

178

that they were happy with each other then, something she had rarely seen. There were old letters to her mother from her grandparents when she was away in school at Tuskegee. They were all stuffed inside a large cardboard box that Celeste had found in her mother's bedroom closet, filled with all sorts of memorabilia. She had only guessed at the significance of some of the things she found, wondering what might have made her mother keep them after such a long time.

She had been completely surprised to spot her 8th grade report card among her things. At first, she couldn't understand how it ever came to be there; her report cards had always been sent to her father, since he was given full custody after their divorce. Then she remembered that she had given her mother the card herself. She had wanted her to see the 'A' she had gotten in her home economics class, all because of a dress she had helped her sew. Celeste had seen how proud her mother was of her that day, and even more proud that she had been the one to help her get the grade.

She had shown her Catherine Ponder's book the day before she and Trazi left for their trip to Ghana, along with several other books she had read recently. She told her God intended that *everyone* should have the best that life had to offer, that everyone should be prosperous in their lives. It was the book, she told her daughter, that had helped her finally see that. That had been the last time she saw her mother alive. She had been so excited that day, more so than Celeste had ever seen her. She told her about other things she had learned from talking to Aunt Kristin, and from studying other metaphysical books like Catherine Ponder's book. She told her the "metaphysical" part meant the books explained the deeper meaning of what she learned as a child in Sunday School. They had helped her mother turn her life around, and Celeste has seen their powerful impact.

Remembering that day made it that much harder for Celeste to accept that her mother's life was really gone, just as she had been getting it under control. And, the two of them had also just begun to know each other too—that was really the hardest part. But she could still feel her presence just as Aunt Kristin had said she would. She sometimes thought it strange that her mother felt so much closer to her dead than she had ever felt when she was still alive. And she knew so much more about her now too.

Celeste had taken the box of memorabilia with her when she left her house for the last time. She had gone through all the things again and read random passages from the books she had also taken with her. They had helped convince her that her mother's passing had been her ultimate healing; the books had helped her see death as a normal facet of the ebb and flow of life.

She had told Celeste that she finally understood the unlimited powers of the Creator; that prosperity was always available to us through our connection to the God-Spirit within. But she hadn't learned that until it was almost time for her to go. Her mission on Earth had been completed and she had experienced all that she intended before she came. Her body was no longer of use to her God-Spirit, nor to her soul. It no longer had a use; that was the real reason it had stopped functioning and caused her death.

Celeste had remembered something else her mother told her that last day too, and it helped her as she struggled to pick herself up after what happened with Ishmael. It made her realize she would have to make the best of a bad situation. Angela had told her it was vital that she cooperate with the Divine Plan for her life, as it unfolded. She said most people were limited in what their imaginations could create for their lives, but the Creator's imagination is unlimited. That was the reason she should always trust in God's plan for her life, she said. She told her to try her best to cooperate with *His* Will for her, and never be so determined to promote her own will if things didn't seem to go her way.

Celeste remembered something Aunt Kristin had told her and Trazi when they were in Ghana too that helped her through her breakup with Ishmael. It complimented her mother's advice and broke through all her tears when she had thought nothing would make them stop. Her aunt had told them that true prosperity meant having it all—including perfect relationships of all kind. She also told them that her life had become much easier after she learned to yield to the natural order of the Universe. She had learned to accept the good that it brought her without question, and she had also learned to willingly release what she had only *imagined* to be good—whenever the Universe took it away.

"No worries," was the way her Aunt Grace and Jamaican cousins usually put it.

Celeste had never known how much easier their advice was to say, than do; not until Ishmael broke her heart. On the day that she had run out of his apartment in tears, she felt terribly hurt, confused, and betrayed. She felt as though her life had just ended because she had lost the love of her life. But she had pulled her mother's books out as soon as she got back to her dorm. The affirmations had helped her once and she felt confident that they would help her again. She had read Ponder's book again and miraculously they were helping her again.

She had looked for the same affirmation she had continuously recited the first time. That time, she had randomly found the verse in the center of the first page she opened. She had felt no conscious connection to its words in the beginning, but something had pulled her to the verse, and she had recited it consistently every day. Before long, she felt a spark as her mind delved deeper into the meaning of the words all on its own. Then, dramatic changes began to unfold in her life; magical changes that she had never expected and some she could still barely believe.

Within two weeks, her father had told her that he and Charlotte were divorcing. When he gave her the news she had to struggle not to jump up and down; not before she searched his face tactfully for signs of how he might be affected. She had been ecstatic to see the look of finality in his eyes, making it clear to her that the divorce had been *his* decision and not Charlotte's. It was a dream come true for her; something she had longed for since the night her brother had left their loft because of their wicked stepmother. Trazi had opted to finish high school from his mother's house instead, on the other side of town.

Celeste had given the affirmation full credit for removing Charlotte from all their lives. Although no one openly admitted it, she knew that everyone else felt as relieved as she did that the marriage was over. Her grandmother would've been the only one to protest the divorce, but she had also passed soon after her mother's death. Charlotte's snow job had been so convincing that her grandmother believed until the day she died that she had been the best thing to happen to them all. But Celeste knew that was because her grandmother had never seen the *real* Charlotte.

It was very clear that her stepmother had served her purpose for being in her life because Charlotte had packed her things and moved out only a few days after her father's divorce announcement—without so much as a good-bye. Celeste's face lit up in a quick smile as she recalled the sight of her going down the stairs for the last time, watching her struggle from her bedroom doorway. Charlotte had stopped to adjust the straps of the over-sized make-up case she carried in one hand, with the brown seal-skinned Prada tote her father had bought her for Christmas, on the other. She had to stop every few steps down to keep the bags from falling from her shoulders, and ahead of her to the bottom of the stairs.

Seconds later, the smile on Celeste's face grew bittersweet as quickly as it had come. It faded altogether as random thoughts of Ishmael flooded her mind. She had never imagined that things would end for them the way that it had. She prayed that the affirmation would restore her; otherwise, she didn't know what she would do.

Then a flash of light beamed through her somber mood once again. This time, there were memories of the first day she had ever seen Ishmael, two years earlier in Summer's Café, a new restaurant not far from her father's office. She only found out later that his parents owned the trendy new restaurant. It was located in a pleasant-looking colorful building on the north side of Georgia Avenue, headed toward Silver Spring. The restaurant had been open a few months before Celeste even noticed it. The word "vegetarian" finally caught her eye because she had been one since her trip to Ghana; she was nearly meat-free now, like Kristin—nearly vegan really, with the exception being seafood of course. She had been looking for a chance to check out the restaurant's menu and thought it would be the perfect place to celebrate her father's divorce.

She had struggled to keep the conversation light as she drove them toward the restaurant, trying to distract him from an aggravating discussion he'd just had with his attorney. They had reviewed the list of assets he had once had but lost in the divorce settlement, and at first Celeste thought that accounted for some of his behavior. She didn't notice at first that the muscles in his neck were tightening as she drove along in the traffic. It wasn't until she turned Kristin's old Saab onto "U" Street, and then north again onto Georgia Avenue that she realized what it was. He was fighting an urge to hold onto the dashboard of the lightweight green convertible, as she quickly maneuvered around buses and cabs on the busy Washington street. The Saab Kristin had given her as a high school graduation present, made it easy to do. And unbeknownst to her father, she often played "chicken" with the pedestrians who would step out onto the street as they saw the car approach. She would routinely pretend not to notice them as she drove around the city; all the while fully in-tune with the rhythm of their movement and prepared to stop at a moment's notice.

When she realized her seeming near-collisions were scaring her father half to death, she had to work hard to keep a grin off her face. But she slowed the car down too because he had no way of knowing that she was in control. She knew that other incident, the one involving his car when she had just been learning to drive, had probably still been uppermost in his mind.

There had been a number of interesting dishes on the menu that was posted on the restaurant's window; prepared, a large sign read, in the West African tradition. Their food was cooked using the same spices and herbs that she and Trazi had grown so fond of when they were in Ghana. It gave the food a familiar savory taste that was hard to describe, and one she had longed for since their return to the United States. According to food critics, who had reviewed the restaurant when it opened, their dishes had a likely appeal to vegans, vegetarians, and non-vegetarians alike.

Celeste had elevated the art of small talk to a new level by the time she and her father were seated. She had been so determined not to bring up the subject of Charlotte, or his marriage, during lunch; but still she felt compelled to talk about *something*. She tried her best not to pry into his feelings because everyone was always saying that she meddled too much in other people's business. So she had talked about anything and everything else she could think of—at least until she spotted Ishmael walking past. After that, her mind had seemed to go blank and she forgot her purpose.

They had both done a double-take after their eyes met, and she was certain she had met him somewhere before. Later, she thought he must have reminded her of someone else she knew, except she never figured out who that person could be. Ishmael had hurried past their table and distracted her from that moment on. Her eyes had followed him around the restaurant and she repeatedly had to remind herself that she had come there to cheer her father up. She waited for Ishmael to walk by their table again, but when he did, he did it quickly. He only glanced back over his shoulder after he had passed, and if she hadn't ventured a quick look herself at the very same time, she might never have known he was curious about her too. They both had looked away after their eyes met that second time, embarrassed that their uncensored feelings had been on display for all to see.

A while later she realized her poor father had been awkwardly trying to keep the conversation going by himself. He had been confused by the sudden change in her behavior, but only for a brief moment.

"Hump, ump, ump ummm." He cleared his throat after he had observed his daughter watching Ishmael for a few minutes. She quickly turned her head toward him as though she had been caught with her hand in the cookie jar. She could tell right away that he was finding it hard to keep himself from laughing at her, and wouldn't be able to hold it in much longer. He had apparently watched the interplay between her and Ishmael long enough to know where her attention lay.

"Now, I know the *real* reason you wanted to bring me here," he teased, and the laughter in his voice caught her by surprise. The sound of it had been missing from her father for a very long time.

"So, you've just been *using* me to try to get close to that waiter over there." He couldn't hold it back any longer and laughed openly as he nodding in Ishmael's direction.

"Daddy! I hardly think he's a waiter." She had instantly defended Ishmael and it made her smile as she thought about it now. She had known nothing about him at all at the time—not even his name.

"The people who *do* work here talk to him like he *owns* the place or something." She had sounded convincing in making the point.

"My, my, my... Aren't *we* the observant ones?" He teased her. "Well, I guess this means my hard-earned money won't be going up in smoke this fall, when I start investing in your education."

He was laughing out loud now, as though seeing her reaction to his criticism of Ishmael was the funniest thing in the world. He kept laughing about it all to himself—like he was at a comedy show or something.

"Do you even *know* this young man?" He asked, managing to pull himself together. He had seen how upset she was and he was frightened of the answer. It was a fear he had developed after she turned thirteen.

"I've never seen him before in my *life*, Daddy." She had answered impatiently. "Are you satisfied now?"

All the time she prayed that she sounded nonchalant. She had been scared to death at the time of what her father might do if he thought she really *did* have an interest in Ishmael. He had done some pretty embarrassing things to her in the past, and sometimes to the unfortunate boy who had shown any interest in her.

"Really?..."

Winston decided to let it go at that, but later she caught him watching her over the rim of his coffee cup. And he had the same amused look on his face. Her heart had raced wildly as her eyes followed Ishmael around the restaurant, up until the time they finally left. She had seen him stop to chat with customers at several tables and had panicked when she realized there was a chance he might stop at theirs. She had been very disappointed when he hadn't, especially after noting the time he spent at all the other tables in their section. She had caught him looking at her a few more times before they left, although he turned away so quickly that she later second-guessed whether she had only imagined it. Somewhere deep down inside though, she knew that she hadn't.

After a point, she realized her father had been watching Ishmael too. What she didn't know was that Winston had noticed him looking at her a long time before she ever did. He also knew that Ishmael kept checking her out whenever he was standing at an angle that kept her from seeing him do it. And by the time they left the restaurant, Winston had his mind made up that he liked what he saw.

✳✳✳

During her junior year of high school, Celeste had finally visited Tuskegee for Homecoming. Her father took her and she had been blown away by the experience. She loved seeing him around his old college friends; seeing how close they still were, even though they only saw each other sporadically now. He had told her lots of stories about his days in school at Tuskegee; about how they had invented their own entertainment in the small historically black college town. She had made up her mind during that Homecoming that she wanted to be a Tuskegee alum too, just like both her parents and Aunt Kristin.

But she had started having second thoughts about going, when her father announced he was planning to divorce Charlotte. After all, her stepmother had been another big reason that she was ready to leave Washington to go to college. With her suddenly gone from their lives, Hunter's appeal began to grow again. She had already applied for admission, just in case she had a last minute change of heart. After all, Alabama was so far away—hundreds of miles, in fact. She wasn't sure that she wanted to be that far away from her father yet, not until she knew for certain that he was okay after his divorce.

But after she saw Ishmael at the restaurant that day, she made up her mind that she would stay in Washington. Anything her father said to convince her otherwise only fell on deaf ears. He was disappointed, but eventually gave up on her going to his Alma mater. He teased her constantly though, asking whether her change of heart had anything to do with the food at Summer's Cafe.

It had been several months later before she literally ran into Ishmael again, in the main campus library. Although she had him figured to be a Hunter student, the university was so spread out that her chances of seeing him again so soon were very slim. And she certainly hadn't expected to see him in the library, and in the secluded area where she always camped out to study. There had always been so much drama going on in her dorm at the time that she found it nearly impossible to study there. The library had become a regular stop on her everyday schedule.

She caught the flash of recognition in his beautiful brown eyes as they

185

made their apologies for the collision. For a split second, she thought there had been pleasure in his eyes too, but his response to her bold introduction had been stiff and awkward. He almost grudgingly told her his name, and the whole encounter was so brief that she was left feeling unsure of exactly what had happened. When she looked back at him, she saw that Ishmael's attention had quickly refocused on his books.

'It's just as well.' The thought was Celeste's attempt to regain her composure. Still hurt by his unwelcoming response, she tried to convince herself that she didn't care one way or the other. But there had been an unmistakable current that passed between them too, just as he touched her extended hand. They had each pulled back at nearly the same time, both clear about the potential for distraction that their being together might bring. Celeste had been determined to bring home good grades each quarter and all her classes were very demanding. She was excited by the challenges they brought up to that point, not at all distracted by the handsome young men of Hunter she had found herself surrounded by.

She caught glimpses of Ishmael a few times after that, always in the same section of the library. He seemed reluctant to make eye contact when their paths crossed, although she felt certain he was aware of her being there. That too became distracting and frustrating too, so she gave up altogether, freeing her mind to study again after adopting a different section of the library. It wasn't until much later that she learned about the commitments he had made to himself. With only two years left in medical school, he had been determined to buckle down; but though he used that term often, in reality, he rarely struggled to maintain his 4.0 grade average. He was in the library every day to get a jump on his internship and to prepare himself for the residency program that would come afterwards. The closest he came to socializing had been what she and her father had witnessed that day at his parents' restaurant; or at least that's what Celeste thought for a long time.

His parents, he said, had worked hard for the money to open it. He knew the cost of medical school wasn't cheap, so he had been determined to graduate with honors to show his parents appreciation for their sacrifices. They, on the other hand, kept telling him that his medical degree would be the best way to do that, since he would be fulfilling his family's dreams in setting up a practice of his own—just as his grandmother had.

He helped out in the restaurant as much as he could, greeting new customers and regulars that he spotted. He later confessed that he had known right away that she and her father had never been to the restaurant before, that it was unlikely he would have forgotten her face. He had been too tongue-tied to visit their table, he confessed, just as he had been back in high school. And he had literally been stunned to silence when he saw her in the library that first time, trying hard to think of something to say that wouldn't sound dumb.

By the time they met again, she was already midway through her second year at Hunter. Still influenced by the designs she'd seen at Exodus Village, Celeste had decided on a career as an architect. She had a heavy project schedule that quarter and was in need of a break by the time Christmas rolled around. She let some classmates drag her to an off-campus party to celebrate; as it turned out, the party was given by some of Ishmael's friends. He was the first person she saw when she and her classmates stepped through the door, and to her surprise he was as drunk as Cooter Brown.

It seems that one of the few underclassmen at the party had thought to spike the punch to liven things up a bit, he said, after he was found out. They had poured a generous amount of sake into what Ishmael thought to be fruit punch; he had been sipping on it for hours before Celeste arrived. Being the non-drinker that he was, he hadn't recognized the effects of the Japanese beverage right away. Brewed in a process similar to making beer, the sake hardly added any taste to the punch that it was mixed in. Ishmael was very relaxed, as his friends kept referring to it, by the time Celeste arrived for the party.

He had walked up to her boldly as soon as he saw her come through the door, barely before she had time to realize he was in the house. Before she knew it, Ishmael was standing very close to her; congratulating her on having the good sense to find another place to study. Not only had he been loud, but Celeste was shocked that he was saying anything to her at all. By that time, she had been convinced there was something about her that had turned him off since he usually refused to acknowledge her in any way. It took a few minutes before she realized he had been drinking, and by then, to her amazement, he had been rambling on and on. He admitted how sidetracked he would have become had she not moved to another area of the library, and he thanked her for helping him realize his goal of graduating magna cum lade. He said it would be all downhill now, since he only had one more quarter to complete before graduating. Then, he had taken her hand and kissed it in a grand gesture for all to see.

"And I'm sorry that I didn't move myself," he continued the apology in a slurred voice, "but the reference books I needed were all in that particular section."

Ishmael had finally stopped talking and seemed to expect some response from her, but she had been too shocked to say a thing. She had been questioning her decision to even come to the party, as she and her friends approached the front door. Now, within minutes of Ishmael's bold confession, she was smitten with him all over again; something she had never expected.

Several of his friends were within earshot of their conversation and found his uninhibited side quite amusing. She could see that he was well-liked among his peers, by the way they gathered around them in good-natured humor. They playfully egged Ishmael on after hearing to his heartfelt confession. Though drunk as he obviously was, everything he said made perfect sense to Celeste. It explained all his past bad behavior and canceled the pain she had felt on being ignored. She was flattered by his surprising admissions but very soon neither of them knew what to say or do next. They stood smiling at each other in awkward silence as the crowd around them grew bored and slowly found other interests at the party. This time, she was sure that it was pleasure she saw in his bright brown eyes, but all too soon his friends were ready to leave. They collected Ishmael forcibly and dragged him away from the party. Gone in a flash, the moment was lost to them and she had found herself missing him before the car he was in drove off the street.

Celeste had very little time to dwell on Ishmael after that, what with the holidays soon approaching. He still brought an occasional smile to her face when she thought about the way he had been at the party, but she was far too busy managing her father's life to give it her full attention. Charlotte had made such a production out of Christmas that she feared her father would miss her during that season if she didn't do something to distract him. Her stepmother had transformed their loft into a winter wonderland—with sleighs, snowmen, and Santa Clauses all over the place. Luckily, her father spoke up in time and confided how glad he was that he wouldn't have to put up with that anymore. Celeste abandoned her more elaborate plans and they decorated a small tree instead, only to give them a place to put the presents they planned to exchange.

She placed a wreath of garland on the front door and draped some over a few pieces of furniture around the living room. Later, Trazi surprised them with a call from the GW Parkway, saying he was headed back to Virginia after a trip to New York. He stopped over and stayed with them for

Christmas too. Everything had been perfect; the first time that the three of them had spent Christmas together since they were children. It lifted their father's spirits and he seemed more of his old self again—like the person he had been before her mother died.

The next time she saw Ishmael was after the holidays, when he was back to his old sober self. He had tried to put the walls back up between them but Celeste told him she was having none of it—not after he had already bared his soul to her in front of a room full of witnesses. She had cornered him in the library and stood her ground, disregarding anything he said contrary to what she wanted to hear. She gave him no choice but to agree, and when she brought him home to meet her father he had flat out told Ishmael he had been wasting his time.

"Not after she's already made her mind up, son," he told a surprised Ishmael. "Save yourself some time and just accept it." He had laughed openly at the younger man. "Just go along willingly," he had urged him, still laughing. "It'll be much easier that way."

And they had gotten along exceptionally well too, just as she had suspected, once he finally stopped fighting her that is. Oddly enough for her, the more time she spent with Ishmael the easier it was for her to focus on her classes. But true to her word, she had made certain there was ample time to study every day. She helped him keep his focus when he had momentary weaknesses, and they became inseparable except for times that they were in class or asleep. She had even started going with him to his parents' restaurant so she could help them out too.

Both his parents loved her and she had never been happier in her life—until the day that she had used the key he gave her to his apartment. He had insisted that she use it many times before, but that day was the very first time that she had. She had stood rooted to the spot for what seemed like hours after opening the door, unable to move. It felt like she had been propelled into a scene from a very bad movie. She had stood there transfixed for several minutes, staring at the love of her life. He had his arms draped around the waist of a young woman her age that she had never seen before. He looked very somber as he comforted her, and she seemed comfortable nestled in his arms.

Celeste had tried to think of some scenario that would make sense out of what she was seeing. She felt her mind go blank as she focused on the words she heard Ishmael saying to the woman. She heard him promise her that he would figure out a way for things to work out; he would find a way for them to get married.

Chapter 16

Distant Lovers

'*M*y dearest Ishmael,' the note began.

'*I feel as though a hole has been punched through my heart, but I do know that was not your intention. In truth, I still love you—very much.*

'*I want you to know that I don't think badly of you either, because of your decision. I will always want that which is for your highest good, Ishmael, and nothing less for everyone else concerned. Considering the timing, it couldn't be more obvious that things were destined to happen exactly as they did. The odds against it, otherwise, would probably be a million-to-one.*

'*I can't say that I expect it to be easy, but I have to accept that it was all in Divine Order; guided by fate. And even though I struggle with it now, I have to believe that it was the best thing for all of us.*

'*I honestly think that only something like this could have ever come between us, and that may be the saddest part; knowing that this thing was already between us before there was an "us."*

'*Please take care of yourself and know that I wish you well.*'

And the note was signed simply, '*Celeste.*'

Ishmael stared down at the neat lettering so evenly written across the single page. Celeste had shown him the note cards only a week or so earlier when he stopped by her dorm for a quick visit. She told him her

190

grandmother had given her the crisp linen stationery, a present for her thirteenth birthday. They had laughed together as Celeste mimicked the lecture she had been given along with the gift, all about the proper etiquette of promptly sending note cards for a variety of itemized occasions. Her reading glasses had been perched on the bridge of her nose, like she said her grandmother had always worn hers. Ishmael could still hear Celeste saying that she couldn't imagine *any* occasion that she would ever use the cards. That phrase kept repeating itself over again in his head.

He had read the note five times already and it still seemed no less surreal. It was hard for him to believe that any of it had happened; Ishmael didn't *want* to believe it. He would've given anything to go back in time to change the way that Celeste found out about everything—about Kendra. He would've sacrificed anything to erase the pain that was etched in her beautiful dark eyes when he finally looked up to see her standing in the doorway. He still had no idea how long she had been there, listening to every word as he had tried to console his old high school girlfriend.

He thought about what Celeste had said in the note and he had to agree with her. He could think of no better explanation for why she had chosen that particular moment in time to use the key he had given her to his apartment. She had been so hesitant about accepting it and had never used it before that day. Ishmael had surprised her with the key because they usually met at his apartment between classes. He had slipped it onto her key ring, proud of his thoughtfulness in having it made; not noticing her startled reaction. He had been concerned about her having to wait outside for him sometimes when she happened to be the first to arrive at his place.

But when he tried to put the keys back in her hand, Celeste had laughingly refused to open it. He remembered how surprised he had been to see her standing so very still, sensing a deeper meaning in his gesture. She looked closely into his eyes as though trying to be sure she could trust what she saw. She looked so serious that he decided to take the key back off the ring. He wanted her to be sure about it and not feel pressured into doing anything before she was ready. He had placed it in a dish that sat on his sofa table, telling her to feel free to take it whenever she felt comfortable in doing so. Two weeks had passed before she finally put the key back on her key ring, and it had been longer still before she actually used it.

When he looked up and saw that she was standing in the doorway, Ishmael had removed his arm from around Kendra's shoulders quickly, as though they had turned into searing lumps of coal. But it was far too late by then; the spell that had kept Celeste rooted to the spot was broken. As soon as he started towards her, she turned and was gone in a flash. When he caught up with her he found her sobbing, broken hearted near the bank of elevators. He had grabbed hold of her arms, instinctively, not knowing what else to do. All he could think of was that if she left the building he would never be able to get her to come back. He had been so desperate to explain what she had walked in on; he kept pleading with her to believe how sorry he was that he had hurt her.

Celeste had stopped crying abruptly. When a blank stare replaced her tears, Ishmael became even more concerned. He considered whether she might have gone into shock, but she flinched as soon as he tried to pull her closer. She had stiffened in his arms as though they were made of deadly poison; when she turned her stare on him, he had released her immediately. It was his turn to be hurt to the core.

He could only imagine how it must have looked to her, and how it felt to hear him reassuring Kendra that he would never abandon her. He had been telling Kendra that she could count on him when he looked up to see Celeste standing there; telling her that she didn't have to worry about him keeping his word.

Ishmael heard the explanations pour out of his mouth, as though someone else was doing the talking from a distance. "Kendra is an old girlfriend from high school," he started, and then looked down with a heavy sigh. He recovered quickly, suddenly aware that there was little time before the elevator would stop on his floor. He could already hear the faint sounds of the bell as the elevator opened on floors beneath them, coming ever closer to Ishmael's floor. He knew he would never be able to stop Celeste from getting on it after it got there.

"I ran into her a few months before we started dating," he said hurriedly. "She invited me to a party that some of our high school classmates were giving and we went there together. I couldn't really tell you why I went."

But in spite of that denial, Ishmael knew exactly why he had gone to the party with Kendra. He just didn't have time to explain it before the elevator arrived. He had been so determined to push Celeste out of his mind so he could study. She had been creeping into his thoughts constantly and interfering with his concentration, no matter how hard he tried to keep her out. She had been a distraction since the first day he saw her and her father in his family's restaurant. He had foolishly hoped Kendra would help him break the spell; desperate to get back to the way things had been before he first saw Celeste, so he could still graduate at the top of his class.

"We weren't sexually active in high school." He paused, ashamed of his confession. "I don't know, maybe that was part of it..." He couldn't help but wonder what Celeste was thinking and he dropped his head again, fearing that it wasn't good.

"We were reminiscing about high school that night at the party and things just ended up going too far, that's all. That's all there was to it, really..." He looked up again, feeling desperate, knowing that the elevator would stop at any moment.

"Please, Celeste...I swear," he resumed his pleading. "That's all there ever was." He forced himself to hold his head up to face her.

"It's not even something I would normally do," he added sheepishly, and that part was true. He had only been intimate with one woman before he met Celeste and he realized his mistake immediately. By the end of the evening, he was convinced that Kendra's renewed interest in him had little more to do with anything other than his being in medical school.

"I never saw her again after that one night," he assured Celeste, "and I never thought about her either, for that matter..." He stopped abruptly, realizing what he was saying would make him seem that much worse.

"She just showed up here today—out of the blue. She had only been here less than thirty minutes before you came." Ishmael looked away again, wondering what Celeste had actually heard him say.

What Kendra came to tell him had been shocking, but Ishmael had only done what he had been taught to do as a man. He knew that the predicament he found himself in would hurt the woman who had won his heart tremendously; he only wished he could have found a more gentle way to let her know. But he was never given that chance. The class Celeste should have been in had been canceled. She had surprised him by showing up an hour earlier than she normally would have arrived.

"Celeste," he said to her finally, "Kendra came to tell me that she was pregnant—with my child." He had taken one last deep breath before saying it, forcing himself to look into her eyes. He had been barely able to manage it because he couldn't believe what he was saying himself. But he had been taught when he was a boy that he must take care of his family when he grew up, no matter what. And since Kendra was carrying his child, she and the baby would be his family now, whether that was what he wanted or not.

He saw that Celeste was speechless so he kept talking, swearing that neither of them had been interested in seeing the other after that one night. He had watched Celeste closely to see whether anything he said would make a difference.

"...And I know she's not the sort of person to plan something like this," he added, defending Kendra. "She's a decent woman with career plans of her own; this baby is causing all sorts of complications for her too..." His voice had trailed off as he realized what he was saying.

Celeste still hadn't said one word. She barely looked at him except for the cold stare that had prompted him to release her arms. He had begged her to believe how much he loved her and his words seemed to propel them onto the set of a very bad movie.

"I would never be able to live with myself if I deserted my child." He blurted after a few seconds of silence.

And just like in the movies, the elevator bell rang out loudly to announce its stop, right on cue.

Celeste had remained perfectly still the entire time as though she was in some sort of trance. As soon as she heard the bell, she gave him one last very focused look and then turned to get on the elevator as soon as the door opened. She had refused to talk to him after that, when he called her later and when he stopped by her dorm to see her.

The first thing he noticed when he opened his apartment door that afternoon was the key that he had made for her. It was back in the dish on his sofa table, and lying across the top was her note.

The love of his life was gone forever, and she had taken his heart with her.

It had been years since Celeste and Malaya had spent time together. Once inseparable, their lives had both taken life-altering turns since they had last seen each other. They had both lost their mothers, though Malaya's mom was technically among the living, and Celeste had finally celebrated the departure of her stepmother. On the day that her friend called to say that she was driving out to see her, Malaya had sensed that she was upset right away. She and SJ had lived with their uncle for nearly four years, yet this would be the first time a friend would visit her there. But although she had finally made a few friends at her new school, her friendship with Celeste had withstood the test of time.

Malaya had made great strides in turning her life around, especially after Uncle Paul became legal guardian to her and her brother. She was free to focus on channeling her lingering pain into her creativity, after her Aunt Anna helped her get into the Corcoran School of Art. She was flourishing at the prestigious school that was only a stone's throw from the White House. Her paintings showed much more depth now than when she first started and she thoroughly enjoyed making her canvases come to life.

Even knowing that Celeste would never judge her, she was still not sure whether she was ready to talk about what had happened yet. Too much of the old hurt still remained and she had made a point of not socializing with anyone outside of her family because of it. The only personal phone call she had made in all the time she lived with her uncle's family had been to her friend, after she heard about Celeste's mother passing. The two of them had talked for nearly an hour that day, and things had almost seemed the way they had been when they were younger. Malaya hadn't been able to bring herself to go the service though—she didn't think she was ready yet to face anyone from her past.

But she had heard the pain in her friend's voice when she called her that morning, and Malaya didn't have the heart to put her off anymore.

She sat on the front porch to wait for Celeste and as the minutes rolled by, she realized she was happy about the prospect of seeing her old friend again. She stood up and watched in anticipation as she parked her aunt's old Saab in their driveway, but as soon as Celeste stepped out of the car Malaya's concerns for her friend deepened. She could see that whatever was bothering her was much worse than it had sounded over the phone.

They walked arm in arm to her grandmother's rose garden. They had played there quite often when they were young girls and Celeste's father would bring her over to spend the day. They sat talking for hours and eventually Malaya opened up about Sam and what he had done to her. Celeste didn't ask her any questions; she just let her friend say what she needed to say. They both cried as she poured out her heart.

"I would give anything to undo it, Malaya." Celeste said during a pause. And they cried again when Malaya told her she wished she could undo it too.

Malaya had given Celeste ample time to open up about whatever was on her mind, but when it was clear that she wouldn't start talking about it on her own she had bluntly asked the question. It triggered a flood of new tears down Celeste's face and between her sobs, she told Malaya all about Ishmael and about walking in on him with Kendra.

"Oh my God, Celeste. I don't know what to say," Malaya managed between her own tears when Celeste finished describing what happened.

Celeste responded that she had no idea what to say to her about Sam either, and then they hugged each other tight again. They sat on the bench in her grandmother's rose garden crying like that for nearly an hour, without any need for words.

After their tears were exhausted, Celeste told her friend that she had decided to transfer to Tuskegee and would finish school in Alabama.

"I just can't run the risk of running into Ishmael with his new family," she explained apologetically. She knew how upset Malaya would be to find out she would be leaving—especially since they had just rekindled their friendship.

"I think I might die if that happened," she finished sadly, hanging her head.

That had been the first time Malaya had ever seen Celeste so unhappy. She had always had a bubbly personality, even with all the stuff going on with her mom. She seemed so unlike herself now; it was like watching a twin sister that Malaya had never known her friend had.

It was hard to think about her moving so far away from Washington but watching the way that her shoulders stooped as she walked her back to her car, Malaya knew that leaving was probably the best thing for her.

As much as she would miss her friend, it was clear to her that Celeste needed to go.

Chapter 17

Pride of the Swift-Growing South
Three Years Later

Celeste frantically searched for her folks among the crowded floor of the Daniel "Chappie" James Center for Aeronautics Science and Health Education. The building housed the nation's only aerospace science engineering program at a historically black college or university (HBCU). It also doubled as the Golden Tiger's basketball arena, and was often referred to as the "new Logan Hall" by her father and his friends. It was always done with much love and respect for the building's namesake though, a fellow alum who had been the first African American to earn the rank of four-star general, in the history of the U.S. military.

She had learned about General James in her transfer-student orientation classes. She found out he had been a physical education major at Tuskegee; hence the odd mix of purpose for the building. He had been taught to fly at Moton Field while he was a student, and had trained pilots for the famed all-Black 99th Pursuit Squadron during World War II. The infamous "Red Tails" had been so-named because of the distinctive red patterns the pilots would paint on the tails of their P-51 planes. Collectively, the group had flown over 15,000 missions as bomber escorts, and they played a major role in protecting U. S. bombers on key missions throughout Europe. All the while, the Red Tails were still being shunned by many in a then-segregated armed forces, but eventually, they were allowed to fly their own missions. They had literally taken off from that point, and are credited as having been instrumental in the Allied Forces' victory over Hitler during the Great War.

After World War II, General James flew combat missions into Korea and Viet Nam before being named Commander of Wheelus Air Force Base in

197

Libya. But, in the tradition of excellence that Tuskegee has been known for since it was founded in 1881, General James hadn't stopped with that accomplishment. He was eventually promoted to a full four-star grade, and with it came his assignment as commander-in-chief of NORAD/ADCOM. In the dual capacity of that promotion, he assumed operational command of all United States and Canadian strategic aerospace defense forces. Later, he was appointed special assistant to the chief-of-staff for the U.S. Air Force, before finally retiring from the Pentagon in 1975.

Celeste had been amazed to learn about the progression of General James' military career. She had also been impressed by the outstanding achievements of many other Tuskegee alumni over the years—in virtually every field she could think of. She was quite anxious to make her own mark on the world and she finally understood why her family had been so persistent in getting her to join the Tuskegee family.

But for right now, she was still looking for her *own* family in the packed arena, and had been for what seemed to be an eternity. She would have settled for seeing *anyone* she knew at that point, because all she could make out was a sea of black robes and gold tasseled caps, stretching out before her as the latest Tuskegee alumni—the Class of 2006.

Most of the new graduates were already surrounded by clusters of relatives and well-wishers, still buzzing from all the joy and excitement of the graduation ceremony. Celeste was almost desperate to find someone *she* knew; someone who could tell her she was not just dreaming—that it really was *her* name printed in fancy lettering on the diploma she clutched in her hands. According to what she read, she had just graduated with honors from Tuskegee's five-year architecture program, but she needed someone else she knew to confirm it.

She thought back to her father's cautions about the time it would take for her to adjust to the slow pace of Tuskegee, especially after having grown up in the nation's capital. But the last three years had been exactly what she needed; living in the predominantly Black college town of less than 12,000 people had been the perfect distraction for her. Celeste had very little time to dwell on her breakup with Ishmael, because she was forced to focus on how she would carve out a life for herself in Tuskegee. The slow pace of traffic in the community had been an immediate relief because she had never felt tense from her short trips around town. But so much of what she had always taken for granted, like being able to hop on a bus or a train when she didn't want to drive, was literally unheard. In many ways, it had been like stepping back into time. It still looked very much the same as how her father, mother and Aunt Kristin had always described it. "It's easy like Sunday morning," her father would usually end, always with a wistful look in his eye.

There were few stores around the town square that Celeste developed any interest in. Her favorite place was the coffee shop that made a variety of tasty sandwiches; she had gone there several times a week. Both her dad and Kristin had been quick to say, "that must be new,'" when she mentioned the shop to them. Nearly everything else seemed as they had always said; the major difference being the main academic building, Huntington Hall, but it had burned to the ground years before she arrived. A few other landmarks had also fallen to the ground or been destroyed over the past few decades.

Had she not been forewarned about the isolation, she was sure she would've been in as much shock as the other city kids, just as her aunt Kristin always said. Luckily, she had agreed to come with her dad for Homecoming during her junior year in high school, and she had already seen the benefits of sticking it out. The close bond that formed between Tuskegee students was significant and it made up much of the inconvenience in her mind.

They had stayed at the Kellogg Hotel and Conference Center, of course, the only hotel in town. It was also in the center of campus activity, and located just inside the university's main entrance, Lincoln Gates. Her father kept saying that everyone in town for the weekend would pass through the hotel at some point or another—at least once. Hotel reservations were always at a premium during Homecoming weekend, but it had been the year of his class reunion so they were lucky enough to get the two rooms.

Celeste had never seen anything like it in all of her life, and she had been very surprised at the fun she had that weekend. As soon as they had boarded the plane for Atlanta and settled in their seats, she had begun having second thoughts about going at all. What had she been *thinking* to agree to spend the whole weekend with her father? She pondered that question in a near panic, thinking how skilled she had been in avoiding it in the past. But she had met so many interesting people just in the hotel lobby when they checked in. There had been hundreds of mostly-Black people everywhere, all smiling and greeting each other with warm hugs, as they struggled to remember names of old friends and classmates from decades before.

She had followed closely on her father's heels as he maneuvered in and around the animated noisy crowds. He would shift directions abruptly whenever an old friend, who happened by, tipped him off to where some mutual friend had last been seen. Her father responded with an impromptu hand signal, waved excitedly, once he finally managed to spot the friend through all the hustle and bustle going on around them. Celeste had wanted so badly to tag along when he went inside the lounge and bar, but no one underage was ever allowed in. He had ducked inside from time to time to talk to Rena, who was Aunt Kristin's sister. Rena was head bartender at the Kellogg Center and she had since become like an aunt to Celeste during the time she had lived in Tuskegee to finish her degree. Judging by all the noise and laughter she had heard coming from inside the bar that weekend, it had been *the* place to be during Homecoming—to see and be seen.

Celeste had still not seen the inside of the lounge since her transfer to Tuskegee. There was a 'no students' policy that was strictly enforced, so she had stood no chance at all of getting inside when she came for homecoming and was still in high school. But her father had always left her in great company, easily passing her off to an old friend he spotted as he made his way inside the lounge.

"Hey girl!" He would say, "this is my daughter. Do me a favor and stay out here with her for a minute or two; I need to run inside the bar for a minute."

Most of his female friends were very funny and Celeste had learned about her father from them. She was very surprised to learn that he had been a ladies' man on campus before he started going out with Aunt Kristin.

Later that night, as they headed back to their rooms, her father told her there was something about seeing old friends during Homecoming that made you believe you would be seeing them again, really soon. He said he had walked away from conversations with several people he hadn't seen in twenty years, like that; so distracted was he by someone else who happened by that he never thought to get the first person's contact information. Kristin had clued Celeste in on another mystery surrounding Homecoming before they even got there, and true enough, she had seen it happening with her father right before her eyes. She recognized it as she watched him search the crowded hotel, looking for the sometimes radically-changed faces of his old friends.

"No matter how hard you try to see everybody that you hear is back for the weekend," her aunt had told her once, "you never seem to be able to do it. There's always that someone that everyone else you run into has already seen—someone who finally made the pilgrimage back to Mother

Tuskegee after many years of being away. And it's usually someone that you really want to see too, she said, but somehow you miss them *every* single time."

Kristin told her that she had usually found out about people who had been there after everything was already over; after the thousands of people who had come for the weekend had left town and Tuskegee once again looked like a ghost town.

"I don't know what it's like now....," Her aunt had started, during one of their frequent conversations after Celeste's transfer, "....but the isolation forced us to really get to know each other. We saw the same faces around campus day in and day out, with very few distractions other than the Tuskegee Relays and the beautiful campus landscape in the springtime. I think that's why we formed intimate friendships that last a lifetime. Our alumni have a unique shared experience, and for many families, one that is passed on from one generation to the next."

By the time they had arrived to check into the Kellogg Center that Friday night, the campus had already been filled with people. Her father squeezed the rental car they picked up at the Atlanta airport into a very doubtful-looking parking space that he managed to carve out between two cars. It had taken a great deal of effort on his part and all three cars were parked very close to the hotel dumpster, to avoid a steady stream of traffic that drove in and out of the parking deck. Their car had been left at such an awkward angle that she wondered how her father would ever get it out.

"That would normally have been a tow-away zone, for sure," he confided about his questionable maneuver. "Except that it's *Homecoming,* and just another part of the weekend tradition."

Celeste had seen so many cars on the campus that weekend, and they were parked everywhere. Her father had explained, "emergency vehicles getting through—yes; but a tow truck? They would be hard pressed to get to any of these cars. There isn't enough room for them to back up so they would never be able to hook up a car and tow it away."

Later, as they approached the first crowd of people they came across on their way into the hotel, her father had whispered to her under his breath, "Okay, remember now, if I don't introduce you to somebody, it's only because I can't remember their names." He had been grinning ear-to-ear as he said it, as they neared an elevator bank in the attached parking deck. It would take them into the hotel and several people were already waiting in front of it.

"Heck. I might not even remember *how* I know some of them—they just look familiar, so I must have known them here when I was in school."

Celeste had felt an immediate surge of the energy that Aunt Kristin told her she would feel in the air. She remembered that her aunt had said Homecoming almost felt magical—and that was exactly the way it felt to her as she followed her father and the small group of alumni they met up with, into the hotel. They had immediately struck up a conversation as they waited for the elevator, and everyone gave each other the same parting greeting that she was to hear so many times that weekend. As they piled out of the elevator and went their separate ways, they all called out warmly to each other, "Happy Homecoming!!"

Her father introduced her to so many interesting people inside the Kellogg Center—all kinds of people. She even had a chance to meet Anthony Jenkins, one of his frat brothers and a nationally-known radio personality. She had been surprised that he seemed to know Aunt Kristin well too; she heard him and her dad mention her aunt's name several times in the short time that the two men talked. She got to meet some of the people who graduated in her father's nuclear engineering program; and she got hugs from a former NFL player, whose name even *she* recognized from watching games on television. Her father had also introduced her to a successful screenwriter and a very interesting frat brother of his who managed the award-winning musical group that formed while he was in school, consisting of several Tuskegee students and alums as well as local musicians. Celeste had even met the guy who invented the water toy that she had whined to get for many months when she was in elementary school, along with many other children in America. She had no idea that her father and he had studied at the engineering building together.

There had been so much love spread around in the crowded hotel hallways. People yelled out nicknames of old friends they spotted, who now had successful careers and no one and probably called them by those names for decades. They all caught up with friends that they barely recognized anymore, sometimes after literally bumping right into them. But as soon as the connection was made again, they would hug each other warmly and start catching up on all the major details they had missed in each other's lives. Sometimes decades might have passed since they last saw each other, but back in Tuskegee, her father had said, it always seemed like it had only been a few days ago.

Some of the conversations she had overheard would likely have been of interest to gossip columnists too. Friends asked about old friends who hadn't made it back that year, and several of them were nationally known. There were tidbits of information being traded here and there that Celeste was certain a celebrity reporter would have been interested in hearing.

And she had been blown away by the colorful parade that Saturday morning, and especially by the football game that came afterwards. There had been literally thousands of Black faces of all shades, sizes and ages. They all milled about peacefully in the stadium that her father and his friends still called the "dust bowl," although the track around the playing field had long since been paved. There were lots of kids and babies too. A good number of the people in the crowds wore at least one item that was crimson or gold, colors representing the Golden Tigers' sports teams. Many others wore the vibrant colors that represented the fraternity or sorority they had pledged years ago. There was lots of picture taking and such a warm energy, as throngs of alumni and friends gathered together in the bright Alabama sunshine.

There was lots of tailgating going on too, including a big setup by her father's fraternity. He told her they set it up in the same place every year and she had a ball that afternoon with him and his friends. Their spot was on a small hillside that sat close to "the shed," the most active area in the stadium. It was where the current students always sat for games, and the Crimson Piper Band was close by.

That semester's pledgees had appeared magically, offering them folding chairs to sit on under the huge tent. Another group of timid young men had offered to serve them food and drinks as soon as they sat down; food, her father pointed out, that they had been forced to stay up all night to cook. Celeste had been amazed by their rhythm and mannerisms until her father pointed out that everything was being orchestrated by big brothers, who were currently on the yard. The pledge line had been given subtle directions by the fraternity's dean of pledgees the whole time, who stood nearby watching their every move.

They had cheered on the Golden Tigers that afternoon, enjoying each other's company as they sang loudly about "...that ole 'Skegee *Spi---rit!*" She and her father had been introduced to several of his old friends' children, who trickled down from the shed one-by-one just long enough to get food and drink. Everywhere she looked, Celeste saw people hugging each other and looking happy to see each other at Mother Tuskegee, one more time. She heard words of encouragement given to those who had seen difficulties since they were last back. But more often than not, there were congratulations to old friends who had joined the ranks of Tuskegee grads to excel in their chosen field.

Celeste had to hand it to her father; he had made sure she understood that Homecoming was about the only time the town didn't seem more like a ghost town. It would come to life again, he had told her, during graduation and sometimes on Founder's Day weekend. If not for him reminding her of that she might have gone into shock after he helped her drive Kristin's car down to school. But just as he and Kristin had both predicted, she had fallen in love with the town's quiet charm in the short time that she had been there. Her grades at Hunter had been good enough to transfer most of her classes toward her degree requirements at Tuskegee, so she had finished the program in only three years.

She had visited Kristin's mother often during that time, and she had insisted that Celeste call her "grandma" too, since she was Trazi's sister. Celeste felt her welcoming energy every time she went to her house for a visit. It had given her a needed boost more than once, as she worked toward meeting one of her tough project deadlines. That, along with her blueberry muffins, broccoli casserole, and famous macaroni and cheese that was absolutely to *die* for, had seen her through. Celeste had made a point of stopping by her house for dinner at least once, every couple of months.

She had still worried about her father from time-to-time too, what with her being so far away from Washington and all. She had hoped that coming down for the weekend would be a nice getaway for him from the long hours he still worked. But he had been on his soapbox since he drove through the main gates; outraged, he kept telling her, by what he called a "callous disregard for the preservation of African American history." He had been very upset in seeing the way that the town had declined over the past few decades, and even faster in the short time Celeste had been there. It was a major distraction for him from everything else for a while, including her graduation. He kept saying over and over how everything had stayed nearly the same in Tuskegee for over one hundred years; only recently had the small town's culture taken such a turn for the worse. He pointed out several buildings around the once-pristine campus grounds that had been allowed to literally rot away—and one of them directly across from the *Architecture* Department.

"It's just outrageous!" He had concluded to anyone who would listen. "Didn't anybody consider that there might be some value in teaching our students the historic preservation of buildings?!"

His questions had sometimes been answered by other alums; someone who happened to be within earshot, and who commiserated with her father and shared in his frustrations. At other times, he had engaged in heated conversations with passersby, who were of a different opinion and believed that the new buildings around campus more than made up for those that hadn't survived. A lively interchange would usually follow as each person shared their thoughts on what constituted progress at the university.

But there was one thing that they had all agreed on, every time—that Tuskegee's rich heritage must be preserved for each generation to come, at all costs. At one point in history, the small town was one of the few places in the entire country where Blacks had been free to pursue their potential, and in a safe environment. All, while being located only thirty or so miles from the old Confederate Capital in Montgomery.

Her father had complained all through dinner the night before graduation that the campus had been given an updated look with no thought about landmarks that were destroyed in the process. It was missing too much of the familiar like the "Little Theatre" and The Fountain, where he kept saying her graduation *should* be held. And her father had been completely devastated after finding out the tree that he kept calling "the wine tree" had been cut down, with all traces of its existence removed. That had sent him on a tirade that morphed into a big discussion about how Tuskegee had changed from the way things had been in the early '70s. He struck up the conversation with a couple sitting at the next table over from theirs in the restaurant. They had come to Tuskegee a few years after her father, mother, and Aunt Kristin had all left.

Everyone was in agreement about the damage done with the disconnect between the school and the community. The consensus was that no one was paying attention to that any more. Celeste understood what they meant because she had noticed it in her interactions with some of the people in the community, people who didn't appear to work on campus or go to school there. Many seemed not to feel any connection with the university at all; the opposite of what it had apparently once been, according to her father and the people at the other table. Many of them flew football banners on their cars for now-integrated universities that had once excluded Black students. It didn't made much sense to Celeste, especially given the demographics of the town. And according to what she had been taught in her orientation classes, it was clearly not something Lewis Adams or Booker Washington intended.

Her father had been agitated all throughout dinner, but as they walked out of Dorothy's Restaurant in the hotel, he seemed to remember finally why he was in Tuskegee in the first place. But Celeste didn't mind; she had been much too excited that her aunt Kristin would be there to see her march into the Chappie James arena with her graduating class. She would have to leave again only a few hours after the ceremony to catch an evening flight out of Atlanta. It was one of the other reasons Celeste had been so anxious to locate her family.

She hadn't missed how quickly her father's mood had changed as soon as her aunt called to say that she had arrived. It made Celeste wonder once again whether her mother had ever noticed the subtle undertones that vibrated between her father and Aunt Kristin. The older she grew, the more Celeste became aware of it—that something changed in the air whenever the two of them were in the same room. She had never felt disloyal to her mother about it either, that she wasn't bothered by what she sensed between the two. Her feelings for Kristin had always been strong and they ran very deep. Their relationship had seemed as natural to Celeste as the one that she had with her father, and one that she might have had with her mother one day, if they had only been given the chance.

Since she hadn't had much luck in the direction she had been going, Celeste abruptly circled back to check the other side of the gym for her family. She maneuvered her way through the crowds, walking behind a small group of graduates until they stopped short to take pictures with friends. They completely blocked her path and after making a quick mental calculation, Celeste detoured sharply toward the right to go around them. She walked though a small opening that formed between another group of graduates that she faced as she walked in that direction. Then she stopped dead in her tracks. There, standing right in front of her was Ishmael, and she could barely believe what she was seeing,

She felt a strong urge to turn quickly and go back in the direction that she had come, but she was paralyzed by the shock of seeing him so unexpectedly. She was unable to move as she had been the day she had walked in on him and Kendra. Suddenly, he turned his head slightly to look her way as though she had called his name. Ishmael had discovered her before she could move away, and now it was too late.

"Celeste!" He shouted out the greeting as he moved quickly toward her.

"What are you doing here?" A wide grin spread across his face as he realized how foolish his question was; she was standing in front of him dressed in her cap and gown. It had been all he could think of to say on such short notice, and he knew that he had to say *something* after he caught up to her. He was as flustered as she apparently was, after running into him like that out of the blue.

"Well, I would think it should be obvious, Ishmael." In her nervousness, her tone had been much sharper than she intended, and she immediately regretted the response. All the while, she was thinking about what Aunt Kristin had told her before she left for Tuskegee. She told Celeste that she was subject to see literally *anyone* in the small town and sure enough, she was right. There was Ishmael standing right in front of her!

Her aunt had rattled off the names of several celebrities that she had found herself in close proximity with while she was a student; people who had come to Tuskegee as guest speakers, performers, or as visitors.

"...And with your father being president of the Student Government Association, we were invited to all the ritzy affairs on campus," she told her. "The list of people visiting the school on any given day could range from local schoolchildren, to heads-of-state, to high ranking officials from all over the world. Your father and I were introduced to top leaders of several countries; to kings, and movie stars, and quite a few wealthy CEO's. All sorts of people would come there to visit the school, the Carver Museum, the Legacy Museum, and the Tuskegee Airmen Museum. We were always invited to some VIP reception or another that the administration was sponsored."

Celeste had already met some pretty interesting people in Tuskegee herself, in the few years that she had been there. But never in a million years had she expected to see *Ishmael!*

It was all so unfair too; she had gone through so much trouble to get away from him. She had upset her entire life; transferring to a school in another state away from her father and her friend, Malaya—all because she thought it would be the one place that she would *never* see him. She could feel her heart racing as it had been doing from the second she spotted him in the crowded room. As he moved even closer, she hoped that her thumping chest wouldn't betray the cool exterior she struggled to show. Her heart was pounding so hard that she feared he would be able to hear it over the crowds.

"What are *you* doing here?" She countered finally, managing to tone down the sharpness in her voice.

"My cousin graduated from the vet school today." His explanation was short. It didn't clear up any of the mystery surrounding how they had been brought together, face-to-face, again.

"Oh...." Her response was brief too, and in a tone that she hoped sounded nonchalant.

"I guess congratulations are in order." Ishmael started a new conversation thread quickly. He was conscious of the longer-than-normal silence that had followed her response. He had hoped she might say more, and now he scrambled to think of something that would keep her from walking away from him again. He could tell that was exactly what she planned to do next; she was already looking past him for some way to exit gracefully.

"Thanks," she answered finally, focusing her attention back to the love-of-her-life-gone-bad, who had materialized again so suddenly.

Then, she added, "I guess congratulations are in order for you *too*." The last part came out a little fast, and once again she regretted the tone that her words had been wrapped around. She had hoped to sound casual and decided to give it one last try, when her comment to him went unanswered.

"So, did you and Kendra have a little boy or a girl?" As she asked the question, she braced herself for the answer, already feeling the pain of hearing it no matter which answer Ishmael gave.

"Oh... That's right..." He mumbled after another pause. A quick look of confusion had briefly crossed his face. He continued talking slowly, after looking down first and then back into Celeste's face.

"...I guess you wouldn't have had any way of knowing..."

"Knowing what?" She had no idea what Ishmael might say.

"...that Kendra and I never got married," he said finally. "She lost the baby, Celeste, so there was really no point after that."

It was *his* turn to immediately regret the words. He hoped that he hadn't seemed too callous in the way that he had just blurted it out. He did care about Kendra; he had known her since they were in high school. But he had also tried everything he could think of to find Celeste after everything happened; when they lost the baby, and especially after he realized she had left Washington.

He forced himself under control. He didn't want her to think that he was some kind of jackass, now that he had finally found her again. But he could see that she was searching the crowded gym again, probably looking for her family. He knew she was also looking for the first opportunity to dash away from him, and he was just as eager to keep her with him.

'What did he just say?' Celeste's face transformed into a deep frown as she struggled to process Ishmael's words. She couldn't be certain of what she had heard because of all the noise in the auditorium. The celebration going on around them had become even louder, as more people connected with the graduates they came to support.

"I'm sorry to hear that," she finally managed. Then, immediately felt hypocritical because she wasn't sure if she was sorry at all. She could feel the deep love she had for Ishmael straining to break itself free again, to reveal itself so that they could pick up where they had left off. But everything was happening much too fast for her.

"I hope it wasn't too hard on Kendra," she heard herself say, after taking a deep sigh. At least she was certain that she was sincere about that.

"It was a little difficult at first, I think." Ishmael was encouraged that Celeste was still standing with him—that she had started a new conversation thread all on her own, He certainly wouldn't blame her if she did decide to leave but he was hoping for a chance to convince her that he wasn't some insensitive Neanderthal.

"We really haven't talked, not since a few days after everything happened," he admitted.

'What was wrong with him?! Why would he say something like that?' He thought better of the comment as soon as it had left his mouth.

"I've just been buried up to my neck with this internship," he added quickly, as though Celeste had asked him for a better explanation. He then realized what he was saying sounded just as heartless as the other remark.

"...Considering the circumstances, I mean. I just didn't think it was a good idea to have her think..." Thankfully, he finally caught himself before he could dig an even deeper hole.

"...Anyhow, I'll be starting my residency soon, and I had a few days off. At the last minute, I just decided to switch my schedule around and come down to help my little cousin celebrate. I've always heard so much about Tuskegee...

"...It was a spur of the moment decision, really; I've been so busy." He kept right on talking, hoping he wouldn't say something that would make her want to leave.

"I had no idea you had transferred here," he started again, stating the obvious. He took a chance and stared into her dark eyes, knowing he shouldn't have done it but unable to help himself. It had taken months to get the image of her eyes out of his mind.

"Well, I've been here for three years." Celeste was still stunned that she was standing there have a casual conversation with him. One minute she had been ecstatic about getting her architecture degree; the next minute, she had fallen right back into her painful past. She looked away from Ishmael quickly and then beyond, finally spotting Kristin, her brother and father in the distance.

It had taken so much time before the heartache of their breakup started to fade; or at least she thought it had faded until she walked right into him. It had taken years before she could push the memory of him standing with his arms around Kendra, from her mind. Tuskegee had been an excellent diversion but now she was forced to realize it had only given her the illusion of being over him. Time had stood still for her in the small town; she had been so busy with her classes, her design projects, and settling into Tuskegee that she hadn't given much thought to her love life after the first few months she was there.

But Celeste couldn't ignore the feelings that she obviously still had for him. They were far too powerful for her to deny, not standing there face-to-face with him, as she was. She had done everything she could to forget about him, but in one instant she could feel him stretched across the center of her heart again, where he had been from the moment they met.

And it was that realization that nearly scared her to death.

"I see my folks over there...I've gotta go." She said it quickly, before he had a chance to say anything more.

"It was nice seeing you again," she called back over her shoulder, giving him something to latch onto. She was already moving in the direction of her family, all smiles as they hurried toward her with their congratulations.

"Celeste!" Ishmael called after her. "Can I call you some time?" His voice was full of hope.

She turned around and stared at him for a second, as though contemplating it. Then she turned back around and continued walking away from him as fast as she could, without saying a word.

Chapter 18

Butter and Honey Shall They Eat

(2007)

*K*ristin stood near a small service area unobserved and looked out onto the crowded ballroom. She was pleased that everyone seemed to be enjoying themselves, and the dishes that their chefs had prepared for the occasion. Candidly, she watched as smaller groups of people talked intently to other guests they had met just that morning, or perhaps at the airport as they all arrived. They would stop their engaged conversations only long enough to sample the delicacies that were being offered by young male waiters in formal dress. The young men zigzagged carefully around the colorfully decorated room, as they were instructed, offering tempting deserts on small sampling platters that they gracefully balanced on larger trays.

A long buffet table had been set perpendicular to the speaker platform on one side; it was filled with an array of eye-catching entrees that the staff was replenishing frequently. Nearly everyone had visited the table at least once during the past hour, as near as she could tell. They brought a variety of appetizing, albeit unfamiliar, dishes back to their assigned tables to enjoy. She knew that most of them had little idea that meat substitutes had been used in preparing the food, and anything that couldn't be positively identified as fish, was strictly vegan.

The feast had mainly been prepared using vegetables grown at Exodus Village. No eggs, dairy products, or non-seafood animal protein was used to make anything their guests were being served. Kristin smiled to herself, satisfied that no one seemed to miss the animal products that their food was lacking. Their chefs and nutritionists had been perfecting the dishes for years, first using feedback from their staff, and later from construction crews who had built the village. They adjusted their recipes carefully over

211

time, studying comments that had been left by their pseudo-guinea pigs after meals. Later, their chefs relied on feedback from their residents to tweak the dishes to final perfection. A blend of savory West African seasonings were used in preparing much of the food they ate, and many dishes were made with soy or moringa leaves as a primary ingredient. Not only did the delectable main courses taste good, but their guests were unknowingly loading their bodies with tons of nutrition at the same time. That element had been one of the key requirements that the Foundation set for any food they would provide to their residents. It had to help them either gain or maintain good health, at least for the five-year period that they would live in Exodus Village.

Kristin quickly scanned the room for Kioni and found him off in a corner talking to someone from the hotel staff. No doubt, he was confirming the details of an event for their now-extended weekend of activities. They had been exactly on schedule as they broke ground for their new cookie plant, and a much smaller celebration had marked the occasion. The production plant for *God's Sunshine Cookies* had taken a year and a half to complete, and they had started the complicated process of staffing it as soon as they broke ground. Along with the new plant, commercial construction was added to the growing list of on-the-job training slots now available to their residents. That would open up many more opportunities when the time came for them to compete with the general population for jobs. And those opportunities would only increase as their Foundation expanded and continued building plants all over the country.

A large number of their graduates had already been hired to work at the new plant, although the majority of positions were reserved for native Ghanaians. They would always have preferential treatment for jobs that the Foundation created in the country. Currently, the greatest number of slots were being held for local Ashanti residents; those living closest to the plant and whose salaries would benefit the surrounding communities most.

Exodus Village had graduated nearly three thousand residents in the preceding years, and they were now full-fledged Ghanaian citizens. With the exception of only a few, they had retained their U.S. nationality too, as had many African Americans who moved to Ghana independently. There were certain advantages in having dual citizenship, with convenience of travel being top among them. Having valid passports that were issued by both countries made visits to friends and relatives in the States a much easier process when they arrived at airports on both ends of the trip. That prompted most residents to select that option during their graduation ceremonies. Getting a travel visa otherwise was a very competitive process; there had always been strict limits on the number of visas the U. S. issued to the nationals of Ghana and other West African countries, at any given time. Choosing to travel without a U.S. passport to the States would make things unnecessarily difficult for them at best. It was that, rather than a hesitancy to adopt Ghana as their new home that was the motivating factor for keeping it. And by re-entering the country using their Ghanaian passports, they could omit having to renew visas periodically when they traveled.

Their residents had been largely welcomed into the communities they chose to live in after leaving Exodus Village, although there had been some minor protests when their pilot group of residents first arrived. After that, the country had accepted them with open arms, for the most part; mainly, she thought, because of the efforts made to reassure native Ghanaians of their intentions. They went to great lengths to make clear that their commitment to the country went much further than the agreements they had negotiated with national government ministers. The Exodus Foundation had also taken strong measures to ensure that its policies would never, in any way, resemble the aggressive antagonistic behavior of the Liberian settlement of African Americans; the first group to migrate home.

That settlement had been sponsored by the American Colonization Society, or ACS, and had been established only after the group forcefully took the land that it was built on from the native inhabitants, and rightful owners. Formally known as the Society for the Colonization of Free People of Color of America, when it was founded in 1816, the ACS had been a very complex organization, to say the least. Its membership ranged from slave owners, to freed slaves, to abolitionists and national government leaders; all brought together by a common thread—a collective desire to return former indentured servants and freed slaves back to Africa.

Slave owners had been highly motivated to rid the country of these "African Americans." They had been increasingly inciting insurrections among the still-enslaved, after their own freedom had been won. The plantation owners feared the influence that this group would continue to have on men like Gabriel Prosser, an enslaved blacksmith who planned a large-scale rebellion in the Richmond Virginia area, in the summer of 1800. His plans had only been thwarted when an informant from his group stepped forward, and revealed the plans to white authorities. Prosser and his twenty-five co-conspirators had been hanged, of course, when they were captured, but the fear generated by knowing how close his well-thought-out plans had come to being carried out left many white Virginians feeling quite unsettled.

Those who had paid to have large numbers of slaves work their plantations were willing to spend large sums to protect their "investments," while abolitionists were intent on ending the practice of slavery altogether. There had been government leaders involved on both sides of the equation, but the financial contributions of the slave owners eventually won out. More and more of them bought membership into the ACS and their money was well-spent.

It bought them leadership and control of the newly formed organization, and the ACS-led brutality in Liberia was instituted as a result. The organization contracted white governors to rule the country during its first twenty years of existence, and there were many decades of violence that took hold as the people who were native to the country defended their homeland. The violence continued for well over a century, until the original peoples' mistreatment became so well-known as to prompt a League of Nations' investigation. That organization, which had been a forerunner to the United Nations, responded to the urgings of many groups to look into their allegations. They found many abuses including the indigenous people of Liberia being sold as contract labor as late as 1927.

In sharp contrast, the relationship between the Exodus Foundation and the people of Ghana had been vastly different. Most noteworthy was the fact that the land Exodus Village had been built on was a gift from the Asante people. Through the use of sensitivity training, any cultural barriers that might have otherwise led to discord were being easily mitigated. Their village existed in harmony with the rest of the Ashanti region, and Heavenly Travel, the company that Kristin and Solomon formed when she had first moved to Ghana, had paved the way for that acceptance. Through its ever-expanding altruistic programs, their travel agency still gave back to the villages where it conducted its business on a regular basis, making it a welcome addition wherever they chose to set up shop in the country.

And as it turned out, the Exodus Foundation had been able to provide jobs to the people in the surrounding region in even greater numbers than originally anticipated, far beyond the mandatory set-asides they had negotiated with the national government. Their latest project, *God's Sunshine Cookies,* was already a big hit. The schoolchildren from neighboring towns had been selected as their test market, and they had fallen in love with the lightly sweetened snack right away. Its popularity quickly spread around the region since the cookies were also filling, and they provided an excellent source of nutrition as an added bonus. The mothers near their village appreciated having the inexpensive snacks on hand to give their children, and so far, the venture had been a win-win situation for all concerned.

Kristin watched Kioni use his hands to emphasize words to the young man he spoke with, making certain that the intent of his instructions were clearly understood. He had been quick to adapt to the local culture, as had his wife, Dina, and their young son, Abraham. Dina had been an unexpected bonus to having Kioni come on board with the Exodus Foundation. As soon as her family had settled into their new home, Dina assumed the role of volunteer coordinator for the village. She now helped their staff produce all the special events that were held at Exodus Village and her position had grown quickly into a full-time job. Dina and Kioni both had played vital roles in their operations in the nearly eight years they had been with her in Ghana.

By the time her star-student from Hunter tracked her down, Kristin had learned not to be surprised by any of the miracles that her life was filled with. Kioni's call had come just as she was concluding they would need to add a new layer to the Foundation's structure. They needed to ensure that all the individual segments of their mission were well coordinated, as they continued to taken on more of their objectives. At that point in time, she was no longer startled when the Universe provided her with exactly what was needed at the time that she needed it. Now, she merely trust that it would always would be the case.

Her confidence in that trust had been bolstered when she learn of the direct translation of Jesus' instructions to his disciples, as he taught them how to pray. The same affirmation of faith that he bestowed on them was now always near the surface of Kristin's mind. When translated directly from the Aramaic language that Jesus spoke, into English, a particular verse from the Lord's Prayer now reminded her of her constant connection to God. It was where her needs would always be met and she now realized that one fact was all she would ever need. The prayer that Jesus taught his followers had put everyone on an equal footing, because he taught them to begin prayer with the words, "*Our* Father."

And, whenever she stopped to consider the direct translation of the verse: '*You give us our needful bread from day to day,*' she felt an instant reassurance in her soul. The King James' translation of the same scripture, on the other hand— '*Give us this day our daily bread,*' was a very sharp contrast in her mind. That interpretation always conjured up images of her demanding stockpiles of a certain level, which by its very definition defied having the faith that her needs would always be met. She had memorized the verses of the Lord's Prayer as a child, growing up in Tuskegee's Emmanuel Baptist Church. It was only later that she found out how much had been lost in the translation that she had first learned. Or, that the ancient dialect that Jesus, his disciples, and the scribes who recorded the scriptures all spoke, was still widely spoken in that area of the world today. The Aramaic language continues to be the native tongue of most people in that region of the Middle East, which was also the physical location for many stories she had read in the Bible.

King James' "version" had been released as the first English translation of the bible in 1611, taking a very colorful route in getting there. The original Aramaic texts had been first converted into a Chaldean dialect, the language that evolved after the confusion of the Tower of Babel. That was during the time that Persian King Nebuchadnezzar had taken control of the region, and ultimately brought the Israelites into captivity as his slaves. It had been years later before that first adaptation was translated again; first into Hebrew, then Greek, and finally into Latin, before King James directed the release of an English translation. A modified Latin Vulgate was used as the basis for the New Testament translation. Even still, the energy of enlightenment from the original scriptures was still so powerful that the King James version still retained much of it, despite its dubious evolution.

But it was the direct translation from Aramaic into English that went deeper into Kristin's spirit, and she felt comforted by it instantly when she first discovered its meaning. She would chant the affirmation from the Lord's Prayer silently to herself, whenever thoughts about the Foundation's needs went beyond her ability to visualize how they would be met. She found that if she didn't, a crease would soon form on her brow as her uncertain thoughts raised concerns about the future. That verse helped her center herself in the present once again; the only place where her connection with God existed. It was there that the path was always clear for manifesting whatever it was that she desired.

Kioni's call had come "right out of the blue," just as she began to realize she would need someone who thought like him to assume responsibility for Exodus Village. A day before his call came, she had happened across the paper he had written for one of the last classes that she taught at Hunter University. She had initially found the paper a few months earlier, during a hunt for something else entirely. It had been stuffed between a stack of personal documents and the second time she came across it, she stopped what she had been doing and immediately sat down to read it.

At the time that he turned in the paper, her schedule had been jammed packed with things that she needed to have done before winding up her affairs in the United States to leave for Ghana. On an impulse, she had given him a final grade of 'A' without actually reading the paper that he turned in. Instead, she had based his grade on all the others papers he had written in her previous classes. It was something that had never crossed her mind to do before, and the only reason that she had done it was because she was so desperate to file her grades at the registrar's office,so she could finally be free to turn her attention elsewhere.

She had found his paper in the same folder where she had also found business cards given to her by some of her other Hunter students, who had set up the tax structure for the Exodus Foundation before their pilot program got under way. She remembered putting Kioni's paper into the folder to bring with her to read later, and she had apparently thrown the business cards in the same folder as she finished up her packing.

She had a vision of him on the morning that he called her about Lawana and her family. This time, she had seen him implementing their policies at Exodus Village. Several of points he had made in his essay influenced her thinking about board policies that had been under consideration during the same time. As she continued reading it, the thought crossed her mind that he would make a perfect addition to their team.

She had continued thinking about that vision as she transcribed notes from their conversation to send to Amina's staff, for follow-up on Lawana's application. Her continued discussions with him about the children's travel status had left plenty of time for her to share some details of the Foundation's activities, as well. Finally, it became clear to both of them that Kioni was the piece of the puzzle that the Foundation had been missing. He came onboard only a year after their pilot residents arrived, although he still maintained control over an engineering firm that he had started back in Maryland. He still took regular trips back to the States each year to keep an eye on his business, which also gave him an opportunity to network with engineers who might be later recruited as technical resources for the Foundation's future projects.

For the first year and a half, Kioni had been assigned to be Amina's assistant, which gave him maximum exposure to the Foundation in the shortest possible time. He had learned a great deal more about the politics of the country at the same time, and as soon as they were all confident that he was ready, Amina began transferring areas of responsibility over to him. Eventually, Kioni assumed the role of Chief Administrator at Exodus Village, with authority over anything directly related to the "underbelly."

Amina retained control over all matters of general involvement in the region, and the Foundation's cultural and legal relationship with the national government. They each had a staggering amount of responsibility resting on their shoulders, but Kristin was certain they were both up to the task. She had only become more impressed with Amina over the years, especially as she realized how challenging it would have been to operate the philanthropic mission of Heavenly Travel without her. That had directly translated into support and acceptance for Exodus Village, and much of their success had been attributed to Amina's knowledge and good judgment. Kristin had come to rely on it heavily during her negotiations involving sensitive matters; Amina had a knack of interpreting Ghana's complicated rules of protocol in a way that she could understand. She had always relied on her heavily; she was one of the few people that Kristin trusted to put the underbelly's interests above all else, and make certain that their needs would always take precedence in what the Foundation was doing.

She felt a similar certainty about Kioni as well, that she could rely on him to do whatever was necessary to keep their village running smoothly. In addition, they each played advisory roles on the projects that came under the other's responsibilities. The three of them had worked together like a well-oiled machine since the year 2000 when Kioni first moved his family to Ghana. She had sensed his commitment in reading all the papers he had written for her classes. She felt his compassion for the underbelly in what he wrote, and she had seen it in action as he went about his duties in Exodus village. It was confirmation for her that at least one of the seeds she had planted in the minds of her students at Hunter, had taken on a solid root. As she watched him grow into his role with the Foundation, she couldn't have been more satisfied. He and Amina provided the steady operational leadership that would permit her to turn her focus toward the second phase of the Exodus Foundation's mission that would begin shortly.

'Who would've ever imagined it?'

The thought kept circling her mind, as Kristin watched smaller groups of people gravitate toward each other on the ballroom floor. Most of their guests were up mingling now and participating in excited conversations. They were getting to know one another as she had hoped they would.

Many of them had traveled thousands of miles in response to their brunch invitation, so she wanted to reward them as much as possible for their unexpected show of support. No sooner had they sent out invitations than they realized a much larger group of people actually planned to attend the brunch, than they anticipated. More than eighty percent of the invitations had gone out with the purpose of providing a courtesy announcement to their key supporters about their new plant. But the rapid rate in which the R.S.V.P.'s had immediately begin to pour in made them realize a different venue would need to be selected.

Their original plan had been to hold a smaller event to celebrate the occasion at their spa resort on Lake Bosumtwe. The only other activity planned at the time, aside from the brunch itself, had been an on-site tour of the *God's Sunshine Cookies* plant, and that had been scheduled for the same afternoon. They had planned to make use of Heavenly Travel's luxury buses to shuttle guests back and forth between the two facilities. The proximity of their resort to Manhyia Palace had also made it convenient for the Asantehene, should he decide to attend. Their plan would have been perfect had their guest count remained below sixty, but it was soon obvious that many more planned to attend. A new venue had to be selected and there were matters of protocol that were brought to center stage, especially in light of the short notice.

Solomon had been immediately dispatched to the king's court to bring the news; he began by offering his apologies, on Kristin's behalf, that the Asantehene's official quarters at Exodus Village were yet to be completed. Because of that, they had been presented with a delicate situation and a few suspenseful days, as they waited for the court to respond. During that time, they had been unsure whether they would have to push the entire celebration back for a few weeks, the minimal time they estimated that the builders would take to finish the king's villa, complete with furnishings. In that case, they would have been able to hold all the events that evolved with their expanded guest count at Exodus Village.

Everyone had been quietly relieved when the king, speaking through his okyeame, or linguist, graciously declined all except the brunch invitation. With that resolved, they were finally back in business, although they had to quickly shift all their planned activities to Heavenly Travel's resort hotel near Accra. There were sufficient accommodations there for the king, as well as all their activities. It had taken a great deal of coordination for everything to go off without a hitch, but so far it had.

Seeing Amina and Kioni spring into action once the new venue selection was finalized, made Kristin feel even more confident that they would be capable of running everything without her, if need be. So much was she convinced, that not one detail relating to the change of venue had ever crossed her mind.

※※※

She stepped forward and onto a raised platform after Kioni caught her attention and gave her a discreet signal. She moved quickly toward the podium, barely able to contain her excitement as she prepared to address the crowded room. There were two flags set on either side of the platform; one bearing the black and white Adinkra symbol of cooperation and inter-dependence that had been chosen as the Exodus Foundation's emblem, and the other bearing the symbol for transformation that she had chosen to represent Exodus Village. In the middle stood the bright red, yellow, and green horizontal stripes of the Ghanaian national flag, with a black star emblazoned in the center of its yellow stripe. The flag had been created when the country won its independence from Britain in 1957; the red symbolized the blood that was shed during the country's revolution; the yellow, its mineral wealth, especially its gold; and the green symbolized Ghana's fertility and its lush vegetation. All three flags waved intermittently in response to a gentle breeze coming from the vents built adjacent to the front ballroom walls, in a steady flow.

As part of her presentation, Kristin would highlight some of the success stories they had been documenting from the experiences of their first graduates. The pilot group had been on their own for several years now and their second and third generation graduates were also living on their own, as well. Many had moved to different regions of the country, including the Northern region with its majority Muslim population. Their guests would be able to see some of the Foundation's other successes for themselves, during the events and tours that had been added to the weekend's celebration.

Heavenly Travel had taken full advantage of the unexpected response to their brunch invitation; they offered special extended-stay packages to those who were in the country for the first time. She and Solomon had guessed right in thinking that the long flight across the Atlantic would encourage those who had the time, to stay longer and see other parts of the country while they were there. Many of their guests had arranged to stay for at least another week so they could get as much out of their trip as possible.

"Akwaaba!" Kristin hailed her guests warmly as she took the microphone in her hands. She greeted them in the language of the Asante, the Twi speaking sub-division of the Akan nation. They comprised the largest ethnic population in Ghana, and their residents and volunteers were all taught beginning Twi, as part of their cultural orientation.

"Welcome!" She smiled, and greeted her guests in English this time, responding to their warm round of applause.

"Akwaaba!...Welcome everyone, and good morning!" She repeated the greeting as the applause gradually began to die down.

"Please..." She urged modestly, motioning with both hands. "Thank you very much everyone...Please, take your seats."

She waited a few seconds more to give those who were still standing time to move back to their assigned tables. Kristin wore a long colorful silk robe with gold threads that glistened, as light was reflected onto it from a dazzling crystal chandelier that hung from the ceiling. A scarf fashioned from the same material was woven throughout her locs that she had swept up and pinned in a formal style on top of her head.

"On behalf of his majesty, the King of Asante," she bowed briefly in direction of the Asantehene, "I welcome you." She looked back toward her audience and after a few seconds of acknowledgement, she then nodded in the direction of the President's sitting area.

"On behalf of the President of Ghana, I thank you for coming. And as Paramount Chief of Exodus Village, I would like to express to you how honored we are that you have joined us today on this very special occasion."

Kristin paused again until a new round of applause began to die down. The title had been given her in her position as CEO of the Exodus Foundation and Exodus Village, although Kioni was officially its chief administrator.

"Everyone, please, if you would," she continued finally. "I would like for you to take a moment to look around at the other guests who have joined you here today. I have been thrilled this morning in observing the sense of camaraderie among you, but now if you notice someone that you have not had an opportunity to greet, I would urge you to take the time to introduce yourself during the course of the next few days."

"You have much more in common than you might imagine, "she added after a pause. "One such commonality is the way in which you have all reached out to our foundation in some significant way. Everyone here has made a commitment to the Diasporan Exodus Foundation's mission, either through your generous financial contributions, your talents, or some other crucial component of our success.

"And more importantly," she went on, "you have *fulfilled* that commitment. I stand in gratitude today, thanking each of you for your help in making our first project in Ghana the remarkable success that it has been. So, please, give yourselves another big round of applause," she urged. "And make sure that you applaud the person sitting next to you, as well."

With that she placed the microphone down and took a few steps away from the podium to clap enthusiastically along with her guests. After she moved back, she had to wait another few seconds before the thunderous applause in the ballroom finally died down.

"I am grateful to have been given an opportunity to personally thank each one of you for your contributions, and that is indeed my goal for this weekend. I thank you for believing in the dreams of our foundation, and I would especially like to thank the largest donor on-record since our first residents began arriving. We have just been blessed with this gift in the last week, but all we have been told about its origin is that it was from an association of professional African American athletes and entertainers, and that the group prefers to remain anonymous. While I am respectful of your wishes, we would still want you to know how *grateful* we are for your very generous donation.

"Thanks to all of you," she told the room full of supporters, with arms extended, "the dreams of nearly eight thousand Black Americans have already been realized. Many of them had little hope before they started out on their journey with us. The dreams of many volunteers have been realized here as well, as they have been given an unexpected opportunity to connect with the Motherland, as they had once hoped they would do.

"We launched our six month pilot program nearly eight years ago, and we are pleased to report that we have accepted one hundred new families each year since that time. They have come to us twice a year from the United States and the Caribbean aboard our ship, the *Black Star,* which bears the name of the ship line that Marcus Garvey had planned to use for the same purpose. Our *Black Star* has made a total of fourteen voyages across the Atlantic, bringing us on average five hundred new residents with each trip. In doing so, we have finally begun to realize the visions that were held by many others before us—people like Paul Cuffee, the mixed-race Mormon abolitionist and shipowner, who had been a forerunner in his attempts to return the African Diaspora in the early 1800s; people like Chief Alfred Sam, the Ghanaian businessman who likely inspired Garvey in his early 1900s attempt to return African Americans to West Africa; and the dream of perhaps the most well-known Jamaican Pan-Africanist, Marcus Garvey himself.

"Our ship travels in the reverse route that was taken across the Middle Passage of the Atlantic Ocean, a route that was used by far too often and by far too many ships during the hundreds of years of the African slave trade." A brief round of applause interrupted Kristin again for a few seconds.

"Our residents here are guided through a succession of programs, both as individuals and as family units. These programs include education, counseling, and on-the-job work experience that has helped prepare them to support themselves at the end of their stay. During our graduation ceremonies, the special citizenship status that each of our residents is extended when they first arrive, is then suspended. Their Exodus Village passports are collected and in its place they are issued their new Ghanaian passport as full citizens. The U.S. passports that we safeguard for them during the five years that they are with us, are returned to them as well, and many have officially chosen the option of having dual citizenship at that time."

Kristin went on with a brief overview of how Exodus Village operated, taking them through the process of receiving applications, how they are considered, and their methods for determining the order of names on the wait-lists they maintain. She also described the process they used for skills assessment; for assigning residents to one of three principal program components that conform to their relocation goals; and requirements that their residents contribute to the communities in which they live. Finally, she gave them details about the relocation status of one family from each of their three graduating classes, as a personalized example of their graduates' successes.

"Our residents are free to pursue their choice of interests at our village, but they are held to meticulous standards," she informed their guests. "They are also held to rigorous social principles, as well, with zero tolerance for things we consider to be unacceptable public dress, like the style that young men in the States have adopted, of wearing their pants to hang down nearly to their knees.

"Our schools are top notched here and our school-aged children are thriving. They are required to wear uniforms at all times that are assigned according to age group. It's an easy way to identify someone who might be out of place at any time. Our children who excel academically are assigned as tutors or mentors to other children, and much of our social focus here is placed on relationship building.

"Life inside our village encourages human interactions, and our success is partially dependent on our ability to maintain a controlled social environment. Our objective is to keep our residents focused on the temporary nature of their residency with us, and that is the primary reason for the systematic moves they are required to make each year. Each move is timed in conjunction with our ship's arrival on January 1st, when we celebrate the Emancipation Proclamation as African American Independence Day. The following day, timed moves take place and each family is moved to a new community.

"The homes in our first community, Marcus Garvey, start out with a much smaller square footage than the residences in our last two communities," she noted. "There is much less closet space in that first community too, which encourages residents to only unpack those items that are essential during their first year." She explained that the Foundation maintained storage units for the rest of the personal belongings that they are permitted to bring with them, or to have shipped later. They are free to remove whatever they want from their units once they have moved into their third community, where the accommodations are much larger.

"The environment in Marcus Garvey community is generally much more nurturing," she added. "We intentionally spoon-feed our new residents and their mentor-counselors, who remain with them during the entire five years they are with us. The first move they make at the start of their second year is into the William Jackson Community, named for the former slave who spied for the Union Army during the Civil War, when Confederate battle strategies were discussed openly in front of him. Residents are assigned a different group of Ghanaian families to assist them in the Jackson community, and they are not nearly as doting as those they probably came to rely on in our first readjustment community. These new resident-managers *are* technically available to them if they need help with some specific issue, but our residents are forced to ask for the help rather than have it provided to them automatically.

"Their next move is into the Rosa Parks community at the beginning of their third year in Exodus Village. That's when their mentor-counselors begin working with them more intensely on their specific plans for sustaining themselves after they graduate. Residents can take whatever they want of their things in their storage units, as I mentioned earlier, and they are also paid for the regular service that all residents provide to the community they live in, beginning with Rosa Parks. But they are only paid in Village dollars, I'm afraid, so the money they make is only good in Exodus Village."

She waited for the laughter to subside before she continued. "They are also required to pay rent for the first time in this third community, using the same currency. They are also given opportunities to earn extra village dollars in a number of different ways. At that point, we also encourage them to start a savings plan in anticipation of their graduation.

"From Rosa Parks, they move into Malcolm X Community; and their next move before they leave us is into Martin Luther King, Jr. Community, at the beginning of their fifth and final year. The restrictions that we impose on them while living in the first three communities are gradually relaxed once they move into Malcolm X. And during their last six months as residents of Exodus Village, they are governed solely by the customary local laws outside the village that they will have to abide by after they leave us.

"By that time, their resettlement plans should be firmly in place, for the most part, and they should be prepared to implement it after graduation. We do provide them with continuing support however, after they leave us, through consultations with their mentors and relocation assistance, including a monthly stipend for six months. Our graduates are free to do whatever they want to do after they graduate, of course, but we feel a continued responsibility toward helping them to succeed even after that. Before they leave us, they can exchange any village dollars they still have remaining in their accounts for cedis, which is the national currency. Because they have opportunities to earn money, it's quite possible for them to leave our village with a nice nest-egg that will help them in their new start.

"We try to make our residents' experiences as pleasant as possible during their time with us," she told their guests, "we want it to be an enjoyable environment to live in. You will notice when you visit the village tomorrow that we have re-introduced the notion of childhood innocence there to our American ex-patriots, and our elderly are fully protected and taken care of. Our young adults are encouraged to participate in many wholesome activities that we provide for them, and as a result, we believe that they are all very happy to be with us. They often tell us that they feel safe in Exodus Village and loved, many for the first time in their lives."

"But, there are some rules that we have in place that have not been as popular, especially with our young single residents," Kristin added after a pause. "We also discourage family expansions and begin those talks as soon as we receive an application—mainly because of space issues. And unfortunately, an unplanned teen pregnancy within the first two years requires that the entire family be removed from the program, temporarily. After we learn the identity of the father, that person's family is also subject to the same actions, in the case of a teenage dad. Neither teen is allowed to return to Exodus Village until the young couple is either properly married, or evidence is provided to show that the young man has otherwise "done the right thing," which includes care for the young woman for a minimum of two years after the birth. But if we find that the father is twenty-one years old or older, and the mother is a teen, then that man may well be turned over to the Ghanaian authorities, depending on the circumstances."

There were audible gasps in the room after Kristin's remark.

"I can assure you that our purpose here is not to dictate morality," she hastened to add, "but as anyone who has experienced a teen pregnancy can tell you, the event can be quite a distraction from the family's goals. I was also reminded by our board during one of our many discussions on the subject, that the last thing we want to do is to unknowingly transplant America's welfare dependency problem to Ghana.

"But I'm happy to report that our mandatory history and cultural enrichment classes seem to be playing a positive role in reshaping the attitudes that some of our residents have when they arrive. We seem to be making a huge impact in reversing the emotion-less attitude about sex in general that has become so prevalent in America. We are helping to dispel the notion of sex as a recreational activity here, with only functioning body parts considered as a prerequisite for engaging in it.

"We rely heavily on the Fruit of Islam, the FOI, to enforce our abstinence requirements for single residents. They have been quite effective in doing so, and we have FOI observation booths stationed throughout each community. They are equipped with security cameras that help minimize the number of violations that might occur. Since our communities are so closely knit, everyone quickly learns their neighbors too. They know who belongs where and they are encouraged to report any offences to the FOI.

"But we do permit and even encourage official dating in Exodus Village—we only require that the couple be chaperoned by our resident managers. Teen dating is also permitted after the age of sixteen, but only after both teens have completed their respective rites of passage programs. We encourage long engagements here, and again that's only because of the logistics involved in arranging for new households outside the normal move-in process. And, extensive counseling is required, at any rate, before a marriage license is granted."

There was another buzz around the room, as guests offered or listened to others' opinions about the social restrictions at Exodus Village.

"Can I please have your attention for just a moment longer. I promise, I have only one last thing, before I let you get back to your conversations..." She said it with an air of mystery.

"As many of you know, Heavenly Travel, the agency I co-own with my business partner, Solomon Esau, has always had an altruistic mission. It is closely aligned with the mission of the Exodus Foundation, though it has always remained a separate entity.

"There were projections made early on about the expected growth in tourism here that would be directly related to our operations. These estimates have proven to be very modest, however, because Heavenly Travel has seen a tremendous growth in business since we welcomed our first residents in 1999. This increase has far exceeded our expectations, and as more and more African American families move to Ghana, we have also encouraged them to invite their friends and families to visit them. We even encourage them to have their loved ones stay over briefly at Exodus Village, though there are strict procedures that must be followed.

"At any rate, as a result, I am very happy to announce that after years of growth, Heavenly Travel has recently purchased a first-rate three thousand passenger cruise liner, from friends in the Middle East who are supportive of our mission. Our unbelievably generous purchase price was contingent on the travel agency donating its space and time in support of the Exodus Foundation's needs, specifically in transporting our new residents to Ghana. Right now, as I speak, the cruise liner is already making its way toward Jamaica with our newest group of residents on board."

A new round of applause greeted Kristin warmly.

"We visualize our new ship as being a means of opening up even more avenues of tourism here. We have received a significant number of inquires over the years about providing an alternative means of travel to Ghana, and it has convinced us that there was a market for those who want to visit Africa but who may choose not to fly across the Atlantic. Therefore, we will soon add a transatlantic cruise to our travel agency's offerings. Our plan is to use the revenue from our travel clients to help fund the future homecoming trips of our new residents.

"And, we have christened our new ship the *Diasporan Black Star,*"

227

she continued. "After a final inspection in Jamaica, it will soon begin its maiden voyage across the Atlantic Ocean. When it docks in Elmina for the first time, there will be a specially constructed pier waiting to lead our new residents through a symbolic Door of Return into Ghana."

A thunderous applause spontaneously broke out again in the ballroom. Everyone rose to their feet, cheering and clapping loudly for several minutes. As Kristin looked out at the audience, she was pleased to see that one of her greatest hopes had been realized, that their supporters begin to take ownership of the Foundation's mission.

"We are extremely proud to be able to add this symbolic ritual to our welcoming ceremony," she continued when she could be heard, "and we believe it will further illuminate the ties that have always bound the Diaspora to the African continent. The *Diasporan Black Star* is scheduled to dock in Elmina during mid-mornings only," she added. "After walking through the Door of Return, our new residents will now be transported to Exodus Stadium, our multi-purpose facility that was built by Heavenly Travel last year. These welcoming ceremonies will now be largely made possible through donations by the anonymous African American association that I mentioned to you earlier.

"Beginning with the first time that the *Diasporan Black Star* docks in Elmina, our new residents will be presented to the paramount chief of that region at Exodus Stadium. He will be joined by an entourage of lesser chiefs from nearby villages, who will greet our new residents and welcome them home to Ghana. They will be given their first true taste of Ghanaian culture there too, with a buffet lunch provided in grand style. The hosting village will lead the celebration that will include ceremonial dances, and a special libation will be poured in honor of our new residents' ancestors.

"It's a remarkable ceremony that I hope you will have an opportunity to witness some day," she added. "At the conclusion of it, our residents will be directed to their pre-assigned buses and brought to their new housing assignments in the Marcus Garvey community." Their guests applauded again, appearing to be moved by her announcements.

"On this joyous occasion," she told them finally, when they had settled down once again, "we mark the beginning of Phase II of our operations—providing support to the Ghanaian economy. On Monday morning, the very first shift of *God's Sunshine Cookies* will begin work promptly at seven o'clock, with a ribbon cutting ceremony immediately preceding that time. As you tour the plant, you will be given opportunities to sample our first line of delicious cookies and you will also get to taste the new flavors that we plan to roll out over the next two years.

"In addition to the tours that we have planned, we also have great entertainment in store for you, as well. We hope that you will enjoy your stay with us as much as we enjoy having you, and we hope that you will return to visit us again and again."

With that Kristin's speech ended, and she moved down from the podium to continue greeting their guests personally.

The rest of the extended weekend went off without a hitch and they received many positive comments from guests who toured Exodus Village and had a chance to talk to residents themselves. Overall, Kristin felt very satisfied with the way things had gone, as she stood in front of the administration building to see off the last of their guests. They had all boarded buses back to the airport, except for those who opted to stay in Ghana for an extended visit, and were scheduled on flights out of the country the following week.

Kristin had plans to catch a flight out herself in another few days. With their new plant celebration out of the way, she was finally free to concentrate on packing for her trip to the States. She had several meetings set up with prospective African American financiers, whom she planned to convince to come on board as backers for the construction of their next commercial plants.

Not surprisingly, there were thoughts of Winston that also popped into her head when her mind grew idle during her packing. They had barely spoken to each other since Angela's death, and she had avoided him as much as possible when she went home for Celeste's graduation. She had far too much on her plate to allow herself to become distracted by her ex-husband on that trip, but she had planned to take a little time for herself this time around.

She found herself wondering whether the time had finally come for her and Winston to face their past.

Chapter 19

The Love We Had Stays On My Mind

*W*inston examined his daughter's profile for the umpteen time, as she concentrated on a slow patch of traffic ahead. He looked for some sign of what she might be thinking, since he had been so careful to hide his own true feelings about their weekend plans. He was curious to know just how successful he had been in concealing them.

'*Fat chance,*' he thought, suddenly realizing that what he had first taken as a smile on Celeste's face, was actually a smirk. It had been there from the point that he had climbed into her car with his bags, making a somewhat weak attempt to appear indifferent about their weekend trip to Maryland. Now he knew that his ploy had been totally ineffective from the beginning.

He had known Kristin was back in the country long before Celeste called to tell him. Everyone knew she was back; the Exodus project had been making national and international headlines for years and he was very proud of her foundation's success. He could still remember their conversations about going to Africa back when they were students at Tuskegee. They had dreamed of taking a trip to West Africa together someday, and he smiled to himself as he remembered how her dark eyes had sparkled at the mere thought of going.

But Kristin's vision for the Exodus Foundation had far surpassed their youthful dreams. She had created a plan that would eventually change the lives of millions, and would have a great effect on millions more. She had found a way to build on the unrealized dreams of those who had come before her, of making it possible for the African Diaspora in America and the Caribbean to return home. The plan she had devised to make it all happen was brilliant, he thought, and the Exodus Foundation had become a powerful vehicle for transformation over the years. Many people now looked to the Foundation for their salvation, and still, the only thing required of them was a genuine desire and a willingness to go through their relocation programs.

At the same time, the Foundation's projects had also helped Ghana advance to a clear position of leadership in Africa again; it had been a win-win situation for both sides of the Atlantic. The world was finally getting a glimpse of how Mother Africa might have evolved naturally over time, had her most valuable resource, her people, not been taken from her and scattered across the Earth.

Her foundation had been doing an exceptional job of inspiring and supporting those who wanted to make radical changes in their lives, the way they were intended. There had been thousands, who had once felt trapped and without any hope at all, who were now following a solid path to a positive and productive future. Kristin had spent the last decade proving to anyone who had once claimed her dreams to be impossible that they were dead wrong. Winston was very proud of her, and he was glad that he would finally have a chance to tell her.

She had been somewhat distant during Celeste's graduation weekend, and they hadn't been able to talk at all in Tuskegee. But that had been an awkward day for both of them, seeing each other for the first time since Angela died. This time, they would have the whole weekend together; they could take things slow and say just what was needed to be said.

He shifted his hip in the well-worn bucket seat of her old Saab, as his daughter headed the car east on Route 50 toward Annapolis. She had been talking nonstop since he got into the car, and he could tell that she was just as excited to see Kristin again as he was.

A few minutes later, he felt a pang of sudden nervousness about their reunion. He had much to say to her and he hoped he would have the chance to say it this time. So much had happened between them over the past twenty-five years, and he wouldn't blame her at all if she wasn't receptive to what he had to say, at first. He had already decided that he would be patient with her, if that's what it took. He hadn't been ready to admit it before, but somewhere in the back of his mind he had always known that his marriage to Charlotte wasn't right—even as they were saying their vows. He had always known in his heart that he was still in love with Kristin. He had been too concerned about how it would look to his kids, that's all, especially to Celeste. He also, hadn't exactly relished the idea of having to face his mother's disapproval either. But she had passed too, so now that was no longer an issue.

But even more than that, he had never been able to face his own guilt about cheating on Angela. And he didn't want his daughter to grow up thinking that he had never loved her mother. He *had* loved Angela once—just never as much as Kristin. He had only done what he thought was best for everyone. He tried to put Kristin out of his mind, but it wasn't nearly as simple as he had once thought. He had never loved *any* woman as much as he loved his first wife and it had taken him all this time to realize it. He was ready to tell her exactly how he felt now; he wanted to tell the whole world.

Trazi had always seemed to know that they had never stopped loving each other, and he guessed now that was the reason his son was so upset with him when he married Charlotte. He knew for sure that his son would be happy to have his parents back together again, and for a few minutes he considered bringing the subject up with Celeste as they drove along. The old Winston would have done it in a heartbeat without giving any consideration to how Kristin might feel about it. But he had decided the conversation with his daughter could wait until after the two of them had a chance to talk. They could decide together when they would tell the children their good news.

He focused his attention back on his daughter, who was still babbling on about something and only God knew what. She and Kristin had always been closer than she had ever been to her own mother. From what he could see, Celeste was elated that she had made a special point of inviting him to join them for the weekend too. And judging by how fast she was driving, he thought it safe to assume that his daughter would approve of them getting back together too.

※※※

Kristin had lined up several meetings with potential African American investors for her trip and the first of them was scheduled for Annapolis. Her board members had voted to support her in soliciting joint venture partnerships in the U.S. and Ghana, as a means of expanding their commercial operations. Her goal for this trip was to convince as many investors as possible to come on board with them, offering them incentives and with very favorable terms in exchange for the working capital that they needed to construct new plants. She was prepared to offer as much as forty percent of their net profits to all their venture partners, collectively. It was a formula that had worked well for them in the Ashanti region during the past few years, and she expected to have similar results as they expanded to other regions of the country. The Foundation's ten percent profit share would be cycled back into paying their ongoing administrative costs for their commercial enterprises. All the remaining profits would be used for the direct benefit of the people living closest to their plants.

Their next phase was planned for the Central Region of Ghana and they had already identified land where their new village was to be built. This time, they wanted their first commercial plant in the region to be operational within the first year, which would give the graduates of Exodus Village - Ashanti an additional opportunity for employment until the residents of the new village started graduating. After their second settlement was firmly established, there were plans to build a third village in the Volta region, on a stretch of land that once belonged to the Ewe people, near Ho.

A non-negotiable requirement was built into all the investment offers they made, namely that the joint venture company formed would sponsor a labor advocacy group that the Exodus Foundation would oversee. The group would be tasked with protecting the rights of their employees, who would be awarded ownership shares in the company after five years of continuous employment, with additional shares after the completion of each five-years.

There had been stipulations placed on how profits allotted to the surrounding communities would be spent. It was to be used almost exclusively to build new schools, resurface and build new roads, establish medical clinics, and other similar projects that would directly affect the people living near the plant. Thousands of jobs had been created in the Ashanti region after their soy and moringa farms became fully operational. Their commercial manufacturing was in full swing there too, including their solar businesses. Many more local businesses had sprung up in support of employees for each new plant, and those businesses had created even more opportunities for the members of the community-at-large.

Kristin had been able to build in a few days of personal time onto this trip, just as she had hoped. She had left Ghana a few days earlier than her business meetings required and the first stop on her agenda had been to her realtor's office. There were closing papers that still awaited her signature to complete the sale of the house she had once owned in D.C. Exodus Village had been built off the beaten path in Ghana. There were no daily

DHL pickups there, unlike in Accra, Kumasi, and other urban cities on the international carrier's regular route. The young couple who bought the house loved it as much as Kristin had though, so they had been patiently renting it until she made time to come to the States again to make the sale official. She had flown into Dulles Airport, where she picked up a car that she would ultimately drive to her friend's house in Maryland. After scribbling her name on several pages, the property was legally deeded to the couple. Next, she drove a short distance from there to drop in on another old friend. She and Niyla had known each other since their freshman year at Tuskegee, and although they didn't talk nearly as much as they once had, they had the kind of friendship that could be easily picked up after years of inattention. There was plenty for them to catch up on too, and it had been well into the afternoon before Kristin got up to leave.

She had felt herself gradually begin to tense as she came closer to completing the thirty-mile drive from Dulles into D.C. She breathed a sigh of relief only after clearing the heaviest traffic on I-295, when she was finally headed northeast toward Route 50. On an impulse, she had decided to stop in on Heavenly Travel's new corporate offices, a few miles south of her turnoff onto the Baltimore-Washington Parkway. Her last visit to the office had been prior to this relocation north of Washington, into a much larger space. She pulled into the parking lot of the stand-alone building and was pleased by first impressions after walking through the door of the tasteful suite. She was greeted warmly by a young female receptionist who had no idea who she was and her mind was put at ease by their interaction.

Their travel agency still played a large role in supporting their Foundation's mission, especially with the new cruise liner in operation that would bring their new residents to Ghana. The agency had developed several exciting travel packages over the years but its specialty was still geared toward the children of the Diaspora, and primarily their African American client-base. They had received some fantastic feedback on their latest itineraries, so far too. They all provided direct contact with the people of Ghana, as their tours had always done. It gave their clients an opportunity to participate in local ceremonies and festivals, in addition to a host of other activities that catered to their stated interests. As a result, their tours had remained very popular over the years and were still being embraced by their clients as deeply pleasurable experiences. Heavenly Travel still depended on word-of-mouth referrals in keeping their business successful. Kristin was well aware that those referrals were often directly related to the image that their staff in the U.S. office presented. It was literally "the face" of their company, with its body operating in their Ghana offices.

When she finally introduced herself to the receptionist after a few minutes of conversation, the young woman became flustered on realizing she had been chatting it up with a part-owner of the company. Kristin made a point of letting everyone there know how much their work was appreciated in Ghana. She had spent the rest of her time talking with the office manager, who had been hired since the last time she dropped in for a visit, over coffee and rolls. She had developed a habit of making personal visits in their early years of operation; only back then, she had been able to drop in much more frequently. Her unexpected visits had paid off for her time and time again. Sometimes, it had earned bonuses for outstanding employees; and at other times, it had set into motion the help that was needed for some employee to move on and into a different space.

As soon as Kristin found out that her first meeting would be in Annapolis, her thoughts had been immediately drawn to a nearby beach cottage that belonged to an old friend. It was built in the charming, privately owned community of Highland Beach in Maryland, and was less than six miles south of the restaurant where she was to meet her potential investor. The well-attended cottage had been in her friend's family for over a century, and it sat right on Chesapeake Bay. Highland Beach had been founded in 1893, the first African American community to be incorporated in the state of Maryland.

She still had fantastic memories from her first visit to the community. She had been a guest of her good friend and graduate classmate, after Winston volunteered to take care of Trazi so she could get away for a long weekend. Their final exams had just ended, and the peaceful Ann Arundel County beach community had been exactly what they all needed. She and another friend had been invited there to recover from their weeks of cramming for final exams and defending the substance of their Master's thesis.

The community was founded by Major Charles Douglass, the son of noted statesman and abolitionist, Frederick Douglass. Charles and his brother Lewis had served proudly as members of the Massachusetts 54th Colored Troop, during the Civil War. But after the war ended, Charles is said to have been refused service at a popular waterside restaurant in Annapolis. The insult apparently prompted him to purchase forty-four acres of tree-lined beach front property, a short time later. He built Twin Oaks as a summerhouse for his father, but the elder Douglass never lived long enough to see it to completion.

Charles established Highland Beach as a resort community after his father's death. It attracted some of America's earliest and most privileged African Americans, and it continues to do so even to this day. Kristin had been fascinated that her friend could trace her ancestry back for over a century, even before the start of the Civil War. She was the first black person that she had met who knew such information about their family, at least until she had moved to Ghana. Her classmate had inherited the house from her grandmother, and she shared stories with them that weekend that had been told to her as a child. There had been many famous visitors that her great-grandparents' entertained in the house, it seemed, including Paul Lawrence Dunbar, Booker T. Washington, and E. Franklin Frazier—all of whom had owned vacation property on Highland Beach at one time.

Kristin had often been fascinated by the bits of colorful African American history she always picked up in and around Annapolis, even before she knew anything about Highland Beach's existence. There had been hundreds of thousands of African slaves sold at the port-side auctions on the bay and they were transported into the Deep South and other areas of the country. Amazingly, there had also been many free African descendants who worked at the Naval Academy and the city docks during the same time—even as business thrived at the auction blocks.

Many of the African descendants who lived in that section of America had been brought to the country as indentured servants. They were freed after a specified period of time and their second generation of descendants had been born free and many had never been enslaved. They shared a similar experience as the African descendants who had lived freely in areas of Florida during slavery. They earned their living in the same way as other free men—as tradesmen and business owners. They had lived as free men as whites did in America, and that was centuries before the Emancipation Proclamation was signed.

Kristin looked over some notes that she had scribbled for her first meeting and reviewed the investor's file. She was depending on the time that she would have on the bay shore to help her unwind and recover from her jet lag. She wanted to be on top of her game during that first meeting, and she had suggested that they meet near the restaurant where Charles Douglass was said to have been turned away. She thought that it would add the perfect climate for her presentation about the Exodus Foundation's mission over dinner, being reminded of the young Douglass' plight and his reaction to it so many years before.

The other two meetings were both scheduled for Chicago, and from there she would have to leave the States immediately bound for the United Kingdom. She had been invited to attend a ceremony there to mark the 200th anniversary of the law banning slave trading by British citizens. From there, she would fly directly back to Ghana, and soon be back on her tight schedule once inside the country again. That had become the norm for her after their official launch of Exodus Village, and had revived itself now that they were at the beginning of phase two of operations.

But she had been determined that she would also make time for Celeste on the front end of this trip to the States. It was her way of making up for having to leave Tuskegee so soon after her graduation ceremony ended— shameless, but it really couldn't be helped at the time.

It came as no surprise to her that she would start thinking about Winston again out of the blue. The secret she had kept from him all those years had never been far away from her mind for long; it would resurface from time to time without any warning or any way for her to stop it. On an impulse, she had decided it was time for her and Winston to have the conversation she had put off having for almost twenty-five years. The feelings that she had about it had continued to haunt her, and it happened at the most inopportune times. She was determined to find a way to let all of it go; both the loss of their baby, and her guilt about never having told Winston anything about it.

She had begun having second thoughts almost as soon as she suggested to Celeste that she bring him to Maryland with her, when she drove up for the weekend. His daughter had been all over it so quickly that there was no turning back once the words were out of her mouth. In a way, she was still glad that he was coming despite all her anxieties. It would finally force things to a head between them, and it was definitely high time for that to happen. It had to be dealt with so she could rid herself of the distractions that it still caused her, after all those years.

Solomon had consistently kept up his habit of introducing her to a variety of handsome and eligible men at every opportunity, since she first moved to Ghana. They were all men who were either wealthy, politically connected, or both, and who had much to offer any woman. None of them had held her interest for very long, but she had recently surprised herself by having a genuine spark of interest in her friend's latest match for her. At least she had thought there was an interest until she heard Winston's voice over the phone. She had listened to the message he left for her several times, and in the blink of an eye she was once again immersed in thoughts about everything other than what she needed to be focused on. She found herself extremely distracted by her ex-husband yet again, and it was only then that she realized how much her past with him had stood in the way of her future.

She had awakened early in the morning after she arrived, and walked to the shoreline for a stroll along the beach; taking in the beauty of the late-summer sunrise coming over the horizon. Afterwards, she sat on the deck that her friend had built some time after her last visit. She lounged on the deck chair and basked in the warm sunshine, allowing her thoughts to drift as she watched the bay come alive. Soon, there were colorful boats that sailed across the water and she could feel the same sense of peace and tranquility that she had felt on her first visit to Highland Beach.

Somewhere in the back of her mind, she knew she would have to call on every ounce of that peace to get her through the conversation she would have with Winston. She had no idea why she had suggested to Celeste that she drive him to Maryland with her. She only wished now that she had thought to invite him up for dinner, sometime later on; perhaps that Sunday afternoon after she and Celeste had time to chat first. She hadn't had a chance to talk with her about Ishmael's sudden reappearance in her life. She had been looking forward to having some girl-talk and finding out what was going on with her on that front.

But she had immediately sensed the eagerness in Winston's voice, when he phoned her to accept the invitation. It had thrown her off completely, even though she had always known in her heart that he still loved her. Her surprise came in the fact that he no longer seemed to want to hide it; that was something that she had never considered that he would do.

Under any other circumstances, she would have been very encouraged by the tone of his voice. After so many years, he was finally giving her a clear signal that a future might be possible for them. She found herself wishing with all of her heart that it was true, that they would be able to get beyond the past once and for all, after everything had been brought out in the open. They could put it all behind them and still have a wonderful future together.

But Kristin already knew that it wouldn't be easy—not by any means.

Chapter 20

It's A Thin Line....

*W*inston chuckled under his breath at the way his daughter kept chatting on and on about anything and everything—except, that is, about Kristin. He couldn't help but notice that her driving skills hadn't improved much either, since the last time he had been a passenger in her car. He became increasingly distracted by her driving; trying not to be obvious, but finding it harder and harder to keep himself from crying out at times.

Celeste maneuvered in and out of the heavy Friday afternoon traffic and for the life of him, he still couldn't remember how it was that she had ended up doing the driving. The muscles in his shoulders were already stiff from bracing himself against the headrest of Kristin's old Saab. After all the years that had gone by, he still hadn't been able to rid himself of the flashbacks from seeing his daughter crash through a wooden fence behind their loft—and in *his* car.

'But that was her first driving lesson,' he reminded himself hopefully, seemingly trying to convince himself. *'And it was a long time ago...'* Winston returned the smile that Celeste flashed after she glanced at him quickly, and he struggled to conceal his mounting anxiety after she turned her attention from the road. He had caught himself digging his feet into the carpet from time to time, bracing himself for what had seemed to be an inevitable crash. It occurred to him that he had been doing such a good job of faking it that Celeste was taking his lack of criticism, as a show of confidence in her driving. She nonchalantly passed every car and truck that she came across on Route 50, as Winston fought against an urge to yell out to her to slow down. The mere mention of her driving skills had been a touchy subject ever since she crashed his SUV, but thankfully, she

239

finally cleared most of the slower traffic that had been heading away from the city, and she started driving at a more even pace all on her own.

She was obviously as excited about seeing Kristin as he was, and he silently prayed that she would get them to Maryland in one piece.

"What's so funny?" Celeste looked over at her father again unawares, and noticed the much wider smile across his face.

"Nothing, sweetie." His response was evasive. "I guess I'm just looking forward to having a relaxing weekend away from the city, that's all."

After another brief interchange, they were both quiet for several minutes, each deep in their own train of thought. As they neared their exit, Celeste broke through the silence. She took a deep breath before announcing her plans to meet up with an old girlfriend from Hunter, later that evening.

"Lisa lives in Annapolis now, but we haven't seen each other in ages." She kept talking about the details of their plans, not bothering to come up with a more elaborate explanation for the absence she was planning.

"We decided to get together for drinks and dinner tonight," she went on quickly. "I told her that I'd probably meet her after work, if we got there in time." All the while, she kept her face glued to the road, not daring to look at her father to see what his reaction might be. They were both silent again for several more minutes.

'Okay, so now I know why she was so keen on driving,' Winston deduced. *'I wonder how long she's been plotting all of this?'*

It was obvious that Celeste had come up with some plan to have him and Kristin wind up alone at the cottage together that night. He knew his daughter well enough to know that it would have been useless at that point to try to persuade her to drop whatever it was that she had planned. At any other time, he would have been furious with her for trying to manipulate his life, and would have at least called her on what she was planning. Now he only looked at his meddling grown-up girl with a big grin on his face. To think that he had been so reluctant all those years; afraid to show his true feelings about Kristin because of the way it might affect Celeste, and what she might think of him because of it.

He was still nervous that she might start digging too deeply later, which was her usual mode of operation. He wasn't ready to have her ask him certain hard questions that he didn't have answers for yet himself—questions about Angela *and* his relationship with Kristin. But he had hopes that by the time the weekend was over, they would be well on their way toward putting their family back together again.

Kristin would still be spending most of her time in Ghana, he knew, but he was sure that wouldn't be an issue for them for long.

The silence in the car continued even after Celeste had veered off Route 50 onto their exit for Highland Beach. And as hard as it was for him to believe, Winston realized his daughter had finally run out of small talk. He, on the other hand, was still lost in his own speculations about what his reunion with Kristin would be like. He allowed himself thoughts about her that had been closed off in his mind for years.

As they got closer to the community, they both stirred in the car and busied themselves looking for the landmark that she had identified for them—Highland Beach Town Hall. According to her directions, they were to make a sharp turn just beyond the small one-story wooden structure that was once home to the community's grounds keeper. Winston was first to spot the sign and Celeste made a quick turn down the narrow roadway that would lead them to the cottage. They followed the rest of Kristin's directions and he could feel his heart beat faster as Celeste finally pulled the car to a stop, in the drive of the house that Kristin had described. It was a beautifully preserved two-story brick framed structure, with a veranda that extended around the right side and ended in the back yard.

Celeste was already out of the car and knocking on the front door before Winston could open the trunk. He could see the two women on the front porch from the corner of his eye, as he pulled out their bags. They were locked in a tight embrace, like a mother and daughter reunited after a lengthy separation. He had begun to feel slightly awkward again by the time he started toward them, and just as he reached the steps Kristin turned to him with a smile on her face that she had no power to dim.

"Come on in, you two." She gave Winston a quick hug that seemed to surprise them both, and then she quickly moved aside so that he could bring the bags in and deposit them inside the narrow doorway.

"How was traffic?" The question wasn't directed at either of them in particular. "I'm glad you guys made it safely, because I know what Route 50 can be like during rush hour—and especially on a Friday."

Celeste led the way inside the house and Winston made a quick face when her back was turned to show Kristin how frazzled his nerves were. His confidence was boosted yet another notch by the second smile she gave him, and from the warm hug that he could still feel on his chest.

His daughter turned around quickly and barely missed the face that he was making, but she did catch the smiling glances that passed between

241

them. She smiled to herself as she turned back around, thinking, '... *executing Plan B might not be that hard, after all.'*

She had called her friend Lisa a few days earlier and told her about the plan she had been cooking up. She had already arranged to spend the night at her friend's apartment, if things developed between her father and Kristin as she hoped.

"What's so funny?" She wanted to know as she turned toward them again, suddenly suspicious of their smiles.

They all laughed nervously in response to her question, although neither made an attempt to answer it.

Kristin felt herself blush involuntarily when she became conscious of how close she had been standing to Winston. That same familiar easiness between them was still there, even after almost thirty years—it was just as it had always been. It was hard for her not to notice how handsome he still was too, standing there against the backdrop of family antiques and heirlooms displayed in the spacious foyer. Apparently, he had been working out again and it took all that she could muster not to stare at his bulging arms, draped loosely in the multi-hued fabric of his linen shirt. She knew his habits well, so she could tell right away that he had paid particular attention to his dress before coming up to see her.

She moved ahead of Celeste quickly to put distance in between them, and called back over her shoulder for the two to follow her on a quick tour of the cottage. Its furnishings were even nicer as they moved further into the living space. Kristin told them that the house had been constructed in 1898, just five years after Douglass had founded the community. She pointed out several framed portraits of family members who had lived in the three-bedroom cottage at the time that it was first constructed.

For the most part, the house was decorated in vintage pieces that had been purchased by its original owners. There was a museum-like quality about the cottage, but it was functional at the same time. Celeste had been immediately drawn to a colorful piece of framed mud cloth from Ghana, and several other pieces of African art that Kristin's friend had added to the décor more recently. Her new pieces had been interspersed between the classical oil paintings that her family bought during different eras of the cottage's history. The blend of African art and early American paintings came together in a style that was quite alluring, and Winston and Celeste were both impressed by the blended results. At some point along the way, Celeste managed to get ahead of Kristin again on their tour, in her eagerness to examine the architecture of the house more closely.

Kristin had already made up the two smaller bedrooms and had placed bouquets of fresh flowers on the antique dressers in each room. A massive oak bed framed the centerpiece of the master bedroom, and it also consumed much of the floor space. It wasn't until after she looked up and saw Winston standing so close to the bed that she realized how similar it was to the one they had slept in when they were married—and that she had continued to sleep in until she moved to Ghana. They had shared many intimate jokes about their need for having such a large bed, and it had been bought as their first major purchase after they finished school in Tuskegee and moved to D.C. Somehow, they would always start on one end of the bed but would end up on the other; unaware that they were moving in the distraction of their intense lovemaking. Neither of them were comfortable in looking at the bed directly, as they walked through the room to continue the rest of the tour.

The master suite included a large sunken tub in an adjacent bathroom, with a bidet that was constructed of ivory and Italian marble. There was a somewhat smaller bathroom that connected the two small bedrooms, and was designed in black Italian marble, as well. Kristin pointed out that the tubs and basins in both bathrooms had been painstakingly restored, and they each had their original claw feet still intact. All the floors of the cottage were covered in a carefully polished hardwood, except for flooring in the newly renovated gourmet kitchen, with its rustic porcelain squares to match a similarly patterned back splash. Kristin told them that the sliding glass doors beyond the kitchen had been installed during the late 1960s. It gave the family more direct access to the back yard, to the newly constructed deck, and the cobbled pathway that led from the center of the yard, through a patch of tall sea grass, down to the shore.

Celeste was impressed by the way that the original design of the cottage had been preserved during its modernization. The contractors had used vintage materials as much as possible, making it difficult for the untrained eye to detect where the renovations began. The overall impression left was that the original structure had remained completely untouched over the years. After they had come full circle and found themselves back in the front sitting room, where they joined in on a brief tirade about the lack of preservation of the historic buildings in Tuskegee. They were all aggravated that so many buildings the original students had so painstakingly built, after first making the actual bricks themselves, had been allowed to deteriorate without any intervention. The buildings had been left to fall apart over time, without concern about the hard work had gone into constructing them.

"Hey, I hope you guys didn't eat anything before you got on the road." Kristin changed the subject after everyone had a chance to have their say. She remembered how Winston's mood would change if his blood sugar dropped too low. She had fought a loosing battle about it when they were married, always trying to get him to eat more foods with a low glycemic index that would keep his sugar levels balanced throughout the day.

"I ordered quite a bit of seafood for us. It's coming from this place just down the road," she went on, smiling. "It looks like your average dive from the outside but they make the best crab cakes than I have ever tasted—and that's saying quite a bit since we're here in Maryland."

Now it was Celeste and Winston's turn to exchange knowing glances; and soon afterwards, Celeste piped up with her surprise announcement for Kristin. As she filled her in on the plans she had made for the evening with her friend, Winston thought he saw a look of panic flash across Kristin's dark eyes. She had finally grasped that Celeste was planning to leave them alone in the cottage for the night, and why he had never moved their bags away from the front door.

'I don't know why I'm even surprised,' she thought to herself, suddenly overwhelmed by a sense of fear. She tried to suppress the feeling of dread that was welling up in her stomach, just at the prospect of being left alone with Winston.

As soon as he and Charlotte started their divorce proceedings, Celeste had become quite vocal to her about her desire to have them back together again. But it wasn't until after she had heard Winston's voice on the recording a few days earlier that Kristin realized it was something that she wanted too. She hadn't even seen her ex-husband much in the last ten years, except for the brief time they had been forced to be in the same space during Celeste's graduation. She had deliberately avoided him as much as she could that weekend in Tuskegee, without bringing too much attention to herself.

Now she realized she really wanted a reconciliation with him badly, but what she had to tell him might very well get in the way of that. She knew that it was quite possible that her news would keep them from *ever* being together again. She had expected that his reaction would be explosive at first, and had hoped that having Celeste in the house would lessen the potential fallout. She figured that after they had made a leisurely meal of the delicious seafood that would soon be delivered, they could relax over a few drinks first to set the mood. She thought that might make things easier for her later, and since they both loved the water so much, she had planned for them to take a long stroll by the bay so they could really talk.

She had counted on having Celeste nearby to act as a buffer in either case, and especially if things didn't go as well as she had hoped. She wasn't at all prepared for the sudden turn of events that would leave her alone with Winston for the night. Her dread quickly turned to a sense of foreboding as she realized it was now inevitable that her secret be revealed. Winston could probably already see that there was something she was hiding, and nothing would prevent him from finding out the truth. He knew her all too well and she wouldn't be able to conceal it from him any longer; even if she tried.

It was obvious now that Celeste had given her plan a great deal of thought too, because she was already moving toward the front door. She scooped up the overnight bag that her father had left on the floor in one move.

"Oh, I almost forgot...I have some photos in here from Tuskegee that I brought to show Lisa." She said it unconvincingly, and didn't seem to care. "Wow—I had no idea it was so late."

Celeste turned around to face Kristin and her father after checking her watch for the time. Kristin was staring at her as though she were in shock.

"Well, I guess I'll just pull them out after I get to her place." She hurriedly finished her tall tale, as she turned back toward the open door. She had moved too fast for Kristin to react. She and Winston both stood paralyzed as they stared after her, like two deer caught in the headlights of a car.

"So, I guess I'll call you guys later, okay?" The words floated back over her shoulder as she made her way out the door. "Just so you'll know I got there alright," she added.

And by that time she was only a few feet away from the car, with keys in hand. Kristin followed her in a daze to the front door but before she could think of anything to say, still, Celeste was already in the car and backing out of the drive.

※※※

"Well... So I guess subtleness was never her strong suite." Winston quipped dryly behind her, after his daughter was out of the drive. He wanted to say something that would break through the awkward silence that had been left in the wake of her hasty departure.

Kristin was still standing next to the front door with her back toward him, but knew she had no choice except to turn around. She started remembering bits and pieces of the carefully rehearsed speech she had thought up during her walk down the shore that morning. The words floated through her mind in random sequence and she had no idea where she should begin. She had been thrown off guard so completely, thanks to Celeste, especially when she knew how upset Winston would be by what she had to say.

"Would you like a glass of wine?" She hoped her voice hadn't sounded as frantic as she felt. "The food should be here any minute now. I hope you brought your appetite with you because it looks like there's going to be plenty now."

She had still managed to avoid looking directly at Winston. Once again, she was having second thoughts about whether it was the right time at all to have the conversation she had planned to have with him. Maybe none of it was a good idea.

"Winston, I...," She managed a start, but wasn't given a chance to say much else. He closed the distance that had separated them almost as fast as Celeste went out the front door. Her reaction wasn't quick enough again and before she knew it, he was holding onto her so tight that she could barely breathe.

"Winston, please, I..." She tried again. Her mind was telling her that she needed to break away from him, but her body was telling her just the opposite.

"Shhhh...," He rejected her protests gently. "Let's not talk yet.." He pleaded with her in a hoarse voice. "Let's just be together first, Baby Girl—we can talk later."

He was nuzzling the back of her neck now and Kristin was thrown into a complete tailspin.

"Oh my God..." She struggled to slow the beat of her heart. She hadn't prepared herself for any of this. What had she been thinking?!

Winston had called her by that name when they were students in Tuskegee. For some reason, hearing him call her that had always made her weak in the knees. He hadn't called her "Baby Girl" in over twenty-five years—that's how long it had been since he had wanted to seduce her. She had forgotten that she was never much of a match for him when he was in that frame of mind. All sorts of thoughts about the good times they had once had together began to flood her mind; it all took her back to a time before they had made such a big mess out of their lives. It was all so overwhelming, and Kristin did what she always did when she could find no other suitable outlet for her feelings. Very soon she was crying softly against his shoulder.

"I'm sorry, Baby Girl." He pulled her away so he could look into her face when he heard her quiet sobs. Then he pulled her back toward him and hugged her close again.

"I'm so sorry." Kristin heard him say through her tears, over and over again. She felt herself lean into his broad chest against her will, as he now kissed the top of her forehead. Then he was kissing her face all over—soft angel kisses, slowly at first.

She wanted to pull away from him so they could talk. She knew that was what she *should* do, but she just didn't have the will to do it.

"I know I've been an idiot," he went on, hurriedly, "But please, don't hold that against me now—don't hold it against *us*."

He pulled her away from his chest again to look into her eyes. He had a look of sincerity on his face that made her feel strangely sad, as he gently massaged the tops of her shoulders and arms.

"You always said I was a Neanderthal," he reminded her, jokingly. "And you were right too."

That comment brought a smile to both their faces because Kristin had often called him a Neanderthal when they had fought during their marriage.

"Please forgive me, sweetheart..." He resumed his pleading, encouraged that she had smiled at him yet again. It had been so long since she had smiled at him like that.

"I know how much I hurt you when I married Charlotte, Kristin. And I'm so sorry." He held onto her even tighter when he felt her stiffen at the sound of his third wife's name.

"Baby, I don't know what made me marry her..." He started, and then stopped in the middle of his sentence.

"Wait, that's not true." He corrected himself and looked slightly ashamed, finally releasing her arms. He was determined that he would be completely honest for once in his life. He stared deep into her dark blue eyes to let her see his sincerely. He wanted to clear the air between them once and for all, so they could start over. He had been thinking about it for days. He knew they would both have to be honest about everything if they stood any real chance of rebuilding what they had once had.

"I *do* know why I married her," he confessed slowly. "It was because of Celeste...My daughter needed a mother, and I guess I figured that if I married Charlotte I might be able to forget about you too."

Kristin was now at a loss for words and could only stare at him. She had never dreamed that he would be so honest with her ever, in saying what he had just said so freely. But she still didn't know whether he was ready to hear what she had to tell *him,* or how he would take it for that matter.

Winston was proud of himself for being open but if he were *really* being honest he would have admitted that his sister, Grace, was the one who had finally got him to see what was so obvious to everyone else. She had read him the "*Riot Act,*" deviating only slightly from the intent of the British law that had come into effect in 1715, as a way of controlling its rowdy citizens. His sister had accused him of *using* Kristin to help him raise Celeste. Grace also pointed out that he was still in love with her, and *had* been the whole time they had known each other. She reminded him of the day that he had called her from Tuskegee to tell her that he had just met the girl he was going to marry.

"I was feeling guilty about Angela too." Winston blurted out the rest of his confession to Kristin, growing unsettled when he saw that his openness was still not having the affect he had expected. "I was too ashamed to face my children with the truth too, especially Celeste."

Kristin could barely believe that it was Winston talking. But why now? Why, after all that had happened and all the time that had passed? She had spent years trying to get him out of her system and she had finally begun to have a *real* interest in someone else before she left for the States on her trip, the latest handsome man that Solomon had introduced her to.

"Please try to understand, Kristin," he pleaded, "and please just try to forgive me." He became hesitant again after seeing an emotion briefly cross her face that he did not recognize. He was desperate to get her to smile again but he could see that she was nearly in tears.

"I'm so sorry for all the hell that I've put you through all these years, Baby Girl." He paused, finally, recognizing the look as pain, "...that I've put *us* through." There was an earnest plea for forgiveness in his voice.

Kristin still struggled with herself, unsure of what to do. There was no doubt in her mind what she *wanted* to do. She had loved Winston for most of her life and she was naturally drawn toward him. She had waited such a long time to hear the confessions he was making so easily now, and she could tell how anxious he was to have her respond.

Winston had feared that she might be afraid to trust him again, but he had already made up his mind and vowed to himself that he would be patient. He knew he could win her over, given time; he was confident that he would persuade her to give him a second chance soon enough.

They were standing so close that Kristin could feel his heart pounding against hers. It had been so long since she felt his warm embrace; the way he touched her made it seem as though no time had passed at all. He turned her head gently toward his and leaned down to kiss her with such passion that she actually began to feel light-headed. She knew that she should stop him, but he was the love of her life and she had always been powerless to resist him.

A small stream of tears began to flow down her cheeks again, yet undetected. Kristin knew that she had to tell him about the baby; she couldn't just leave what she had to say to him unsaid. She had to tell him *everything*. That was the only way they would ever stand a chance of getting things back to the way they had once been between them—to the day before the day that she had watched him walk right out of their marriage.

And she knew that if she didn't do it now, she never would. It would be something that would always hang invisibly between them, and over time, he would feel it too. He would know that she was keeping something from him and those feelings would only grow stronger until he was eventually hurt by them. It would gradually erode the trust that they had managed to hang onto, even with everything else that had happened between them.

Kristin loved him too much *not* to tell him, so she gathered every ounce of strength she had to pull away from him. He looked puzzled at first, and then hurt. He started to say something else but she cut him off before he could speak.

"Winston, please..." She pleaded. "You have to listen. You know that I've always loved you and that's never changed. I doubt that it ever will.

"But there's something that I have to tell you first..." She had said it finally, and she just let the words hang in mid-air.

Her mind was in a race to find the right words to say to him. She tried to remember the speech that she had prepared when she walked by the shore that morning. She had opened the door to their past now and there would be no turning back until it had been properly dealt with.

"I want to be with you too." She whispered hoarsely, searching his face with pain on her own. "You have no idea how badly I want that...But I have to tell you first."

He had been stroking her arms still with his fingers, making it difficult for her to concentrate on what she was trying to say. It had always taken a long time for her to say what she needed to say to Winston, and she knew that he would soon be aggravated if she didn't just spit it out.

"Please Winston...This is very hard for me." She stepped back from him, her words stopping him cold. She could still feel the heat of his hands on her arms from when he massaged them. His hands fell abruptly to his sides

249

when she moved away.

"Can we just sit down and talk?"

And right on cue, the doorbell rang. They both looked out the front window to see a skinny Black teenager standing on the porch in an oversized tee shirt and jeans. He was holding a large box that was packed with Styrofoam containers filled with food. Kristin wiped back a stray tear on her way to the door.

The rich aroma of food drifted out of the box as the young man brought it in and put it on the kitchen counter. The smells reminded Winston that he hadn't eaten anything since breakfast that morning, and he had worked right through lunch so they could get an early start. He had a client meeting scheduled for the following Monday morning so he had organized himself for the meeting before he and Celeste left D.C. Work was the last thing he planned to have on his mind that weekend.

He watched Kristin search through her purse for money after waving away his offer of a credit card. After she had paid for the food and the young man left, she moved around the kitchen quickly placing everything they would need on the table. She tried to make her actions seem as close to normal as possible, given the scene that the delivery guy had just interrupted. She avoided looking into Winston's eyes as she spooned food onto their plates, and during all that time she became even more anxious.

She managed a few weak smiles across the table as they ate—quietly, at first. The energy between them felt stranger than it ever had and she could see that he was quite curious now about what she had to say. He was wondering what it was that could be so important?..And what made her push him away.

Winston's first thought had been that he had waited too long to tell her how he felt. But could it be possible that there was someone else in her life? He quickly dismissed that thought because he didn't think she would invite him to Maryland to tell him that. He was very puzzled by her behavior but he had decided he would be patient. He would wait until she was ready to tell him whatever it was, and in her own time. He felt that he owed her that much.

After a minute or two more, the silence became almost unbearable and Kristin broke through it herself once she was satisfied that Winston had really backed off. She was pleasantly surprised once again by the changes he had made in himself since the last time they were together.

The seafood and all the side orders were just as good as the smells from their containers promised. Gradually, she and Winston relaxed as they ate;

their conversation began to loosen too. They found that they had plenty of other things to talk about—like what was going on with Celeste and Trazi. She and Winston compared notes on both kids, just as they had done when they were much younger. He had never realized before that Kristin's work hadn't kept her from following what was going on in their lives.

And she, on the other hand, as surprised that Winston seemed genuinely fond of Ishmael. Kristin still hadn't met yet, but from what she heard about him from Celeste, she would like him too. They were both glad that she and Ishmael were back together again, especially since Celeste told them she planned to move more slowly with their relationship this time. He had seemed to be a great match for her, but Kristin had always been doubtful whether Winston would consider *any* man good enough for his daughter.

Once they had finished the main course, there was coffee and a piece of apple cake that Kristin baked as she waited for them to arrive. She moved deliberately slow as she cleared the table and put away the leftovers. Winston could tell that she was stalling again, but eventually she joined him on the large, surprisingly comfortable, sofa. She only did it, when she could think of no other reason to be in the kitchen, and she sat as far away from him as possible; a fact that didn't escape his focused attention. He had been struggling to remain open-minded about whatever it was she had to say, but now he had a sinking feeling that it wouldn't be good at all.

Kristin had always found it difficult to look in his face when she knew that he felt hurt—even if they had been fighting and he was hurt by something she said. He was the one man that she knew who had a puppy dog look that would actually affect her. That made it doubly hard for her to start a conversation that she was certain would only cause him pain. '*Did she really have to tell him?'*

"Winston," she began nervously. "Do you remember the day that you and Angela were leaving the hospital with Celeste, after she was first born? We all ran into each other in the hospital parking lot..."

'*What?'* Now Winston was at a complete loss. Kristin had a knack of coming at him from out of nowhere with things, but this time she had outdone herself. Why on Earth would she be bringing up something like that now? And what could it possibly have to do with the two of them?

"*Of course*, I remember, Kristin." He said it a little too quickly, and hoped that he hadn't sounded annoyed.

"It was one of the happiest days of my life—how could I forget? And I remember that you never came by to visit Angela either, not before she and Celeste left the hospital," he reminded her.

"Wait. Is *that* what this is all about?" But even as he was saying it, he knew that was off-base. That explanation didn't fit in at all with her behavior.

"Well, that's part of it..." She was still stalling for time, but she knew that he was growing irritated that she hadn't just come out and said whatever she had to say. She knew how much Winston disliked having people beat around the bush the way she was doing now. And she knew there was no use in stalling either. She had already opened a door that Winston would never allow her to close again, not before he found out exactly what it was all about.

"There's something that I never told you about that day," she started again, after exhaling deeply.

"I had just been discharged from the hospital myself—just a few minutes before I saw you. That's why I never visited Angela..."

"What?" Winston startled her by the simplicity of his question.

"What do you mean?" He asked, after getting no response. He couldn't imagine what to make of what she was saying.

"Please, just let me finish everything," She begged him. "This is very difficult for me to tell you."

"Okay, I'm sorry." He backed up because he knew that if he didn't, she might retreat even further and it would take even *more* time for her to spit out what she was trying to say.

"But I have no idea what you mean, okay, so why don't you just say it?" He urged, trying to remain calm. "What's all the mystery about?"

She held her head in her hands for a few seconds and then forced herself to continue. She could feel Winston's patience wearing thin, despite the attempts he was making to conceal it. She was just so nervous about his reaction to learning the truth that she would tell him, something she had been keeping from him for years.

" I knew it was one of the happiest days of your life too," she agreed finally, ignoring his other questions. "That's *why* I didn't want to tell you."

She heard herself still speaking in riddles but she couldn't seem to control it. "I didn't want to spoil your happiness," she said in the same mysterious tone. "And I couldn't dream of what I would say to dear Angela."

"*Angela*?" Winston asked the question with as much patience as he could muster. "What do you mean, Kristin? What does *Angela* have to do with anything?" Her name instantly brought back a flood of guilty feelings that he had carried around for years.

"She has everything to do with it, really." Kristin blurted out another cryptic response before she could stop herself.

"Do you remember the night we were together at my place?" She had waited until she could gather herself again; until she felt her emotions were under control. "When Angela was pregnant?..."

Winston flashed a smile of recognition, flooded by sudden memories of their passionate night together. But he was still confused by the timing. And what would make her think he would forget something like that?

He had subconsciously relaxed after she mentioned that night. Now, as he looked at her closer he could see that she was shaking. He got up from where he sat on the sofa quickly and moved closer to comfort her.

"Kristin, what on earth...?" He put his arms around her shoulders and tried to draw her nearer.

"No! Winston." She pulled away more forcefully than ever.

"I have to tell you this before I loose my nerve!" She had shouted it, as the pain that had been buried with all the emotional trauma from that day began to quickly rise to the surface.

"Okay. I promise." He stood up and took several steps back.

"But just say it, okay?—Whatever it is!" The pitch of his voice had risen slightly, despite his intentions. His nerves were starting to get the best of him because he still had no idea of what she might be getting at.

Kristin took a deep breath and was silent for a few painful seconds while she held it in.

"We made another baby that night..." She started and then let her voice trail off again as she exhaled.

"What do you mean?" A confused frown had quickly covered his face, even as he realized how ridiculous his question had been. What else *could* she mean? His thoughts began to race wildly. What was she really saying? Was she trying to tell him she had an abortion?"

He tried as best he could to associate some type of time line involving events that had happened decades ago.

But that makes no sense, he concluded, still uncertain. Surely, Kristin hadn't done something like *that*. He let out a big sigh before speaking.

"Why didn't you tell me?" He managed an anguished demand for more of an explanation. He was grateful too that she had allayed his worst fears, with a look she flashed him after reading his mind about the abortion he suspected her of. At least she hadn't done something *deliberately* to hurt their child.

"I couldn't tell you." She wanted desperately to make him understand, but she had no idea how she could when so much time had passed.

"At the time, you could barely stand to even stay in the same room with me. And I knew how you felt about betraying Angela, because I felt the same way."

After their one night of passion together they had both known it wouldn't go any further. The main reason was because Angela was already pregnant with Celeste, and they had both been consumed by guilt.

"But I *wanted* to tell you, more than anything, Winston..." She was suddenly worried again that she had made a big mistake in telling him about the baby at all. All of it had happened so long ago. There was nothing he could do about it now, and nothing to be gained from telling him. Maybe she should never have said anything to him at all.

His eyes narrowed as he searched her face. She was someone he had always thought he knew so well, but now he questioned whether he knew her at all. He would never have believed she was capable of keeping something so important from him, especially for such a long time.

"I decided not tell you about it because everything was already such a big mess." She was desperate for him to understand, and got up to stand near him.

"Angela was having such a hard time with her pregnancy," she reminded him. She started to cry again from all her guilt, remembering how they had betrayed her friend.

"I knew even then that to do the honorable thing meant everything to you, Winston," she said through her tears. "And I also knew you would've been torn apart if you had known about our baby. You would have been consumed by guilt at causing Angela even *more* pain, and I know you would've wanted to do the right thing by me, too.

"It was just an impossible situation," she reached the same conclusion then as she had so many years ago. More tears began to trickle down her face as she relived the trauma that had been a part of her for so long.

"What happened to the baby, Kristin?" It was all Winston could manage to say. The coldness in his voice surprised them both.

"I didn't know *what* to do at first," her tears were flowing freely. She was strangely relived that everything was now out in the open.

"I never *dreamed* of *not* having our baby, though, not for one second; but I knew that I couldn't tell you about her either," she finished in tears.

She stopped for another brief second and took in a deep breath, trying to control the flow of her tears. She walked back to where she had been sitting on the sofa, and her knees buckled slightly as she sat down again.

When she finally looked up at him, his face was still frozen in shock.

"After I had some time to think about it, I decided I would make up a love interest to explain the baby's father," she told a surprised Winston.

"I had planned to start talking about him gradually, and then after a few months I would announce that I was pregnant." She made an audible deep sigh. She felt a great wave of relief after finally removing the weight of the deception that she had carried around for decades.

"I thought I would say that I had broken up with my mystery lover some time later, and then I would just raise the baby on my own..."

"You would've been involved in her life, Winston, " she added plaintively, and to Winston it sounded more like an afterthought.

Kristin was aware of how upset he was on hearing her plans about their baby; she only hoped that he would understand her reasoning, somehow. She got up again to stand by the sliding glass doors and looked out into the back yard toward the bay.

"You just wouldn't have known that the baby was yours, that's all." She still faced the yard. She had really given what she was telling him a lot of thought at the time; but as she said it out loud now, she realized how ridiculous it must have sounded.

"*Her* life?"

When she finally turned to look at him again, she had hoped she would see some degree of empathy for the dilemma she had found herself in. She looked for some sign that he understood why she hadn't told him about it before, a sign that he knew she had only been trying to protect him. But instead of empathy there was a coldness on his face that she had never seen before.

"I was *desperate*, Winston." She turned her head away to avoid looking into his eyes. "It was the best I could think of under the circumstances," she offered.

"It was *your* plan, Kristin!" His voice boomed, forcing her to face the coldness that had caused her to turn away from him.

"What happened to the baby?" He repeated his original question more quietly, as though nothing else she said to him had made a difference.

"What happened to *our* baby."

She had watched his expression change from bewilderment to astonishment, and finally to anger as she told him about the baby that he had known nothing about until that day.

At one point, his expression had taken a definite turn as he struggled to wrap his mind around what she was telling him. As he listened to her talk, he thought about the number of years that he had known her and about all the things that they had gone through together. Never in a million years would he have considered her capable of deceiving him in the way that she had, and that she would have, no doubt, continued doing. All the time he had known her, he had been operating under the assumption that their relationship was based on honesty. He thought he could trust Kristin when he couldn't trust anyone else. But how could an *honest* woman make the kind of decisions she had made without even mentioning it to him?

"I lost the baby, Winston," she sighed again. "I had a miscarriage."

"Our little girl died on the same day that Celeste was born," she said finally. "I had a miscarriage—that's why you couldn't reach me. And I had just been discharged when I saw you and Angela bringing Celeste out of the hospital to your car."

She stopped again to catch her breath. She wanted to tell him all of it now, so that she could finally be done with it. She could tell that he was getting more upset but she had to get it all over with.

"The orderly who pushed Angela's wheelchair to your car had just wheeled me out to mine." She relived the details of her ordeal as she told him what had happened.

"You were so excited about Celeste that you probably missed the puzzled look that he gave me, when I first walked up to you and Angela.

Winston still stared at her with a look of utter disbelief on his face. Could all of that really have been going on that day?

"The timing of everything was just a hideous coincidence," she kept going, hoping to be done with it all soon.

"I was still trying to get myself together to drive home. That's when you saw me sitting in my car and I didn't have much choice after that."

There, she had finally told him everything, but why didn't she feel the relief she had hoped for now?

The silence in the cottage grew so loud that she thought her eardrums might burst. Winston sat back on the sofa and continued to stare into space, refusing to even look in her direction. He was still trying to process what she had told him, but he just couldn't make it all fit.

After a few more minutes of silence, he got up and headed toward the front door. "I've got to get out of here," was all that he said.

Chapter 21

'Til You Come Back To Me...
1983

Dr. Foster's words were clearly irrevocable but Kristin still prayed that he would follow them by saying something else that would take it all back. She had hoped that he would tell her he had made some hideous mistake; that what he said hadn't been meant for her at all, and he had been thinking of some other patient when he said those horrible words. Otherwise, it would mean the nightmare she had been living since she came to the hospital wasn't just a dream. And if that was the case, she didn't know what she would do.

When it was clear that what she had hoped for would never happen, her instincts immediately took over. Her inner strength stood guard over her sanity as the machines that had monitored her and the baby were methodically disconnected. It was done by the same nurse who had been in and out of the room since she was first wheeled in that morning. A few seconds later, an orderly came in and together they rolled her to the room where she had spent most of the day. They were back again a few minutes later; this time they wheeled her to a different room at the far end of the floor, one that she had never been in before. The new room had far less sunlight than the other; it held a dark energy that she clung to as though her survival depended on it.

She spent the next hour trying to guess the average length of recovery time for women her age who had undergone the same procedure that was performed normally after miscarriages. It was the first thought that came to her mind and she hung onto it, dismal though it was. It seemed far less painful than focusing on the baby she had just lost. She couldn't imagine how she would ever recover from that ordeal and she had clutched at anything that showed promise of keeping her mind from slipping away.

She had been completely enamored by the precious little life that she had carried for nearly five months. She and the baby had developed a daily routine and her sudden absence felt as Kristin imagined it might feel to have someone cut a hole through the center of her heart. She vowed to herself through tears that she would never forget her beloved little angel who she had come to love so much in such a short time. In the brief period that she had been a part of her life, Kristin had pictured her baby as she would have looked when she was a little girl and sometimes she would see her as a teenager. She knew that it would be hard to erase those images from her mind but she also knew she had to find a way to do it.

And even as she made the solemn promise to the baby's Spirit as she felt it leave her body, she knew she would have to pull herself together. She would have to figure out how to go on with her life; as though the bond she had felt with her sweet love child never existed. She would have to do it for Trazi and she would have to do it for herself—though she couldn't imagine how she ever would. How would she keep up such a charade when a part of her heart was now missing?

During the next few hours in the lifeless room, her mind had circled in cycles of random thoughts. It never seemed to hit on a particular theme that would hold her attention for more than a few seconds, but it had kept her from thinking about the baby and so it seemed vital to her survival. She felt so helpless and all she could do was cry because she couldn't think of anything else. She cried for the baby she had lost, and she cried because she was going through the worst experience of her life alone. She cried for Trazi because he had lost his little sister, and for Winston because he didn't know the child she had almost given him had ever existed.

She felt in her heart that the baby had been the daughter that she and he had fantasized about having once, when they were at Tuskegee and had just started dating. They stayed up all night one night talking, and in the process they had first discovered their love for one another. They plotted out their life together that night for hours, talking about the first child they would have, a daughter. They planned the entire first half of her life in great detail; even down to her wedding, which would be a grand affair. They kept adding litte details onto their make-believe daughter's life until they finally fell asleep together, just as the sun was rising.

Winston had been thrilled, of course, after Trazi was born, but she had always suspected that he held out hope for the daughter of their dreams, as she had. And now their little baby girl was dead.

She started crying all over again about their lost baby and she soon found that she was unable to stop. She cried for hours—sobbing loudly at times, until eventually she cried herself to sleep. The next morning when she awoke, she didn't remember any of what had happened for the first several seconds, or even where she was. As her groggy thoughts began to clear, she remembered that she was in the hospital and soon the events of the previous day began to flood her mind. She had only vague recollections of Dr. Foster prescribing a sedative for her, and cloudy memories of the medicine being injected into the bag of fluid still attached to her hand.

Her nurse had asked her several times whether there was someone she might call for her, but Kristin could never manage a reply. She knew that Niyla would have gladly been there with her through it all, but her friend had been out of the country vacationing at the time. Besides, Winston was the only person she really wanted to have comfort her, and since she knew that was impossible she was content to be alone.

Thankfully, Trazi had been spending a few weeks with her folks in Tuskegee. She used the phone next to her bed to remotely check for messages on her home phone to see if he had called. There were no messages from her son but there were a string of messages from his father. She had already known Angela was in labor; Winston had called to tell her before she had to leave for the hospital herself.

On the first message he left, he had happily announced the birth of his baby daughter. According to the timestamp, she had been born a short time after Kristin's miscarriage. Each message he left after the first one had been a little more persistent, and she could sense his curiosity about why she hadn't returned his calls. She kept replaying his messages in her mind after she had put her phone back in its cradle. She found herself crying all over again—only this time she cried for herself.

Eventually, she learned to force back her tears whenever a nurse came into the room. The last thing she wanted was to be sedated again, so she called on her stoic will to help her appear as calm as would be expected under the circumstances. Her tears were all that she had left now, the only weapon against the pain she felt in her heart. Still, she knew she would have to pull herself together before she was confronted by Winston's happiness.

Eventually, sleep rescued her from her torment and this time she dreamed that her baby girl was still alive. She was holding the chubby little infant in her arms and her little girl had looked up at her with an indescribably sweet smile on her round face. When she woke up the next time, her nurse told her that she had developed a slight fever and warned that Dr. Foster wouldn't discharge her until her temperature was normal again.

The relationship that she had with her doctor up to that point had been friendly, but it had never crossed professional bounds. She could sense Dr. Foster's concern that she had no friends or loved ones at the hospital to comfort her during her sorrowful times. When her fever persisted throughout the day, he confirmed what the nurse had said as he made his rounds. He seemed pensive as he interacted with her, and she knew he was probably wondering about the baby's father for the first time.

She found that she was grateful for the delay that her fever had caused in her release. It gave her more time to pull herself together and come up with a plausible explanation about her disappearance. Most new parents would likely be so distracted with the new baby that they would take little notice of her absence. But she could hear in his tone that Winston had already noticed and he would be looking for an explanation of some kind.

She was glad that her son was still in Tuskegee; it would have been next to impossible to hide her misery from him. She was also glad that she had listened to her intuition, one that she had always considered a gift from God. She decided to take the summer quarter off that year from teaching, the first time she had ever done so in her career. Thankfully, she was spared the ordeal of inventing an explanation for having to rearrange her classes; because there was no way she would have been ready to resume her schedule any time soon. The methods she often used in her lectures brought up emotional issues for her and her students, as they delved into subconscious feelings and examined old wounds. She could only hope to have time alone to deal with her anguish in private, and until then, she couldn't imagine having to face Winston, Angela, or their new baby girl.

By the next morning her fever had finally subsided. She put all her energy into a pretense of calm acceptance, as she slowly dressed to leave the hospital. She prayed that she would be able to contain her grief until she was home and free to mourn for the loss of her baby girl in peace.

The pleasant young orderly made small talk as they got onto the elevator and headed for the ground floor. Her response to his questions had been polite, though brief. It was standard policy for discharged patients to be wheeled out of the hospital but her only desire had been to be left alone in her sorrow. She would have much preferred walking to her car on her own instead. The young man registered surprise when she directed him past a stand of waiting taxis near the front entrance, and had him take her to her car that was still parked in an adjacent lot. He seemed unsure whether she should be driving alone, as he helped her out of the wheelchair and into her car. She paused to collect herself for a few minutes, but when she glanced out of her window again, her uneventful morning had taken a sudden turn.

Much to her dismay, she saw Angela holding her new baby in her arms, being pushed from the hospital's entrance by the same orderly who had just deposited her into her car. And walking along beside them, of course, was Winston, grinning from ear to ear. Kristin had been so wrapped up in the turmoil of her feelings and the strain of holding her emotions in check all morning that she hadn't noticed his car parked close to hers. At almost the same instant, he looked straight in her direction and their eyes locked from a distance. He seemed excited to see her and waved in a way that let her know he made the assumption that she had just pulled into the lot.

"You're too late!" He called out happily, barely able to contain himself. "We're already on our way home with our little girl," he shouted the obvious, from a distance now of only a few yards.

Kristin had been shocked by the unimaginable timing that had led them all to the parking lot at the exact same time. She couldn't believe that she had been discharged so close to the time that Angela was, but she saw little choice other than to get out of her car again to greet them.

'How could he be this happy when our baby just died?' The thought reverberated in her mind as she walked toward the small group. Winston was still grinning and she had to struggle with her grief as she came closer to them. She forced her mind to believe it was happening to someone else, just as she had done in Sister La La's Speech and Drama classes at Tuskegee, when she was called on to make her presentations.

"Congratulations, you two." She gave Angela a quick mechanical hug, mustering as much excitement in her voice as she was able to manage. She was careful to avoid direct eye contact with Winston and with the orderly she could see from her peripheral vision. The young man had seemed quite bewildered by her behavior. She knew he must have been wondering why she would conceal that she had just been released from the hospital herself. He had seemed to sense her anxiety at the awkwardness of their situation though, and was kind enough to avoid further eye contact with her.

She had prayed silently that her body language wouldn't give her away. She hoped her smile didn't look as forced or weak as it felt; the last thing she needed was to give Winston a reason to start probing her with his questions, ones that she would have found impossible to answer.

"Where have you been?" He had demanded an explanation as soon as they moved closer to his car, and the orderly had helped Angela to her seat inside. Kristin only imagined how curious the young man must have been to hear her answer, but he had thankfully left them in private afterwards and headed back toward the hospital. She had made an impromptu decision to stick with the same story she had concocted to cover her baby's paternity. Keeping Winston's avid curiosity in mind, she had rehearsed several different scenarios. She had practiced in her mind enough to feel comfortable in believing that she might actually be able to pull it off.

"Don't be so nosey," she had teased him, with an artificial smile flashed to cover her nervousness. "I'm sorry I didn't get here earlier, Angela," she turned toward her friend. "But if you must know," and she had said that looking directly at Winston, "I spent the evening with a friend a few of nights ago. I ended up having car trouble just as I was about to leave, but that just makes a long story get even longer..."

She let her voice trail off so Winston's imagination could fill in the blanks. His expression had changed dramatically from the moment she insinuated that she had been on a date. For a brief second, a fierce scowl appeared replaced quickly by a forced grin. As she had suspected, her plan worked. He didn't ask her any more questions because he was unwilling to hear her talk about being with another man.

She had dreaded the time when she would have to come face-to-face with his and Angela's baby, from the moment she had heard his message announcing her birth. But when he pulled back the colorful blanket that had shielded her tiny face from the morning breeze, Kristin felt her entire being light up. She had been overcome with sudden joy after one look at the cherub face nestled in the blanket, a shower gift to Angela.

"Baby Blue," as Winston called his new daughter when he first introduced her, was without a doubt the most beautiful baby Kristin had seen in her life. And that included her son, Trazi, who she had always believed to be the reason the sun rose and set. As she started to tell the proud parents how beautiful she thought their baby was, the tiny infant's dark eyes had focused directly on her face. She smiled the sweetest smile imaginable and from that moment on, Kristin had been completely enchanted. She and Celeste had an instant and surprisingly deep bond from the very beginning, and those feelings had only grown stronger over time.

She had stood almost transfixed for a few seconds as she looked down at the tiny baby, still unable to utter a sound. But the strangely loving interchange that had taken place between them had also intensified her already charged emotions. With all that she had gone through in the past forty-eight hours, to find that she would be so drawn to Winston's new baby had been a bit much for her to digest.

"You did good, Angela." She told her after she had managed to recover.

"Thank you, Kristin. I never would have been able to make it without your help." Her friend acknowledged, gratefully.

"Well, you know that I love you," she answered, and to both of them she added, "I'll stop by to see you guys in a few days, after you've had time to settle in with the baby."

By then, Winston had started to recover from her candid disclosure about her mystery date. She was sure he was curious about who she might have been with, but he had certainly been in no position to make demands. She made her way back to her car so she could finally go home, but there was little that she remembered about her trip.

When she turned the key in her front door finally, she was still in a daze from the events of the past forty-eight hours. She tried to wash the whole painful experience away with a long hot shower; afterwards, she sank down beneath the thick covers of her own bed, and stared blankly at the ceiling. Finally, she got up to make herself a strong cup of chamomile tea, in the hopes that it would coerce her into the peaceful night's sleep that she so badly needed. She craved a silencing of the random thoughts that had repeated themselves in her head over and over in the last two days.

Kristin took her steeping tea back into the bedroom to cool down enough for her to drink. On an impulse, she opened one of the dresser drawers that held some of the baby's things. She had tried to resist shopping for her, but there were things that she had been unable to resist buying and now wondered idly what she should do with them. She had already taken them out of their packaging and washed them in baby detergent, in her eagerness to have everything ready when she and her baby came home.

When no ideas came to her right away, she sat down in the rocker that she had bought before Trazi was born. She ran her fingers along the embroidered designs of a tiny pink jumper she held in her hand, and before she knew it she was crying all over again. She climbed back into bed and sobbed inconsolably for hours, as her tea grew colder on top of the dresser.

Then, something miraculous happened. An image of Winston's tiny baby suddenly flashed across her mind of her squirming in Angela's arms. She remembered the incredible smile the baby had smiled at her, as though she had been waiting a long time to see her.

And remarkably, given everything that had happened to her in the past few days, she fell asleep with a smile on her face.

Chapter 22

I've Got To Go On Without You...

Winston's bag was still parked on the floor of the foyer where he had dropped it as soon as he stepped inside the cottage. He had hoped it would make its way back to Kristin's bedroom later that evening. He thought for sure that things would be right for them this time, and he would once again be with the woman he had been in love with for nearly thirty years. As soon as he saw the sunken tub in the master en suite, he had immediately started fantasizing about them soaking in it later—after they made up for all the years that they had missed.

He picked the bag up on his way out the front door but it wasn't until after it closed behind him that he remembered Celeste had driven them to Maryland. And the minute that he stepped onto the porch, he also remembered he had left his cell phone in his office in Washington. He had discovered it was missing shortly after he and Celeste turned onto Route 50, but didn't bother having her go back for it. After all, he had no business plans scheduled before Monday morning and his daughter was the only other person likely to have called. He had been in a such a hurry to get to Maryland to see Kristin.

Kristin.

He agonized now at the mere thought of her name. He had no intention of asking for her help either, so he found himself stuck on the front porch of the cottage when all he wanted was to get as far away from her as he could. He tried to think of something else he could do and he even thought about trying to find his way back to the service station they had passed near their turnoff into the community. But he couldn't be sure of the turns after they had left the main road.

Since he couldn't see walking as much of an option, he finally plopped down on the top step with a heavy sigh and looked out toward the narrow road in front of the cottage. After a few seconds, he realized how heavy he was breathing and tried to make himself slow it down, thinking of other things that might distract him from the spiraling anger that he felt still.

He turned his attention to the design of the cottage and began to imagine how it might have looked when it was first built. He speculated on the political conversations that had likely taken place in it, picturing parties and other social events and the spectrum of guests who had likely been in attendance. From what he had learned from Celeste, the quiet elite community had seen many well-known Black actors in its time too. There had been entertainers and political figures who vacationed in Highland Beach since the town was founded. Many of them owned property there and Winston imagining himself at some of their parties, mingling with the likes of W.E.B. DuBois, Langston Hughes, and Booker T. Washington.

He thought about a number of things that he never would have likely spent much time thinking about, but he welcomed any thoughts that had nothing to do with the interchange that had just taken place between him and Kristin. He was willing to think about anything except what she had just told him.

Kristin was still frozen on the living room couch, sitting with her hands clasped together tightly. A steady stream of tears rolled down her cheeks every few seconds, disbursing themselves onto the silk fabric of her sheer pink blouse on contact. She knew that Winston had forgotten he came to the shore with Celeste as soon as she saw him head for the front door. She also knew better than to say *anything* to him when he was as angry as he appeared to be. He had seemed to loose touch with reason at times like those, until he had once again regained his equilibrium and was ready to be civil again. Thankfully, he had never been one to get angry very often; but whenever he did, she had learned to be mindful of what she said or did around him. Hence, she had done nothing to keep him from walking out the door and putting himself in the position that he currently found himself in.

'Now what?'

She was just starting to recover from their emotional scene herself. She knew him very well and had expected him to be upset after he found out she had kept so much from him. But she had never been prepared for all of this. Had she waited too long to tell him? Had she made it impossible now for him to forgive her, for not letting him know anything about the baby sooner?

The shrill sound of her mobile phone startled her out of her daydream. And thank God she thought to check the caller id before she answered it.

"Hey! What are you guys doing?" Celeste's voice teased happily from the other end. "Wait, wait...Don't tell me....I may be too young to hear this..." She was obviously happy at the thought of her and Winston being together. She spoke quickly and with light laughter in her voice. She hadn't given Kristin a chance to say anything since she answered the phone.

"Celeste..." She interrupted her before she could say something more embarrassing. "I'm glad that you called..."

Winston had already told her about leaving his cell phone at his office, so she was very much aware that he was stuck out on the front porch.

"Your father forgot about some business that he needs to take care of in Washington," she lied quickly. "It's urgent, actually, so he needs you to come as soon as you can so you guys can head back." She knew how obviously untrue what she told her sounded, but she was too upset to care.

"Are you just about ready to head this way?" She tried to sound light and casual and hoped that her voice didn't betray the pain and confusion she felt. What she was saying didn't make any sense, she knew, because it had been clear to everyone after Celeste's abrupt departure meant she had no intention of returning to Highland Beach—at least not that night.

But Kristin didn't care what she thought; she only needed her to come back to the cottage to get her father as soon as possible. She prayed that she and her girlfriend hadn't been drinking, but she knew Celeste didn't care much for alcohol, so she figured it was a safe bet that she would be okay to drive. And since she was young, she was probably good for making it back to D.C. that night too, in case Winston didn't feel up to driving.

The younger woman was truly thrown by what Kristin was saying to her. She was sure that she had seen a sparkle in her father's eyes before she left. She couldn't imagine anything that would make him want to leave Aunt Kristin so soon. So what on Earth could possibly have happened?

"Sure... I guess..." She floundered, hoping to pick up some hint about what was really going on from Kristin's voice. Had she been crying?

"Where's Daddy?" She thought she still might be able to prolong their reunion just a bit longer, since it had taken so much time before they had even attempted this one. The image of the two of them on the photo she had found at Kristin's house before she moved to Ghana, had always stayed uppermost in her mind. It had been taken at Tuskegee when they were still students, and she had seen how much love there was between them. If there had been some kind of disagreement between them, she thought maybe she could help them work it out. It would give them a little more time together before Kristin had to leave the country again.

"Huh?... Oh..., Well, we ate so much of that seafood, you know, that I think he's out walking some of it off." She kept up the lie without giving any pretense that it was anything other than a lie. She knew that Celeste would never believe the explanation she was giving her, and she had *never* lied to her before—or to Trazi, for that matter.

But she couldn't handle any more emotional trauma that day, or one more revelation of truth.

"Okay..." Celeste was reluctant to give up but she recognized a lost cause when she heard one. "Tell Daddy I'll be there in about thirty minutes, then." She still racked her brain to figure out what was *really* going on.

"Great...I'll tell him." Kristin's tone was conclusive and an abrupt indication that she was about to get off the phone. She knew that Celeste was already thinking up a thousand questions to ask her.

She had no intention of delivering any message to Winston either, although she could see him sitting on the steps from where she stood. He had been in the same spot for nearly an hour and she was sure that he had heard her cell phone ringing. Maybe he had even heard parts of her conversation, but either way, she had no intention of going anywhere near him again.

"Be careful driving back." She reminded Celeste, and hurriedly ended the call before the young woman could ask anything else.

Kristin sat back down on the couch quietly again until she heard her old Saab engine as the car pulled into the drive. She tried to imagine what Winston might be saying to Celeste to keep her from coming in to say good night. But whatever he said her prayers had been answered and she heard the car engine start again a minute or two later. She waited a few seconds to be sure that they were gone and then she walked over to the bay window in time to see the car disappearing down the narrow road.

The moment that Celeste saw her father sitting on the front steps, she knew he would be in no mood for conversation. They rode all the way back to Washington in silence, but when they reached the loft, Celeste drove straight past the back door and into Charlotte's old parking space. When her father turned toward her to protest, she had answered him with a determined look. He could see that it would be pointless for him to try and persuade her otherwise; since he was still exhausted from his ordeal with Kristin, he pulled both bags from the car instead and they headed toward the back door together. Each of them had such high hopes before they left the city and they had both come back feeling weary and defeated.

As soon as they had stepped inside the doorway, Winston mumbled a quick good night to his daughter and walked up the stairs toward his bedroom without waiting for a response.

Celeste followed him up the stairs and pulled out her cell phone as soon as she had thrown her bag onto the bed in her old room.

"Aunt Kristin...?" She ventured hesitantly.

"Celeste...Please. Don't ask—okay?"

Kristin cut her off before she could go any further. She had been expecting her call, of course, and had tried briefly to think of something she could say without actually telling her the truth. There wasn't anything, of course, and she was too emotionally drained to try.

"...I know that you're concerned, honey," she told her quickly, without giving Celeste a chance to say another word. "And I appreciate it...I really do... But this is something that's between your father and me, okay?"

Neither woman said anything for a few seconds and the phone's white noise was the only thing that connected them.

"Is he okay?" Kristin asked, resuming a conversation she had just made clear that she didn't want to have.

"I guess..." The younger woman responded, even more puzzled now by her aunt's question.

"...He won't say anything either," she added, still straining for a clue about what had happened. Otherwise, how would she ever fix it?

"Just try to give him a little space, okay?" Kristin made the appeal as though she had read Celeste's mind.

"Alright, I'll try to leave him alone." She finally gave the promise that Kristin had been waiting for. She didn't know what else to do.

"And Sweetie, I hope you don't mind...," Kristin said quickly, "but I have to hang up now.

"...I'm glad that you called though, and let me know that you guys made it back okay." She brought their conversation to a deliberate end.

"I really need to get some sleep now."

After they had hung up, Celeste was more confused than ever. She had heard the love in Kristin's voice when she asked about her father. The whole thing was even more of a mystery to her now.

Was Aunt Kristin involved with someone else?

Chapter 23

I've Gotta Use... My Imagination...

Kristin felt numb when she woke up the next morning and the emotional meltdown she had with Winston gradually played across her consciousness again, word for word. She lay motionless on the oversized bed in her friend's cottage for several minutes, wondering how things had possibly turned out the way they had. She was at a loss to explain how any of it could have happened, since she had barely thought about Winston as she boarded her flight from Accra. She had been so focused; so intent on raising the capital that the Foundation needed for its commercial projects planned for the Central region of Ghana.

But now, she couldn't think straight at all. And she certainly was in no state of mind to conduct business; she was far too distracted by Winston's explosive reaction from the night before. It had become a heightening mystery to her and caused her emotions to be scattered all over the place. She still had no earthly idea why he had reacted the way he had; and to make matters worse, she would now have his unexplained anger to add to the emptiness she already felt about the saddest day of her life.

Her mind kept turning back to his anger. She couldn't remember a time when he had been so upset with her and had no idea what to expect next. It hadn't been the first time that they had been annoyed with each other by far; they had been married for four year and it had happened many times, especially in that last year. She had expected him to be upset when he found out about their baby girl, but he had gone way over the top.

The one thing she knew for sure was that she would have a day to be alone before her first meeting. She was grateful that it had been scheduled over dinner and she hoped she could use the extra time to help her pull herself together. Being close to the water would be a tremendous help in that process; it centered her the same as her daily meditations did at the mountain retreat she had carved for herself near Exodus Village. She wasn't able to meditate now because her thoughts could not be quieted enough. But as difficult as things were between her and Winston, her investor meetings were far more important and would have to be her priority. There was no longer a point in denying that she still loved him, but she would have to be on top of her game. She had no idea what their blowout might mean for her future, but she had come to realize the Exodus Foundation's mission was far more important than what might happen between the two of them. Still, she had to summon her strength to get out of bed that morning.

When the phone rang, she was so sure that it was her son that she didn't bother to check the caller id. From the day that she and Winston brought him home from the hospital, she had been aware of a psychic attachment between her and her son. He had always seemed to know the exact second that she woke up in the mornings when he was an infant. She had tried to lie perfectly still, hoping for a few minutes to collect her conscious thoughts before her day began. But Trazi had always sensed when she was awake, no matter how careful she was not to stir or make the slightest noise.

"Mom?" His tone confirmed her suspicions that Celeste had called him as soon as they had hung up the night before. Winston's daughter had most likely given her brother a complete play-by-play of everything that she knew to have happened. And Trazi, of course, would be calling her to find out the rest.

"Are you okay?" She heard the concern in his voice and knew that he could tell that she had been crying as soon as she answered the phone. She struggled, even then, to hold back more tears.

"I'm fine, sweetie." She lied to her son. First to Celeste, and now Trazi; she had lied to both children that weekend for the first time in their lives.

"Did Dad do something to you, Mom?" He was direct in his question and didn't pretend not to know that something was going on. He knew that his mother would have anticipated Celeste calling him, so as far as he was concerned there was no need for pretense. He wanted to find out what was going on, so rather than beating around the bush he got straight to the point.

"Do you need me to come up there?" He asked, after she didn't answer him right away. His voice was heavy with concern and she found it touching that he wanted to protect her.

"No, no, baby. I'm fine—really..." She lied to him easily again.

Hearing the anxiety in his voice caused the tears she had been holding back to flood unhampered down her cheeks. He was so much like his father—so caring and so sweet. She remembered that when Trazi had been little, the three of them would do things together as a family on the weekends. He had been like a carbon copy of Winston then, and he was the same now that he was all grown up.

"Mom, what is it?" He was shouting into the phone now, aware that his mother was crying again.

"Did Dad hurt you?" His anxiety rose as he asked the question again, not sure how he might respond if his worst fears were realized. Kristin knew that if something didn't add up for him, her son would press until he discovered the missing link.

It had taken much effort for her to get father and son moving back toward each other again, and although they had made substantial progress, his suspicion now of his father as an abuser told her just how much work was left to be done.

Trazi hadn't been concerned when Celeste told him she had found their father sitting on the front steps when she got back to the cottage. But after she told him that she hadn't actually seen his mom, he found himself becoming alarmed. Now his mom was being evasive so his imagination began running wild. He became more apprehensive the longer she was silent, and he thought up all kinds of scenarios to explain what might have really happened between them.

He had been too young when they were divorced to be affected by it much, and he had to give it to both of them for the way they had handled everything. He had never felt separated from either parent and now that he was older, he could appreciate the seamless transition that their divorce had been for him. It wasn't until after he was an adult himself that he became aware of the unspoken love still between them, and that it had never been interrupted.

Trazi loved his father as much as Celeste did, but there was still a subtle undercurrent of their past separation that blocked the two men from being as close as they once had been. He kept thinking about Malaya's stepfather—he had seemed like a nice guy too, and everyone thought they knew him. He had never suspected his father of being a violent man before, but what if it was something that had he kept hidden from him. A sense of alarm quickly evolved into panic as he waited for his mother to answer him, or say *something*.

"Look mom, it'll only take me a couple of hours to get there." He was already frantically looking around the room for his gym bag to throw a few things in it before he hit the road.

"No! Wait Trazi..." Kristin was finally moved to speak once she realized her son was about to get on the parkway.

"Please...Don't come up," she pleaded. "Your father didn't hurt me at all," she assured him, "at least not physically. He would *never* do anything like that."

There was silence on the other end of the phone as Trazi evaluated her response.

"Okay. Honestly?.. I'm not really okay yet," she confessed. She was desperate to convince her son not to drive all the way to Maryland from Virginia.

"I just need a little time to pull myself together. I really will be okay after that," she added quickly. "And that's a promise. I just need some time, okay?"

She paused to catch her breath, waiting to see whether she had gotten through to him. She forced herself to stop crying because she didn't want him be even more upset than he obviously was. And she *definitely* didn't want to undo all the progress that he and his father had made.

"Trazi. Honey, this thing between me and your father isn't his fault, okay? He didn't do anything to me." She stopped short, not wanting to say more. "I promise."

"I'd still like to come up to see you, Mom." There had been a long pause before he spoke again. He was being persistent, although he tried his best to sound more composed than he was.

"I'd just like to see for myself, if you don't mind," he offered. "I don't mind the drive and Celeste told me that the house where you're staying in is pretty nice."

"No, Trazi. Please!" She said it again, more forcibly this time. She knew that if her son came to Highland Beach she wouldn't be able to keep what really happened between her and Winston from him. She had no idea how *he* would feel about it. There was no way for her to tell him only a part of what happened and not give him a real explanation. It was all too complicated still and she hadn't sorted it out for herself yet. She had far too much on her plate for this trip already and there was sure to be an even greater distraction if her son came to see her.

"Listen, baby," she told him finally. "What happened with your father was my fault, okay, not his. He didn't do anything," she repeated herself.

"It was all me, okay?"

Trazi was still silent on the other end. He was trying to imagine what might have caused both his parents so much heartache when they obviously still cared so much about each other.

"Please, Trazi," She kept talking because she knew he was at least considering what she said.

"I love you baby, and I appreciate how concerned you are about me—really, I do. But I don't want you to drive all the way up here, okay?" She pressed, hoping that she hadn't said too much already.

"It's not that I wouldn't love to see you, but I really need to pull myself together. I have some key meetings scheduled over the next couple of days," she told him, honestly. "I need to get my act together and if you come, I won't be able to concentrate on my presentations like I need to do. This is really important for the Foundation.

"Okay, sweetheart?" She ended, hoping that she had convinced him.

"Are you sure Mom?" He asked her again. He still didn't feel right about her crying, and he was more puzzled than ever about what could've happened. Still, he was starting to be convinced.

"Yes, my sweet baby," his mother answered him, "I'm very sure."

She was relieved that she seemed to have gotten through.

"And Trazi..." She started again.

"Yes, Mom." He answered, still not feeling good about her being alone.

"Please promise me that you won't say anything to your father about this. Trust me; it would only make things worse.

"Stay out of it, okay?" She pleaded. "I guess you've always known that your father and I have never really stopped loving each other," she admitted finally. "But I really don't know how this is going to turn out, okay? It's just something that the two of us will have to figure out."

She hoped that she sounded confident.

"Okay, Mom," He conceded, sighing heavily. "If that's what you want."

"It is, baby. I promise you that it is."

"So, how long are you planning to be in the States?" He changed the subject after another pause. "Will you have time to get down to Norfolk before you leave the country?"

"Not this trip I'm afraid, sweetheart," she said it hurriedly, hoping not to upset him further. Sometimes it seemed as though she spent more time with Celeste than she did her own son, but she knew he didn't mind. Besides, Celeste had always been like a daughter to her, all of her life.

"I'm due in London the day after my last meeting in Chicago," she explained, "so I have to cut this trip shorter than I originally thought."

She told him about a last minute invitation she had received from the Archbishop of Canterbury to celebrate the law that ended British participation on the slave trade. Exodus Village and the Exodus Foundation were to be recognized as part of the planned events.

"It's all going to be held at Westminster Abbey," she added, "so it's going to be a pretty big thing. The press coverage will mean a lot of publicity for our Foundation, and we hope it will translate into a significant boost in donations. She told her son that she had only agreed to do interviews after the commemoration ceremony because it would benefit the Foundation.

"And I have to be back in Ghana shortly after that," she went on. "My input and sign-off is required on some of the promotional campaigns we're creating for another line of soy cookies that just went into production. And we're also about ready to break ground for our first soy bean production plant in the Central Region. The money I'm trying to raise here is for the other plants we'll need built to manufacture our soy milk, soy cheeses, flour, tempeh, burgers, and different variations of tofu in that region. It's all going to be set up similar to our Ashanti production plants.

"Each of them are really big deals for the Foundation right now, sweetie. So, I'm sorry but this will have to be another short trip for me.

"It's okay Mom, honest." He didn't know how it had happened, but all of a sudden *he* was the one who was being comforted.

"Celeste and I both understand how important your work is. And Dad does too," he added after hesitating for a second. "He's been telling everyone how proud he is of you."

Kristin was caught off guard again by her son's comments about his father, but grateful for that signs that the two men she loved most were still at least working on their relationship.

"Well, call me before you leave the country, then," he added, after she failed to respond to that comment. He restrained himself because he didn't want her to think he was prying.

"I hope everything goes well with your meetings."

"Thanks baby," she told him, relieved that she had convinced him not to come.

"Me too."

She let out a big sigh of relief after they hung up. She had been bracing herself for Trazi's call, knowing that he would be a much harder sell than

Celeste had been. She had kept him on the phone deliberately so that he could see that she was okay, switching to a different subject that had nothing to do with Winston.

It was still early yet, and the sun hadn't made it too far above the waters of the bay. As she and her son talked, she had pulled on her pants and a loosely fitting shirt and she was sitting on the deck by the time they ended their conversation. She grabbed a light parka and tucked her cellphone into her shirt pocket as she started out down the cobblestone path that led to the sandy beach of the bay. She was counting on a walk along the shore to help her clear her head and a strong breeze blew in to greet her when she reached the water's edge. She quickly donned her parka and pulled the hood over her head to keep the cool wind out of her ears.

She had finished the bottle of wine that Winston opened for their dinner after he left, and eventually she had cried herself to sleep. Now that the conversation with Trazi was behind her, she was free to let her tears flow again. She didn't expect to hear from Winston, although she knew that he had thought of many more questions to ask her by that time. Knowing him as she did, he had probably spent the night thinking back almost twenty-five years, trying to put a sequence of events from their past together in his mind.

Kristin pulled the hood from her head again. She had walked a half mile away from the cottage before she turned to head back in the direction she had come. On her return trip, she faced east and the breeze coming in off the bay felt much warmer now against her face. She sat down on a small sand dune as she neared the cottage and watch several groups of elderly couples who took a daily walk along the beach. Most of them still held hands and they seemed to naturally enjoy each other's company.

It was what she had envisioned for herself when she and Winston were on their honeymoon in Jamaica. Would it ever be impossible now for them to have something like that one day when they grew older?

The odds against it seemed greater now than they had ever been. She kept replaying the scene in her head that had hurt her most of all. It hurt so much because of the truth in what Winston said. Honesty had *always* been something that they both felt was paramount in their relationship. They had talked about it when they first met, and again for hours before they started dating. Honesty was just that important to them both. But, for the first time, their trust in each other had taken a major hit. It had been seriously eroded and Kristin didn't know whether it could ever be repaired.

He had made no secret about his interest in dating Angela, for instance, when he first had the idea to go out with her. They were, after all, already divorced, and she could remember thinking at the time that she probably knew more about his plans than Angela did. At first, she had thought it was because of Trazi being so young and their determination that he not be negatively affected by their divorce. Now she had to wonder whether that had been Winston's way of shaking things up between them a bit; something that would spur them into counseling or at least try to work it out themselves.

She hadn't realized how much she had missed him until he was holding her in his arms the night before. She had been so tempted to give in to him, to wait to tell him about the baby until they woke up that next morning. She could have waited one more night to tell him the truth. Pulling away had been one of the hardest things she had ever done, especially when he finally admitted to the truth, that he had never stopped loving her either.

Kristin kicked her shoes off and walked back down to the edge of the water to stick her toes in. The temperature was much too cool for her so she began dodging the gentle tide that moved in ever closer to the shore. She walked back to sit on the sand dune again and allowed herself to remember how good it had felt to have Winston's long arms wrapped around her. His body pressing against hers had felt as muscular as it had the last time they were together.

She had been busy with the Foundation's business for years with little time to dwell on him, before this trip. She had easily pushed seeing him again out of her mind again after she was back in Ghana from Celeste's graduation. But she had never dreamed that he might be ready to make things right again, himself. She had been flustered and totally unprepared for his eagerness to be with her, with no time to think how she should respond. She could still feel the faint imprint of his desire branded on her thigh after he had pressed himself against her. Their passion for each other had been pent up for even longer this time, and it had been determined to find a way to express itself.

She couldn't remember when he had kissed her that way before, so tender and oh so sweet. It had made it very hard for her to hold back, to stop him from sweeping her up and carrying her off to the oak bed they had both found so familiar. She had an almost desperate need to feel him inside of her again, to hear the whispers of his love as he kissed her ears and caressed her neck.

But as bad as things were between them, she knew that they would've been far worse if she *hadn't* stopped him. That last bit of dishonesty would surely have ended things for good. At least now there might be another chance for them some day, and timing would likely be an important factor. She knew that she had done her best all those years ago, under the circumstances. Her heart had been in the right place, for sure, so she had that to hang onto.

The fresh hole that she felt in her heart would keep her from pretending that she didn't care anymore, but there was nothing she could do about any of it now. She could only pray that their love wasn't lost forever—that some day they could recapture it after Winston's trust in her had been restored.

And no matter what, she still believed that telling him had been the right thing to do. He had a *right* to know, and her only regret was that she hadn't done it sooner. It was more clear to her now than ever that they belonged together, but she had no idea how long it might take before Winston believed it again too.

The one thing that she *did* know was that she couldn't afford to keep sitting around crying or waiting to find out what he might decide. In spite of the deep love that she felt for him, she was even more attuned to the higher purpose of her being. At this point in her life, she wouldn't let any trouble between them stand in the way of doing what she had come to the earth to do.

Looking back, she couldn't imagine now what had made her decide to see Winston *before* her meetings. The accusations and insults from their argument still swirled around in her head.

She went back into the cottage and warmed some of the leftover seafood for her breakfast and brought it back to the deck to eat. She continued to stare out at the water, and permitted herself to cry again whenever she was overcome by sadness and felt the need.

After a few hours, she took another long walk on the beach that ended just as the sun prepared to set. By the time she was back at the cottage this time, she was ready again to focus on the reason that she had come to the States.

She had decided that it was time for her pity party to be over so she could get back to work. As she left Highland Beach for her first meeting in Annapolis the next afternoon, her mind was once again crystal clear.

Chapter 24

Love Is A Hurting Thing

*C*eleste heard her father up and moving about his room early. Apparently, he was working out on his exercise equipment that he had set up after Charlotte moved out. To keep herself from looking at the small clock on her dresser every two seconds, she decided to divert her attention by going through her old closet. She had only packed casual clothes for their trip to Highland Beach and she hoped to find something suitable to put on so she wouldn't have to go all the way back to her apartment before she went out.

She had never officially moved out of her old room in the loft. Instead, she had only taken things as she needed them at any given time. Her room still looked pretty much the same as it had when she had been a sophomore at Hunter, and that had been nearly six years ago. Many of her clothes and books were in the same place where she had left them when she transferred to Tuskegee to finish college.

Ishmael had teased her once and asked whether she would ever be willing to live more than a few miles away from her dad. There had been an air of mystery in his question but he had refused to say more when asked. Ironically, it hadn't been long after that before she moved hundreds of miles away from both him and her father.

Now that he was back in her life, she had found a way to smile again about the good times they had shared at Hunter. It was surprising to her still, although they weren't nearly as close as they once were. That had been her decision, and so far, Ishmael was respecting it. She was glad that they were seeing each other again; ecstatic, if the truth be known, but she was also afraid of getting too close. All the suffering she went through the last time was still too fresh in her mind.

And she couldn't get past thinking about Kendra, and that she had lost her baby so soon after she had showed up unannounced to tell Ishmael she was expecting. In all the time that Celeste was gone, they had never been married or lived together. Ishmael had confided to her that they had never been intimate again either, so it meant that the years that they had been apart were for no good reason. She had moved to Tuskegee when everything happened but they might have easily still been together all that time, even if it meant having a long-distance relationship.

When she first left D.C., she had thought about something Kristin had said to her once, whenever she had trouble getting Ishmael off her mind. Her aunt had told her that people who were meant to be would always find a way to be together—and without much effort required on their part. The situation with Ishmael had appeared so hopeless at the time that she assumed it implying that she and Ishmael weren't meant to be together. Then, the next thing she knew, they had literally run into each other after her graduation from Tuskegee. She still wasn't clear on all the answers, but she had at least resigned herself to being open about where things might lead in time.

She had called him shortly after talking to her brother the night before and when Ishmael found out she was back in the city, he had invited her out for brunch. Celeste was hoping that her brother would call before it was time for her to leave to meet him. Her cell phone rang just as she stretched her hand out to open her closet door. She hurried to the other side of the bed to grab it before it could ring a second time.

"Trazi?..." She asked anxiously.

"Yeah, it's me," Her brother's response was short, his usual.

"Well, what happened?" She had been dying for him to report back to her on what else he might have learned.

"What did she say?" Celeste hadn't given him time to respond to her first question.

"Well, you were right," he answered quietly. "Something is definitely going on and it's peculiar, whatever it is..."

He had never been sure how concerned he should be about anything his little sister told him. Everyone in the family knew that she was prone to exaggeration at times. But there was definitely something amiss with his parents and now he was just as curious as she to find out what that was.

"What did she say?" Celeste repeated her question.

"Not very much, I'm afraid..." Trazi gave her his usual cryptic answer. He had always made her drag information out of him; sometimes it drove her nuts.

"The only thing that she was definite about was that it *wasn't* our father's fault, whatever happened. She kept insisting that it was something that *she* did, but I still have no earthly idea what that could be."

What he had failed to mention to her was the suspicion he had harbored for a while that their father might have physically harmed his mother. The rift between the two men had gradually started healing over the past few years, especially after he divorced Charlotte. They had begun to rebuild the relationship they once had, but there had been the occasional setback too. Sometimes, Trazi felt the old distrust of his father coming back again, in spite of himself. And since it involved his mom this time, he had decided he would find out for sure if there were any merits to his suspicion, before mentioning anything to Celeste. There had been no sense in getting her all riled up for nothing, and now he was glad he had waited because his fears had apparently been unfounded.

"I couldn't get her to say much else beyond that," he added, "*except* that she wants us to stay out of it. She made me promise that I wouldn't say anything to Dad before we hung up."

"...But did she say *anything* else?" Celeste pressed him. She was having a hard time accepting that her dream of getting her father and Kristin together had drifted away like stormy clouds. She kept thinking about the pictures she had seen of them at her aunt's house when she had been younger. They had been so young themselves then, and so obviously in love. It made Celeste realize over time that she had always seen the same love between them for most of her life, and especially when they first arrived at the cottage where Kristin was staying.

Everything had seemed so promising for their reunion too. Aunt Kristin had even asked her to bring her dad along to Maryland, without *any* involvement on her part. She had believed it would take much maneuvering and a much longer time to get them together, but Kristin had proved her wrong.

She could see how hurt her father was too by whatever it was that happened at Highland Beach. It was killing her not to know; she had to find out to be able to help them get past it.

"I'm afraid that was pretty much it," her brother answered reluctantly. He had known that his report would disappoint her because he didn't find out one thing that she didn't already know.

"...I had the feeling that she didn't want to say *that* much," he added. This is a real mystery to me too, Celeste. And it has to be serious, whatever it is."

His sister agreed with him and then offered a few more theories to explain their rift.

"I don't know about any of that," Trazi responded, "but I think we have to respect their wishes for now and just leave it alone."

"Okay. I know, you're right...But it's so hard because *anybody* can see how much they love each other," she argued. "Maybe if I drove back up there..."

"No, Celeste. I don't think that would be good at all." He interrupted her train of thought just as she had seized on a new plan of action.

"Mom told me about these financial meetings she has scheduled here and they all sound pretty serious. She has to stop over in the U.K. for a few days too, on her way back to Ghana. She'll have to deal with the press and that whole thing there, and I think she needs some time to herself to regain her focus."

"What?" Celeste was surprised by his news. "She's leaving again so soon? She just got here!" She had been so intent on leaving Kristin and her father alone at the cottage that she had missed out on that bit of information.

"Well, she's leaving again," her brother stated the obvious. "I had been hoping to get her to come down to Virginia for a few days, but that's not going to happen either." He was still working for a major alternative energy company assisting in sustainable energy research for a Navy project, but had left their Washington area office in Alexandria to return to the Virginia Beach office after Celeste left for school in Tuskegee.

"...Are you sure there's *nothing* else we can do?" His sister persisted; she was still reluctant to accept that things wouldn't work out as she had planned.

"It doesn't look like it," Trazi answered and she could hear the sadness in his voice. "And from what you've told me about how Dad is acting, I don't think we have much choice but to leave them alone. Especially, since we don't know what this is all about."

"Yeah, I guess you're right," she agreed reluctantly. "...But it's really hard knowing how upset they both are." Celeste sighed heavily, disappointed.

"I know. But like I said, I really don't think there's anything we can do—at least for now.

"But I *have* been thinking about taking another trip to Ghana," he added. "I think I'll call Heavenly Travel tomorrow and get them started on looking for a decent fare before the end of the year—maybe some time in December. I'll go see Mom to make sure she's okay."

It made Celeste feel slightly better after hearing about her brother's plans; maybe she would even go to Ghana with him. She had been dying to get back, and she didn't even have a chance to say goodbye to Kristin before they left Highland Beach. Their father had made sure of that.

"...Well, okay. I've gotta go then." She conceded the point and agreed to her brother's suggestion that they drop it. "I'll just keep an eye on Daddy and try to be there for him in case he *does* want to talk."

"Okay. I think that's best. But I don't think there's much chance of him doing that." He made one final attempt to lower his sister's expectations before they hung up.

※※※

Winston waited in his room until after he was certain Celeste had left the loft. Only then did he venture down the stairs at the urgings of a hunger that surprised him. He rambled around in the kitchen looking for something to satisfy it and his stomach grumbled fiercely as he scoured the sparse refrigerator. It almost made him miss Charlotte for the first time; his third wife had always kept something good on hand to eat. But he was also well aware of the reason he hadn't restocked the fridge yet, himself. He had expected to be away with Kristin for the entire weekend but that plan had fizzled in only a few hours after they arrived in Maryland.

He wasn't much in the mood to go out to eat either, not after all the drama from the day before. He didn't even feel like walking around the corner to the pizza place that he liked so much, to pick up a couple of slices. He looked into a few plastic containers in the refrigerator instead, but found very questionable contents. It had likely started out as leftovers, no doubt, but now looked more like materials needed for a science project. Eventually, Winston came across some soy cheese that Celeste had made the last time she stayed over. Satisfied with this discovery, he put on some coffee and cut a few slices of the cheese onto a plate, adding some of the not-so-fresh-looking strawberries he had discovered. He carried his find into the living room and then plopped down on his brown leather sectional, still wearing the Scooby Doo pajamas that his kids had given him a few Christmases ago.

He stretched his tall muscular frame across two sections of the couch, propping feet that extended well beyond it onto a nearby ottoman he had dragged closer. Winston settled back into the soft leather pillows on the couch and nibbled at a piece of the cheese that he decided wasn't half-bad. He started picking his way through the strawberries, hoping to spot one or two that weren't too far gone. But when the strong aroma of the brewing coffee hit him, he immediately abandoned the fruit and responded to his need for caffeine. Winston filled a large mug that he reserved for his weekend coffee and took his first grateful sip. After as he did, he looked around the kitchen with wider eyes, seeing it all clearly for the first time that morning. It was only then that he noticed the note that had been left for him by his daughter, propped up against the Lazy-Susan on the breakfast table.

'Bless her heart.'

He knew that by now, both his kids were probably worried sick about him, but he was grateful that they were also respecting his privacy. He knew how hard that was too, especially for Celeste.

She had written on the note that she had picked up some muffins from a vegetarian market around the block. He peeped inside the oven and sure enough, there was a basket filled with carrot walnut muffins still warm to the touch. They had large chunks of walnuts sticking out of their ruptured tops and he plucked one of them from the stainless steel mesh basket that his daughter had placed them in. He covered the other muffins back up with a large cotton cloth he had found across them, with plans to eat more later that afternoon. He made a small cut across the top of the muffin he had selected, adding a large dollop of soy butter that had also been courtesy of his daughter. He carefully placed it on a paper towel and then into the microwave to heat for a few seconds. Once the butter had melted, he carried the hot muffin into the living room and placed it on his plate right next to the cheese, dumping the wilting strawberries into the trash.

He had to admit to himself that his little girl had finally grown up. She had shown considerable restraint over the past few days. He knew how hard it had been for her not to ask a million questions on their drive up to Maryland, he was sure that she had probably thought of a million more questions by now. Both his children would want to know what had happened between him and Kristin, he was sure, but he had no idea what he would tell them.

'Kristin!' His agony renewed itself at the very thought of her name.

Less than twenty-four hours earlier, he had been so optimistic about what the future might hold for them. His sister, Grace, had finally forced him to see how stubborn he had been about everything. He had phoned her thinking that he might have a sympathetic ear, as he and Charlotte were going through all their divorce drama. His sister had given him an earful alright, but it was doubtful that anyone would have called it sympathetic.

She had reminded him of how excited he'd been the first time he mentioned Kristin's name to her. He had called her from Tuskegee—the same day that they met. It was funny how he had forgotten all about it until his sister brought it up that day. He remembered that he told her he had just found the woman of his dreams, and he had described Kristin by saying that God had created her just for him. Grace had forced him to remember it all that day and before he could get comfortable in his thoughts, his sister had abruptly pulled him out of his reminisces. Grace had demanded to know how many more lives he planned to mess up, and then she added that she hoped his experience with Charlotte had helped him finally grow up. And with that, she had hung the phone up—right in his face!

For the next day or two after his sister's tongue-lashing, he had continued to reminisce about how happy he and Kristin had been in Tuskegee. He had gone to see her at Highland Beach ready to own up to all his past foolishness; he had planned to apologize for how he had been acting toward her, especially after he and Angela divorced.

But that had all been before Kristin dropped her own little bombshell; before she told him about the baby—*their* baby, their little girl. He had almost had another daughter twenty-five years ago and couldn't believe that he never knew a thing about it. He knew in his heart that she was the daughter that he and Kristin had dreamed of having once; and she and Celeste would have been around the same age.

Now, he had no idea what he should think about *any* of it. He had been blindsided by Kristin and the biggest surprise had been how nonchalant she seemed about the whole thing. Did she even care?!

Once he was certain Celeste was tucked away in her room for the night, he had gone back downstairs to pour himself a generous shot of Glenlevit and carried it and the bottle back up to his room. The strong taste of the scotch had burned his throat at first, because he had gulped it, rather than sip it. He willed himself not to think about the scene that he had with Kristin earlier, otherwise he knew he would never get any sleep. But after several hours he still had no success so he decided he would force his attention on the memorandum of understanding (MOU) he had just signed with the Army Corps of Engineers.

His company was to provide the hydraulic cylinders and controls that were needed to operate lock guards and service gates, for a lock and dam rehab project they were awarded. It was a substantial three-year contract that was just beginning to take shape, and Winston wanted to make sure he stayed on top of the project time line. But he was far ahead of schedule; they had several months of prep time before his crews would be required on site everyday. The meeting he had been getting ready for on Monday morning would be with one of the companies that would supply the raw materials that his company would use throughout the project.

Combing over the MOU had given him something else to focus on for a while, until he realized he had been unconsciously comparing the project's milestones against their family calendar. And as far as he knew, there had been no updates made to it at all since Charlotte moved out of the loft.

'I guess old habits are hard to break.' He thought about how Charlotte had finally cajoled him into referring to the family's calendar of activities before he set any of his project deadlines. She had him check for any conflicts with the milestones in particular, to minimize any clashes with her social plans. It had kept her from throwing her infamous hissy fits, so going along with her hadn't seemed too high a price. He had to laugh at the irony now, because he could remember a time when her pouting had seemed cute to him.

But that was all before he realized he had merely been the main character in a script she had created for her life. He knew now that the part he played was completely interchangeable; it could be played by virtually any man who had a solid financial future. He hadn't expected her to skip a beat before she found a replacement, and as it turned out he wasn't wrong. The script had been an eight-year run of their marriage, but they had played their last scene so now the show was over.

He had finally seen their marriage for what it was, and once he had, he grew resentful of Charlotte—especially in the months leading up to their divorce. He finally saw the destruction and havoc she had wreaked on his family, and he had no patience with her at all, after that. He had no interest in hearing anything she had to say to him either, and he had adamantly refused her attempts at marriage counseling. He felt no need to sit around with a stranger to dissect their marriage, he had told her, because by then he only wanted to be done with it once and for all.

The final straw had come on the day that she had the nerve to suggest that they start a family, of all things! After that he *knew* he had to do something—and fast. That was the day he decided he couldn't take it any more, and he invited her to dinner that night so they could talk. He took her to one of her favorite restaurants—a really posh place that he thought was very fitting for the occasion. He began by telling her what he had envisioned their marriage would be like, thinking it might be a way of preparing her for where his conversation was going. In mid-sentence, he remembered he had said something very similar to Angela. It caused him to loose his train of thought for several seconds while he recovered from the feelings of déjà vu.

When he looked back on it now, he thought he had been pretty nice to Charlotte, especially considering the deliberately untruthful insinuations she had made about his son. It was only luck that he still had any kind of relationship with Trazi, after her. Her lies had put a serious strain on their relationship for years—to the point that his son had actually left his home to be away from that lying....

Winston had been determined he would remain civil and willing to compromise as they worked through their divorce, even to the point of conceding that he had been the cause of their marriage failing. But Charlotte had still not been satisfied, so she kept taking things farther until she finally went too far. She had the gall to bring up his children, and she even tried to convince *him* of all people that she had been a good mother to them. It was such an obvious lie that Winston tuned out everything else she said after that. He was just glad that she had finally revealed her true colors, because it completely absolved him of any guilt that he had started to feel.

But Charlotte didn't even stop with his kids. He had sat quietly listening to her as she berated him and his mother, who she had managed early on to convince that she adored. He was glad that his mother wasn't there to witness her betrayal of their friendship; glad that she would be spared Charlotte's indiscriminate bashing.

By the time their desserts arrived, Winston had heard more than enough from his soon-to-be-ex-wife. He had been letting her talk as much as she wanted; his lawyer had advised him ahead of time to let her vent. It was part of the reason for the posh restaurant he selected, because he knew she wouldn't make a scene in public. He had given her as much rope as she needed to hang herself and he sat quiet until after their waiter had put their desert plates on the table and left.

Then, he turned to her and said, "Okay, I expected you to be upset by what I told you, so I've let you have your say.

"But here's the bottom line: I know that I said, *"I do"* when we took our wedding vows, and at the time I honestly thought I did. But, as it turns out, I really *don't*. And I'm sorry Charlotte, but I can't see anything changing in that regard. So, I am filing for divorce tomorrow morning and really just wanted to let you know that."

He could see that he had caught her off guard; she sat rigid like a statue for a few seconds with her mouth partially open. Winston could actually see the color rise across her cream-colored face; "high yella" his grandfather had called it. She got up from the table and threw her napkin down on her plate, glaring at Winston before she turned and stomped out of the restaurant.

And needless to say, she had put him through an extremely trying experience before they finally reached a divorce settlement. She had hired an attorney from hell to try to take him for all he was worth. But he had no regrets about the way he had ended their marriage; he thought it entirely befitting of such a greedy vindictive woman as Charlotte turned out to be. To Winston, it had been worth every penny that it took to get her out of their lives. And it wasn't until after it was all over that he admitted to himself that he had never loved her. After the business of their divorce was done, he had seldom given her a second thought. He had rearranged the loft almost immediately after she left, to get it back more to his liking. In many ways, it was as though Charlotte had never even been there. And good riddance!

But on that morning he was glad to have her in his thoughts. It helped him avoid the painful memories of his confrontation with Kristin; he couldn't believe she had kept something so important from him.

'And why? Why wouldn't she just tell me?' He kept asking himself the same question over again, but he already knew the answer. In his heart, he knew she hadn't told him because there was absolutely nothing he could have done about it, just like she said. Deep in his heart he knew that she was right; he would have been devastated had he known they had conceived the baby daughter they had once dreamed about, only to loose her just as Angela was giving birth to Celeste. And it would've been a horrible mess for him to contend with. He wouldn't have been able to comfort Kristin—not in the way that he would have wanted.

'But how could she just make that decision for me?' Each time he thought about it, Winston became even more infuriated.

He couldn't help but wonder what would have happened if their little girl *had* lived. Was Kristin really that cold? Would she have let him bond with their daughter and still not tell him that she was his?

And what about the child? Wouldn't she have the right to know who her father was? Kristin had never answered that question and it bothered him almost as much as finding out he had lost his daughter. It had all happened years ago but he still felt a great sense of loss. The night that they had conceived their baby daughter had been very special for both of them—or at least it had been for him. They had been together for the first time in years and there had been no doubt that they still loved each other, in spite of the mess they had made. He had been consumed by guilt in the days that followed, and was something not able to look her in the face, just as she had said, but those few hours they spent together had been a bright light that they had both badly needed in their sea of darkness. And to now find that they had created a child that night, after all these years!

He was feeling less sure of Kristin than he had ever felt before, and that was the main reason for his pain. His feelings had taken a turn for the worst from the moment she revealed that she had hid the baby from him. It was obvious that she was remorseful that she hadn't told him about it sooner, but as hard as he tried, he couldn't remember a time when she had seemed upset enough to have just lost a child. He thought about what she had said, about sitting in her car after being released from the hospital to pull herself together. That was a day that Winston remembered very clearly; he didn't remember anything that would suggest that she had been upset in any way. He knew that he would have noticed if she had been, even in all his excitement over Celeste. What he remembered was that she had been the opposite of upset that day.

He realized his thinking wasn't rational because no one could say that Kristin hadn't been an excellent mother to Trazi—and Celeste too. Grace had reminded him of that. He thought back to the times that she had been at their house helping Angela with Celeste in the first few months. Now he knew that it had only been a short while since their *own* baby had died, at least according to what she said. Nothing that he remembered around that time had seemed out of the ordinary for her at all to him.

Could he have missed it? Could Celeste have been that much of a distraction that he hadn't realized Kristin was silently suffering? Or maybe the truth was that their baby's death had been a relief to her. After all, it did save them from having to admit that they had betrayed Angela. But had their little girl's death really meant nothing to her?

❋❋❋

Angela had begun withdrawing from him soon after they were married, so much so that Celeste's conception had been a miracle in itself. Their marital relations had become less and less frequent within the first six months of their union. And to make matters worse, Angela's emotional state had begun an accelerated decline around the same time. She had made it painfully clear that she wasn't happy about the baby she was carrying all throughout her pregnancy. She made her arrangements for prenatal care and everything else involving the baby in a very impersonal manner, as though she were imagining that it was happening to someone else. Winston blamed himself for all of her problems, and felt guilty at being so happy about the baby that was making his wife so miserable. He had been at his wits end trying to make things seem normal for Trazi, and he had no idea how he would have managed without Kristin's support.

He had silently watched Angela for months, deluding himself into thinking that she would eventually snap out if it. He reasoned that as their baby grew inside her and began kicking, she would plug back into reality and take on more than a superficial interest in her pregnancy. But that time never came. She even responded with an almost comical robotic reaction whenever Celeste took to plummeting her with her tiny appendages, a reflexive movement of her hands across her belly.

Kristin and Angela had grown as close as sisters by that time and Winston felt he could speak freely about Angela to her. She would seek her advice from time to time, just as he would have sought advice from Angela's sisters, had they lived closer by.

He and Kristin had never entertained the thought of betraying her, or acting on their obvious attraction to each other that had never died. They never considered being together again—not as long as Winston was still married to Angela, and especially not while she was pregnant. He had been grateful to Kristin for helping him take care of his wife and their new baby too. It had been Kristin who kept up with all the doctors' appointments; she even started going with Angela after Celeste was born, to make certain nothing was going on that they needed to be aware of.

Sure, he felt awkward at first, but he was even more reluctant to discuss his wife's peculiar behavior with his mother. She had always considered Angela a much better "catch" than Kristin; based, no doubt, on the fact that Angela's father was a general at the Pentagon. But his mother's fondness had more to do with her disapproval of Kristin, than anything else. She had never considered her family to be in a high enough social class for her son, not for her to marry him and have his children. Her opinion about Angela had changed, of course, in the end, but she had welcomed both of Kristin's replacements, just as soon as Winston introduced them.

And he knew that asking Grace for help was out of the question. She had barely concealed her opinion about Angela, and it definitely wasn't a good one. Her assessment of Charlotte had been no better. After he introduced them, Grace had grunted under her breath loud enough for him to hear, "that's two for two." And later that same afternoon, she had phoned to tell him that Charlotte was a gold digger who wouldn't give him the time of day if he didn't have a comfortable six-figure income.

Winston had been happy at first that Angela had no interest in his career. He didn't mind at all that there had been no questions for him as soon as he got home every day. He had stopped appreciating Kristin's attention to his daily work experiences long before their divorce, somewhere around the time that he was promoted at Goddard space center. That never stopped her, of course, but he had to admit that whenever she pressed him about something that he had mentioned to her earlier, he would usually conclude later that she had called attention to some significant factor that he might have otherwise overlooked. How she did it, he couldn't say. Half the time, he would be talking about something highly technical, like some aspect of nuclear propulsion. Without any foreknowledge of the subject, she seemed to understand enough of what he said to influence his consideration in areas that he often hadn't thought of before.

Angela had been different from Kristin in many more ways. His second wife had been very secretive for one thing, but he didn't mind that either. He even appreciated the mystery and after they first started dating, he decided the less complicated their relationship was, the better. It never occurred to him until later that the reason he didn't mind her being so secretive was because he didn't want to know that much about her. At that time, the most important thing to him was that she was nice, in an artsy kind of way—and she was cute.

Apparently he had learned little from the mistakes he made with her, because he made some of the same ones with Charlotte. He had married both of them thinking they would help him raise his kids; and the irony was that neither of them contributed much at all in that department. Angela and Charlotte put together weren't half the woman that Kristin was. And that's why it made no sense now that he hadn't fought for their marriage. He couldn't even remember why they got a divorce—one day they were married and the next day they weren't. At the time it seemed like the logical thing to do, but now it just seemed stupid. Kristin had been his closest friend from the time that they had met, closer even than most of his frat brothers.

And now he had lost his best friend.

They had agreed when they split up that it would be best for their son if he found a place close enough for him to easily stop by Kristin's house on his way home, if there were a need. And Trazi had given them plenty of justification for him doing it—to pick up a toy or to drop one off. Winston would come by to collect a pair of pajamas, or a robe, or *something* that was always left at the house where Trazi *wasn't* sleeping that night.

He had still worked long hours for NASA back then but only because Angela didn't care whether he was home or not. He had his eye on another big promotion that would mean more money and far less hours at work. But as things stood at the time, his working as much as he did left little time for him to consider how miserable his life really was.

He had stopped by on the night they ended up together to talk to Kristin about a conference they needed to have with Trazi's teacher. Winston readily admitted that he was glad to have the excuse to visit her because he always left her house feeling much better about everything in general. He had even questioned himself that night whether he might be taking unfair advantage of her, as he pulled his car into her drive. She had never seemed to mind it though; he could talk to her about anything too, including what he was going through with Angela.

Neither of them had reason to think that anything would be different that night than it had been any other time he had stopped by. He could sense that she was upset about something as soon as she opened the door, and he had offered her the support he would have given to any friend. His intention had been to lend a sympathetic ear and commiserate, but that had touched off something in both of them. In an instant, the barriers they had normally kept in place between them, disappeared. They were suspended in time and in a place where only the two of them existed.

He still couldn't say what had been different about that night. All he knew for sure was that his carefully controlled will power had suddenly vanished without warning. His conviction for doing the right thing was long forgotten and he was overtaken by a fierce yearning for the love of his life. Before he realized it, they were locked in a passionate embrace that was too powerful for either of them to resist. Their first kiss ignited a desire that had been simmering just beneath the surface for a long time. They no longer denied their love for each other, that one night. They had both savored every touch and every caress, as though they had all the time in the world. And when their passion could no longer be contained, all judgment was suspended and they had found contentment in each others arms.

Their mangled bodies glistened with perspiration and they had fallen asleep together with their very breathing in synch. But a strong dose of reality had greeted him as soon as he got up to go to the bathroom. It shouted out to him and reminded him that he was married to *Angela* and not Kristin; Angela, who was nearly five months pregnant with his child, and who was at home that very moment in the fragile state she had been in for months, waiting for him to get there. He was also reminded that his small son was with her and that he had been expected home almost an hour earlier. Even at that he still climbed back into bed with Kristin, desperate to hold onto the moment that he knew would soon fade. It was a half hour later before he could force himself away from her again.

He had stood over her and watched her sleep, knowing that what they had shared that night would be gone again the second he left. He couldn't imagine how *anything* would be the same for them again, but he also couldn't see a way for anything to be different. He was already weighed down by guilt by the time he dressed to leave and left Kristin asleep in their old bed.

When he thought back to how close they had been that night, he was even more baffled that she didn't trust him enough to tell him about the baby. He was still bothered that she seemed so unaffected by their little girl's death. Was it because there had been so much time that had gone by? Had she moved beyond her grief?

He could always sense that she felt guilty about betraying Angela too, but as hard as he tried, Winston couldn't remember a time when she seemed upset at all about loosing their baby. He kept thinking back to different times that he had been around her after Celeste was first born. He couldn't recall that she seemed grief-stricken at all, or when she had acted in a way that he imagined a woman who had just had a miscarriage, would act.

Was she that good of an actress?

No matter what she said, he just didn't think he would have missed it. He could only presume that loosing their baby hadn't meant as much to her as it did to him.

That hurt him to his core, and he wasn't sure it was the kind of thing he would ever get past.

Chapter 25

One In A Million, Chance Of A Lifetime

"**D**addy?" Celeste called out to her father softly as she peeped around the doorway of his office. "Do you have a minute? I need to talk to you."

"Hey baby," Winston looked up from his computer pleasantly surprised, until he noticed the distressed look on his daughter's face.

"Sure, come on in. What is it?"

Celeste had stopped by to chat with him more frequently when she first started working with at their firm. But once she learned her way around and got involved in her own projects, she rarely had much time to stop by at work anymore.

She took a deep breath as she crossed the threshold and sat down across from father's desk. It had been nearly a year since the fiasco at Highland Beach and every time she saw him he seemed less affected by whatever happened between him and Aunt Kristin there. He had been down in the dumps for months after that weekend, but still hadn't given her as much as a hint about what caused their big blowout.

She only hoped that enough time had passed for him to accept what she had come to tell him.

"What is it sweetheart?" Winston asked the question again and with a hint of concern in his voice this time. He was bracing himself for whatever it was his daughter came to tell him. He had seen her tussling with something for the past several days and knew her well enough to know that something was heavy on her mind. Judging from her recent behavior, he had guessed that it might be serious.

Celeste sighed deeply before she answered. "Well...," She hesitated in

293

starting. "I'm not sure how you're going to take this, Daddy...but I've been thinking a lot about Aunt Kristin's foundation lately. I've been thinking about going to Ghana to live with her for a while, to help her out with some of the designs they need for the next set of commercial buildings."

At first she had directly at her father so she could gauge his reaction, but then she changed her mind and dropped her head quickly to avoid his eyes.

Winston didn't respond at first to his daughter; he had to let what she said sink in for a while. He couldn't believe what she was saying really, and realized he had been *way* off in guessing what might be on her mind.

He had made no secret that he admired what Kristin was doing in Ghana, in spite of everything that had happened between them personally. Her foundation's success had not only benefitted Ghana but it had been a welcome relief to the federal budget in the U.S. too. Money that had once been spent for entitlement programs was on the decline, as more and more benumbed Black American began to realize who they were and how they got to where they are today. Many of them had already left for Ghana to have their souls restored in West Africa, and many more who had opted not to participate in Kristin's programs, were still developing a '60s-like pride in themselves. They were pulling themselves up in America again, and from what he had been reading in the papers, there had been thousands who had graduated from Exodus Village to become healthy and prosperous human beings.

He knew for a fact that many of the people who had initially balked at the idea of moving back to Africa, and had first resisted any connection to the Exodus Foundation, were also starting to come around. It was just like in the '60s. Black people like his mother and her friends had been so indignant with James Brown and his controversial hit song at first. Brown had urged Black Americans to say out loud that they were Black and proud—something literally unheard of at the time and frowned upon by many.

Back then, most of the detractors found their outrage at the song lessening over time too. Black Americans soon grew to not only accept the distinct features of their African ancestors but they developed a great sense of pride in them as well. There had been a revolutionary shift of energy in the '60s, as the world felt the effects of a major astronomical/astrological event; one that was 2,100+ years in the making. It was energy being ushered in by the new Age of Aquarius, with far reaching changes brought to the world to last for another 2,100 years.

At the time of Marcus Garvey's Universal Negro Improvement Association, the word "Negro" had literally kept the coloreds in Jamaica, like his mother, who had European ancestry as well as African, from identifying themselves with the word in any way. When the British military excluded Jamaican "colored" soldiers from being promoted beyond a certain rank during World War I, even in their outrage, they had still distanced themselves from Garvey and his movement. All because of the word "Negro" which means "black" in Spanish, something they had adamantly refused to associate themselves with.

Winston was secretly proud that his daughter wanted to play a more active role in Kristin's mission, beyond the regular charitable contributions that she already made. It was obvious that the Foundation carried the Aquarian energy of brotherhood and concern for all fellow human beings. And he knew that Celeste had passionately embraced its mission since her visit to see Kristin when she was still in high school.

But the thought of having her moving so far away was another story altogether. She had been working at his firm since her graduation from Tuskegee, and it wasn't long at all before she had established herself as more that just the boss's daughter. Celeste found her niche in designing energy efficient commercial buildings; she also developed a talent for incorporating green technologies into contemporary concepts. She was good at what she did, and she was starting bringing in a significant amount of business. He had just made her a full partner a few months earlier, as they celebrated her twenty-fifth birthday.

His first company had been dissolved during negotiations for his last divorce settlement. Charlotte had been vindictive enough to insist that he sell the company right away , so she could have the money that she was entitled from it. He had waited patiently until after their divorce was final before he resurrected a new company. And as it turned out, she had actually done him a favor instead of the intended harm. His newly restructured company had already made more money in the first couple of years than his previous one had during the entire time he owned it. And to make things even better, Trazi had finally agreed to add the third "Bailey" to Bailey, Bailey and Bailey Architectural and Engineering Designs. His son had finally gone to college on his on and earned an engineering degree. He had already started work on developing a new alternative energy division for their company. The Bailey's had evolved into an excellent team, except now his daughter was sitting across from him telling him that she wanted to leave.

"Dad?" Celeste broke through his silent thoughts. "It's not that I don't love working with you and Trazi—I do. But this is something that I've dreamed of doing since I was fifteen years old. I think that it's time for me to make my contribution to the Exodus Foundation, that's all," she offered her rehearsed explanation.

"I really want to help Aunt Kristin in Ghana, and I know that the solar experience I've gained here can be put to good use for the Foundation." She still avoided looking directly into his eyes and he suspected there was something else that she was not saying.

"This is an opportunity for me to be a part of history, Daddy—a one in a million, chance of a lifetime." She made the attempt at humor to lighten the mood, and then she was quiet again.

"Well, it certainly seems as though you've given it a lot of thought." Her father's comment bridged the silence that had dropped after her last statement.

"I've been thinking about this for a few months, off and on." There was a delayed reaction in her response, as though her mind had drifted for a time until she was drawn back into their conversation. "I really could get a lot of experience there too and our company would definitely benefit from it later—after I work for a year or two in Ghana.

Winston's eyebrows shot up when she mentioned being away for two years.

"I think that it'll only benefit us in the long run..." She kept talking, because she wasn't ready to hear what her father's response would be.

"...It would really be more like a leave of absence than anything else."

She braced herself and finally looked directly into her his eyes. It nearly broke her heart when she did because he looked so hurt and sad.

That was when Celeste decided she had to tell him all of it. She had to tell him the other reason that she wanted to go to Ghana now—the main reason.

"There is something else, Daddy," she finally admitted. "...And it's just as important."

There was something in his daughter's voice that made Winston look at her more closely. When he did, he could see that she was close to tears.

"Sweetheart! What's the matter?" He moved around to the other side of his desk quickly, so that he could take her hands in his. "What has you so upset?"

"It's Ishmael, Daddy," she answered him simply, and a lone tear rolled down her coffee-colored cheek. "I have to put some distance between us."

"Well, that's an awful lot of distance, sweetie." He smiled, trying to lighten her mood, but the intensity of her eyes told him she wouldn't be receptive to joking.

"Well, what happened?" For the first time he noticed the pained look on her face."I thought everything was going okay with you two."

"It is..." She was quick to reassure him. "...Well, at least, sort of..." Her contradiction came just as quickly and on realizing it, she stopped herself with a heavy sigh.

"Okay, Celeste." Her father had already grown impatient waiting as she went around in circles. "Just tell me what you're trying to say. What's going on?"

"Okay," she agreed quietly. "But first, you have to promise me that you won't get upset with Ishmael."

"Just tell me." He was more adamant this time, already upset at the thought of Ishmael doing *anything* that would hurt his daughter.

Celeste interrupted his menacing thoughts as she began to open up finally. "This is about something that happened a long time ago," she began, "before I transferred to Tuskegee."

'Why did that sound so familiar?'

Winston remembered how evasive his daughter had been about why she wanted to transfer. He had always hoped that she would want go to his Alma mater so he hadn't pressed her for any details about her sudden change of heart.

Celeste took another deep breath and told her father everything that had happened before she left for school in Tuskegee. Winston listened in disbelief as his daughter described how she had walked in on Ishmael and some other woman, in a small quiet voice. He couldn't believe that he was just hearing it for the first time, especially since his daughter had obviously gone through such a traumatic experience.

"Why didn't you tell me, baby?" He pulled her close to his chest as though protecting her. "I'm so sorry that you went through all this."

Silently, he had to wonder why the women in his life withheld such important things from him. Did he come across as being that uncaring? Were they afraid they wouldn't be able to trust him with their pain?

"I was too upset to talk about it, Daddy." She answered, and then she started to cry again. "Besides," she said between sniffles, "there wasn't anything you could have done about it. There wasn't anything *anyone* could have done," There was such sadness in her voice that Winston could hardly stand to hear it.

"And I couldn't be mad with Ishmael," she persisted. "It's not like he had planned it or anything. It was something that had happened before we even started dating.

"...And I certainly couldn't be upset with him for wanting to be a real father to his child either, or for being decent enough to be supportive of Kendra when she needed him."

Winston suddenly realized why everything his daughter said seemed so familiar. The conversation he was having with her bore an eerie similarity to the one he had with Kristin a year before.

"But what happened to the baby?" He heard himself ask the question, already knowing the answer.

"She lost the baby, Daddy," Celeste sighed in frustration, "shortly after I got to Tuskegee—I just never knew anything about it.

"And that's the part that has me so out of whack now. I refused to talk to Ishmael after that day in his apartment, so I never knew about the baby until I ran into him after graduation."

Winston still stared at his daughter in disbelief.

What could this all mean? It was like watching the second act of the same bad play.

"How could Ishmael *keep* something like that from you?" He heard himself suddenly explode, unable to control his anger any longer.

Celeste had been crying softly with both hands over her face, but after her father's outburst she stopped crying. She lowered her hands slowly so she could look at her dad because it had come as such a surprise.

"I never told him where I was going, Daddy," she said it hesitantly, not sure what had caused his reaction. But she instinctively defended Ishmael as she had since the day they met.

"We never talked about Tuskegee at all. And I'm sure he didn't want to run the risk of asking *you* where I was."

Winston had barely heard most of what she said. He was still too stunned by all the similarities in their situations.

"His cousin graduated with my class at Tuskegee," Celeste told her father, still not sure what had set him off, "from the vet school. We ran into each other after commencement, when I was still looking for you guys. That's the only reason that I know anything at all about what happened."

She looked over at her father when he didn't respond, to see if he was still okay. He seemed alright, but his mind had obviously gone far away.

"Ishmael wants things to go back to the way they were between us," she confided a second later, "before everything happened. "But I just don't know if I can forget about it."

"He really *is* trying to be patient with me, Daddy. I'm just so scared...

I'm not sure whether I can trust him with my heart again yet."

"Of *course* you can't trust him," Winston angrily agreed, forgetting himself again. "Why *should* you trust a man who would keep something like that from you?" He didn't even seem to hear her explanation about Ishmael not knowing where to find her. Then it seemed to dawn on him that the outburst he made had been inappropriate for what she was saying. He looked at his daughter sheepishly and tried to pull himself together.

"Daddy, is everything okay?" She had temporarily forgotten about her own dilemma and was now looking at her father very carefully.

Were those *tears* welling up in his eyes?

She leaned over to comfort him with a hug but she was still alarmed. She had *never* seen her father so upset; such an emotional display was completely out of character.

"What's wrong Daddy?" "Please, tell me... Are you all right?"

He finally changed his position in the chair so he could look at his daughter head-on. He let out a big sigh of his own before he answered her question.

"Yes and no, sweetie." He was aware that he wasn't making any sense, and that now *he* had begun speaking in riddles.

"Do you want me to call someone?" Celeste was suddenly terrified that something was really wrong with him. Maybe he was sick or something.

"No, no, baby." He was agitated with himself that he couldn't control an unexpected flow of tears.

"Just give me a minute." He tried to stall for more time but he realized that wouldn't work either. He had no choice but to tell his daughter what was really bothering him. He had to tell her *something* after that outburst, and all the crying. Otherwise, she might think he was insane.

"Okay..." Celeste compromised, "but you're starting to scare me."

"I'm sorry, baby...I guess I just needed some sort of release, that's all." He was still having a hard time pulling himself together. He had never once considered that he might need to mourn the loss of his baby daughter, but now he knew how much he needed to do just that.

"Does any of this have to do with what happened at Highland Beach?" Celeste had a clear picture in her mind of how upset he had been that night too, when she had come back to find him sitting outside the house on the steps.

"How did you know that?" After he asked, he quickly realized it would be the only logical conclusion that she *could* reach. He had responded to her question without even waiting for a response to his own.

"...Yes, it has everything to do with that. But you have to promise me that you won't say anything to Kristin, or to Trazi," he pleaded with her.

"I promise, Daddy." She still hesitated for a second, racking her brain while wondering what could make her father go through so many changes.

"You can talk to me about it Daddy, whatever it is." She was silent again after her reassurances.

Winston hesitated for a few seconds more before he finally told his daughter about her little sister who had died on the same day that she was born. It was hard for him to look at her as he confessed to having had a brief affair with Kristin during the time that he was still married to her mother. But he did, and he forced himself to look her straight in the eye as he fully owned up to what he and Kristin had done. He ended his shocking confession by telling Celeste that he had only found out about the baby when they saw Kristin up at Highland Beach, the previous year.

She had remained quiet during the whole time he talked so he would have a chance to say all that he needed to say. Celeste couldn't have been more astonished and she found it impossible to imagine that any of it had happened. If someone other than her father or Kristin had told it to her, she would have never believed that it was true. For some time, she was very confused. She didn't know what to think about *anything*.

Winston had been looking for signs that her daughter would hate him, once she had found out about his betrayal of her mother. But all he saw was love in her dark blue eyes instead, mixed with a great deal of bewilderment.

"Daddy, do you think my mother knew?" She asked the question after a few minutes of silence. "Is that why she always had such a hard time?"

Her innocence made his tears start again. He braced himself to answer the question he had dreaded since the day she was born.

"I honestly don't think she did, baby," he said slowly. Your mother and Kristin were like sisters, which only made what we did that much worse.

He knew that the turbulence he saw in his daughter's eyes only mirrored what she must have been feeling. He hesitated, not sure if he should say anything more. He tried to anticipate how she might feel about the rest and couldn't be sure whether to say it. Finally, he decided that it was best to be totally honest with her because she was too smart not to guess the truth.

"Kristin and I have always loved each other," he heard himself say. He felt an instant relief as the weight he had been carrying around was lifted from his shoulders. "We've been in denial about it for a long time."

"But I did love your mother, too," he hastened to say. "It's just that I honestly never stopped loving Kristin, that's all."

She could see how torn her father was and she hugged him again to let him know that she wasn't upset. He had told her something that took a great deal of courage to say; she knew how difficult it must have been but still, there was a lot to process. As she thought back over her life it all began to make sense. *Everything* made perfect sense now after what her father had told her.

They were both quiet until a puzzled look grew across her face.

"Wait...I don't understand something. Why were you so *angry* with Aunt Kristin? Why are you *still* angry with her?"

Winston hesitated before speaking. He didn't want to say anything that might cause his daughter's opinion of Kristin to change, especially in light of what she already knew. But there was no turning back now because only the truth would satisfy her. He took another deep breath before answering.

"It's because I couldn't...I *still* can't understand how it could be so easy for her," he confessed to his daughter.

"Kristin acts as though our baby's death meant *nothing* to her. I've been over it in my head again and again, and I can't remember anything that suggests she ever mourned for our baby girl. It seems as though it didn't matter to her at all. I'm pretty sure she would've been able to *hide* something like that from me," he concluded.

Celeste was now even more surprised than ever. She didn't believe for one second that Kristin had been unaffected by her baby's death. She would've been upset to know of *any* baby dying and she must have been devastated about loosing her own. She immediately regretted having promised her father that she wouldn't say anything to Kristin. He had to be wrong in his suspicions and Kristin was the only person who would be able to prove it.

"There has to be some other explanation." She told him confidently. "I don't know what it is yet, but there *has* to be something else."

Her father looked at her with an expression that she couldn't define.

"I must admit this has taken me by surprise," she told him, thinking he might be anxious to hear how she felt. "And it's sad too, because I almost had a sister. I've wanted one for a long time..."

Hearing the wistfulness in her voice made Winston remember that *she* had been the one to come to see *him*. He apologized after it dawned on him that he had somehow turned her conversation about Ishmael into one about him and Kristin.

Was he really as self-centered as his sister had accused him of being?

As hard as it had been for him, he was glad that he had finally told his daughter the truth. In the process, he had rid himself of guilt he had carried around for twenty-five years. It felt good to be relieved of it, despite the awkwardness of the situation. He had never realized how much he needed to talk to someone, because he had apparently been weighed down since their trip to Highland Beach.

"I love Aunt Kristin too, Daddy," Celeste told him, after a minute or two of silence. "I always have."

Winston couldn't believe how lucky he was that his daughter possessed such understanding.

After another big sigh, he told her that he understood why she needed to get away from Ishmael and that it was okay with him.

"And I promise not to tell him where you are, if he comes looking."

They both knew that Winston would be the first person Ishmael would come to this time. The two men had become much closer and they had developed a relationship all of their own. Winston knew he was a good man, and in spite of his daughter's plans to leave the U.S., he had every reason to believe that Ishmael would still become his son-in-law one day. But he would keep the promise he had made to his daughter and stay out of it. Ishmael would have to capture her heart again without his help.

"I'm going to hold you to your promise though," he reminded her, "that you'll only be gone for two years."

He had come to depend on Celeste in many ways and he made sure that she knew he would miss her terribly after she was gone. He had only realized at that moment how much she *had* been helping him hold it together since their brief trip to Highland Beach.

They spent time talking about who would cover for Celeste during her absence, and how she would roll off the projects she was currently working on. She left him to go and call Kristin once everything was settled to make arrangements to join her aunt at the Exodus Foundation, who was pleasantly surprised to hear the news. After they had hung up, Celeste called Malaya next to share the news with her. She and her friend had seen each other occasionally, but she still had not resumed being the Malaya that she used to be. Celeste had already begun daydreaming about her friend coming to visit her in Ghana, by the time they got off the phone.

This time, she decided she would send Ishmael a letter to let him know she was leaving Washington. She wouldn't say where she was going yet, but she would ask him to be patient and give her time to clear her head.

Chapter 26

That Midnight Plane...

*I*shmael boarded his connecting flight and leaned back to settle into his seat for the second leg of the trip. He had been a child the last time he had seen his grandmother and he was excited that he would soon see her again. They had spoken on the phone often as he grew up, and those conversations had become more frequent once he enrolled in medical school. They had talked even more during his internship and residency at Hunter University Hospital. He heard in her voice how pleased she was that he had chosen to follow in her footsteps.

At one time, he had thought that he might be bringing Celeste along with him to meet his grandmother, as he readied himself to start his own practice. But she had been gone for nearly a year now, and without a word. He had no idea where she was nor whether she ever intended to come back to Washington at all. Her father had seemed sympathetic to his cause but Ishmael soon realized it was a wasted effort to try and persuade him to tell him where his daughter had gone.

He didn't blame either of them; he knew that he had messed things up pretty bad but he would've done anything in the world to fix it. He had noticed the struggle in her dark eyes when they were together and sensed she was having flashbacks about Kendra and the baby She had tried hard to forget about the whole thing. But how could she? He had started feeling her pull away from him for months before she actually left; it happened whenever they were alone together, and especially if they seemed to be getting close. He wished that he had found a way to restore her trust in him. He could only hope that her pain would pass in time or at least start to fade. He was still optimistic that she might give him another chance some day to prove himself, and to show her how sincere he really was.

He had prayed that she wouldn't bring up Kendra though, as he watched her struggle. He wouldn't have been able to lie and it would have been a tough conversation for both of them. Now, looking back, he wondered if it was one that they needed to have. When he looked back at the way that things had transpired, he couldn't honestly say that he would've done anything differently, given the circumstances. His parents had raised him to be strong and be responsible as a man. His family was very important to him and as difficult as the situation was, he had never *dreamed* of abandoning his child. And he wouldn't abandon Kendra either, especially not as long as their baby was small.

Still, he would've given anything to go back in time to change the way that Celeste had found out about the whole thing. He loved her more than anything and would never have hurt her intentionally—not in a million years. Everything had all happened so quickly. He still hadn't had time yet to digest that Kendra was pregnant himself, and then he turned his head to find Celeste standing there watching him comfort his former girlfriend. He would have given anything to have found a better way of telling her—anything to keep her from finding out in the dreadful way that she had. And to make matters worse, Kendra had always been an attractive woman, though she couldn't hold a candle, in his eyes, to Celeste. She had turned more than a few heads in her day, but she just wasn't the woman for Ishmael. That had been the only reason they weren't already together at the time that he met Celeste.

He only had himself to blame for missing out on his opportunity to make it right too, or at least give it more of a try. Everyday, he found himself wishing that he had done something different, something other than just waiting for things to right themselves. He should have used the short time he had with her more wisely, after she graduated and moved back from Tuskegee. He should have tried much harder to reach her, to convince her that he had never stopped loving her. He should have tried to make her understand that he had to do what he had done, and that now he planned to dedicate a lifetime to making it up to her.

He wished there was some way to erase the image of him standing with his arms around Kendra from her mind. He knew that it was still etched there and he couldn't imagine how he would've reacted had the shoe been on the other foot. She had heard him tell another woman that he would marry her, for God's sake, so he could only be grateful that she had agreed to try again after that.

The whole episode had been bizarre from start to finish. For one thing, it had been out of character for him to be with Kendra in the first place, and especially without having taken some precautions. They had only dated for a short time when they were in high school. There had been some history between them before that night, though never the kind of intimacy it evolved into. They hadn't seen each other for years until she had come to his parents' restaurant looking for him. It was only a few months after he and Celeste started running into each other at the campus library. Kendra had managed to convince him to take a short break from his studies, and they ended up at a party together with a good number of their old high school friends. Everyone had a nice enough time that night and they had all danced quite a bit. He enjoyed the mini-reunion and the company of his former classmates, but things had changed radically when he and Kendra danced to a song that she had once called "their song."

It started them down a long road of reminiscing that had eventually gotten out of hand. He had no excuse really, because at the time he had planned his entire life around going to medical school. He knew exactly where babies came from, but what happened between them had been less a romantic reunion than a case of post-teenage hormones. Kendra had a few drinks that evening before they walked onto the dance floor, and it seemed to have prompted her to be friendlier with him than normal. He had allowed things to go too far as they danced, and he had beaten himself up countless times over his lapse in judgement.

But the most bizarre part of all was Kendra losing the baby, and that she had only been pregnant long enough to break him and Celeste up. He had been genuinely sad for a while when he got the news that the baby didn't make it, but now when he looked back on the whole episode, it all just seemed odd.

He thought back to how intent he had been on staying away from Celeste when they first met, afraid that she might distract him from his studies. His grandmother had been right, as usual, when he talked to her about how he felt. She had warned him to be careful what he wished for, because there was good chance that he just might get it. She had also taught him as he was growing up that there was no such thing as coincidence. He had puzzled about the timing of everything because Celeste had never used his apartment key until that fateful day.

If he could have gone back in time, he would have said something to her about all of it before she left Washington again. Maybe if they had talked, they would have found a way to work things out. They might have started couples counseling or something. Maybe, if he had just been honest and talked to her about everything that happened, she wouldn't have left him again.

Ishmael stared out the small window of his plane and prayed that they would find each other again somehow. Their chances had grown even more slim now because he had left Washington too. Her father hadn't budged an inch when he stopped by to tell him that he was leaving, so he still had no idea where he could even start looking for Celeste. He looked out the tiny plane window again and into the moonlit sky. He vowed to himself that he would never let her go again if he were lucky enough to find her some day. He was convinced more than ever that they belonged together, and that she was the only woman for him. He wouldn't stop until he persuaded her to trust him with her heart again, when he found her. He was miserable without her in his life and he had to make it all right.

Ishmael had promised his grandmother that he would set up a clinic in her community; he had finished his residency, so that was precisely what he was on his way to do. There was an urgent need for pediatricians there and his grandmother had sounded pleased when he called to let her know he was on his way. Once he had the clinic set up and operational, he would call Winston again. He would let her father know where he could be contacted, and maybe by then, Celeste would have had a change of heart herself. Maybe she would be ready to see him again.

He had just begun to stir from a short nap when he felt the plane begin its final descent. As it prepared to land, Ishmael gratefully accepted a warm damp towel from a flight attendant as she passed his row of seats. It had been a long flight, but he felt refreshed again after wiping his face. His grandmother had sent a driver to pick him up, and he would be at her house soon enough. He spotted the young man in the airport terminal, holding a sign with his name written across it in large neat lettering. As soon as he had collected his things and they were loaded in the trunk, the driver had them out of the airport in no time and on their way.

Ishmael leaned back in the seat as the young man cruised down the main street that would carry him out of the airport. His grandmother's house was just over 54 kilometers away, or just under 35 miles. Ishmael decided that he would take another quick nap on the way to her house. He had spent the past six months doing double shifts at the hospital; he hadn't realized how tired he was until after he had boarded his plane.

The next thing he knew the driver was tapping him lightly on the shoulder to let him know they had arrived. Ishmael stretched his long legs after he had stepped out of the car, and hurried toward the front door of his grandmother's house. The driver, in the meantime, pulled his bags out and followed him inside.

"Nana!" Ishmael called out to his grandmother. He pulled open the front screen door and walked inside still calling her name.

She had been standing in the middle of the living room and turned toward the front door seconds before her grandson's voice rang out.

"Oh good mercy, me—my grandson is finally home!" Nana quickly moved toward Ishmael as he rushed forward to meet her. He was overjoyed to see his grandmother and gave her a gigantic warm hug. Her house was instantly familiar to him from the summer he had spent there as an eight year old.

Nana pulled back from him almost reluctantly so she could trace her fingers across his face. Both of them were totally oblivious to the driver, who had quietly deposited his bags inside the door before leaving.

"Well, well..My little boy has come home a man—and a doctor at that!" She smiled her approval as she updated the mental picture that was stored in her mind, adding to it a now ruggedly-handsome face.

Ishmael still felt a bit disoriented from having gone months without a good night's sleep and now, added to it was the long time difference. As he sought to regain his equilibrium, a shadowy figure that had been just out of his immediate vision on the right side, caught his eye. It was only then that he realized his grandmother had a visitor, and as he turned fully to greet them he could only stare in disbelief.

"What are you doing here?" Celeste and Ishmael asked the question at the exact same time. She had stood rooted to the floor from the second that she had heard his voice on Nana's porch. Her mind refused to accept that it was possible, at first. How could Ishmael possibly be standing in Nana Adwoa's house?

Neither of them could do anything except look dumbfounded at the other. Ishmael broke through their daze by releasing his grandmother abruptly; he hurried to where Celeste stood. He gave her an even bigger hug than the one he had given his grandmother, as they both smiled happily, in curious wonder. They were like two children on Christmas morning, who had unwrapped presents to find the very thing that they had hoped to find. They hugged each other again after a brief interval, and neither of them were able to imagine how they had found each other in such an unlikely

307

place. That curiosity was suspended as they indulged in the contentment of familiar warmth; they each felt a completeness in being together again.

Nana Adwoa stood back with a big smile pasted across her smooth ebony face. She didn't seem at all surprised by what had transpired, but for the first time she wished that she had her sight. She wanted to see it for herself, to witness the joyous reunion of her grandson and his bride-to-be.

"...Wait...You mean Nana Adwoa is your grandmother?" Celeste asked. She pulled back to search Ishmael's eyes, finally finding her voice. Her mind had just processed his earlier conversation with Nana. It was starting to sink in that Nana and Ishmael were blood relatives. But how was that possible? And how could Ishmael be standing right in front of her, just like that?

She had visited Nana regularly during the year she had been in Ghana, and they had become quite close. She had thought about Ishmael constantly since she arrived and she had finally confided everything to Nana one day—about Ishmael, Kendra, the baby, and finding them together at his apartment. She had looked to the older woman for advice on how to get past it, but Nana had only listened to her instead. She would not tell Celeste what she should do, not even when she asked her directly. She would only tell her that she would know what to do when the time came. And she had been right too, because she knew she belonged with Ishmael the minute he walked through the day.

She remembered the first day she had met Nana Adwoa, and felt wobbly for a second as she took it all in. It had been not long after her fifteenth birthday, when she and Trazi visited Ghana together for the first time. She remembered how puzzled she had been that day too. Nana had come directly to her when she, Trazi and Kristin walked into the room. She had called her "granddaughter" and they had all thought it strange at the time. Now it all seemed even more strange—but in a way that was good. Kristin had advised her to accept that she wouldn't necessarily understand everything Nana said to her or did. She had added that she was a very wise and intuitive woman though; no one questioned her judgement about life in general or about healing herbs in particular.

But how could she have possibly known about her and Ishmael all that time ago?

He finally released Celeste so that he could go over to his grandmother and hug her again, and give her big wet kisses all over her face. His mother had always told him that her mother could do magical things. She had given him something that was special to him, each and every time he saw her. She had done it all his life, and he could never figure out how she always knew exactly what he wanted. There was no doubt in his mind that she had arranged everything for him, somehow. Celeste had been the best present that his grandmother had ever given him, and he still didn't understand how it was possible.

But he finally remembered Celeste's lingering question. "Yes, she sure is my grandmother," he answered her in amazement, "but I haven't seen this beautiful woman since I was eight years old. I spent the summer here all that time ago, but now it seems like it was just yesterday."

"But how do *you* know each other?" Ishmael looked to her to help him clear up the mystery. He already knew his grandmother would never give him a straight answer. He was momentarily distracted by Celeste's beauty and that she was really standing right in front of him. He remembered the vow he had made on the plane and smiled inwardly to himself.

"I can't understand how she could be your grandmother! I've known Nana since I was fifteen years old." Her answer only served to astonish him further.

"I met her on my first trip to Ghana." She walked closer to where Ishmael and his grandmother were standing. He was smiling broadly at her and she smiled back in her own mysterious way.

"I never knew you had been to Ghana...But both of us came here years before we even met." They turned to look at Nana, who seemed to be having the time of her life.

There was obviously much about each other that they had never bothered to learn. The incident with Kendra had happened early on, when they were still giddy from all the newness of being together, but otherwise focused solely on their classes. When they were together again after her graduation, they had mainly gone out with friends. Except for an occasional brunch or lunch date, they had spent little time alone.

"How could you have possibly known all this?" Celeste turned to Nana, certain she had a hand in getting them back together again. Nana Adwoa's smile only brightened. Celeste had a clear memory of how she had embraced her that first day that they met.

"An old woman *always* knows these things," she said in her still-mysterious tone. And apparently, that was all the clarity she intended to provide. She chuckled to herself as Celeste and Ishmael stood on either side, hugging her warmly between them in a surreal moment.

As soon as they released her, Nana excused herself and waddled down the long hallway that led to her bedroom.

"There is food prepared for you my grandson, whenever you are ready to eat," she said over her shoulder. Then she stopped abruptly and turned partially toward them before retiring for the night.

"I trust that our dear Celeste will be kind enough to serve it to you."

After that, she turned and continued down the hallway toward her bedroom.

"I hope you will both excuse a tired old woman," she called back over her shoulder again. "It's been a very long day for me and now I must rest."

"We can talk more tomorrow, my grandson," she ended, "and you can tell me all about your plans for our new clinic."

And with that she disappeared inside her room, leaving a still-astounded Ishmael and Celeste alone for the first time. Both of them felt as though they had fallen into a wonderful dream.

※※※

"Daddy...Hi! You'll never believe what happened!" Celeste was shouting into the phone as though it would compensate for the distance.

Winston could tell right away that his daughter was happy about something. She was practically singing out every word.

"Hi sweetheart...What's going on?" He was glad that she was in a better mood than she had been the last time they talked. She had sounded awfully sad that day.

Celeste had only been in Ghana for a year, but she had started making a name for herself right away. She had taken the lead in the expansion project for the Foundation's solar panel enterprises that operated in the Ashanti region. Their plant produced enough panels to supply to a good portion of the commercial builders across the country. Trazi had helped her develop a set of strict protocols that they had used for handling the raw materials. It was designed to minimize exposure to their employees and the environment at the same time. The new regulations were being strictly enforced and the Foundation had encouraged whistle blowers.

All workers were required to wear protective suits during their shifts that would prevent them from inhaling or ingesting the hazardous fumes from the soldering guns, and any skin absorption of the materials that they worked around in the plant. They were also required to shower before they left work, to prevent any contamination of their street clothes as well.

Winston knew all about the air filtration system that Celeste and Trazi

310

had collaborated on. It was specifically designed for a solar plant work environment; their system used bentonite clay to neutralize the toxins that would otherwise be released in the air as fumes. It was considerably less expensive than the one it had replaced too, and from what Winston understood the cost savings would be considerable.

He had gotten his information second-hand from his son, who was still in frequent contact with his mother. Winston had been worried about Celeste before she left, but from what he was hearing she had been doing just fine. According to Trazi, the money saved after implementing her initiatives had resulted in a significant increase in the Foundation's profits.

"...So, I've been hearing a lot of great things about your work lately," he complimented her proudly.

"Thanks, Daddy, but my news is *much* bigger that!" Her voice was animated and her behavior made him curious.

"Are you sitting down?" She was so excited that she could barely contain herself.

"I'm getting married, Daddy!" She blurted it out, without stopping long enough for him to sit down if he *had* been standing.

"You're what?" Winston was alarmed, to say the least. He couldn't believe that his daughter was serious, that she would be so hasty in making such a big decision. He hardly thought a year was enough time for her to meet someone and make *that* kind of commitment already—especially when there were cultural differences to consider. His experience with Kristin had made him aware of that. She had felt so left out at times around his Jamaican relatives, especially around the females who had always insisted on calling her "Yankee" and who had held her in contempt for the longest time.

And where did his daughter even find this person anyway? No one had even told *him* she was dating.

"Did you just say you were getting *married*?" The connection was clear but he had to ask again, in case he had somehow misunderstood.

"Yup...That's right," she was shouting through the phone again, obviously as thrilled as he was horrified. "I'm getting married!"

"You'll never guess what happened..." She rambled on before Winston had time to speak. He was wracking his brain for something he could say that would get her to slow down. Where was Kristin?

"Ishmael is in Ghana, Daddy!" She blurted it out, interrupting his thoughts. "I was at his grandmother's house last night when he got here. He just walked through the door, right in the middle of our conversation.

311

Can you believe it?"

She still hadn't given him a chance to say anything, but Winston could feel a flood of relief as soon as she mentioned Ishmael's name. But he missed the part about his grandmother.

"Did you say his grandmother?" He wondered whether he could have heard his daughter right again. "How do you know his grandmother? She lives in Ghana?"

"Yes, she does. Do you remember the woman I told you about before, when Trazi and I came here to visit Aunt Kristin?"

He had vague memories of being somewhat alarmed by someone who was a stranger to him having such an attachment to his daughter. But Kristin had seemed to think she was harmless, so he had let it pass.

"As it turns out, Nana Adwoa is Ishmael's maternal grandmother!" Celeste still felt amazed each time she heard herself saying that.

"You're kidding!" Winston was just as surprised as she had been. "I can't imagine the chances of that happening. Did you know his parents were Ghanaian?"

"Ishmael swears he told me right after we met," she answered, "but I can't imagine that I would have forgotten that. I never told him that I had been to Ghana. I knew his parents were West African, but our conversations are usually on a different level most of the time..."

She realized she was blushing and finished quickly.

"Neither of us have had time to digest all of it yet, but it turns out that I met Ishmael's grandmother almost five years before I even met him. He was born in Washington, and it never dawned on me that we would know any of the same people in Ghana.

"We stayed up all last night and talked about *everything*," Her voice sounded even more content.

"We watched the sunrise, Daddy, and it was so beautiful! Ishmael proposed just as the sun rose above the eastern horizon." She stopped to experience it again as she remembered the moment from the night before.

"And we don't want to wait either, Daddy," She was distracted for a second or two, but she focused her attention back to their conversation. "We've decided that we've wasted far too much time already."

"...So, we want to have the ceremony really soon." She was almost giggling as she told him.

"Well, that's wonderful, baby." He was finally able to get a word in. "I'm so happy for you, and please give Ishmael my congratulations too."

He was happy that things were working so well for his daughter, and

312

started calculating whether he could get Grace to come down to spend some time with him in Washington. She would be the perfect person to help him get ready for Celeste's wedding, especially on such short notice.

"Okay, I'll tell him...But there's something else that I have to tell you..."

He immediately picked up on the hesitancy in his daughter's voice, and wondered what might be the cause. At least she didn't make him wait very long to find out.

"Ishmael is going to practice medicine here, Daddy. That's why he came to Ghana. He's planning to open a pediatric clinic outside of Winneba; that's a town near Nana's house. He promised her that he would do it before he started medical school. He came back to get started on the clinic as soon as he finished his residency."

Winston had been so relieved that she wasn't planning to marry some stranger that he had missed the obvious, at first. Of course, it would mean that she would renege on her promise to only be gone from the business for two years.

"Well, I guess that means you won't be coming back next year." He decided he would spare her from having to say it. "I'm happy for you, baby, but it's going to take some time to get used to you staying there permanently."

He felt crushed by that portion of her news, but even with her being a partner in the business he knew it was a matter of time before she got married. There had always been the chance that she might move away from Washington.

"But I'm going to try really hard, I promise..." He thought about his sister's criticism—that he had a habit of making everything that happened, be about him. He didn't want to be that kind of person any more.

"We'll miss you here for sure. But don't worry, we'll figure it all out."

"Oh, thank you Daddy...We're so happy that we're almost giddy, and the lack of sleep isn't helping much either." She was laughing now that the pressure of having to tell him she would be living in Ghana permanently, was behind her.

"And I know this is all short notice and everything, but how soon do you think you could possibly get here?"

Everything had happened so fast that he had little time to fully process his daughter's news still. Before the phone rang, he had been deep in thought trying to decipher some technical specifications to make a decision on purchasing a new piece of heavy equipment that the company needed. He hadn't expected anything like this at all before he picked up the phone.

"We don't want to wait, Daddy," his daughter said for a third time.

"We're hoping that everyone who'll be coming from the States will be able to make it here in about two weeks..." She ended wistfully.

"Do you think there's any way you can get here that soon?" Aunt Kristin has a friend who says she can contact the embassy to get your visa processed in time, so that won't be a problem."

"You're planning to get married in Ghana?" He tried not to sound too disappointed, but he had never pictured himself walking his daughter down the aisle in Ghana. But when he thought about it, he realized it made little sense for them to come all the way back to the States for the wedding. Most of their guests would only have to turn around and fly back to Ghana almost as soon as the ceremony was over.

"You're right, of course, I guess that does make more sense," he conceded. "But you know your Aunt Grace isn't going to get on any airplane, let alone one that flies across an ocean *and* a desert."

"I know." There was suddenly a hint of sadness in her voice.

"I wish she could come too, but I'll call her in a few hours to tell her about it. ...Maybe I can get her to change her mind," she was hopeful.

"You can always try...But I really don't think it'll help," he warned.

"Okay, I'll tell you what I'll do. I'll see what I can do to clear my schedule, and give you a call later this afternoon."

After he had hung up the phone Winston leaned back in his chair. He released a sigh of contentment at the thought of his daughter being so happy. He didn't even want to think how much he would miss her, but he was glad that she and Ishmael had finally worked everything out. He was looking forward to walking her down the isle and giving her away.

But he wasn't looking forward to seeing Kristin at all.

Chapter 27

What Does It Take?

*K*ristin was almost exhausted from all the effort it had taken to keep a safe distance from Winston for the past three weeks. At first, she had been encouraged when he cancelled some of his meetings in the States so he could arrive in Ghana a week *before* the kokooko, or "knocking on the door" ritual began. It marked the beginning of the traditional marriage ceremony that both kids wanted to have, although many others in the country now opted for a more westernized marriage ceremony. But Ishmael and his family had literally come and knocked at the door of her apartment two weeks earlier, to ask their permission for Ishmael to take Celeste as his bride.

As soon as she had seen his flight information, Kristin realized Winston would have a lot of free time on his hands once he got there. She had high hopes at first that he might be ready to talk things out with her; but if she had been available when he called, she would have known better. More than likely, she would have picked up the coldness in his voice and that would have prepared her for the way he had been acting since he got there. When they were married, she had used his tone of voice as a barometer to tell her whether she should tread with caution around him, or not. She could usually tell if she had offended him in some unknown way that he then intended to make her to pay for. But still, she had done everything she could to keep him occupied and entertained in Ghana—as long as he was kept away from her.

She remembered how much he had wanted to travel to Africa himself when they were students, almost as much as she had. So she made certain that he got to see as much of the country as possible, but nothing seemed to work with him—no matter what she did. And by that point, she was well beyond caring. As far as Kristin was concerned, he needed to get over himself—that, and stay far away from her.

Back when they were students at Tuskegee, her friend Niyla had taught her a few basics from her study of astrology. It had come in handy over the years because she had enlightened Kristin about some of the traits that were typical of men who born under the astrological sun sign of Cancer, like Winston. When she first heard Niyla's description of that energy, she and Winston had only been dating a few days. Most of what her friend read to her had sounded wonderful at the time. It was confirmation that she hadn't just been imagining what a sweetheart he could be. It felt like they were meant to be together, she remembered, because, like other men born in late June or early July, he could be very affectionate, sweet, thoughtful, and caring. He had been unbelievably nurturing and loving to her for most of the time they were together; the perfect match for Kristin' sun sign of Taurus.

Niyla told her the attributes of the Taurean earth energy included being solid and fertile, while the Cancerian water energy was nurturing. It was the perfect blend to create nearly anything together—or at least it could have been. In retrospect, she recalled that her friend had warned her that there was a flip side to Cancerian men too, just as there was for all the other signs of the zodiac. She had carefully explained that together, the twelve astrological signs represented the 360 degrees of a circle.

Each 30 degree segment of energy that an individual sign carried was necessary and vital to the whole. She told her there were extreme energies expressed through each sun sign; one on either end of the spectrum. And as always, that energy was perfectly balanced in the center, where the two extreme expressions of the same trait met. It was at that precise point that the elevation of spiritual consciousness related to the sun sign's energy expression occurred.

But, should a healthy balance be missing in a Cancerian's expression, her friend had told her, what normally would be a positive trait of affection might come off as being clingy, instead. And a caring attitude might be expressed as being overbearing. Her friend had kept stressing that there were two other things that were noteworthy about the men who were born under that particular sun sign, and she had urged Kristin to always be aware of it. One, was their unusual attachment to their mothers in most cases, or something else going on about their mothers that was significant. The second, and most important thing, she had cautioned, was that

Cancerian men, including men with key personal planets in their natal charts in the sign of Cancer, were *always* super-sensitive. The tricky part, she said, was that they were usually masterful at hiding it.

In all the time that she had known him, Kristin had never been able to tell exactly when she said or did something that Winston took as her being insensitive. Over the years, she had spent much time looking back at the crazy mess they had made of their lives. She had much to regret for having paid so little attention to Niyla's cautions, because if she had, things might have gone over much better at Highland Beach.

She still had no idea what *that* was all about, although she had thought long and hard about his anger on her flight back across the Atlantic. But, since she had been unable to figure it out by the time her plane landed in London, she saw no other choice but to put it all out of her mind. Otherwise, it would have distracted her from all the work that lay ahead of her, and she had been determined not to let that happen at any cost.

She had expected that Winston would be upset about the baby she lost; that she hadn't told him about it when it happened, and all. But she still had no idea why he had taken such offense. *She* was the one who had suffered, after all, and she had done it all by herself. Besides, it had been two years since she finally told him everything about loosing the baby, so no matter *what* she might have done to hurt his feelings at the time, she couldn't believe how big of a jerk he was being now.

The only reason he was in Ghana was to celebrate his daughter's wedding; while she, on the other hand, had been working tirelessly to make it all happen. Quite a bit of work had gone into making sure the ceremonies and all the festivities they planned would live up to Celeste's dreams about her big day. Kristin had been as happy as Winston's daughter was when she called to share the news about Ishmael being in Ghana. She was so glad they had been able to work everything out; as well as being floored, of course, to learn that he was Nana Adwoa's grandson of all things.

She had a thousand questions for the woman now, but once again, her respect for her as an elder had prevented Kristin from pressing her for an explanation. She could still recall clearly the day that Celeste had met Nana, when the woman had surprised them all. She recognized Celeste immediately as Ishmael's future bride, on the day that Kristin had brought Celeste and Trazi to her house to meet her. But how? How was that even possible?

In all the flurry of activities that had been generated after Celeste said "yes" to Ishmael's proposal, Kristin's mind had kept finding its way back to Nana Adwoa and that same question. It was all a mystery to her, but it had also helped keep her from being completely distracted by Winston's antics. The elderly woman's mystique had only heightened after she learned of Ishmael's connection to her, but Nana had been a mystery to her from the day she had first called her "Moses." That had been on *their* first meeting, during the time that she had been teaching at the University of Kumasi on a two-year sabbatical from Hunter.

Now, just like that, they were permanently linked together by a much more solid bond. They had become family after the marriage ceremony that had taken place that morning, and now their relationship went much further than the friendship they had developed over the years. Her thoughts kept going back to Nana's initial reaction on meeting Celeste, and it stayed on her mind as she readied herself to receive their wedding guests. Somehow, Nana had known from the beginning that Celeste would marry her grandson, and the knowledge of that only deepened the surreal tenor that had engulfed Exodus Village when the couple innocently announced their plans for a brief engagement.

At the time that Celeste called to give her the news, Kristin's executive team had been in full swing making arrangements for the construction of their third village, to be built in the Volta Region. Its infrastructure plans were already in place and they were turning their attention to the communities they would build for village residents. It would house a more limited number of people who would be returning home to Africa from Mexico and several South American countries, Brazil being top among them.

They would come as other residents from the Caribbean and North America had been coming to the Ashanti region, and would soon continue into the Central Region, after that village was completed and made ready for occupancy. The Foundation's guiding principles would remain intact in Exodus Village-Volta region, as with the other villages. The same emphasis would be placed on learning the history of their enslavement; as well as cultural awareness education to prepare them for life in the Motherland after their first five years back home. Kristin's intent for all their residents was for them to be taught as much about their collective history and heritage as possible before they arrived. She was as convinced now, as she had always been that it held the key to their former-underbelly residents' now-proven abilities, to unlock the chains that had bound them long after their ancestors won their freedom.

The village in the Central Region had already gotten off to a fantastic start; they had completed three of the five communities that it would eventually contain. The money that was currently being generated by the Foundation's commercial projects in the Ashanti Region, all from the ten percent share of profits it retained, was more than adequate to supplement donations that were still regularly flowing in from all over the world. The combined resources of the two was sufficient to cover their operating expenses for all three villages.

Their applicants would soon be able to select a preference of locations in Ghana, which they would try to accommodate whenever possible. Soon they would even consider allowing village transfers between the Ashanti and Central regions, during their yearly relocations. Their new village in the Volta region, like the two others, would have its own attraction to newcomers; based, in part, on the unique training opportunities it would offer. Their graduates from Exodus Village-Ashanti had been proving for years to all that they were capable of living up to their potential and making their dreams come alive.

There had been a steady stream of both mentor and resident applications for their resettlement programs, and they had maintained a consistent number on their waiting lists since the beginning; as more families left for Ghana and new ones took their place. Exodus Village-Central Region would absorb some of the backlog when it opened, but it would soon have a waiting list all of its own. Their village in the Volta region was expected to follow a similar path. The demographics of their applicants had changed as well, as the passion grew among the Diaspora around the world, and more became intrigued by the possibilities of Africa.

Kristin and her foundation had started looking even further toward the future. The Foundation had already expanded its readjustment assistance programs that were provided to their graduates. Now, they offered assistance in relocating them to areas of Ghana, as well as an increasing number of countries across Africa. They would also soon offer DNA testing to applicants so they could identify their native lands.

They had their sights on an expansion of their own mission in other countries, as well, starting with West Africa, when the majority of captives had been taken. In the long range, there were plans to extend their programs to countries all across the continent, whose residents had been taken during the slave trade.

They had just mapped out a schedule that would allow her to travel to as many West African countries as possible over the next several months, when Kristin got the news about Celeste's engagement, to get started on their expansion plans. They would reach out to those who had lost large populations in particular—those countries that were closest to Ghana and also bordered the Gulf of Guinea. After her return from each trip, they planned to invite the traditional and contemporary leaders of those countries to come to Exodus Village-Ashanti. They would show them what the Foundation had to offer, and demonstrate how well the regions where their villages were located had profited from the operation of their commercial plants. And she would always highlight the Foundation's community involvement through Heavenly Travel, outlined well thought out plans to do the same in their respective countries.

From that point, they would arrange to hold talks on the specifics of what it would take to establish a new Exodus Village in their country. And later, they would work out the details of having the *Diasporan Black Star* bring new residents into one of the forty or so castles that once operated along the gulf and was still inhabitable; one that would provide an easy route to the new village. Each new village was to be modeled after the original Exodus Village in the Ashanti Region, with adaptations made to more appropriately fit the local culture. For each, their administrations would be structured with the same care and attention as their villages in Ghana.

Kristin and Solomon had already agreed they would open satellite offices of Heavenly Travel in those same countries, in advance of the Exodus Foundation's entry. They would immediately begin building support among the people through the travel agency yet again, and create a new framework of contacts they would need in establishing a new village. They had completed plans that would take them through the first critical phase of their expansion, and had been close to working out a schedule of follow-up meetings to checkpoint milestones. The schedule would be tight but everyone had been eager and ready to move forward with the plans that had been approved by their board of directors only the day before.

And then, virtually everything had come to a screeching halt. Everything that everyone had been working on had to be immediately set aside. Like it or not, their main focus had to be shifted to the production of Celeste's wedding. They had all soon realized it was inevitable that it would become the talk of the Ashanti region, if for no other reason than her relationship to Kristin. Given the circumstances, there had been little choice for them but to turn the dinner and reception that was to follow the ceremony that morning into a spectacular extravaganza.

Celeste and Ishmael were already satisfied with having a small private ceremony and had been no problem with the Foundation mixing business with pleasure. But no one could have predicted how much time and energy they would spend on it over the next six weeks; certainly not Kristin, who, along with her team, had once again turned on a dime and come through in a pinch. Neither bride nor groom had been in Ghana long enough to appreciate how unacceptable their original plan had been, to only have a quiet ceremony. As Winston's first wife, many of her associates considered her to be Kristin's daughter, as much as if she had actually given birth to her herself. She and Ishmael had no inkling of the kind of offense that might well have been taken, had she excluded the Foundation's business associates and major donors from such an important occasion as her daughter's wedding; or their travel agency's VIP clients, for that matter.

So, the first thing on Kristin's agenda had been to put her foot down about the timing; she had told the couple in no uncertain terms that they were not having the wedding in two weeks, and that was that. With only one solid month of planning before the first ceremony was to take place, she informed them of how close they were pushing it with even those dates in mind. She added that she also had the Foundation's benefactors in the States to consider, and Celeste had become very popular in Exodus Village in the short time she had been in the country. Most people who met her seemed to love her—including their VIP travel clients who she sometimes mingled with at their travel agency's social events. Kristin told them that some of those clients wouldn't have been happy at all, had they been excluded from the festivities—especially when it was well known that travel wasn't an issue.

Amina volunteered to coordinate all the plans, since decorum for the Foundation fell within her arena, she said. Once again, Kristin had been most grateful for her help. She had been a guest at several of the traditional weddings that had been performed in Exodus Village over the years, including Lawana's, but she had never participated as a "supporter" of the bride or groom. She was yet unfamiliar with the protocol so Amina had sat down with her and Celeste to go over all the events that were planned. They discussed the menus for all the dinners and the other get-togethers planned for the two families between the ceremonies.

Amina created a master list of tasks from her notes when she got back to her office. She passed it along to her assistant, who divided the list and assigned tasks to volunteer groups. Amina prioritized each of the tasks and provided clear enough details so that the appropriate number of volunteers could then be recruited. Celeste had made so many friends in the year that she had worked at Exodus Village-Ashanti that they ended up with far more volunteers than were actually needed.

Nana Adwoa volunteered to bring as much of her family's kente cloth as was needed for the wedding, and Kristin had only been slightly caught off guard, this time, by the offer. Nana's driver brought her to Exodus Village the very next day with two large containers filled with the fabric. The design had been created centuries earlier and the green and beige silk threads woven into the cloth represented Nana's family lineage. Her family could be traced back to the 15th century, and she had proudly proclaimed to Kristin that the shade of green in the fabric she brought was an exact match to the original design.

She had brought enough of it to use as accents around the grand ballroom, where the dinner and reception were being held. They had used it to decorate the bridal table at the front of the ballroom too, and tied strips of the cloth around the bouquet that Celeste had carried in the bridal party's procession. There had been still more of the cloth left to attach strips of it as ribbons on the silk pouches they had given their guests as wedding favors.

The pouches had been a special gift from Lawana, who had contacted Kristin to make the offer, as soon as she learned that Celeste was getting married. She said she wanted to contribute something special for the festivities, to show her appreciation for everything that the Exodus Foundation had done for her and her kids. She had created a special heart-shaped design for the pouches to commemorate the occasion, with Ishmael and Celeste's initials stitched across the front. The students in her design class had happily taken on the project; they hand-sewed the elaborately constructed lined bags, and embroidered them under Lawana's careful supervision.

Kristin was still proud of the way that she and her family had blossomed with their new start in Ghana. Lawana had embraced the skills training she was offered and found her passion in designing women and children's clothing. In only a few years after they arrived, she had met and married a Muslim brother that Brother John introduced to her. Her husband was near the top of the FOI organization at Exodus Village, and they were both well respected in all the communities. Her children were doing well too: William had followed in his stepfather's footsteps and was working his way up through the ranks of the FOI. George had become quite the gifted musician; he played the lead guitar in the band that had been hired to entertain their guests that evening. And Lacrecia had done very well in school there;

she was already making plans to continue her education at the University at Kumasi, after she completed her last years of secondary school. In the meantime, she had been a big help to her mother in keeping up with their baby sister in the afternoons, so that Lawana could devote more time to building her business.

She now owned and operated her own clothing store, in addition to the design classes she taught at Exodus Village. Her store catered to an increasing number of Black American tourists who now visited the country year-round. She had been doing quite well with her designs and Celeste especially loved the way that she blended West African and Black American styles together. Celeste had become one of her best customers since moving to Ghana, and she had been thrilled when she was told about Lawana's gift; especially since her new family's kente would be used in the design.

Their traditional ceremony had been a small and intimate affair, the last event in the formal rites of the "knocking at the door" ceremony. There had been an official announcement of the couple's marriage at the end, although some in Ghana had begun to think of the traditional ceremony as more an engagement, rather than a marriage event. It was but one part of a colonial influence that had been ingrained throughout the original culture.

Two weeks earlier, Kristin and Winston had opened the door of her apartment together after Ishmael, his parents, Nana Adwoa, and several other elders literally knocked on it at a pre-arranged time. Ishmael's father had stepped forward eagerly to speak on behalf of his son. He offered them several small gifts, including two bottles of Schnapps, as a gesture of his family's good will. Winston accepted the gifts and according to tradition, he had signaled his willingness to hear what the family had come to say. Ishmael's father had then opened a third bottle of Schnapps for libation, pouring some of the liquor onto the ground as he said a traditional prayer to God and the ancestral spirits.

After the prayers were ended, Winston invited Ishmael's family in, and directed the group to the same ballroom where the official ceremony had taken place earlier that morning, as the culminating event. He then led Kristin, Trazi, and Malaya, who stood in for Celeste, as her maid of honor, into the ballroom after the others. The room had been elaborately decorated with cowry shells, as a symbol of the couple's fruitful union. They sat down with Ishmael and his family to formally discuss the purpose of their visit. Solomon and his wife, Liyana, were already seated when the two families arrived; along with Amina, Amad, and several supporters for

Ishmael's family. They were all there to serve as character witnesses, if such assurances were proven necessary during the discussions that followed.

After everyone had been seated, Ishmael's father came forward. He asked Celeste's entire family to grant his son permission to "uproot" the "beautiful flower" that Ishmael had seen at their house, referring to Celeste. According to tradition, the bride's family was to be given an opportunity to carefully look into the background of the would-be groom and his family at that point. If they hadn't already been familiar with them, custom dictated that the intended bride's family be given time to assess whether the groom's family had a good reputation. They could investigate whether there had been a history of chronic illness, genetic disabilities; or whether any close family member had been known to be a thief, prostitute, or murderer; and whether the groom had another marriage or children outside of marriage. It was only after those hurdles had been cleared, or waived, that the attention would then turn to the groom's character in and of itself.

Ishmael's father offered up his clan's history to those who were assembled in the room, going back for many generations. After he had finished proclaiming his family's good standing in the community, his son surprised everyone by asking for permission to speak. It was normally unheard of during the ceremony for the groom to speak himself, but Ishmael wanted to stand before the group and explain his past relationship with Kendra, voluntarily.

First, he apologized to Celeste's family publicly for all the pain that he had caused their daughter. He offered his regrets for having hurt her as he had and he declared his intent to sign a certificate at the local registry that would make their marriage legal under the Marriage Ordinance. That would be more in keeping with civil law, and it had been an added step to the traditional ceremony by many of the couples who still had them. Another addition to the Ghanaian culture as a by-product of colonialism, the Marriage Ordinance was now considered by many as the only "official" proof of marriage. Some touted it as a proper legal remedy, on a more practical level, in the event that something happened to the groom. The ordinance would ensure that the wife retained all property rights of her husband, so that she would be able to support herself in the case of his untimely demise.

Ishmael had looked directly into Winston's eyes as he told them all that he intended for his to be a monogamous marriage, as well. He wanted Winston to feel at ease about that since the practice of polygamy, like many other traditions in West Africa, had never been entirely discontinued during the British occupation. Like so many other customs, it had only been driven partially underground.

Since it was customary for the bride to be represented by her family and maid of honor during the first ceremony, Celeste hadn't even been in the room while everything was being said. Ishmael had only been given glimpses of her earlier that morning, as she passed near his family as they made their way into the ballroom. As everyone else sat and listened to the traditional rites unfold, there had been surprising sparks of interest among the western guests in attendance. They all considered the widely encompassing factors that were involved in the Ghanaian traditional marriage rites, and each of them thought of the high rate of American divorces, in turn. They had to wonder whether that increasing statistic might actually decline over time, if there were as much attention and consideration given to the groom and marriage in America, before the marriage ceremony took place.

It had seemed very strange to Malaya at first that Celeste should be excluded from participating in the ceremony. Then, as the process of evaluating Ishmael's suitability as her husband continued, along with the opportunity given to investigate the groom and his family's reputation, as well, she began to have an appreciate for the custom's value. She imagined what her grandmother, Uncle Paul, and the rest of her family might have uncovered about Sam at such a ceremony. She then realized they would have only been successful in extracting the truth from him, if her mother had been kept out of the room. Otherwise, she would have distracted them from a full examination of the facts about Sam for sure, because she had already made up her mind early on that she would marry him. And Malaya could only imagine the emotional appeals she would have made during such an inquiry. If she had been allowed in the room, she knew her mother would have done all she could to keep family members from questioning Sam's character and putting him on the spot.

No one seemed surprised that Winston opted to ask Ishmael a few pointed questions, when it was time for his response. They were all fairly certain that Celeste wouldn't have appreciated her father's intense interrogation of her fiancé, although the questions he asked clearly showed that he had her best interest at heart. Once Winston was satisfied with Ishmael's answers, he had agreed to give his daughter to him in marriage. He invited him and his family back for the private ceremony that had taken place earlier that morning, and had been witnessed by fifty of their closest family members and friends.

His family had to ask for Winston's permission once again during the second ceremony; this time Celeste was allowed to be present for much of it. Each family and their supporters sat facing each other in the ballroom, with Ishmael's kente added to the cowry shell decorations. Elders from both families poured libation to acknowledge their ancestors; they offered prayers for the success of the marriage, as well. There were introductions made of all family members present, and afterwards Ishmael's parents came forward to present the gifts that Celeste had requested as a dowry.

Malaya, who was dressed in a stunning green robe of silk that matched the colors of Ishmael's kente, got up and made a careful visual examination of what they had brought. There were mainly trinkets, some cloth, and photos of Ishmael taken as a child. After Malaya confirmed that the family had brought everything that Celeste had requested, the bride-to-be was finally led into the room. She wore an elaborate white silk wedding gown that was beaded in pearls; suddenly feeling bashful, she had stolen a quick glance at Ishmael before lowering her head.

After she was seated, Ishmael's father advised him to take a closer look to confirm that she was indeed the woman that he wanted to marry. His eyes were misted with tears as he took in the beauty of the woman that he so adored, and he quickly corroborated her identity. Then, Celeste was given an opportunity to inspect the dowry he had brought her for herself. When she saw Ishmael's expression, she had a burst of confidence and she smiled broadly at him after looking at her gifts. She indicated to all that she was happy with what she saw and once she had, her father asked her whether she agreed to marry Ishmael, asking her three separate times.

"Yes." She had answered almost immediately after the question was posed the first time. She confirmed it twice more and then her father formally asked her whether she accepted the gifts that Ishmael had brought for her. Her husband-to-be came to stand next to her, as everyone waited for Celeste's response. As soon as she had indicated that she accepted the gifts, Ishmael quickly slid her wedding ring on her finger. They hugged each other affectionately, and when they released each other, they were immediately directed to sit in the two chairs that had been placed at the front of the small room full of people.

As was required by tradition, they sat unsmiling while the elders from each family came up and gave them advice about their marriage. After everyone had passed on their words of wisdom, Nana Adwoa presented them with a bible to help them remember to make God and their spirituality a large part of their union. She offered prayers and blessings to them, and then officially declared that they were married.

The dinner and reception had begun only a few hours later, with continuous entertainment provided for guests who had arrived early. The final two events had been anything *but* small and intimate. At the height of the reception, there had been close to five hundred people in the ballroom. The partitions between the smaller rooms had been removed to create a grand arena that was still crowded with people after several hours. It had been beautifully decorated with ice sculptures everywhere, made by the students in their catering classes. There were magnificent flower arrangements too on large pedestals placed all around the floor, with exquisite lighting that made everything magically come alive. Partitions had been removed from the standard wall on one side of the ballroom to reveal a second glass wall. The glass enclosed atrium was on the other side of it and led to the Olympic-sized swimming pool that was also surrounded by tempered glass. The atrium had been decorated as an overflow space for those guests who might not want to be as close to all the dancing. But for the most part, everyone had remained inside the main ballroom and they all seemed to be having a wonderful time.

As soon as they had agreed on a date for the dinner and reception, Amina had drafted a quick email that Kristin sent out as an announcement. In only a few short sentences, she had alluded to the couple's rocky history without giving any specific details. It offered an explanation for the breach of protocol in giving such short notice, and made clear at the same time that Celeste and Ishmael had known each other for a number of years.

Kristin had spent hours making personal phone calls in advance of sending some of the emails, since their unconventional invitation was being sent out so late. There were people that they couldn't afford to alienate by not contacting personally, but she and Amina had been able to whittle down the list to only fifty or so. She had prayed for voice mail each time she dialed a number; if someone answered, she had told them as briefly as she could, without making it sound hurried, that the email she would send shortly included all the details. Her tone had always been apologetic, yet curt, about the short notice; she did her best to sound understanding, instead of relieved, when someone responded that they wouldn't be able to make it. For everyone else, she ended her recorded message with a polite insistence that they respond by the date requested. She stressed how vital it would be to know exactly how many people *would be* attending, so that proper arrangements could be made.

Aside from the people that Kristin had to phone personally, the rest of the emails had been sent as a courtesy more than anything else. But, for the second time as they planned one of their events, there had been many more people who indicated they would come than had been expected. Luckily, the timing of the events couldn't have been more perfect for accommodating their guests. They would still have at least six weeks left after the wedding was over, before their latest group of residents were scheduled to arrive. The Marcus Garvey community was already vacant, since it's previous residents had moved on to the William Jackson community, as they worked their way through the Foundation's programs. Kioni had merely moved up his schedule for renovations by a few weeks. The houses had been repainted and spruced up in time for their wedding guests' arrival, and there was more than enough space to accommodate everyone. They had also offered to host their VIP clients at their resort in Accra instead, and provided luxury buses that shuttled them to Exodus Village.

Kristin had been working her way around the ballroom all afternoon. Her feet were starting to hurt from having to stand in heels that she was no longer used to wearing. But she had been determined to personally thank as many of their guests as possible for coming, and she had made a special point of being welcoming and hospitable to Ishmael's extended family, as well. There had also been a sizeable number of Heavenly Travel's clients who came for the festivities, along with tribal chiefs and their families from the surrounding area. There were government officials and other business contacts that she also needed to acknowledge and spend at least a few minutes of time with each one.

At the beginning of the reception, their guests had been entertained by talented drummers and dancers who had stirred up excitement in the ballroom, before the wedding party paraded in. Celeste and Ishmael had worn matching white silk garments, and had been seated in chairs that were also covered in white silk and placed in front of the bridal party's dinner table. Kristin and Winston had come forward, with Nana Adwoa and Ishmael's parents following close behind. They had all greeted the newly weds and presented them with gifts and well wishes. After they had been seated again, there was a long line of guests who had also offered their congratulations and presents. There had been so many people in attendance that it had taken well over an hour before everyone in the line had been received.

Celeste had mentioned that she and Ishmael planned to donate any monetary gifts toward the construction of the pediatric clinic Ishmael planned to build. Kristin included that information in her emails and a large number of guests had responded with donations. In keeping with tradition, they had touched the money to Celeste's head lightly before dropping it into one of the tall wicker baskets that sat on either side of their chairs.

Dinner stations were set up all over the ballroom for an exquisite buffet supper that their chefs had prepared for the occasion. The main courses were accented by a variety of mini dishes that had been prepared by their culinary students. There were jazz and traditional musicians that serenaded them while they ate the food, and later, they brought on the band that changed the pace of the evening, and was still going strong. A large area of the floor had been sectioned off for dancing, and it quickly filled up as their guests finished eating. There were many guests who had been dancing almost non-stop since the reception began, and the music the band played was a definite hit for the crowd.

Amina had hired George's band, of course, as the main entertainment for the evening. Everyone at the top level of their Foundation had more or less adopted Lawana and her children; mainly, at first, because of her connection to Kioni. They had all been pulling for them over the years, especially the boys. George's group had been formed with several of their former residents who had joined with musicians from a small village outside Obuasi, the gold-mining town that was a short distance away. The members of "Sankofa," as the band was called, were all talented musicians and singers. The Adinkra symbol of a bird flying backward with an egg in its mouth, expresses the importance of learning from the past in order to create the future. They had become quite popular around the country in the past few years, and played a blend of Ghanian and African American tunes that everyone seemed to enjoy.

Kristin was glad that the formal events were finally over and that she had talked to nearly everyone that she needed to thank personally for coming, and for supporting Ishmael's clinic. Were it not for Winston, she would have finally been able to relax and enjoy the party herself—heaven forbid. But her ex-husband had a way of getting under her skin as no one else had ever been able to do. She would have avoided him altogether once the reception started, had she thought it wouldn't be considered rude not to introduce the father-of-the-bride to some of their associates.

Even still, she had only approached him when he was talking with someone else, and when she thought he might offer the least amount of resistance to her efforts. She would watch him for a few minutes and then take a deep breath before approaching him, assuming a persona to keep the attention away from her true feelings. She would keep it up just long enough for the required pleasantries to be exchanged with whomever had introduced him to, and after a reasonable amount of time transpired she would excuse herself and leave Winston to hold his own. She could only hope that she was giving off an adequate appearance of normalcy, because she would shed the facade as soon as she was free to move away.

By the end of Winston's first week there, she had begun to wonder whether she might have had a successful career as an actor. She recognized the obstinate expression on his face immediately, as she greeted him when he arrived at the village. At first she thought he might have been miffed that she hadn't been at the airport to personally greet him when he flew in. She had offered an explanation, saying there was still a large amount of work they were still involved with in preparing for the wedding. She had hoped that would pacify him enough to drop the hostile stares, and had even explained all they had been doing to get ready for the festivities, and what was still been left to be done.

But she had soon realized his attitude had nothing to do with her not being at the airport to meet his flight. Within the first few minutes, it had become clear to her that the reconciliation she had hoped for would be out of the question. Still, she had resigned herself to make the best of things while he was there, and she had done everything she could think of to be cordial —in spite of the way he continued to respond.

Amad had driven him all around Exodus Village the next day after he arrived. They drove through all five of their communities and she found out from Amad later that he had asked him to stop the cart a few times. Winston had talked with several of the residents they came across and later, he had gone inside the entertainment complexes in some of the communities. Once he got his bearings, Amina had given him a solar cart of his own to use. He entertained himself for the next couple of days, driving around and visiting their various processing plants and their farms, and any other place inside the village that he wanted to go.

After the first part of the knocking ceremony was over, Kristin had asked Amad to drive him and Trazi, who had arrived with Malaya by that time, to see some of the sites in nearby regions. They had started with Accra, so that Winston could see more of that city than the airport, and next, Amad had driven them to the Central Region so they could visit the site of the relocation settlement that would operate there. Their trip had taken several days, and as they circled back to Exodus Village, they had toured two of the solar construction plants that Celeste designed, so Trazi could see the hazmat systems they had worked on together for himself.

330

He stayed at Exodus Village for a few days once they were back, during which time there had been dinners and other social events for Ishmaels family and friends and their own. Then he was off again, but this time they took one of the larger vehicles, and Celeste, Ishmael, and Malaya went along too. They drove up to Kumasi and the trip had taken two more days. They visited the markets and the King's palace; on their way back to the village, Amad took them on a tour of their soybean farms and some of their processing plants in the Ashanti Region. Aside from all the other trips, Celeste and Ishmael had also taken her father to Winneba, to spend time with Nana Adwoa and learn more about her work with medicinal herbs.

Kristin had bent over backwards to make sure that he got to see everything she knew that he would want to see in Ghana. And in spite of it all, he had still refused to budge. He had kept up the same sour demeanor when he was around her, as when he had first arrived. Every time she would look at him, all she saw was the same pigheaded expression on his face.

She was getting really tired of seeing it too. Kristin was tired—period.

His return flight to the U. S. was scheduled for the following evening, and she only hoped that she could make it until then. Midway through the reception, she realized she was gritting her teeth sometimes when she was around him, just to be able to get through it. But she kept a smile pasted on her face as she glided around the ballroom floor, in the blue and green silk dress that Lawana had made for the occasion. The eye-catching print combined a western and Ghanaian design. She had been aware of the stir she caused in the close fitting dress, as she joined the rest of the wedding party for their parade into the ballroom.

She could tell Winston liked the dress, because his eyes had betrayed him for a split second when she first walked through the door. The latest man that Solomon had in mind for her seemed to like it too. She could feel his eyes and Winston's on her at different times during the evening, and she would catch them both staring at her from across the room from time to time. But Winston's stares would usually become quite unfriendly as soon as she caught him at it; as though it was *her* fault that he liked what he saw. She had already been counting down the hours until the celebration would likely wind down, because of him. She was far too tired from having to react to his nonsense all the time.

She only hoped Solomon's friend would understand why she hadn't been able to spend much time with him that evening. She was beginning to feel a real attraction for the man, but she couldn't be certain how Winston might have reacted to her attention to him, and the very last thing she wanted was to cause a scene. She had already felt Winston's eyes glaring at her, the one time that she had agreed to dance with her handsome would be-suitor and Solomon's. She might have had a good time with him too, were it not for Winston. For some reason, and in spite of everything, he still had the nerve to feel entitled to an opinion about who she should spend her time with. But knowing how he could be at times, she decided she would keep her distance after that one dance with Solomon's friend.

Everyone else seemed to be enjoying themselves and Kristin could tell that the party was just getting started. She had asked for Amina's help in keeping Winston occupied between her introductions, but that didn't seem to be working out either. Amina would lead him off in a direction that was far enough away from where she was; but before she knew it, he would be back again—turning up just like a bad penny. He would position himself so that it was hard for her to avoid seeing him, or the accusatory looks that he had been so intent on giving her since he got off the plane.

She still had no idea what his problem could be, but her feet were beginning to hurt in the *comfortable* shoes that she had switched to—a pair of silk flats that were a perfect match for the green in her silk dress. She was in no mood for Winston's foolishness, not after everything she had gone through to make sure that things had been perfect for his daughter's wedding. Since she had wanted to be personally involved in everything, Kristin had put most of her appointments on hold so that she could concentrate on the wedding activities. All the late night entertaining had begun to take its toll on her however, since that was something that she had never been used to doing. But it was a once in a lifetime celebration for Celeste, so she didn't mind the sacrifice that it had taken to make it special for her.

Now, it looked as though her father intended to make his pouting the main agenda for the rest of the evening, but Kristin had taken just about as much from him as she planned to take. Yet, she was *still* trying her best to avoid the confrontation that he seemed so determined to have with her. It had been two years since they had seen each other at Highland Beach, but she had nearly forgotten about her earlier optimism that Celeste's marriage might lead to a new starting point for them. She had thought it might be another chance to put all of their old hurts behind them, but Winston's behavior had dashed those hopes as soon as he arrived.

She had thought for certain he would be willing to put aside his anger long enough to get past his daughter's wedding day. But thanks to him, poor Celeste had probably been put on the spot more than once, having to explain why her parents were always seated so far apart. And it was all because Winston couldn't stop thinking about himself for more than five minutes. Kristin became more angry each time she thought about it, and her aching feet didn't help her very much. It got harder and harder for her to keep her composure whenever his and her paths crossed in the ballroom.

As a final resort, she had decided to look for an opportunity to take him aside and appeal to his sense of reason. By the looks of the crowd, they still had several more hours left to go, at least, before the celebration was likely to die down enough for them to be able to leave. She would ask him if he would *please* put aside their differences for only a few more hours, until his daughter's wedding celebration had ended and the majority of guests had left. Winston had been making things awkward for *everybody,* because both Trazi and Solomon had made comments to her about him. She had to talk both men out of confronting him right then and there, because that would have been all she needed on top of everything else. And it wasn't until after she had introduced him to Solomon that she noticed the lukewarm reception her friend and business partner had given him. It was only at that point that she became aware of how strongly her friend felt about her ex-husband.

※※※

Kristin finally spotted a perfect opportunity to talk to Winston when she noticed him standing alone in the patio area. She quickly followed him through the sliding glass doors and into the two-story atrium, and they faced each other on that side of the ballroom's glass walls. It was the first time they had been in direct contact alone since they had prepared to greet the couple at the start of the reception dinner.

"Winston..." She found herself suddenly nervous as she approached him, and she was also struggling to keep her temper under control.

"Can we talk for a minute?" She tried to make her voice sound light, with a friendly tone added. It was forced and she hoped that it didn't sound that way.

"I don't think we have anything *else* we need to talk about." His response was terse and very childish. He partially turned from her after saying it.

'Did he just say anything else*?'* As she realized that was exactly what he had said, Kristin was stunned. Apparently, he had not moved one iota in thought from their last conversation the night he had walked out on her at Highland Beach. They were suddenly thrust back into the beach cottage

with all the hostile feelings that had just surfaced there.

"Winston...," She tried again, after taking a few moments to make sure she could control her tongue. She tried to keep her focus on Celeste and her purpose for trying to talk to him.

"I just wanted to make an appeal to you, for Celeste's sake...Now, I can see that you're still upset with me, although I frankly don't understand why... But this reception is the last of all of it...It's the last of their wedding events. Everything is going to be over after tonight...

"Don't you think that it's possible for you to look beyond your anger toward me for just a few more hours? He had turned back toward her.

"I wanted to make this celebration special for your daughter," she pleaded with him, encouraged that he was at least looking at her now.

"*You're* the one with the problem caring for your children, not me!" He had raised his voice and the expression on his face had suddenly changed into an icy glare. He was so focused on his own apparent hurt that he didn't notice the flash of anger that exploded beneath Kristin's dark eyes.

"*What* did you just say to me?" She shouted the question to meet the intimidation in his voice, her eyebrows raised at an inquisitive angle.

Kristin moved toward Winston quickly without further warning, temporarily forgetting all about the wedding guests and everything else that was going on around them. Several people turned to look in their direction as the sound of their voices traveled through the glass. The guests who were closest to the wall could hear the sound clearly, but fortunately they were standing at too great a distance to make out what was being said. Their body language, however, made it clear to anyone who was watching that they weren't having a friendly conversation.

"You selfish, pompous, idiot!"

Kristin heard herself shrieking at Winston as she closed the distance that still separated them. Before he had any time to react, she had smacked him squarely across the middle of his forehead with the palm of her hand. The impact made such a loud noise that it echoed around the glass enclosure where they stood.

"Everything isn't always about *you* Winston!" She snarled at him now, clinching her teeth together to keep herself from exploding further.

When she realized what she had done, Kristin was mortified—nearly as shocked as Winston apparently was. She had actually hit him!

Realizing it, she turned around in horror and quickly walked away, leaving him rooted to the spot and completed flabbergasted by what she had done.

Chapter 28

Family Secrets

"**A**unt Kristin?" Celeste called from the other side of Kristin's bedroom door.

"Are you okay?" She knocked on the door softly.

Reluctantly, Kristin got up and unlocked it, still horrified by the very conspicuous meltdown she had with Winston.

"Honey, I am so sorry...," She was sheepish, as she pulled Celeste into the room, quickly closing the door behind her.

"I'm so sorry that I've ruined your wedding, sweetheart." Kristin was very remorseful and held her head low. "I only wanted to talk to your father, that's all. I just wanted to *reason* with him, to get him to stop making things so uncomfortable for everybody else.

"I swear, Celeste...I never intended to hit him."

She kept on talking which kept Celeste from responding. She didn't look at the young bride so she didn't notice the shocked expression on her face.

"Everything just happened so fast, and your father can be so *aggravating* at times." She was still too embarrassed to look directly at Celeste.

"And my hormones have been all over the place lately. I guess I just finally let Winston get the best of me..."

"Wait!...Do you mean you actually *hit* Daddy?" Celeste finally interrupted her after she found her voice Now, she was laughing hysterically and holding her stomach at the same time.

"You mean you didn't see it?" Kristin ignored Celeste's question in her eagerness to hear an answer to her own. She could remember seeing her near the atrium shortly before she had gone out to talk to Winston, and she had just assumed that his daughter had seen them. The glass walls had

335

extended the view from that side of the ballroom, making it appear to flow into the atrium where they had been standing in clear sight.

But if Celeste didn't see them, maybe there was hope. Maybe she hadn't caused an outrageous disaster to ruin the evening, as she had imagined. She still couldn't believe that she had lost control of herself like that—and in front of all their guests.

"...Thank goodness!" No further confirmation was needed as to her good fortune, after Kristin realized the questions Celeste had asked her, made clear the answer to her own.

"If *you* didn't see anything maybe no one else did either." She was hopeful that she wouldn't have to think up some off-the-wall explanation for anyone who might have seen them.

"Wow..." Celeste had finally stopped laughing, but she was still grinning openly. "I can't believe you really *hit* him. And I can't believe that I missed it, either! Man!"

She remembered that when she had been in high school, her father had told her that Kristin waited for him to get out of class one day, on what the students at Tuskegee had called "the Ignorant Bench," a central place on campus for the male students to watch the female students walk by. The entertainment value in that area of campus where "the bench" sat had greatly diminished by the time Celeste was there, but from what her father told her, most female students wouldn't have dared to sit on the concrete bench at the time. It sat directly across from an entrance to the cafeteria and the student union, and was one of the busiest areas on campus back then. There would usually be a group of popular guys sitting on it at any given time, and they could be so intimidating, in a humorous way, that some young women wouldn't even look in that direction as they passed it on their way to and from class.

Her father told her he had opted not to say anything to Kristin about sitting there, because he knew that she was already mad at him that day. He said he had much preferred having his friends heckle him instead, and Celeste had just assumed at the time that he had been exaggerating. But now she believed him. After what had apparently just happened, she understood why he had chosen the option he had.

"Not to worry, Aunt Kristin." Celeste was not bothering to hide her amusement about the incident. "I don't think anyone saw *that* part, but you could definitely tell that you guys were arguing." She knew that a few people in the area where she had been standing definitely knew they were arguing and had watched them for a few seconds as she had. It didn't seem too serious though, but it had been enough for Celeste to feel the need to check on her.

"Oh...Thank goodness!" Kristin was obviously relieved to have a verbal confirmation, as well.

"Maybe everyone will just chalk it up to the bride's parents blowing off a little stress, after planning for all the wedding festivities." She was hopeful as she considered that possibility for a few seconds. She looked up quickly after realizing what she had said and was flustered all over again.

"It's okay, Aunt Kristin," Celeste saw the look of embarrassment and hastened to assure her.

"I guess I've always thought of you as my mom, anyhow," she admitted shyly.

"You have?..." Kristin felt tears begin to form in her eyes.

"Yes, I have..." Celeste walked over to her and hugged her for emphasis. "Always...And *no* mother could have done a better job with their daughter's wedding, either.

Ishmael and I *both* appreciate it; everything you've done. You and Amina and all the others did a spectacular job. Everything was beautiful, from start to finish."

A second or two later she released Kristin, and broached the subject she had been hesitant to bring up—mainly because she had promised her father that she wouldn't.

"...but there is something else that I need to talk to you about..."

She started, unsure exactly what she would say to Kristin. She had kept her father's promise to this point, but after what had just happened it was clear that she needed to say *something*. She only hoped that her father would forgive her some day after he found out.

Kristin detected the note of seriousness in Celeste's tone, and immediately shifted her focus to finding out the cause; the way any mother would do.

"Is everything okay with you and Ishmael?" There was a hint of concern in her voice.

"Huh?...Oh, yes...We're fine. Definitely," she added with a big smile. "I don't think we could be any happier." The mention of her new husband's name distracted Celeste for a second. Their wedding ceremony and the reception had been everything she could have dreamed of and more. She and Ishmael were still having a great time and neither of them could believe how many people actually came, or all the money they had donated for Ishmael's clinic. She had left him dancing with his cousins though, as soon as she saw Kristin leaving the atrium and heading toward her apartment.

"...It *does* have something to do with Ishmael, though....Kinda," she added.

"Remember when I told you about his old girlfriend, Aunt Kristin?... Mom?" She corrected herself. "...and finding out she was pregnant?"

Kristin's brow was quizzical. "Of course I remember that, honey. How could I forget?" She was puzzled to find out what Celeste might be trying to tell her. No one had said anything to her yet about what had transpired during her first "knocking" ceremony, the one that she hadn't been present to witness. Ishmael's declarations of love had touched them all, and everyone there could see how much he truly cared for her. He had told them in great detail about Kendra and how she had come to become pregnant a few months before he and Celeste started dating.

Celeste, herself, had called her in tears one day, to tell her she had just found out about Kendra and the baby. They had talked for hours and Kristin postponed an important meeting so she could keep talking to her as long as she needed. It had been very difficult for her to hear how upset she was from such a distance. She had encouraged Celeste's decision to transfer to Tuskegee to finish school, knowing that the distraction of living in the small town would be the best thing for her.

"...I'm so glad that everything has worked out the way that it has too, sweetheart," she added, "although no one wanted to see the other young woman hurt either. All anyone can ever do in a situation like that is to put their trust in their Creator. The Universe always evolves in such a way that we're led to our highest good, no matter what; even when we can't visualize how it'll happen ourselves."

When Celeste brought up the subject of Kendra's miscarriage, her thoughts had been immediately directed to the baby she had lost herself such a long time ago. Nana Adwoa had helped her quite a bit before her blowout with Winston on Highland Beach, so she could concentrate on the Foundation's business at hand. She had finally gone to her for advice on the situation after she had been unable to get any work done once the sadness overcame her She had asked Nana how she might reconcile her emotions about the baby so that she could find some peace about what happened to her.

"I'm been waiting for you to ask me, my child." Nana had smiled a gentle smile in response to the question. It made Kristin suspect that the woman had somehow known about it all along.

She could tell from Nana's expression that she knew all about the pain that was still suffering after all those years; that would come from out of nowhere to haunt her, though happening far less frequently now, than in the past. Nana had explained to her that the energy of the baby's placenta had responded to her pleas not to leave her body. It had attached itself so that it could stay with her forever, just as Kristin had asked it to do. It made the tender spot inside her heart its home, and it became despondent whenever it could sense Kristin no longer wanted it there. Nana told her the energy of the baby that had been left inside her through the placenta, had been added to her own sadness to weigh her down.

They had talked about everything she had gone through that day in the hospital, all alone in her misery. She talked about how she felt after loosing the baby, and afterwards, the older woman performed a ceremony to encourage the baby's remaining Spirit to leave her. At the end, she performed a burial rite under a large tree in Nana's backyard. It would ground the connection that she would always feel to her beloved infant, Nana said. And although Kristin still thought about her baby from time to time, the deepest emotional scars she had were now gone, because the baby's Spirit no longer added its sadness to her own. Winston had never given her the chance to tell him all that part before their explosive blow-up at Highland Beach.

Kristin realized her thoughts had drifted and she wondered again why Celeste had brought up Kendra on her wedding day.

"The timing just wasn't right for you and Ishmael back then," she suggested, "that's all. You both needed to do the things that you ended up doing in the years that you were apart, like you finishing school in Tuskegee. That wouldn't have happened had you and Ishmael stayed together. Maybe you really would've become a distraction to him at Hunter." A slight smile was on her face again.

"Well, I *am* glad that I followed your advice and went to Tuskegee," Celeste confided, "that's for sure. It's still hard to believe we found each other again, especially so far away from where we knew each other... and at Nana's house of all places."

She and Kristin talked for a bit about Nana Adwoa and all of her mysteries. There had been things that neither of them had been able to make sense of, and talking about it was a diversion that seemed to help Kristin relax again.

"Aunt Kristin," Celeste started again after a pause. She hoped what she would say wouldn't be too shocking coming from her.

"What I have to say is about Daddy too." She said it slowly, poised for Kristin's reaction.

"What does *Winston* have to do with anything?"

Celeste could almost see her anger rise again at the mere mention of her father's name. He must have really ticked her off this time.

"I didn't know that you had even *told* him anything about Kendra." Kristin took a deep breath before saying it, trying to regain her composure. Celeste had made her promise that she wouldn't say anything to Winston about Kendra or the baby, after the two of them had talked.

"I didn't tell him....," She answered slowly, "at least not until right before I came here to work.

The two women had grown even closer after Celeste moved to Ghana. Kristin understood how difficult it had been for her to be around Ishmael, especially since she didn't trust her love for him anymore. They had talked about all kinds of things since she had arrived, anything, that is, except for Winston. There had been an unspoken rule between them since the weekend that she and her father had driven to Highland Beach to see Kristin. The topic of the man that they both loved so much had still been off limits between them, all this time. Kristin couldn't understand why Celeste was bringing him up now.

"...I told him about the baby just before I left the States...and that's when he told me what happened with your baby..." Celeste blurted out the last part without thinking. She searched Kristin's face to see what impact the abrupt mention of the baby had on her.

"What?" Kristin responded in distressed surprise. She had been completely thrown off guard by this unexpected revelation.

"You mean, you know?...Winston told you?..." She felt her anger rise again. She couldn't believe that he had actually told Celeste, that she knew what they had done. It was a moment that she had dreaded for over twenty-five years; having to face Winston's daughter with the truth.

Despite all the discord between them now, she was still glad that she had finally told him about their baby. She felt relived because of it, and it helped her release a part of her past, for good. The lie of omission that had been between them was no longer there, and now apparently, it would no longer be between her and Celeste, either.

"...Oh dear God, Celeste!" Kristin moaned, and turned her head away in anguish. "I don't know what to say to you..."

She wasn't ready to face her yet, and especially not on the night of her wedding. It was too difficult to be confronted with the truth, so abruptly, after she had avoided it for such a long time. She was already tired physically, after having put so much energy into preparations for the wedding for the past six weeks. It had turned out to be a much more emotionally charged day than she could even have imagined.

First, the wedding itself, which had been more emotional than she had been prepared for; then the thing with Winston. After she came to her apartment to recover from that, there had been the emotional acknowledgement between her and Celeste about their special relationship; and now this. The last few weeks had been less than cordial too, thanks to Winston. She had such high hopes for a reunion between them when they had planned the activities that would bring the two families and close friends together, to celebrate the marriage.

"I can't believe he actually told you!" She was still outraged by his betrayal.

"Aunt Kristin...Mom, please...It's okay, really." She walked across the room to stand next to Kristin, who had placed her hands over her eyes until Celeste gently pulled them away.

"Please, don't be so upset, Mom," she pleaded, wiping away a stray tear from Kristin's check with her hand. She hugged the woman that she had always thought of as her mother, closer to her.

"...And trust me, Daddy definitely didn't intend to say anything," she defended her father as she always had.

"It happened the day that I went to his office to talk to him—to tell him that I wanted to come here for a while, to work. I didn't intend to tell him about Ishmael and Kendra either," she added, "but he just looked so sad that I felt I had to tell him the real reason that I needed to get away from Washington.

"I was so upset myself that day, after I started talking about it. I didn't notice right away when he started getting upset himself. And right in the middle of me telling him about Kendra's baby, he started having some kind of melt-down or something."

Kristin's eyebrows knitted together quickly to match a sudden frown that was on her face. She had already had it with hearing about *Winston's* feelings. What about *her* feelings?

"I've never seen him that way before..." Celeste missed Kristin's reaction, and her voice was still filled with concern as she thought about her father's behavior that day. "It was even worse than when we drove back from Highland Beach that time...

"Oh..., I'm sorry, if that sounded insensitive Aunt Kristin..." She finally looked up at her after realizing her statement lacked any empathy for what her aunt had gone through that night, too.

Kristin was staring at Celeste in shock. It was still too hard for her to accept that Celeste knew all about the brief affair she had with her father, and the child they conceived that night. She had known before she arrived in Ghana, a whole year before.

"Daddy begged me not to say anything." Celeste read her thoughts and explained. There was much regret in her voice; she knew she had betrayed her father in telling Kristin about their conversation that day in his office. "He made me promise that I wouldn't tell Trazi, either."

"Trazi knows about this too?" Kristin misheard what Celeste said, and she sounded horrified at the thought of having the same conversation with her son.

"No, he doesn't know anything...at least not yet... And Daddy's going to be furious with me when he finds out I told you. It's just that after what happened earlier...Well, don't you think this has gone on long enough?" Celeste paused in mid-sentence, hoping she had at least started to get through to Kristin.

"And I promise...Trazi *still* doesn't know anything about it; and I won't tell him, either." She offered the reassurances, hoping to restore some degree of comfort after she had upset Kristin so much.

She waited until after a minute or two of silence. "Aunt Kristin...Daddy told me how much you've always loved each other, too."

"He did?" Yet another surprise, she sighed heavily in response.

"He did...He told me that he had loved my mother once too," she persisted, dropping her head, "and I believe him..." She lifted her head again. "He just never loved her as much as he loves you," she added, smiling again.

Kristin was at a loss for words so she didn't try to say anything.

"It's obvious to everyone really," Celeste went on, "nothing compares to the way that he feels about you."

She had been a "daddy's girl" all her life, her father's biggest fan. Kristin could see how hard Celeste was trying to fix things for him again, as she had always done.

"Celeste, I..." She tried to speak after another minute of silence. She stopped to search for the right words.

"...We never meant to hurt Angela—honestly, neither of us did..." She was still hesitant. "Your mother was like a younger sister to me....and what happened between Winston and me...Well, it just happened...once." She added the qualifier in hopes that it would make a difference.

"I know, Aunt Kristin, I believe you." Celeste assured her and fell silent.

It was surprising how easy it had been for her to have such a sensitive conversation. But Kristin had always been in her life; she had been more like a mother to her than her own mother had. She could see how much the past was still hurting her, and she wished that she could do something to ease her pain.

"There's something else...and I'm really sorry to be bringing any of this up now." Her tone was apologetic again, as she rubbed her hands across Kristin's shoulders. "...The only reason that I mention it at all, is that... Well, it's because Daddy also told me why he's been so upset with you.

"...Okay, why he's been acting like a raving lunatic," she corrected herself, and the quip helped to lighten the mood for a few seconds. Celeste hoped it would help to soften what she had to tell Kristin next.

She leaned forward to hear what she would say, and seemed to be trying to prepare herself to hear it at the same time. She had no idea what Winston's explanation might be but she had searched for that answer for nearly two years. Celeste took a deep breath before she finally told her.

"Daddy has convinced himself that you never cared about loosing the baby." She stopped and braced herself for Kristin's reaction.

"He what?" Kristin heard herself shout, despite her intentions to remain calm.

"Celeste, is that some kind of sick joke?" A deep frown had crossed her face as she struggled to understand.

"Did he actually *say* that to you?" Her aggravation with Winston began to grow again in leaps and bounds.

"...Well," Celeste sighed, I'm afraid he did." She had grown hesitant again because she had never seen her aunt look so angry. Far too late, she began to consider that it might have been best if she had kept her mouth shut about the whole thing. She had only wanted to help turn them back toward each other; she never wanted to make things worse.

"Believe me..." She countered quickly, hoping to calm Kristin down a bit. "I tried to tell him that he was wrong but he just wouldn't listen. He kept talking about the day that he saw you at the hospital, when he and mom were bringing me home."

Kristin winced at hearing the matter-of-fact tone Celeste used to talk about the most painful day of her life.

"Daddy kept insisting that he has an excellent memory," she went on.

"He kept saying that he remembered everything about that day clearly," she finished. "Apparently, he's gone over it in his mind a few times and he's absolutely convinced that you weren't upset at all during that time. He says he would have known if you had been."

Celeste looked away from Kristin again. She had only then realized she had been oblivious to the effects that what she was saying might have on her. She knew it had to be difficult for her to hear, but she had only been concentrating on getting out everything that she felt Kristin needed to hear.

"Daddy says he can't forgive you for not caring about the baby," she told her finally. She had deliberately averted Kristin's eyes as she spoke. When she finally looked at her and saw the pain that was etched in them, she realized just how far off the mark her father had been.

"Aunt Kristin, he actually cried when he was telling me all this." She had waited a few minutes before speaking again. She could only imagine how upsetting it all was for Kristin to hear. But she told her because she had to know why her father was being such a jerk about it. She had to know that he was just genuinely upset about the baby.

"...I don't remember seeing him cry about *anything* before this," she ended.

Both women were quiet again for several minutes and Kristin sat perfectly still. She was partially in shock from hearing Celeste talk about the affair she had with her father so casually. She had been much more understanding about everything than Kristin had dared to hope. But it was still such a delicate situation, and she debated with herself about how much more she should share with her.

'And why on Earth would Winston think that I never cared about loosing our little girl?' Her thoughts kept going back to what Celeste had said about Winston. Suddenly, she felt tired and very offended.

Kristin sat down on the side of her bed and all her defenses were now down. "Of course, I cared." She let out a big sigh, and she began to cry in spite of her resolve.

"I cared so much that I thought I would go off the deep end, at one time." She stood up again and looked straight into Celeste's dark pupils; eyes that had always been so much like her own. She took a deep breath again before speaking.

"I know this may sound strange to you, Celeste, but you were the one who actually saved me." She spoke the words softly, as she took the young woman by her hands.

"I've never said this to anyone else before, but I begged our daughter to come back to me that day; as soon as I realized she was really going to leave me. I've never felt so alone in my life as I did that day. I had nothing else to cling to so I kept begging her to stay with me until I felt that she would do it."

Tears had started to fall from Celeste's eyes too, as she listened to Kristin's painful recount.

"You were born less than fifteen minutes later and I was so grief stricken when I first saw you that I actually thought you were my baby girl, the one that I had just lost. I thought you had answered my pleas, Celeste, and had come back to me as I had asked. And that was the only thing that kept me from falling apart."

Kristin paused for a moment, and it was her turn to wipe away Celeste's tears. "The first time we saw each other, you looked into my eyes and gave me the sweetest smile. I swear, it was the sweetest smile that I've ever seen; as though you recognized me too, right away.

"I know that it doesn't make much sense," she said, as she turned away from her. "But that was what held me together." Kristin turned back around to face Celeste, again. "I believed with all my heart that day that you were actually my little girl—that somehow, a miracle had happened and my baby daughter had been brought back to me.

"*You* were the only thing that kept me from loosing my mind."

Celeste had put her arms around Kristin and tears were now streaming down both women's faces. They stood holding onto each other as they cried softly and time seemed to stand still. They felt an even stronger bond grow between them, and for the first time Celeste referred to Kristin as her mother with more confidence in her voice.

"You're going to have to tell him, Mom,"

She kept saying it softly, over and over as they rocked back and forth in the middle of the floor.

"You've got to tell Daddy, so you can make him understand."

Chapter 29

Stop In The Name Of Love

"Celeste?" "Honey, what's wrong?..."

Things had finally calmed down enough for Winston to feel safe to duck out of the reception again for a few minutes, without being attacked. He saw that Kristin had returned to the party; she looked okay from a distance, but it was too hard for him to tell for sure. He decided it might be best for him to avoid her altogether, since she was clearly on the edge. There had been far too much commotion between them already and he was determined he would prevent any more from happening. As it were, he had practically held his breath after the ceremony that morning, to get through that lengthy photo shoot. They had been forced to stand close and smile at each other—all for the sake of his daughter's pictures.

But he did have to hand it to her, she had done a magnificent job with the wedding—both the ceremonies and everything that led up to that last fabulous evening. Everyone had been telling him how beautiful everything had been all night. And their guests were clearly having a great time; more than half of them were still up dancing with no apparent plans to end the evening anytime soon.

After his last run-in with Kristin, Winston decided to join the others on the dance floor for a while. He had surprised himself that he remembered so many of his old moves from back in the day. He kept Ishmael's mother entertained for quite some time, in fun, and he had even danced with Malaya a few times.

He wondered whether he was the only one who had noticed his son was paying more than just polite attention to his sister's childhood friend? He had to wonder whether there might be a romance brewing that Celeste had been too distracted by her wedding details to take notice of yet.

He had take the steps that led to the 2nd floor balcony two at a time, to look out over the atrium and investigate whether Trazi and Malaya might indeed be a couple. No one had questioned their plans to travel from the U.S. together; could it have been more than mere coincidence?

He ran into his daughter unexpectedly as he walked past the first set of tables and moved toward the potted plants that bordered the side walls of the balcony. She was crying quietly and she was there all alone.

"What is it baby?" He asked her, anxiously. "What happened? Did Ishmael do something to you?" He was instantly protective of her, as he had always been; alarmed, because he couldn't imagine what would cause her to be so unhappy on her wedding day.

"No, Daddy." She was laughing through her tears.

She hadn't been able to get the conversation with Kristin out of her mind since she left her apartment. She had come outside to the balcony to be alone for a few minutes, before it would be time for her and Ishmael to leave for the evening.

Kristin was right—the last few weeks had been an emotional whirlwind for all of them. She had been moved to tears as she thought about how much closer they had become after they talked. Hearing about the connection she felt to her after loosing her own baby seemed perfectly normal to Celeste, and it had only strengthened their bond.

She didn't hear her father as he approached her, and she clearly couldn't answer his question truthfully. Then, she thought that maybe the angels had sent him so that she could do something to fix things between him and Kristin. And as soon as he asked her about Ishmael, she knew exactly how she would do it.

"Ishmael hasn't done anything to me," she said hesitantly, "...At least not yet..." She looked up at her father innocently.

"What do you mean, not yet?..." He was confused and still didn't get it because she was speaking in riddles. He opened his mouth to tell her as much and then stopped dead in his tracks. He frowned at her slightly and bent forward so he could look at her face more closely.

'Was it possible?' He was squinting his eyes at her, looking at her closer still.

"Celeste, are you trying to tell me that you've never..." His voice trailed off after he saw that her eyes had begun to tear up again. She really wasn't faking that part because she had started getting nervous as the evening wore on, and it grew closer to the time that she and Ishmael would leave the party.

Winston was at a complete loss for words.

"I don't know why you're acting so surprised!" Her nervousness turned into aggravation, and she raised her voice to her father before she knew it. She had been proud of her decision to remain a virgin until she married. The whole thing with Ishmael and Kendra had brought home to her the perils that went with having casual sex, and had reinforced it. But now she suddenly felt embarrassed that she would find herself being so inexperienced on her wedding night.

"*You* were the one who kept telling me *not* to!" She said to her father, in an accusatory tone.

"I know that's what I said, sweetheart, but are you saying that you have never?..." He couldn't help from asking her a second time. He was blown away and pleased with himself at the same time. He had done a remarkable job of raising his daughter, but in the same instant he realized he had nothing to say to her that would help her in any way.

What could he possibly say?

"Well,..." He heard his daughter go on, "there *was* this one time, when I..."

"Wait! No!" He cut her off. "Stop! That's way too much information at this point—I don't need to hear all the details," he said hastily.

It made Celeste laugh again but the tears kept streaming down her face. She had started out with one purpose in mind but her true feelings had taken over. She found herself crying to her father as she had always done, whenever she needed to be comforted. Winston held out his arms to her and took her in them, searching through his mind for something he could say, *anything* that would give her the help that she needed on her wedding night.

He gave up after only a few seconds, giving her arm a quick squeeze as he turned to leave. "Wait right here," he told her. "I'll go and find Kristin, so the two of you can have a talk."

"Thank you, Daddy." Celeste dabbed at tears with the white lace handkerchief that Nana had given her before their wedding ceremony that morning. Shedding a few tears had helped to rid her of anxieties about her wedding night, and she had known that it would be just the thing to get her father to go looking for Kristin.

"Daddy..." She called after him. "If you see Ishmael, please don't tell him where I am, yet."

"Don't worry, baby." He called back over his shoulder. "If I see my new son-in-law, I'll just take him for a little walk so we can have a man-to-man chat, that's all."

"Daddy, no!...Please!" Celeste was instantly alarmed by the thought of what her father might actually say to her new husband.

"Don't worry, pumpkin." He was quick to add, and he turned the corner and left her sight. "I was just kidding."

But they both knew that he wasn't kidding at all.

※※※

"What is it now Winston?" Kristin had been instantly annoyed as soon as she saw him approaching her table. She was still furious with him for blabbing to Celeste about their indiscretion, because it hadn't been his alone to tell. And it had already taken her well over thirty minutes to recover from their last interaction, that and the intense conversation she had with Celeste. She had finally managed to pull herself together to fix her makeup and rejoin the festivities. She had worn the same smile pasted across her face as she mingled with their guests again, for well over an hour since her return. She had been going from table to table to personally make sure that everyone left was still having a good time. She decided to take a quick break after she discovered a quiet corner of the ballroom where she could get off her feet for a few minutes. She had been watching their guests idly from her secluded spot and trying to prevent the conversation she had with Celeste from resurfacing. She would think about all that tomorrow; she couldn't afford to think about it now, not when they still had over three hundred guests left to entertain.

Amina had prepared a breakdown of their benefactors and business associates who had accepted their invitation to the wedding reception. After Kioni looked at all the names, he had the brilliant idea of mixing business with the joyful occasion of the wedding. He had noticed right away that many of the meetings they had been forced to cancel were with the very same people who were planning to come. Kristin had to admit that only a man would have thought of such a plan, but it made even more sense to her after he reminded them all that there was only so much small talk any one person could participate in during a three to four hour time span. Taken together, they had calculated that the dinner and reception would last for well over five hours. That would certainly give them enough time to conduct business at some point, once their guests had relaxed and enjoyed an entertaining evening first.

The Foundation had literally suspended its non-essential appointments for over a month so that everyone on staff could concentrate on the wedding plans. There was to be lots of rescheduling afterwards, and Kioni had devised a way to use the reception to further the Foundation's goals at the same time. Dina had her volunteers create name tags for everyone in a way that would make them easily identifiable, based on the person's relationship with the Foundation. The name bags for residents of Exodus Village, who were in attendance, were created using the same system. The designs for all the badges were similar enough to seem identical to anyone out of the loop, at first glance. But there were subtle variations on their badges that would reveal how long a resident who was at the dinner and reception, had lived in Exodus Village, for example.

Their volunteer hostesses could also tell in one glance whether a guest was a friend or relative of the bridal party, or whether they were associated with the Foundation in some way. Kristin, Kioni, and Amina relied on the designs as they introduced their benefactors and business partners to their residents and to each other. During the last few hours of the reception, they had been covertly working the crowd to form as many new associations with the stakeholders, as possible. Residents, who were heavily involved in a specific program in Exodus Village, for example, were seated at the same table as the major contributors of that program, wherever possible.

That was another of Kioni's ideas too, and a brilliant one, Kristin thought. She had such an appreciation for his ability to think outside the box. Arranging for personal contact with their residents, for instance, had turned out to be a much more effective way of furthering some of their funding goals than their normal presentations would have been. Kioni's creative thinking had made it possible for them to resume their meetings and negotiations on a much more productive note.

※※※

She braced herself as Winston walked much further into her space than she had anticipated. She was already agitated at the thought of him starting up with her again. She couldn't believe all the nonsense he had been telling Celeste, either, but she was still partially ashamed about the way she had reacted the last time they had been close, when she had lost it completely.

In all honesty though, she couldn't really say that she regretted having hit him either, because he had driven her to it. Doing so had apparently gone a long way in helping him get over himself. She had noticed how he suddenly started acting like someone who had good sense for a change, when she came back to the party, just like a miracle had been performed. The last time she saw him he had been was dancing like everyone else, and finally focusing his attention on something other than *her* for a change. Except, here he was again.

"It's Celeste." He dropped his cryptic statement on her like a bombshell, not trying to hide his displeasure at having to talk to her at all.

"What *about* Celeste?" Kristin was already well on her way to fuming again. She got up abruptly and turned away from Winston, scanning the ballroom for his daughter. The dance floor was *still* crowded although it was starting to get rather late. She didn't see Celeste or Ishmael among the crowd of people who were within the line of her vision.

"Where *is* she?" Reluctantly, Kristin turned to face Winston again with the question. She sat back down when he didn't respond right away.

"I left her on the balcony." He answered after she was seated. His tone was blunt enough to emphasize that he was talking to her under duress.

"She's upset and she needs to talk to you," he added, grudgingly.

"What's wrong with her?" Kristin was back on her feet again and already halfway into her shoes. "Why couldn't you just say that from the beginning?"

She looked in the direction where Winston pointed, not giving him a chance to respond to either question. Then, she brushed past him as her concern for Celeste took center stage. What on earth could cause her to be upset on her wedding day?

She hurried to the second floor of the atrium but Celeste was nowhere to be found. Puzzled, Kristin turned to head back down the stairs only to find Winston blocking her path.

"She left a note." He held up a folded piece of paper that he had spotted and picked up from the table where his daughter had been sitting.

"It says that she went to her room."

Winston handed the note to Kristin, who took it from him without responding. After verifying it's contents for herself, she hurried past Winston and headed back toward her apartment. He followed, only after giving brief consideration as to whether he should tell Kristin that there was nothing seriously wrong. But when he thought about what she had done to him earlier, he decided he would let her suffer.

※※※

"Celeste?" Kristin called out as soon as she had her apartment door open. She had made it there in record time considering that she had been forced to slow down as they passed through the ballroom. She didn't want to alarm their guests unnecessarily so she made up the time as soon as she had cleared the door.

"Baby?..." She called out to Celeste again. "I'm here, Celeste. It's Kristin. Are you all right?"

"Not really..." She could hear the faint answer from inside Celeste's bedroom. "Are you alone?... I'm in my room."

Her voice sounded shaky and it alarmed Kristin even more. She hurried toward has, as distant thoughts registered surprise that the lights were off in the sitting room. They had been on when she was in the apartment before; not knowing why they had been turned off only added to her sense of anxiety. She moved quickly toward the dim light of the bedroom.

"Your father is with me, honey," she answered. "Why are you sitting in the dark like this?" Kristin hurried inside the room and toward the overhead switch against the left wall. She had to see for herself what was going on with Celeste, and it had taken several seconds before her eyes fully adjusted to the brightness of the room from its previous dimness. Winston had come in right behind her, now alarmed himself. He thought that something else must have happened after he left his daughter on the balcony.

As soon as he had crossed the threshold into her room he could feel Celeste scurry past him. The bedroom door was closed behind her with a loud thud just as the overhead light came on. Shortly afterwards, they heard a similar sound coming from the door that led through the adjoining bathroom into Kristin's bedroom. A few seconds later her bedroom door slammed shut, and finally the door leading out of the bathroom into the sitting room closed with a bang too. Before either of them could react, Winston and Kristin heard the sound of something heavy being dragged across the rug outside, and pushed up against each of the three doors leading to the outside, one after the other.

"What on earth...?" Kristin had already been overstimulated by everything that had been going on over the past few weeks. She felt overwhelmed, like she had been stuck on a carnival ride for all that time, and now this. She hadn't been able to fathom what might be happening for the first several minutes, but now it was quite clear.

"I'm sorry, sir." They heard Ishmael's voice speaking above Celeste's sudden peal of laughter.

"I'm sorry too." Her voice came from the direction of the sitting room, and there was nothing about it that sounded sorry.

"And I really *was* upset a little, Daddy," she offered, "but Ishmael found me after you left the terrace. We had a nice long talk about it. Everything is okay, now."

"What in the...?" Winston couldn't get anything more out of his mouth. He had tried all three doors that led from Celeste's bedroom, but he had been too late. The bathroom was as far as they could go; he and Kristin were locked inside his daughter's bedroom together.

"Celeste!" He yelled through the door. "I don't know what you're trying to prove but you'd better open this door, and right now!" It was only after he said it that he realized he was talking to her as though she was ten years old again.

"Sorry Daddy, but I can't." She answered him in a nonchalant tone that made her pretense of remorse that much more unconvincing.

"You and Aunt Kristin really left us no choice," she said, making Ishmael an official co-conspirator. "We couldn't very well go off and be happy on our honeymoon, not with things the way they are between you."

She started giggling again. The whole thing had been much easier to pull off than she had ever expected.

"Celeste, please..." Kristin tried a gentler approach.

"Honey, why are you doing this?" There was pleading in her voice.

"I'm really sorry, Aunt Kristin." This time she at least sounded sincere.

"You've got to tell him." All the laughter had left her voice, and she paused a few seconds before she said it.

"Tell me what?" Winston demanded, although he was afraid to hear the answer. He had already had his share of surprises in the last few weeks.

"Celeste, please don't do this," Kristin urged, still not acknowledging Winston at all. Her brain was still trying to register what was happening and what she might do to prevent it. She refused to believe it at first, that Celeste had actually locked them in. "There has to be another way..." She offered, in a compromising tone.

"But I've already tried that," Celeste sounded regretful this time. "I really am sorry, but this was the best I could come up with on such short notice." She gave the explanation as though it made sense, as though what she was doing to them was rational in some way.

"We're heading out for the airport early tomorrow morning for our flight to Harare," she reminded. "I never would have been able to enjoy myself at Victoria Falls, Daddy. Not knowing that you would just get on a plane tomorrow evening and go home without even talking to Aunt Kristin.

"I really do wish there was some other way," she finished, " but as they say—desperate times call for desperate measures..."

Ishmael had moved her bags from her bedroom into the sitting room before Winston and Kristin got there, hence the darkened room. The only thing he had forgotten was the small bag of cowry shells from their ceremony that Celeste wanted to keep with them on their honeymoon. He had collected her bags and started toward the front door to load them into their golf cart when he remembered the beads, but opening one of the doors was out of the question.

Kioni had transformed one of the single residences in the Garvey Community into a honeymoon suite. He and Celeste would be the building's only occupants for that night.

"I just couldn't let this go on forever," Celeste called back apologetically, as she turned to follow Ishmael out the door.

"I would really love to stay and chat with you guys some more, but Ishmael and I have an appointment..." She was laughing again, this time nervously.

"So, is that it?...You're really just planning to leave us in here, Celeste?" Winston was trying to be more cautious with his tone, as he made one last ditch plea. In reality, he was so upset with his daughter in that moment that he could barely speak. But he managed to find his voice quickly after he realized no one would hear them banging on the door—not over the loud music coming from the ballroom.

"...I'm afraid so, Daddy...But don't worry, Trazi knows where you are. I told Amina where you were too, Aunt Kristin," she assured her. "I only left out the part about your being locked in here, that's all. But I did ask them to bring you breakfast in bed tomorrow, so someone will be by in the morning for sure.

"They can let you guys out then...That is, if you still want to come out." She laughed at her own joke.

"...Oh, and one last thing..." She turned back toward her bedroom door, holding her mouth for a couple of seconds to keep herself from laughing out loud.

"I took the liberty of checking the room to make sure there were no guns or blunt instruments in there that you guys could use as weapons. I'm sure that you'll both thank me for that later." She giggled out loud at her own joke once again, as she headed for the door behind Ishmael.

"Oh, and thank you soooo much for our beautiful wedding! The only thing that would have made it better is if Aunt Grace could have been here for everything too." Kristin and Winston both knew she meant both the wedding as well as Grace knowing that they would be locked in the bedroom for the night.

And those were her last words before she closed the apartment door firmly behind her.

Kristin was completely speechless after she heard the door close. She had been in denial up to that point, convinced that Celeste would never really leave them locked in the room together. She stood rooted to the same spot for ten minutes after she and Ishmael had left, as though her feet were attached to the floor. She kept her eyes closed with one hand resting across her brow, unable to think of what to do next.

She walked around to one side of the bed finally, and sat on the edge with a heavy sigh, acknowledging the reality of their predicament. She often made the same sound to underscore her troubled thoughts, when she faced a situation that wasn't to her liking.

She only noticed the large tray of food that Celeste had apparently left for them, after she sat down. There were also two bottles of champagne chilling in a large metal ice bucket, with two flutes sitting next to the bucket. Kristin still couldn't believe that she was really locked in with Winston. Her mind began to replay all the activity she had been involved in since Celeste had announced her engagement. Everything had been thrown into high gear immediately, because of the time crunch. She had been involved in so many conversations with so many different people during the last six weeks, and she had participated in many activities with several different groups of people, in the last two weeks alone.

But this had certainly topped them all.

※※※

Eventually, Winston plopped down on the other side of the bed, and there they sat, without one word between them for nearly an hour; not ever looking in the other's direction. Celeste and Ishmael had thought to remove the two chairs that were normally kept in the room so their choices were to remain standing, sit on the floor, or share the bed.

Kristin felt light headed after a while and that was when she realized she had hardly eaten all day, except for occasional hors d'oeuvres she had grabbed from a passing tray. She got up to fix herself a plate of food and grudgingly asked Winston whether he wanted something too. She did it as much for her benefit as for his, because she knew his behavior might become unpredictable if his blood sugar level went down too low. The *last* thing she needed was another blow out with him, especially with them locked inside such a small space. She could see that he was so angry with Celeste that he could hardly see straight. Kristin chose to put all her effort into remaining calm. They would have a quiet uneventful evening and someone would come to let them out of the room in the morning.

"Thanks." It was all Winston could trust himself to say.

The silence resumed,as they picked through the food on their plates. They were both in a daze, and neither of them was yet willing to believe that Celeste intended to keep them locked in the room all night.

After another thirty minutes or so of silence, Winston turned abruptly so that he could look directly at Kristin. He locked his gaze on her, although she pretended not to notice him.

"Why did we get a divorce?" He finally broke through the silence with the question. He decided he should at least make an effort to talk to her, so they would have *something* to show for the ridiculous situation his daughter had placed them in.

"You should know!" Kristin snapped at him, with an undeniable anger in her voice. She had forgotten all about the resolution she had made not to get in a fight with him.

"You're the one who wanted a divorce." The statement had sounded like more of an accusation, and Kristin regretted her words. She had no idea how Winston could push her buttons so easily.

She finally calmed down enough to give him an answer to the question he had asked her, but it was after several more minutes had passed.

"I honestly don't even remember why anymore. I've asked myself the same question more times than I could say."

They were both quiet again for a long time after that. They each searched their own memories of their early relationship and marriage. They couldn't help but think about how differently their lives would have been, had they not divorced. Their thoughts drifted to Celeste at nearly the same time. Neither could truthfully say that they regretted the relationship Winston had with Angela, because of his daughter. Kristin couldn't imagine her life without Celeste in it, any more than Winston could. And she also couldn't imagine her life without the Exodus Foundation either.

If she had stayed with Winston, it was doubtful that she would have pursued the opportunity that had presented itself to her, and had led to its creation. She couldn't imagine herself not doing the work that she had been doing, or her not living in Africa, for that matter.

The conversation she had with Celeste earlier had still weighed heavily on her mind. Now, she debated with herself whether she should to say anything to Winston and began to realize that Celeste was right. They had to talk about it because she was struggling with her anger that he should somehow think she hadn't cared that their baby died. It was outrageous and Kristin made a decision that he should probably know she felt that way.

"Celeste told me why you're so upset with me," She had mulled over what she would say to him for a few minutes, and then decided she would just say it.

Winston turned towards her again, wondering just how many more surprises were in store for him that night.

"She always *did* have a big mouth," he said of his daughter, dryly. His comment made them both smile involuntarily, and they forgot themselves for a moment. It cleared the air a little and kept Celeste as their target to focus on, instead of themselves for a while longer.

When she had been younger, they would talk about how she had constantly tattled on poor Trazi. Celeste would quickly spill the beans about anything he did when they weren't around. They had all called her "the little tattle tale" behind her back. Winston and she had always felt bad for Trazi, because he would look so betrayed when she did it. They all knew that he literally would have done *anything* for his little sister, and even her tattling hadn't change that.

"Winston..." She started again. "What would make you think something like that?"

He could hear pain in her voice as she searched his face for an answer.

"Don't you know me at *all?*" Her shoulders had drooped as she asked him the question.

"I thought I did," he responded hotly. Then he wished he could take back what he said, so he could say it in a different way.

"Okay, look Kristin...," He started again in a more agreeable tone.

"I know more than anybody that it doesn't make much sense," he admitted. "You've always been an excellent mother to Trazi, and Celeste too, for that matter. I realize that and I thank you for it.

"But I keep playing that day over again in my mind. Believe me, I would give anything to make it stop."

Kristin had to grit her teeth to keep herself from saying anything. She would keep quiet so that he could say what he had to say.

"I know I was preoccupied with Celeste after she was born—and with Angela too, trying to juggle everything and all. But whenever I look back, I just can't remember *any* time that you were sad, or even seemed really that upset. I just can't believe I would have missed something like that."

She could see that he was honestly confused about it, now. She could hear Celeste's voice in her head, urging her to tell Winston everything, but she had to wonder whether he would even understand it. He seemed to have made up his mind already.

"I can't help it. I think you were relieved when it happened." He hadn't stopped long enough for Kristin to have an opportunity to speak, and also hadn't paid much attention to her reaction to what he was saying.

"...I guess that's understandable in a way too, considering... I know how close you and Angela were. You must have felt at *least* as guilty as I did about what happened. You had to be worried too that she would find out about it one day, but with the baby gone..."

Kristin was staring at him in disbelief with a deep frown on her face. What he said had hurt her deeply, way down to her core. She felt as though he had taken a razor and sliced across her heart with it; the man she had loved all her life was now apparently out to destroy her. She couldn't imagine another reason that he would be saying the things that he had said.

When he finally stopped talking he looked at Kristin directly and saw the pained expression on her face. She had been looking at him as though she was seeing him for the very first time. Then the pain he saw had quickly transformed into anger again, anger that she no longer had the will to control it. Winston had taken a cheap shot at her, and it was all too much for her to take. She had no choice but to release it, everything that she had been holding back. She felt her anger well up inside of her and it grew into a quiet rage.

"Well, tell me Winston..." She said quietly. "What is it that you would you have me do?"

The calmness in her voice gave no indication of the looming explosion, or that he had crossed the thin line into hate.

"Did you want me to say that I was sorry that I lost our baby?" She asked him evenly. "Is that it? Will *that* make you feel better?"

"Okay, then..." She was suddenly agreeable. "I'm sorry..."

The tears had begun to form in her eyes; she couldn't believe his insensitivity to her feelings.

"I'm sorry that I lost our baby, she said calmly. "I'll even go as far as saying that I'm sorry I kept my pregnancy from you, although you couldn't even look me in the face at the time."

Winston had been looking down at his hands, but he looked up as Kristin kept talking. What she said was true; he had been in terrible shape after that night they spent together. He had been burdened by his conscious, as had she. It wouldn't let him forget what they had done, and so he had avoided Kristin and would often leave the room if she had entered it, for quite a long time. He could no longer deny that he was still in love with her; but he had been almost eaten alive by guilt because Angela had been so close to an emotional breakdown. He couldn't trust himself to look into Kristin's eyes; he felt terrified that he would be mesmerized by them again, and hopelessly lost.

"I'll admit that I was wrong in trying to protect you, Winston." A trail of tears slowly rolled down both her cheeks, as she started to cry.

"You're absolutely right. I should *never* have tried to shield you, to keep you from having to make more difficult choices in an already impossible situation." Her rising anger had finally betrayed her facade of calm.

"I guess I should've just called you back, after you left those message about Celeste being born.

"You're absolutely right!" She was shouting now. "I should've called you back right away and told you that *our* baby had just died. I should have told you how much I needed you there with me, to *hold* me, and keep me from falling apart."

Her voice had grown louder still and she got up from the bed abruptly. She moved as far away from him as she could manage in the small space.

"I'm sorry that you missed your chance to be with me in that cold room, Winston." Her voice was softer again, coming from the other side of the room.

"And I'm really sorry that you didn't get to feel our baby's *life* slipping away like *I* did.

She turned her back toward him and burst into tears. He got up to go to her, but she moved away before he could reach her and shrank away to avoid his touch.

"And I'm so *sorry* that I figured out how to keep from loosing my mind!" She was shouting at him again.

"I'm guessing you would have found *that* much more convincing!"

The memories of that day had completely flooded her mind again, and Kristin broke down in sobs. Winston felt helpless and guilty too for having caused her so much heartache.

"Oh, and I'm sorry that I figured out how to stop crying too," she said, when she had pulled herself together and could talk again, "...so my doctor would stop sedating me long enough for me to leave the hospital!"

"Believe me, Winston. I'm truly sorry that I didn't share all this pain with you, so you could feel it too." She choked on her words, sadly.

"If I hadn't kept it all to myself like this, maybe I would've been able to put it behind me a long time ago."

"So does that make you happy?" She was yelling at him again, and suddenly moving towards him.

"Are you satisfied?" Her fists were clenched, as her shoulders heaved up and down sadly. "Is this enough pain for you?"

Winston was crying now too, and he reached out to try and comfort Kristin again. He was so ashamed that he had caused her to relive something that was so obviously painful to her. He had been such a jerk, and once again he had hurt the woman he had always loved so much.

Kristin tried to pull away again but this time he was quicker. He grabbed hold of her arms and pinned them to her sides. It took a few minutes, but she finally stopped resisting him. He held onto her, and rocked her gently from side to side. And they finally mourned together for the baby girl they had lost.

"I'm so sorry, Kristin." He kept saying it over and over.

"I'm so sorry you had to go through all of this alone. Please forgive me for being such a jackass."

She still struggled against him, telling herself that she had really had it with him this time. She had stopped wrestling just long enough to regain her strength, and to try to free herself again from his grip as soon as his attention had turned. He seemed to sense her intention beforehand, to be done with him once and for all. Because no matter what she tried to do to get away from him, he refused to let her go.

Kristin wanted nothing more than to be as far away from Winston as she could get, but he kept holding onto her firmly. They stood in the middle of the floor like that for what later seemed to be hours. All the while Winston kept holding her, and kissing her through her tears, until finally, they stopped flowing.

And after a time she relaxed in his arms.

Chapter 30

That's The Power Of Love

*K*ristin sat very still on one side of the love seat in her office. She sipped at the tea she had made from some herbs sent by Nana Adwoa, waiting several seconds between each swallow that she took. To see her sitting there, as she had been for the past half-hour, one would never guess there were as many details left as there were to be confirmed. She only had a short window of time to get through the items on her list too, but she had been brought to a virtual standstill again, this time by issues with her stomach that had plagued her for the past few days. She prayed that the tea would bring her relief soon, and in the meantime, she tried as best she could to be patient and to give it the time it needed to work its magic.

Everyone had to work much harder this time than normal to get ready for the *Diasporan Black Star's* arrival. Kristin had been determined she would do her part too, despite her upset stomach, since much of the extra load was due to the ground they needed to make up after Celeste's wedding, when their business activities had been suspended for weeks. But, things were finally getting back on track—partially because Kristin had pushed herself again for six weeks after the wedding, day in and day out. She knew she had allowed herself to get run down in the process, but certain milestones had to be checked off before their ship docked again.

She made a guess that Nana would have advised her to get more rest, to help fight off whatever bug she apparently was trying to catch. Since taking time off to rest was out of the question, she had purposely delayed going to see her. She phoned her about the symptoms she was having instead, and Nana had sent her driver with the tea the very next day. It had seemed to help her at first, but now the tea appeared to have lost its powers. Kristin had been debating with herself whether she should take the time to visit Nana after all. She would need something to help her make it through the next hectic round of activities.

An increasing number of African American tourists had been coming to Elmina twice a year, to witness arrival ceremonies for their new residents. Heavenly Travel, and most other travel-related businesses, had seen dramatic growth since their Foundation originally began its mission. There were now more and more African Americans who vacationed in West Africa, in general. Their tours of Exodus Village had become one of the most popular destinations requested too, and all the business that these new tourists generated was having a very positive impact on local communities. Kristin was proud that their foundation had lived up to the meaning of the Adinkra symbol that represented it. A solid system of cooperation and interdependence now existed in Ghana with the Exodus Foundation, as the African Diaspora continued to make its way home.

A series of events had snowballed to make the reception of this latest arrival of residents an even more special occasion. Kristin had been approached by her public relations department a day or two after Celeste's wedding, about posting a video of their arrival ceremony on YouTube. Her staff had convinced her that there were people they might reach through the popular internet site, who would want to see what the ceremony was like in person, if they could. The comments from her staff got her thinking and she had made a few calls that started the ball rolling in a much bigger direction. Now, the arrival would be important to Exodus Village for another reason, and Kristin was very anxious to have everything run smoothly.

Tony Jenkins would be on board the *Diasporan Black Star* when the ship arrived, along with nine hundred and fifty of his crew, listeners and fans. Tony was one of the most successful radio broadcasters in American history. He had a popular syndicated radio show that was broadcast everything in the U.S., and even to the U.S. troops overseas. He was also an old friend of Kristin's from Tuskegee, and one of Winston's frat brothers and closest friends. Tony would be covering their next arrival ceremony for his show, and he had invited his fans to book passage on the *Black Star* with him, to join in the experience.

Anyone who had listened to his show would tell you that it was usually hilarious, but it was also very socially and politically conscious at the same time. His comedic façade had helped him build a reputation for "going there" with his interview guests. Tony was known for asking the questions that many other journalists wouldn't dare to ask, but they were usually questions that his audience wanted to have answered. His listeners had developed confidence in him that he would bring out the truth during any of his interviews. He and his cohorts on the show had gone so far as to reveal the secret dating tricks that single Black men often used on women, during one show; after Tony had remarried, of course.

He already started taping on board their luxury cruise liner during the two-weeks it had taken to sail from Jamaica to Ghana. Tony was documenting the journeys of four new resident families in particular, and he planned to broadcast their interview during a full four-hour show, live from Exodus Village. It would be taped every day for an entire week and was a major deal for the Exodus Foundation. They had all been busy once again, getting prepared to put their best foot forward.

As soon as all the arrangements had been set, their agency put together some travel packages that were heavily discounted for Tony's listeners. There was an additional discount given to anyone traveling to Africa for the first time, with an even better deal for those who opted to spend at least a week in Ghana, after they arrived. Their travel agency had booked flights back to the States for those who wouldn't stay over, and they would be departing in the first three days after the arrival ceremony. And there were others who had booked a return passage on the *Diasporan Black Star,* which would leave for Jamaica again within the next two weeks.

Tony had announced the trip on his radio show as soon as Heavenly Travel sent him their pricing samples, and the nine hundred and fifty tickets they had reserved for his fans sold out quickly. They had all traveled to Kingston, Jamaica in time to board the *Black Star* there, after all their new residents had been checked on-board first. From all accounts, Tony's fans had enjoyed the ship's luxurious accommodations for the long voyage across the ocean. There had been the usual musical entertainment booked as part of this special cruise, so his guests could party with Tony and his crew with a special purpose in mind. The finale would be the experience of the arrival ceremony when their two-week journey came to an end in Ghana.

His producers had contacted the Foundation ahead of time to let them know the type of residents they were interested in interviewing in Exodus Village. Kioni had put together a list of possibilities, along with a brief description of the family's history. He had added some of their more seasoned residents to the list, along with graduates who lived in the area from as far back as five years. Kioni even had an alternate list of names in case the first group was too far off the mark.

Tony planned to continue taping the four families he had started interviewing in Jamaica, as well. He would record their first moment-to-moment reactions to being in Ghana. He planned to document their thoughts and feelings as they began their transformation in Exodus Village too, and he would do periodic follow-ups in the years to come. His listening audience was so large that the Foundation would get priceless exposure from his visit. Kristin wanted to make sure that they took full advantage of the opportunity. She wanted his listeners to hear first-hand how well their residents were adapting in the country, and how they were blending in with the culture after they had graduated from the Foundation's programs.

She agreed that Tony should interview residents who were having problems adjusting in Ghana too, and he would, no doubt, ask them pointed questions in his usual direct style. The bit of humor that he always added to his journalistic probing seemed to put most people at ease fairly soon. His technique netted a more in-depth response to his questions; making his interviews more informative for listeners while he entertained them at the same time.

Tony had planned to highlight the intermarriages that were commonplace across the country, and the new generation represented by their offspring. The Foundation had made certain that there was a good mix of children in their schools early on, through busing. There had always been children who were brought in for school inside Exodus Village, and they had also bused children from Exodus Village to neighboring schools. Ghanaian women had taken the lead in running all their day care facilities, and they exclusively taught their children from preschool through the third primary grade. The main purpose had been to ensure that an adaptation to the culture remained constant. The natural outcome of having African American and Ghanaian children go to school together had also been to have them grow up as friends. They formed strong bonds with each other that had often translated into marriage. Their offspring were of particular interest to Tony; the new Ghanaians, who were a living testament to the cultural blending taking place.

He had interviews lined up with their Fruit of Islam security force as well, with a special segment dedicated to their own "Department of Please," as their residents of the village had affectionately nicknamed the FOI. It was the same name given to the make-shift security force that had assumed responsibility during Woodstock in 1969, for the five hundred thousand mostly white young people who had descended on the Catskills for a weekend of partying and music. The "Please Department" had controlled that massive crowd on the six hundred acre dairy farm for the whole three days, taking care of minor emergencies and keeping the peace, just by asking people nicely to follow their instructions.

The FOI had used a similar gentle, yet firm system for enforcing all the regulations in place at Exodus Village; and they had always had quite a few. Their reputation for enforcing security had preceded them, so there had been few challenges to their authority over the years even from people who had seemed immune to walking the straight and narrow before they arrived. Many of them had been in frequent contact with the American justice system before they left for Ghana; but thanks to the FOI, there had been no need for that kind of structure at Exodus Village. They had a very high success rate for their graduates, and they were proud to let the world know about it.

When they had spoken on the phone, Tony shared with Kristin that his listening audience was especially curious about FOI's role at Exodus Village. His interviews would highlight the range of services they provided in each community—from helping new residents learn their way around, to making sure their male residents kept a respectable distance from the single females, in particular, when they weren't in the company of their chaperone. Their no-nonsense authority had been unquestioned since their pilot residents came to live there. They had never been required to use, or even threaten physical force, and they always carried a strangely similar sense of caring as had the Please Department at Woodstock, even beneath their stern businesslike exteriors.

And just like the young people at Woodstock, it was very clear to Kristin that their residents were glad to have them there.

※※※

Tony's crew was to film the entire arrival ceremony and record the reactions of their new residents as they walked through the *Door of Return* into Ghana. The hosting village would get to see the fruit of their labor once again, as the five hundred or so people from their ship walked through the symbolic reentry point that had been constructed on the pier. Tony's listeners would be directed to leave the ship by a different route, and after the arrival ceremony there would be buses waiting to take them all to Exodus Stadium for the welcoming ceremony that would be held there. Tony's crew would film highlights of that event too, and parts of it would be broadcast live to his mainly African American audience.

Each local village had tried to outdo the other, when it was their turn to host the arrival ceremony, treating their newest residents to a more memorable and welcoming reception than the group who came before. Volunteers from Exodus Village usually worked around the clock as the ship sailed nearer to the shore, decorating the stadium, putting up welcome-home signs, and cooking the food that would be their residents' first meal in their new home

The talking drums already sent word out about the ship's imminent arrival, when it was two days away from Elmina, as the excitement continued to build. Two of Amina's assistants and three agents from Heavenly Travel had been assigned exclusively as concierges for Tony and his crew. Although he kidded around on the air quite a bit, Kristin had known him for a long time and she knew Tony to be a consummate professional. They had grown up together in Tuskegee and he had even stood up as Trazi's godfather during his christening. She had regretfully lost contact with him after she and Winston divorced, and his broadcasting career had taken off shortly after that. They had been trying to work things out to have him broadcast his show from Exodus Village, for years. The timing had always been off until now, but her phone call to him about their next arrival ceremony had come to him at the right time.

He and his crew were to be the first members of the Western press who would be allowed inside Exodus Village. She knew he would give his listeners a complete picture of what their residents and volunteers' experiences were like. Tony planned to shoot enough material to produce a prime-time television special much later too, beginning with the footage he had taken inside their Jamaican hotel, before they boarded the ship. He would broadcast portions of their history and cultural sensitivity classes for his special, that he had taped while they were still in Jamaica.

He would do a lot to showcase the Foundation's successes while he was in the country. His show catered to the same "old school" crowd that matched exactly with the descriptions of volunteers their public relations department targeted in their recruitment campaigns. Kristin hoped that his radio coverage would give them the extra boost they needed to bring the right people together for their new expanded programs into other West African countries.

And of course, they all hoped the exposure from Tony's broadcast would attract the attention of the new American President, who was scheduled for a visit to Ghana in four months to address Parliament. The President, though himself a native son, had a personal relationship to African slavery only through his wife and daughters' ancestry. His paternal ties to Africa would still make him a welcome guest to Exodus Village and they hoped to have him visit. And personally, Kristin hoped for an opportunity to speak with him about his impressions of the slave castles that he and his family were scheduled to tour.

With everything nearly in place now, it was hard to believe that the option for Tony's broadcast had only come up a few days after Celeste's wedding. Once the opportunity presented itself, things had started to move fast quick; Kristin could only imagine how overwhelmed she might have been were it not for Amina and Kioni. There had been so much going on that she was having a hard time keeping up with all their reports. She had even caught herself napping once, as Amina was going through the schedule of events with her for the arrival ceremony.

She looked up from a report she had been reading, in reaction to a new sensation in her body. It ended the debate she had been having with herself about whether she would stop by to see Nana. She remembered that she had a bit of a headache that morning when she woke up too. She was beginning to have her suspicions about the cause but she thought it best that she see Nana and find out for sure. She found that whenever she was in the woman's presence, she would always somehow know what was needed to restore Kristin's health. Nana was an absolute marvel, and she prescribed herbal medicines that had the least evasive impact on the body. She had taught Kristin how easy it was for the body to heal itself, as long as it was given the right food, water, exercise and proper elimination.

She knew she couldn't afford to be sick with everything that was going on over the next few weeks, so she decided she would make the time to go to Nana's house to see her. When she walked into her sitting room, Celeste froze like a deer that had been caught in the headlights of a car. Unfortunately, she had been in the back of the house when Amad drove up, so she missed the sound of the Land Rover as it pulled to a stop in the front yard. She also missed her opportunity to disappear into one of Nana's back rooms as she had rehearsed. She had known that it was quite possible for Kristin to stop by Nana's house at any moment, and she had planned to wait in one of the back rooms until after she had figured out what kind of mood Kristin might be in.

She and Ishmael had come back from their amazing honeymoon trip almost three weeks earlier, to the day. Victoria Falls had been as amazing as she had imagined it would be; but she changed her mind about the bungee jumping in a hurry, after she saw the actual distance she would have to fall. They had gone to work on Ishmael's clinic just as soon as they got back from Zimbabwe. Kristin had made no objection about her taking the six weeks off that she had requested in advance for their honeymoon. In fact, everyone thought it was a great idea that they have a leisurely trip, since they had such a rocky start to their relationship, and Ishmael would soon be busy enough after the clinic opened. The money they had been given as wedding presents was substantial; they had more than enough to get started on the building, as soon as her designs had been approved. Celeste had been creating preliminary sketches for the various rooms he would need in the clinic first, and she would design the outer building around their shapes, after factoring in the sunlight. She had drawn initial sketches on each room based on its functionality. They had already made quite a bit of progress, but all the time her family had been in the back of her mind.

She had hoped that she would have talked to Trazi by then at least, and certainly before she found herself face-to-face with Kristin or her father. She still had no idea yet how bad the fallout had been, when some unsuspecting soul had gone to let them out of her old bedroom. She had already left several messages for her brother, but he had yet to call her back. Celeste wasn't taking that as a good sign at all, because Trazi had *always* returned her phone calls.

She knew that it would be time for her to get back to work at the Foundation soon. There would be meetings with the surveyors and engineers to evaluate the suitability of the properties they had under consideration for plant construction in the Volta region. She and Ishmael decided to stop by for one last visit with Nana Adowa, before it would be time for her to head north to Exodus village and face the music. She knew it would be tough going, but she had hoped to have time to at least prepare herself.

And, unbeknownst to her, Kristin had glimpsed her silhouette as she was getting out of her car. She knew beforehand that Celeste was in the house.

"Hi, Aunt Kristin...er...Mom..." Her greeting was hesitant and riddled with guilt. She still wasn't able to gauge much by Kristin's expression or her body language either, for that matter.

"Oh, Celeste...So, you're back." Kristin merely glanced in her direction briefly and acknowledged her in a nonchalant way. She gave no indication that she had already known she was in the house.

"So how was Victoria Falls?" Her question was casual, and in a tone that

368

said she had no stake in the answer whatsoever.

"I've only been to Harare once," she continued indifferently, "but that was for a meeting, so I didn't get to see much of the city." Kristin changed her focus to some plants that Nana was growing near the front door. Her back was turned away.

"It was great!" Celeste was beginning to feel even more uncomfortable now. "We had lots of fun..."

"I'm glad." Kristin interrupted her, but still displayed little emotion. Celeste wasn't sure whether she cared one way or another how her honeymoon had gone. She had never seen Kristin that way before, not ever. She didn't seem angry with her exactly; it was more like indifference. She was being cordial but it felt like she was talking to someone she hardly knew.

What she didn't know was that Kristin, Winston, and Trazi had all decided they would not say one thing to Celeste about the stunt she had pulled on her wedding night, locking them in her bedroom for the night. They had all decided they would act as though it had never happened, when they saw her. Eventually, Celeste would be forced to be accountable for her little prank.

Trazi had been angry with his little sister for the first time in his life. It took him several days to get over the fact that she had set him up the way she had, leaving him there holding the bag. He had been the one who had unknowingly stopped by the next morning, to check in on his parents. He had hoped they would end up together somehow during the wedding festivities, just as Celeste had. He had already arranged to stay in one of the residences in Marcus Garvey Community with Malaya, so he could keep her company since they were traveling together. He had no idea that his parents had been locked in all night until he stopped by the next morning with their breakfast. Everything had worked out for the best in the end, but none of them intended to let Celeste off the hook so easily.

"Do you know where Nana is?" Kristin changed the subject casually. "I need to get over to the stadium for a walk-through, but I wanted to talk to her before I headed over there."

As if on cue, she heard Nana Adwoa making her way down the hallway.

"Good morning, my dear Moses," she called out. Kristin hurried forward to greet her with a warm hug.

"I was expecting you by this morning. How are you and our little one doing this morning?"

"Good morning Nana," She greeted the older woman with a kiss on her smooth ebony cheek. She had known her for almost twenty years now, and was accustomed to her perceptive abilities. She wasn't surprised at all to hear Nana say that she had been expecting her.

"Well, that's the reason I came," she answered. "I was hoping there might be something else that you could give me to settle my stomach." She looked hopeful. "I've been drinking the teas you gave me but they don't seem to be working anymore."

"That's not at all unusual, my dear," Nana said, confidently. "There are other herbs, of course..." Her voice trailed off for a second.

"It would be best if you didn't take any of them though, especially at this stage..."

"Then what do you suggest?" Kristin was puzzled by Nana's vague responses. She had long since given up on understanding her colloquial expressions, but Nana was usually much more direct when she prescribed her herbs. Kristin had already told her what her schedule was like these days. She had too much work to do and she couldn't afford the time off for an illness. She thought that she might have a minor bout of malaria, and only wanted Nana to give her something that would relieve it.

"You should try to get as much rest as you can," she advised, just as Kristin suspected she would. "And keep eating lots of fruit and those soy bean products of yours," she finished with a sweet smile.

Kristin wasn't surprised by Nana's suggestion, even with everything that the Foundation and Heavenly Travel had going on over the next few weeks. But how could she possibly expect her to get any rest?

For the first time since she met her, Kristin wondered for a second whether the woman was starting to show signs of slowing down finally; but senility was not as commonplace in Ghana.

And as soon as she mentioned eating the fruit and soybeans together like that, it made her want to...

Kristin stopped in the middle of her thought. "Oh my God! Nana!" She looked at the woman in disbelief, hearing, finally, everything she had said to her on a delayed reaction. She stood staring in amazement as the old woman's smile grew even broader.

"What do you mean?" Kristin stopped and tried to calm herself after asking the question. The bemused look on the woman's face confirmed her suspicions about the impossible answer she would give her.

"Don't tell me you didn't know?" Nana was chuckling now.

"Know what?" Celeste was feeling more secure since Kristin was obviously distracted. She moved closer to where the two women stood so she could hear their conversation better.

"...But how is that even possible?... They had both completely disregarded Celeste and her question. Kristin was beginning to feel dizzy and her heart was racing so fast that she felt as though she might go into shock.

"Well, my dear one," Nana was laughing openly at her, "if you have to ask the question, then perhaps that might explain everything." She clucked like a hen and laughed out loud again.

"What are you two talking about," Celeste asked more forcefully this time. At first, she had been concerned that there might really be something wrong with Kristin, but Nana's laughter made it clear that wasn't the case.

Kristin felt as though her knees would give way. She sank down into a chair next to the sofa and covered her face with her hands, still in disbelief.

"Why, you're going to be a big sister. You're going have a little baby brother or sister," Nana told Celeste in a matter-of-fact tone. "I'll have to wait another week or two before I can say which."

"And you my dear," she turned back towards Kristin, "are going to have to find some way to get some rest, as I said." She had finished in a stern tone. "You can stay here with me for a few weeks, if you'd like," she offered matter-of-factly. "I would love to have the company."

She knew already that Kristin would have some concerns about the baby's wellbeing, and she could sense the worry taking form across her face.

"I'd be able to keep an eye on you that way..."

"You're kidding!" Celeste interrupted Nana after she was finally able to react. "My goodness. That's wonderful!"

"Oh, well, I guess that means you and Daddy got along pretty good, when I locked you in that room, huh Mom." She was smug now and grinning from ear to ear.

"Don't you dare tell him!" Kristin dropped her hands so she could glare at Celeste with a threatening look. Then she finally smiled, because the reality of what Nana told her was beginning to anchor in her mind. She had been afraid at first to believe it was true.

"And don't you tell anyone else, either" she added weakly." "I have to be the one to tell your father." Her tone was much more serious. "Although, I'm not sure whether he's going to believe me."

She starting thinking back and she realized she had been having headaches in the morning frequently, and she had begun to tire easily too. She had chalked it all up to her need for time to recover from after all the activity from Celeste's wedding. And then they had to get right into making preparations for Tony's broadcast after that.

Now it all made sense. She didn't have malaria after all, and she hadn't ingested some strange bacteria that had found its way into her intestinal tract. She was fifty-one years old and she was pregnant again. She and Winston were having another child!

Her mind flashed back to some of the material she had read as she got ready for her first trip to Africa. There had been documentation on the affects of the tropical climate in West Africa on some people. One such report had specifically stated that many older women who traveled there resumed their menstrual cycles like they were young women again. There had been stories about women who had previously gone through menopause, but their bodies had been suddenly rejuvenated by the tropical climate, and they were once again capable of bearing children. They became as fertile as the soil that grew the lush vegetation of the rainforest.

She was having another baby!

Her immediate thoughts been for the baby's welfare, and she had frightening memories of the baby she had lost once again. She tried to remember what Nana had told her about miscarriages; and the Akan practice of not prolonging the mourning of an unborn or newly born baby. Many people believed them to be mischievous spirits, who were capable of returning whenever they pleased. Little thought was given to them at all after the mother made her physical recovery.

Kristin was reminded that the sight of Celeste lying in Angela's arms had kept her from loosing her mind. It made the remaining aggravation that she still held for her melt, and she smiled at the young woman again who had always been her daughter in her heart.

The trick she had played on them turned into more of blessing than she could have imagined. And Nana was right, of course. She would have to take things much easier than she had been doing. She had gratefully accepted Nana's invitation to stay with her for a few weeks once Tony and his production crew left Ghana. In the meantime, she would move into her suite at their Cape Coast hotel. That way, Amad could drive her to visit Nana every day if need be. The most important thing now was to make sure everything was okay with the baby, their baby—hers and Winston's.

"What about the ceremony tomorrow, Nana?" Her mind suddenly refocused on the flurry of activities that were about to descend on them. "Do you think it's okay if I go? Will I be alright if I'm not on my feet too much?

"I do need to spend some time with Tony, and at least show my face to welcome our new residents to Ghana."

"The baby will be fine, my child...Don't worry, it will all be fine."

✳✳✳

Kristin broke the news to Amina and Kioni first, of course, as soon as the filming had wrapped up on the welcoming ceremony at Exodus Stadium. Their new residents had been moved by the ceremony, as was Tony, his crew, his fans and listeners who came with him. Their residents were all on buses now and headed to their new homes in Exodus Village.

Amina and Kioni were both ecstatic about the baby, and they adapted to their hastily revised roles with Tony's production company with ease and confidence. The three of them met so they could go over Kristin's schedule for the next few weeks, and she had hastily reassigned all the meetings that she couldn't postpone. She would remain on the coast as long as possible after Tony left, so she could be close to Nana.

Her first meeting with him wasn't scheduled until the day following his arrival, but she had sent word to him that she needed to speak with him on an urgent matter. And just as she had expected, he went into hysterics when she told him that she had just learned she was pregnant. And it only got worse after she told him Winston was the baby's father.

After he finally stopped laughing long enough, Kristin told him about the baby that she and Winston had lost after Trazi. She didn't get into any of the sordid details, but she explained that she would have to reduce her schedule to make sure that her pregnancy went okay. They arranged to do the interview he had planned with her from her hotel room, and he had jokingly tried to coerce her into letting him give Winston the good news during his show.

Kristin had been mortified by the thought of course, and she had to promised him an interview with Nana Adwoa if he would agree to drop his threat. He had become fascinated by Nana's work, after Kristin told him why she would be staying with her for a few weeks.

"I'll do my best, Tony," she promised, "but please don't mention the baby on your show—at least not until after I get in touch with Winston."

She had already left two messages, asking him to call her as soon as he could. She had decided to wait to call him the following afternoon; with the time difference she had hoped to catch him as he got started with his day in Washington. She found herself in a panic whenever she heard her phone ring after that; her heart seemed to stop for a second until the caller

ID told her someone else had called.

They had been talking pretty regularly since Winston left Ghana to go back home; they were communicating openly now for the first time in a very long while. She didn't know whether it was because they weren't living in the same space or not; all she knew was that it felt really good and she didn't want it to stop.

She was about to start feeling paranoid that he hadn't called her yet, then it dawned on her that she had placed both calls within the same hour. She forced herself to calm down, reminded that he could be tied up for hours if he was meeting with a client. Winston usually turned his phone off then, or whenever he got really involved in something he was working on.

Lying flat on her back all day had made the hours seem to drag by. Nana had suggested that Kristin stay in bed for most of the day, since all the commotion from their new residents' arrival was now over. She had entertained herself by watching the goldfish swim around in the small tank that Celeste had brought her, waiting for the phone to ring. The movement of the fish had a calming affect and she found it soothing to watch.

She kept going over the plans in her head, for Amina and Kioni to keep things going until she felt she was balanced in her pregnancy. Every day, Kioni was to feed his activity reports to Amina for review, and she would do the same for him. They would each fax their daily reports to Kristin's hotel, for them to be delivered to her at the same time in the late afternoon. That way, they would all be kept in the loop about everything that was going on.

At an appointed time, Kristin would join Amina and Kioni on a conference call every evening too. They would only discuss those things that she needed clarification on or required her input. They were off to a great start and Kristin felt very comfortable with their arrangement. She wished she had been at the Village for Tony's interviews, but she wouldn't run the risk of the long drive up from the coast just yet. Luckily, she had Amina and Kioni to stand in for her. If it had been any other news organization, she would have tried to cancel the whole thing, or at least scale it back. But she trusted Tony completely with the process, and she had no qualms about what he might produce while she was not there.

But she didn't trust him not to call Winston at all—she knew it was much too big of a temptation. She kept checking her watch every few minutes and finally picked up her phone to dial Winston's number a third time. When she looked down at the display and saw his name and number, there were several seconds that passed before it registered that he was already on the phone, and holding for her on the other end. He had apparently called her at the exact moment she was opening her flip phone to dial his number, before it had the chance to ring.

"Kristin?" He said it hesitantly. He sensed that she was there, although he had never heard the phone ring. He wasn't certain that he had made a connection at all, but somehow he knew that she was there.

"Winston!" She was suddenly nervous all over again now that she finally had him on the phone.

"I've been trying to call you..." She stalled for time.

"I know... I'm sorry, Baby Girl, I was tied up in a meeting all morning.

"Is everything okay?" He asked the question with a thin layer of concern in his voice.

"What's going on?"

"Yes. It's more than okay..." She answered in her usual cryptic way. She began to feel a little more confident again after hearing his voice.

"....I do have something important to tell you, Winston..." She started.

"Does it have anything to do with the Foundation?" He interrupted her. He could already tell from her voice that she was calling with good news.

"No, this isn't about the project at all," she answered, smiling.

"Are you sitting down?"

"He could have added fortune to fame,
but caring for neither
he found happiness and honor
in being helpful to the world."

—Epitaph on the grave of Dr. George Washington Carver

~ ~ ~ ~ ~ ~ ~ ~ ~ ~ ~ ~ ~ ~ ~ ~ ~

"By the blessing of God, I will argue the case
before the Supreme Court - I implore the mercy of
God to control my temper, to enlighten my soul,
and to give me utterance, that I may prove myself
in every respect equal to the task."

—John Quincy Adams, as he prepared to defend the African men
who had killed their captors aboard the slave ship, *Amistead*

www.ingramcontent.com/pod-product-compliance
Lightning Source LLC
Chambersburg PA
CBHW030240030726
47493CB00023B/270